august 2, 2011

WHEN PASSION RULES

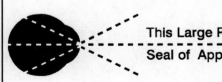

WHEN PASSION RULES

JOHANNA LINDSEY

THORNDIKE PRESS
A part of Gale, Cengage Learning

GALE
CENGAGE Learning™

Detroit • New York • San Francisco • New Haven, Conn • Waterville, Maine • London

GALE
CENGAGE Learning

LIBRARY OF CONGRESS CATALOGING-IN-PUBLICATION DATA

Lindsey, Johanna.
    When passion rules / by Johanna Lindsey.
        p. cm. — (Thorndike Press large print basic)
    ISBN-13: 978-1-4104-3839-3 (hardcover)
    ISBN-10: 1-4104-3839-2 (hardcover)
    1. Mistaken identity—Fiction. 2. Large type books. I. Title.
PS3562.I5123W46 2011b
813'.54—dc22   2011020933

Published in 2011 by arrangement with Gallery Books, a division of Simon & Schuster, Inc.

WHEN PASSION RULES

PROLOGUE

Leonard Kastner had been thinking of retiring for good. He should have done more than just think about it. The timing was right. He had made more money than he had ever dreamed possible merely by using his talents. He was at the pinnacle of his career, his successes unblemished, and he'd never refused a job. His clients knew that. Details weren't important. Half the time they didn't provide them until he'd accepted a job. But he was finding his occupation more and more distasteful, and he was losing his edge. When you didn't give a damn, nothing mattered. When you started to question what you were doing, it did.

Long since wealthy beyond his needs, he didn't need to take risks any longer and certainly didn't need to take this particular job. But he had been offered more money than he could possibly refuse, more than he'd made in the last three years, and half of it had been paid in advance. And no wonder the fee was so enormous. This was one of those rare jobs the lackey who had hired him wanted his full agreement on before Leonard was told what was required of him.

He'd never been hired to kill a woman. But he was going to end his career with an even more abhorrent crime, the killing of an infant. And not just any infant, but the heir to the crown. A political assassination? Revenge against King Frederick? Leonard hadn't been told and he didn't care. Somewhere along the way he'd lost his humanity. This was just another job. He had to keep telling himself that. He was *not* going to end his career with a failure. If he found the job distasteful, it was only because he liked his king and loved his country. But the king would sire more heirs once he was out of mourning and had remarried. He was still a young man.

Getting into King Frederick's palace during the day was easy. The gates of the palace, located in the courtyard of the old fortress that overlooked the capital city of Lubinia, were rarely closed. The gates were certainly guarded, but few were ever denied entrance, even when the king was in residence. He wasn't. He had retired to his winter chalet in the mountains directly after the queen's funeral four months ago to mourn in peace. She had died only a few days after giving him this heir that someone wanted dead.

Leonard would have been stopped at the gates if he'd given the slightest hint of who he was, but he didn't. He had a nefarious reputation, but it was under the false name of Rastibon. He had a price on his head in his own country and in several neighboring countries. But no one even knew what Rastibon looked like. He had been careful about that, always being hooded, meeting his contacts in shadowed back alleys, disguising his voice as needed. He had always planned to retire right here in his own country with no one ever suspecting how he had acquired his wealth.

He lived in a prosperous section of the capital city. His landlord and neighbors weren't overly nosy, and when asked about his work, he merely alluded to an export business in wine to explain his frequent absences from the country. Wine he knew. Wine he could talk about freely. But he made it clear he didn't have time for idle talk, so he was generally considered an unfriendly sort and was usually left alone, which was the way he preferred it. A man in his profession couldn't afford to make friends unless they were in the same profession. But even then competition would get in the way.

It wasn't as easy getting into the wing of the nursery, but Leonard was resourceful. He discovered which women had the care of Frederick's heir and picked the night nursemaid as his target.

Helga was her name. A plain-looking young widow, she had an infant of her own that she was still nursing, which is why she'd gotten the palace job. It took him only a week to woo her into his bed during her brief visits to her family in the city. But then he was a personable young man in his late twenties, somewhat handsome with his dark brown hair and blue eyes, and he even dredged up some old charm from the days when he hadn't been a cold-blooded assassin. He was going to have to kill Helga, too, if he wanted to be able to retire in his homeland. If he let her live, she would be able to identify him.

It took Leonard another three weeks to arrange a rendezvous in Helga's room in the palace's nursery wing on a night when the other nursemaid had time off and wouldn't be there. Even though Helga had assured him that no one ever visited the

10

nursery at night, other than the two guards who made their rounds twice nightly, she was still fearful of losing her job if he was somehow discovered there. After all, the number of guards stationed at the palace was doubled at night. But passion won in the end and the right doors were left open for him. He only had to remain hidden briefly until the two guards left the nursery wing.

He didn't kill the woman after all. That had been the logical thing to do. He had used yet another fake name with her, not to hide his intended crime, but to prevent her — or anyone else — from connecting Leonard Kastner and Rastibon. He had no intention of hiding his crime. Whoever had hired him would need to hear of it. But there was no reason to kill the nursemaid, too, when he could simply render her unconscious with a sleeping potion in her wine. He had a moment's regret even over that.

He'd grown fond of Helga in the month he'd known her. It changed his original plan quite drastically. It meant he wouldn't be retiring in his own country after all, when she would be able to identify him. But he'd made this hasty decision just today, and the only sleeping powder he'd been able to find quickly was unfamiliar to him, so he didn't

11

know how long it would last, forcing him to hurry. He made another last-minute decision: to bind her hands behind her back so no one would think she was complicit in his crime. But worse, he couldn't bring himself to kill the child there in the nursery where the woman would wake up and see it. She adored the king's child, claimed she loved it now as much as her own.

Leonard *had* intended to finish the job on-site. Much less risk involved. But after glancing at Helga lying on her bed, soon to wake, he began looking for a sack instead. He couldn't find one in the main room. The royal infant was being raised in the lap of luxury, fed with golden spoons, her bassinet worth a fortune, lined in satin and the finest lace, circled with gems. A shelf was filled with fancy toys the baby was too young for. Numerous bureaus lined one wall, with so many clothes she would outgrow most of them before she could be dressed in them all.

The nurses had no cots to sleep on in the nursery. They weren't allowed to sleep while they were on duty, which was why the princess had two nurses. Each had a small room attached to the nursery where they slept when they weren't on duty and cared for their own babies. In a corner of the nursery, Leonard saw a stack of pillows of every size imaginable, which were probably used when the baby was allowed to play on the floor. Leonard grabbed one of the larger ones from the bottom of the stack, cut it open along the seam, and pulled out the stuffing. Then he cut out three small air holes. It would serve his purposes.

He lost no time stuffing the child into the pillow casing, though he did so carefully so as not to wake her. She was four months old. If the baby woke, she might cry. He had one long hallway and a narrow corridor to traverse to reach the stairway to the side door he'd entered from, and two guards to work his way around. Easy enough to do as long as the baby didn't cry.

The previous night he'd secured a rope to the fortress's back wall, which faced away from the city. He'd left his horse near there tonight in a grove of trees. He'd made these preparations because the fortress gates were closed and heavily guarded at night, and he needed another avenue of escape. But the fortress walls posed another challenge. Although Lubinia wasn't at war, several guards still walked those ramparts at night.

Luckily for him, it was a moonless night. Lamps lit the courtyard, but they were a boon, creating shadows where he could hide as he slipped quickly across the courtyard. He made it to the fortress wall without incident and climbed the narrow stairs to the top. The baby still slept; the guards were presently on the front wall. A few moments more and Leonard would be out of the fortress. He had to tie the improvised sack to his belt because he needed both hands to climb down the rope. The sack swung slightly on his way down, banging once against the wall. A mewling sound came from it, not loud, and no one but he was close enough to hear it.

Finally, he was safe, on his horse. He tucked the sack inside the front of his jacket. No other sound came from it. He rode hard over the Alpine hills, rode until dawn. He finally stopped in an open glade, far from any towns, far from any intrusion or pursuit. The time was at hand. He would do the deed swiftly. Each day since he'd been told what this job entailed, he'd been sharpening the knife he was going to use.

He took the bundle out of his jacket, opened the pillow casing, and let it fall to the ground. He held the sleeping baby with one arm, drew the knife from his boot, and placed the blade against the tiny neck. This innocent didn't deserve to die; the one who was paying him did. But Leonard had no choice. He was only the instrument. If not him, someone else would be doing this. At least he could make it as painless as possible.

He hesitated a moment too long.

The infant in the crook of his arm had awakened. She was looking directly at him — and smiled.

CHAPTER ONE

The long blade of the rapier bent as Alana pressed its tip hard against the chest of the man in front of her. It would have been a death skewer if not for the protective padded jackets they both wore.

"You should have accomplished that move three minutes ago," Poppie said, removing his mask so she could see the disapproval in his sharp blue eyes. "What's distracting you today, Alana?"

Choices, she thought, three too many! Of course she was distracted. How could she concentrate on her lesson with so much on her mind? She had a life-changing decision to make. Of the three completely different directions she could take, each held its own special appeal, and she'd run out of time. She was eighteen today. She couldn't put the decision off any longer.

Her uncle was always so serious about these fencing lessons. Now was not the time to tell him of the dilemma she'd been grappling with. But she did need to discuss it with him and would have done so much sooner if he hadn't seemed so preoccupied himself these last few months. It wasn't like him. When she'd asked him if anything was wrong, he'd fobbed her off with a smile and had denied it. That wasn't like him either.

She'd been able to hide her own preoccupation — until today. But then he'd taught her how to hide her emotions. He'd taught her so many odd things over the years. . . .

Her friends called her uncle eccentric. Imagine, his teaching her to use weapons! But she would always defend his right to be different. He wasn't an Englishman, after all. Her friends shouldn't try to compare him to one. She'd even lost a few because of the wide-ranging education Poppie insisted she receive, but she didn't care. The snob who had moved in next door was a prime example of such narrow-mindedness. Alana had mentioned some of her recent studies and how fascinated she was with mathematics when she first met the girl.

"You sound like my older brother," the girl had said disdainfully. "What do you and I need to know about the world? We just need to know how to run a household. Do you know how to do that?"

"No, but I can skewer an apple tossed in the air on the tip of my rapier before it hits the ground."

They never did become friends. It was no loss. Alana had many others who marveled at her diverse education and just chocked it up to her being a foreigner like Poppie, even though she'd lived in England her whole life and considered herself an English-woman.

Poppie wasn't her uncle's real name but the name Alana had given him when she was a child because she liked pretending he was her father rather than her uncle. She was average in height herself, and he wasn't much taller than she was. And although he was in his mid-forties, he didn't have a line on his face yet to prove it, and his dark brown hair was just as dark as it had always been.

Mathew Farmer was his real name, so English-sounding, which was funny, because his foreign accent was so pronounced. He was one of many European aristocrats who had fled the Continent during and im-mediately after the Napoleonic wars, to start new lives in England. He'd brought her with him because he was the only family she had left.

Her parents had died when she was an infant. Tragically, in a war they weren't even fighting in. They had tried to visit Alana's maternal grandmother in Prussia because they'd received word that she was dying. They were shot on the way by overzealous French sympathizers who mistook them for enemies of Napoléon's. Poppie guessed it was because they were obviously aristocrats, and the simpleminded peons considered all aristocrats to be enemies of France's. He didn't know the details, and it made him sad to speculate. But he did tell her so much about her parents when she was young that she felt as if she had real, firsthand memories of them.

As far back as she could remember, her father's brother had always been her guardian, her teacher, her companion, her friend. He was everything she could want in a father, and she loved him as one. What had happened to her parents was horrible, but she had always been grateful that Poppie was the one who ended up raising her.

Because he was wealthy, her life with him was a mix of privilege and the unexpected. She'd had a long stream of tutors, so many she'd lost count. Each taught her something different and each stayed for only a few months. Lady Annette was the only one who had stayed with her longer. An impoverished young widow forced to seek employment, Lady Annette had been hired by Poppie to teach Alana all aspects of being a lady, then he'd continued to employ her as a chaperone, so Annette had been part of the household for nine years now.

Alana's days became even busier when she turned ten and her martial training began. Poppie himself taught her how to use various weapons. The day he took her into the room that had been cleared of furniture and whose walls were now lined with rapiers, daggers, and firearms, she recalled something he'd told her when she was younger and probably thought she wouldn't remember: "I used to kill people. I don't anymore."

She'd known he'd fought in the wars that Napoléon had instigated all over the Continent, the same wars he'd come to England to escape, but that had been an odd way to refer to it. That day he'd put the rapier in her hand, she'd asked him, "This is the weapon you killed with?"

"No, but I trained myself to use all weapons, and this one offers the most exercise and requires the greatest dexterity, quickness, agility, and cunning, so training in its use has more than one benefit. But for you in particular, it will teach you to avoid grappling, which a man will most definitely attempt with you, thinking he can subdue you with his superior strength. So it will teach you to keep your distance no matter the weapon at hand."

"But I will probably never be required to use it to defend myself?"

"No, you won't carry a rapier to defend yourself. You will master the pistol for that."

Sword fighting was simply a form of exercise to keep her fit. She understood that. She came to look forward to those practice sessions with Poppie as the highlight of her days. Unlike some of her other tutors, he was always calm and patient with her.

Annette had risked losing her job when she'd confronted Poppie about the new turn Alana's studies were taking. Alana had caught the tail end of that argument as she passed Poppie's study one day. "Weapons? Good Lord, she's already too bold and opinionated, and now you put weapons in her hands? You've given her a man's education. How do you expect me to counter that at this late date?"

"I don't expect you to counter it," Poppie had calmly replied. "I expect you to teach her that she will have choices in how to deal with people. What you criticize as being too bold, manly even, will only be a benefit to her."

"But it's *not* ladylike, not in the least."

Poppie had chuckled. "It's enough that you teach her manners and all the other things a lady should know. Keep in mind, you aren't creating a lady out of thin air. She's already a lady of the highest caliber. And I'm not going to deny her a real education just because she's a woman."

"But she questions *every*thing I'm trying to teach her, just as a man would."

"I'm glad to hear it. I taught her to be thorough, even meticulous, in the analysis of any given situation. If anything strikes her as odd, she's not to shrug it off, but to find out why. I have confidence you will persevere without disrupting what she's already been taught."

With that remark sounding like a warning, the discussion had ended right then and there.

Now, Alana stepped back from Poppie and moved to the wall to put her weapon away. It was time for her to tell him what was distracting her. She couldn't put it off any longer.

"I have some unexpected decisions to make, Poppie. Can we discuss them tonight at dinner, or as soon as I get back from the orphanage?"

She knew he would be frowning now. He might not have forbade it, but he didn't like her going to the orphanage even though it was *his* orphanage. When she'd found out last year about this institution he had established soon after they'd arrived in London and had been supporting ever since, she'd been incredulous. She didn't know why he'd never mentioned it to her. Because her later education had leaned toward turning her into a lady? And ladies shouldn't associate with urchins from the slums? But his explanation had been simple.

"I was given a new life here, a second chance. I felt unworthy of it. I needed to give something back, to try to give others the same chance I was given for a new life. It took me a few years to figure out that the people most in need of my help were the most hopeless, the homeless street urchins."

A worthy cause. Could she do any less? It had seemed so natural for her to decide to teach there. Her education had included so many different subjects and skills that she was far more qualified than any of the other teachers. She *loved* doing it. Whether she should continue to teach at the orphanage was one of the decisions she had to confront because teaching wasn't at all compatible with the other two paths she could choose.

"I've made a decision as well," he said, standing behind her. "I never thought this day would be so momentous for you, but I cannot put off this matter any longer. Come to my office now."

Good Lord, was she going to have even more choices set before her? She swung around abruptly and saw how uneasy he looked. He couldn't see the apprehension in her gray-blue eyes through the fencing mask she hadn't yet removed. *Momentous?* That sounded so much more important than her own dilemma.

He turned to the door, expecting her to follow him. "Wait, Poppie. The children have planned a birthday party for me. They'll be disappointed if I don't visit the orphanage today."

He didn't immediately answer. He had to think about it? When he cared for those children as much as she did?

He finally said, "Very well, but don't be long."

He left the room before he could see her hesitant nod. By rote she removed her mask, the padded jacket, and the tie that bound back her long black hair. Now she was filled with dread.

CHAPTER TWO

The party didn't help Alana to relax or to stop thinking about what lay ahead of her. If anything, the children's squabbling exasperated her today, enough that she snapped at Henry Mathews, "Do I need to box your ears?"

Henry was one of her favorites. Many of the children at the orphanage who didn't know their real names had adopted Poppie's surname with his permission. Henry had had to be different, though, and had picked Poppie's first name instead.

But Henry was also different in other ways. He didn't just show a keen intelligence by quickly grasping everything he was taught, he'd also discovered and developed a talent that would serve him well when he left the orphanage. He could carve the most beautiful things out of wood: ornaments, people, animals. He'd given Alana a carving of herself. She'd been so touched the day he'd thrust it into her hands then run off in embarrassment. She'd repaid Henry by taking him on an outing in Hyde Park and had encouraged him to bring along some of his carvings. One of the vendors there had paid Henry several pounds for them, more money than he'd ever before had in his pockets. It finally convinced him that his talent was worthwhile.

She'd caught him just now grappling with one of the younger boys over one of his carvings. But to her threat, he just grinned cheekily at her. "You wouldn't box me ears. You're too nice."

No, she wouldn't. She had a better tool to use. She gave him a look of disappointment. "I thought you were learning to share your carvings with those less fortunate than you."

" 'E ain't less —"

"That you agreed it was the charitable thing to do," she reminded him.

Henry ducked his head. But he shoved the toy soldier at the younger boy, who immediately ran off with it.

" 'E breaks it and I'll break 'is bleedin' neck," Henry mumbled.

Alana tsked. "Perhaps we should work on attitude? Being generous should have warmed your heart, particularly since you can replace that toy easily."

He gave her a stricken look. "It took me four 'ours to make that. I stayed up late to do it, then fell asleep in class the next day and got punished for it. 'E took it from me chest. Maybe you should be teachin' 'im not to steal instead o' teachin' me to give away me 'ard work."

She groaned and put out a hand to stop him from running off, but Henry was too fast. She'd been too stern with him. Her being worried was no excuse. She'd apologize to him tomorrow, but right now she had to get home.

But Henry caught her at the door as she was tying her cloak on and wrapped his arms tightly around her waist. "I didn't mean it, I didn't!" he said earnestly.

She patted his head. "I know, and I'm the one who needs to apologize. A gift isn't a gift unless it's given freely. I'll get your toy back tomorrow."

"Already 'ave it back," he said, letting go of her. " 'E were just pullin' me strings to rile me. 'E went straight back to the dormitory and tossed it on me bed. And it were for you, teacher, for your birthday. Can't 'ave the other carving standin' alone, eh?"

She took the carving he held out to her. The little soldier was carved in meticulous detail. She grinned. "You see me paired with a soldier?"

"They got courage. It will take a bunch o' that for a man —"

She caught his drift and interrupted with a laugh. "Come now, I'm not so intimidating that a man would need to be courageous to marry me?"

"It ain't that, it's wot you got up 'ere." He tapped his head. "Women ain't suppose to be as smart as you are."

"My uncle disagrees. He arranged my education. And we've moved into an enlightened age, Henry. Men aren't the barbarians they used to be. They've opened their eyes."

He mulled over that for a moment, then said, "If Mathew Farmer thinks so, then it must be so."

She raised a brow. "No further arguments to support your contention?"

"No, ma'am."

His quick reply made her laugh. The children idolized her uncle. Of course they wouldn't disagree with anything he said or did.

She ruffled Henry's hair. "I'll put the soldier by the other carving anyway. He'll be her protector. She'll like that."

He beamed at her before he hurried off again. Henry had just made her decision for her, she realized. How could she not continue teaching here?

A gust of cold wind almost dislodged her bonnet as she stepped outside and hurried to the waiting coach. She hoped Mary had the brazier burning. She'd been Alana's nanny before becoming her maid and occasionally served as her chaperone, but Mary was getting old. She could have come inside the orphanage to wait, but she preferred the quiet of the coach, where she could knit in peace.

Alana thought it was silly for the coach to wait at the curb for her. It could just as easily have returned for her at an appointed time. But it waited at Poppie's insistence. She was never to be kept waiting anywhere and never was to leave the house without a full escort, which included two footmen and one of the women to serve as her chaperone.

Lady Annette had been Alana's chaperone for the first six months she had taught at the orphanage. While Lady Annette supported charitable endeavors, she'd firmly disapproved of Alana's actually teaching there daily because it had the appearance of being a "job." But Annette had grown as fond of the children as Alana had, and Annette had even started teaching a few classes. She'd seemed to enjoy it, until Lord

Adam Chapman came upon them leaving one day.

"Alana?"

The footman who had been holding the coach door open for her closed it again for Mary's sake as Alana turned at the sound of her name. Speaking of the devil, she thought with some amusement. Adam was doffing his hat to her. She gave him a warm smile. She was always relaxed in his presence and attributed it to his amiability and wonderful sense of humor.

"I didn't forget what day this is," Lord Chapman continued, and handed her a bouquet of yellow flowers. "A momentous day for most young ladies."

She wished he hadn't used the word *momentous*. It reminded her of what awaited her at home.

"Thank you," she said. "But where on earth did you find flowers, so late in the year?"

"I have my sources." He grinned mysteriously, but then laughed and confessed, "My mum keeps a hothouse, well, her gardeners do. Wouldn't catch her mucking about in the dirt, even for pretty results."

His parents lived in Mayfair, but Adam had told her he had his own flat just down the street from the orphanage, and once or twice a week she would find him passing by. He always stopped to converse with her, listening to her anecdotes about the children with interest, and divulging bits and pieces of his own life.

Alana had met Adam because Annette had known him before she'd married Lord Hensen. He'd been walking by the orphanage one afternoon when Alana and Annette had been leaving, and he'd greeted Annette warmly. He'd kept showing up to try to renew their acquaintance, but while Annette was polite, her manner turned cool and aloof every time she saw him. She would never say why, despite Alana's probing. But she'd stopped accompanying Alana to the orphanage. That, however, didn't stop Adam from showing up.

Alana had been flattered when he'd turned his attention to her. How could she not be when he was so handsome and charming? He was in his early thirties, the same age as Annette, but he looked much younger.

Alana thought about once again inviting Adam to dinner so he could meet Poppie, but — no, not today. She'd invited him a few times before, but her timing hadn't been good because he'd already been committed elsewhere. But soon.

It was getting too cold to stand there on

the curb for these little chats, though, and Mary must have thought so as well because she opened the coach door to remind Alana, "It's time to go, m'dear."

"Indeed," Adam agreed, and took her hand to help her into the coach, then said with a jaunty grin, "Until the next time we happen to cross paths."

Alana laughed as he closed the door. Their meetings always seemed to be happenstance, but they weren't. He knew exactly what time she left the orphanage, and that was always when he would walk by so they could have one of their chats at curbside.

An earl's son, his family rich, Adam was the kind of young man Poppie would certainly approve of. And he'd given her flowers today! That was definitely a sign that he was ready to take their relationship up a step. Had he only been waiting until she turned eighteen to start courting her? Quite possibly. He'd even mentioned the word *marriage* last month, though she was pretty sure it had only been something about how the time was approaching for him to start thinking about it. She couldn't even remember why he'd mentioned it, though that was when he'd actually become her third decision. Or he would be, *if* he got around to courting her in the proper way.

33

CHAPTER THREE

Alana was rarely nervous. Perhaps she felt a little apprehensive when a new tutor was scheduled to arrive, but that was nothing compared to what she was feeling now as she walked down the hall to Poppie's office. What if Poppie insisted she keep to the path Lady Annette had laid out for her two years ago? Annette had been preparing Alana for her come-out in London society. She assumed that Alana would want to do the same thing other young ladies her age were being groomed to do. Alana *had* been looking forward to the endless round of balls and dinner parties where she would meet potential suitors — before she'd discovered how gratifying it was to open young minds to possibilities they'd never before considered. She couldn't imagine quitting her work at the orphanage.

But she knew the two worlds weren't compatible. "You'll have to give up teaching, you know," Annette had recently warned her. "You've spent a year there, which is very generous of you, but it's got nothing to do with your future."

And her friend Harriet, who was the younger sister of one of Annette's old friends, had echoed Annette's warnings: "Don't expect your husband to allow you to be so charitable with your time. He'll expect you to stay at home and raise your own children."

There was Alana's dilemma. That was why she favored Adam and wished he'd be more clear about his intentions. Not because she loved him, but because she appreciated that he admired her dedication to the children. He had said so a number of times. He wouldn't forbid her to continue teaching if *he* was her husband.

Her feet moved more briskly now as she made her way to Poppie's office. Henry had helped her to make her decision. She was nervous, yes, but only about what Poppie had on his mind, not about her own decision. She just hoped he wasn't going to tell her that her trips to the orphanage must come to an end now that her come-out was almost upon them and the Season was about to begin. That was the only thing she could imagine he'd been brooding over.

His office was one of her favorite rooms in the large, three-story town house. It was cozy, especially in winter when the fireplace was lit. It was bright, too, because it was a corner room with two walls of windows and light cream-colored wallpaper that contrasted with the darker furnishings. She'd spent many a night there reading with Poppie, sometimes aloud. Or just talking. He always wanted to hear about her studies.

Poppie said nothing when she quietly entered the room. He wasn't sitting at his desk, but in an armchair close to the fireplace. He remained silent when she sat in the chair across from him. When she looked at him, she suddenly realized, incredulously, that he was more nervous than she was!

She'd never seen him like this, ever. When had this bulwark in her life ever been apprehensive about anything?

His hands were tightly gripped in his lap. She didn't think he was aware of it. Nor would he meet her gaze; his dark blue eyes were riveted on the carpet. Such tension was in his posture and in his face! She could see that he was gritting his teeth. He was probably trying to appear deep in thought, but she wasn't fooled.

Loving him as she did, she put aside her own fears and tried to ease his by beginning with the least of her concerns. "There is a young man I like who might soon come to ask your permission to court me. This would negate my need to have this come-out that Annette has been preparing me for. I've been at my wit's end trying to resolve this in my mind, but —"

She stopped abruptly. His eyes were on her now, and narrowed, but not for the reason she thought. "Who has dared to approach you without my permission, before you've even come of age?"

"It's perfectly innocent," she quickly assured him. "We've just run into each other so often outside the orphanage that we've become friends — curbside friends, you might say. But he mentioned recently that he's finally reached an age to start thinking about marriage, and I had a feeling, well, it was more a hope, that he was thinking of me when he said it."

Poppie sighed. "Then your feelings are involved?"

"Not yet," she admitted. "I like him, certainly, but the reason I would favor him is he's an English lord, yet *he* doesn't mind that I want to continue teaching. He even admires my dedication in doing so. And I do want to continue teaching, Poppie."

There, she'd said it. She held her breath,

waiting for his reaction. But all he did was sigh again before he said, "You could have done so."

She scoffed. "Annette said I'd have to give it up, that a husband will never allow it. If that's the case, I simply won't marry."

She was relieved to hear him chuckle. "Stubborn, princess? Over trivialities?"

She loved when he called her by that endearment. It always made her feel special. She was glad that odd tension had left his demeanor, but she certainly didn't consider any of this trivial. This was a turning point in her life they were discussing.

But he wasn't finished. "I suppose I should have been more specific instead of just suggesting that you don't need to follow the pack if you don't want to. Alana, I didn't want you to marry yet. I don't care if it's a social standard. You're young. There was no hurry. And I wasn't ready to face . . ."

"Losing me?" she guessed when he didn't continue. "That won't happen. But I *really* wish we'd had this talk sooner. I let all this converge on me as if there were a deadline on making a decision — today."

She chuckled at herself, relieved, but only for moment. Poppie looked tense again. She realized two other things that brought back her own dread. He'd said she *could have* continued teaching, not that she *could* continue. And she'd just made an assumption when he'd taught her never to do that, and he'd let her because it was a way of delaying what he had to tell her. *His* momentous decision.

Hesitantly, hoping he'd deny it, she said, "None of this matters now, does it?"

"No."

"Why not?"

"I always knew this day would come, when I would have to tell you the truth. I thought I would have more time, a few more years at least. I thought you could have this introduction to society with your friends and simply enjoy it without feeling pressured about marriage. You've worked so hard at your studies, I wanted you to have a little fun and frivolity. I felt you deserved it. But I was taking a risk in allowing it."

"A risk for me to have fun? That makes no —"

"No, a risk that despite my assurances that you didn't have to think of marriage yet, some young man still might have caught your fancy at one of the many parties you were to attend. That would have forced my hand because your marriage is much too important to squander here."

"Here? But you like the English! You raised me to be English. I've spent my whole life here, so where else would I marry — ?" She cut herself off with a gasp. "Surely not Lubinia!?" He didn't deny it, which made her incredulous enough to remind him, "When I asked you about our homeland, you said it was a backward country, nigh medieval in some ways, that we were lucky to escape it. You warned me never to tell anyone that we were born there, that we should say we are from Austria instead, because they'd end up looking down on us if they knew we were Lubinians. And I didn't tell anyone the truth because even the one tutor I had who included Lubinia in my studies didn't contradict what you said. He confirmed that it's a backward country whose progress has been hindered by its isolation. You can't possibly want me to marry *there*," she ended with disdain.

He was shaking his head at her, but she knew immediately that it was because he was disappointed by the abhorrence she'd just revealed. "It's highly doubtful that you will have to, but it's not our decision to —" He stopped, waving that thought away to address her attitude. "I am surprised at you. From a few remarks you developed contempt for your own country?"

"That isn't fair. *You* didn't want me to even claim it as mine. What else was I to think?"

"There was a reason for that, and not the one I gave you. But I expected you to form your own opinion someday when you had more facts, when you could read about the beauty of the country and its culture that lies beyond its rough edges. Obviously it's my mistake for not instilling in you some pride in our homeland sooner, and there *is* much to be proud of."

"Perhaps — I overreacted," she said, abashed.

He smiled at her with a light reprimand. "Yes, and to an issue that isn't even an issue yet. You don't need to think about a marriage that isn't even remotely imminent. I only mentioned it to explain what would have eventually been the catalyst for this discussion. But something else has occurred recently and became the catalyst instead."

She didn't want to hear it when instinctively she knew what had changed his timing — he'd been told he was dying. He never dressed warmly enough when he went out, and he went out so often, to the orphanage, to the wine shop he owned; and at least once a week without fail, warm weather or cold, he took one of the orphans on a special outing. Oh, God, what had he caught that was killing him? He didn't look sick. . . .

"I love you, princess. Never doubt that. But you and I aren't family. We aren't related at all."

Her panic receded immediately. That news was — distressing, shocking. But it certainly wasn't as bad as what she'd just been thinking. Was she the first orphan he'd helped? He'd helped so many, it wasn't really surprising that he'd begun doing so by taking in one to raise.

"Did I really have to know that?" she asked.

"That is only a minor part of what I have to tell you."

Oh, God, there was more? "Why don't we have dinner first?" Alana quickly suggested.

He gave her a knowing look. "Calm yourself and don't jump to any more conclusions. You know better."

She blushed. These were things he'd taught her. Facts first. Intuition only as a last resort. And he was giving her facts. She just didn't want to hear them!

Obviously he guessed as much because he remarked, "Before we got here, I actually thought about farming."

That was so out of context, she blinked.

Was he trying to distract her to calm her down? It worked — a little. But then it clicked. "Farmer isn't your real name, is it?"

"No. But when we arrived in this bustling city, I realized the best way to hide us would be in plain sight right in the city, so I gave up any thoughts of farming. It was still a good name, solid, and it didn't sound foreign. It fit in, just as we fit in." He smiled when he added, "I did try gardening, though. I even found it rather peaceful for a few months, but then I gave it up."

"Too boring compared to what you used to do?"

She was thinking of the wars he had fought in on the Continent. She had learned about so many wars when she'd studied the history of Europe.

"Perceptive of you. Good." He paused for a moment, even cast his eyes down at the floor again. "I told you once that I killed people. You were rather young. You might not remember that, and it wasn't something I wanted to repeat."

"I remember. Why did you even tell me that?"

"You were a darling child, beautiful, inquisitive, and I was becoming much too attached to you. I threw it out there as a buffer, so you'd think about it and maybe come to fear me. But it didn't work. No barrier formed between us. You were too trusting, and I was already too attached. I love you as if you were the daughter I never had."

"I feel the same way, Poppie. You know that."

"Yes, but that will change today."

Her apprehension was back, a hundred times worse. Good Lord, what could he tell her that would make her stop loving him? She couldn't voice the words to ask, and her mind jumped frantically ahead, but absolutely nothing occurred to her that would explain what he'd just said.

And he didn't explain it either. He turned reflective instead. "I didn't intend to raise you like this, you know. I had envisioned isolation, for your own protection, and so you would learn not to depend on others. But in the end, I couldn't deny you a normal life. That may have been a mistake I'll have to live with. But until you are settled, it is imperative that you trust no one."

"Even you?"

"I believe I am the exception. I could never harm you, princess. That's why you're here."

"What do you mean?"

He closed his eyes for a moment. She was reminded that he didn't want to tell her these things, that something else was forcing this confession.

He gave her a direct look. "I told you I used to kill people. I was —"

"You *just* told me it was a lie," she cut in sharply, "that you only said it to put distance between us and it didn't work."

"No, I didn't say it was a lie, you chose a more palatable interpretation. The simple truth is, Alana, that I killed people for money. It was a lucrative career and one I was adept at because I had no care for my own life. I was an instrument of death for other people to wield, and I never failed a job I was hired for. My record was spotless. Not many hired assassins were as dependable as I was."

Her mind was in absolute denial. He was describing someone else. Had he hurt his head? Could he not remember his real past?

"For whatever reason you believe you used to do this, it's *not* true!"

"Why not?"

"Because you are a kind, caring man. You took in an orphan to raise. You have given others a chance for a decent life they wouldn't have had without your help. You're not a killer. Just because you know about weapons doesn't make you a killer!"

He tsked. "Use the intelligence we have honed. It's what I was. It's not what I am now. I wish it wasn't so, but it is. I wish someone had killed me long ago, but I was too good. I wish I couldn't remember my real past, but I do."

She made a mewling sound. "You really did this?"

"It's all right if you hate me now," he said in a pained tone. "I have expected it."

"I — I'm trying to understand how you could do this. Help me!"

He sighed. "I wasn't going to share this, but perhaps you should hear how it began. My real name is Leonard Kastner. My family were winemakers. We grew grapes in the fertile mountain valleys of Lubinia. Ours had been a large family, but many members were old and died of natural causes before I was grown. But then my father was caught in an avalanche and my mother succumbed to an illness that same winter. There was grief, despair, but my brother and I continued on, or tried to. He was barely five years old, so of no real help. And nature conspired against us again. We lost the grapes that year, and our home, since we could no longer pay the rent to the nobleman who owned the land. He would have taken as-surances from my father, but he wouldn't from me."

"What you're describing is pitiful, but . . ."

He waited for her to finish that thought, but she couldn't. She didn't *want* to con-demn him out of hand, but how could she not? She slumped back in her chair, saying instead, "Go on, please."

He nodded, but there was still silence. He was staring at the floor again, but sightlessly, the memories in his mind so obviously pain-ful that tears formed in her own eyes.

She jumped to her feet. "Never mind. I will endeavor to try —"

"Sit down," he snapped without looking at her.

She didn't. Her only thought was to flee because she knew what was coming. He was going to tell her that he'd killed her family, had been paid to do it, and she feared what he was going to ask her to do. *I wish some-one had killed me long ago.* Is that what he'd raised her for, why he'd trained her to use weapons? So she could avenge her parents' honor and be the one to kill him?

CHAPTER FOUR

Calmly this time Poppie said, "Sit down, Alana. This tale is only half-done, and it will never be spoken of again. *You* helped me to bury it. You took away the nightmares. You gave me back my humanity. You deserve to know what you saved me from."

Slowly, she took her seat again, but only because she was feeling faint. She felt sick to her stomach — oh, God! She'd thought she'd solve her own dilemma today. She'd never thought she'd be shocked, again and again, by things too horrible to contemplate.

"It was a struggle at first after my brother and I lost our home. We moved to the city, where jobs were plentiful, only to find that no one would hire me when I was not quite a man yet. But I supported us meagerly with menial jobs until a watchmaker took me on as his apprentice. It was precision work. I enjoyed it much more than growing grapes. And it supported us well. He was a kind man who lived alone with his only child, a daughter younger than I. It was impossible not to fall in love with her. Several years later she agreed to be my wife. I felt blessed. She was the most beautiful woman I'd ever seen — and she gave me a son. They meant everything to me, they were my life. And then they were taken from me, my brother with them, in a senseless accident."

"I'm sorry," she gasped.

He didn't seem to hear her, he was so deep in his memories now. "I was consumed with rage — and possibly a little insane over how painful their deaths had been. They burned, trapped inside their coach, which had been pushed over into one of the contained street fires that are used to melt the ice. If the coach had covered that fire completely when it toppled onto it, it might have snuffed it out. If the wagon that crashed into them hadn't been overladen, the oxen might have been pulled back off the coach in time, instead of making escape impossible. It had been an accident, but the driver of that delivery wagon was drunk, so it was an accident that never should have happened. That is why my rage wouldn't go away, and why I finally found that drunken old man and killed him. But that didn't make the rage go away either. Everything important in my life had been ripped from me. With nothing left to live for, I wanted to die. So I sought out the owner of the company that drunk had worked for and killed him, too. I wanted to be caught, but I wasn't. I couldn't bear to see my father-in-law again because he reminded me of my wife, so I stopped working for him. I was starving by then and spending every last coin I had on drink so I could stop remembering what I'd lost. And then I heard of someone who would actually pay me for what I'd been doing."

And this is how a killer was born? Alana wondered. But Poppie wasn't like that. She'd lived with him all her life. Nothing, ever, had prepared her to deal with this tale.

"Were they at least deserving of death, those you were sent to kill?"

"Is anyone, really?"

"You say that now, but what about then?"

"No, back then I did the job mindlessly and collected the money. I didn't care. But, yes, some were deserving. Other jobs, the ones who paid me were the ones who should have died instead. I didn't value my life any more than I valued the lives of those I was sent to kill. There were so many reasons to hire men like me, politics, revenge, simply eliminating business competition or enemies. And I certainly wasn't unique in my profession, far from it. If I didn't take the jobs, someone else would have been hired for them."

"You can't claim that as an excuse. Fate might have decreed it otherwise."

"True," he agreed. "Yet that justification was still somewhere in the back of my mind. I was good. I could kill mercifully. Better me than a butcher who enjoyed his work too much. I was known only as Rastibon, and as Rastibon, my fame quickly grew."

"Another false name?"

"Yes, a name that wasn't associated with my true identity in any way. And eventually I actually valued my reputation for never having failed a job. I'm not even sure why. Pride in a talent, I suppose, even if it was a despicable talent. After seven years I began to think of retiring Rastibon with that perfect record, before it was tarnished by a failure."

"Was that the only reason you considered quitting?" she asked.

"No, the rage was gone, it no longer governed me. The desire to be caught so someone else would end my life was gone, too."

"You couldn't do it yourself?"

He gave her a wry look. "I remember trying several times during the worst of my hell, only to find my sense of self-preservation hadn't died with my morality. But that morality began to assert itself again, making me question what I was doing, and if no sense of justice was involved in a job, making me disgusted by it. So it was a good time to quit."

She had to ask it. "You've trained me to become an assassin like you, haven't you? Why else would you teach me to master so many weapons?"

"Don't be absurd. I trained you in weapons so you would be able to protect yourself and use your body effectively as a defense."

"Why would I need to?"

"Because of who you are, Alana."

"And who is that?"

"You are a Stindal."

The name sounded familiar, but she couldn't place it, not with so much horror clouding her mind. Did it mean she had family still alive, or . . . ?

"How did you come by me? And please, Poppie, please don't tell me you killed my parents. I don't think I could —"

"No, princess," he quickly cut in. "I wasn't hired to do that. I never had to kill a woman, although I thought I could. I even thought I could kill an infant."

Nothing surprised her at this point. "You were hired to kill me, weren't you?" she guessed.

"Yes."

"Then why aren't I dead?"

"Because you smiled at me. I had the knife at your throat, but you smiled and I couldn't do it. I decided to end my spotless career with a blemish after all, though until this day, only one other person knew that I didn't kill you."

"What do you mean?"

"I was paid to get rid of you, half the gold paid in advance. To 'get rid of you' could mean only one thing. I didn't doubt what the job was. And yet it could be open to interpretation. I never went back to collect the rest of the payment, letting them assume I died while completing my task. And your disappearance spoke for itself. The job was done to the letter, as it was described. I had gotten rid of you. That the ones who hired me assumed you were dead was of no consequence to me and a benefit to you. It meant they wouldn't be sending anyone else to kill you."

"Did you let my parents think I was dead, too?"

"No, actually, I didn't. You were quickly teaching me compassion, and giving me back the feelings of a parent. I thought I would never feel such things again. Your mother had already died of natural causes, but I sympathized with your father and sent him a missive several months later to tell him I would keep you safe until he found out who wanted you dead."

"He's alive?" she asked in a small voice.

"Yes."

"He's that one other person you just referred to, who knew you failed to complete that job?"

"Yes, the only one I ever told."

"Thank you for letting him know."

"Don't thank me. I'm not even sure he got my missive. And the news of your disappearance traveled so fast, I heard of it before I got too far from Lubinia, since I was delayed by the necessity of finding a nursemaid for you who would be willing to travel with us. Your father only thought you had been stolen. I don't doubt he expected you back after he satisfied a demand for ransom. My missive may have been harder for him to bear because it indicated that you wouldn't be returned to him until he eliminated the enemies who had tried to harm him by killing his daughter."

"So my death was only to be a means of hurting him?" she guessed.

"Of course."

"But eighteen years have passed, Poppie. In all this time he didn't find out who did this?"

"He's a good man, but in matters of intrigue, he has proven to be utterly incompetent," Poppie said with some disdain. "He had to have known who his enemies were back then, yet no confession was ever obtained."

"How do you know? Do *you* know who it was?"

"No, I would have told him if I did. But I rarely ever dealt directly with my employers. They were typically too fearful of having a finger pointed at them later, for having hired an assassin. Some of my clients came cloaked, disguising their voices. Most of them sent lackeys to hire and pay me. A few times a voice would whisper to me from the shadows and a purse of gold would be tossed at my feet. I didn't care. They were making me rich and I was living a dead life, devoid of happiness, devoid of anything to care for — until you entered my life."

"How have you kept apprised of what my real father has or hasn't done? Or is he English? No, that was a stupid question. Of course I'm not really English. You wouldn't hide me in the same country you took me from."

He raised a brow. "Assumptions, Alana?"

She blushed. "Ignore them and answer the original question please."

"I monitored our country indirectly. I joined a gentleman's club that catered to European émigrés and was also frequented my members of His Majesty's Foreign Office, who knew the latest information about foreign affairs. They were willing to share that information as long as it was common knowledge in those countries rather than anything secretive."

"*This* was your source of information?" she asked incredulously.

"It was a safe way to find out what was going on without drawing attention to us. And it did produce results. It took four years before your father's name was mentioned, but it wasn't the news I sought, merely that he had remarried finally. When you were seven, there was another tidbit, that with so much time having passed, it was now presumed you were dead."

Two things occurred to her immediately. Poppie didn't really want to give her back, and her father, with a new wife, probably didn't want her back.

"How could you be so passive about finding out what was going on in our homeland? How could you leave it to chance like that?" she exclaimed. "Why didn't you go back yourself and find out for sure?"

"I wasn't going to leave you for that long a time or take you with me. Our homeland isn't exactly close to England."

"I don't believe you! Admit it. You love me too much. That's why you haven't made any real effort to find out if it was safe to return me to my father."

He didn't try to calm her. The tender smile he gave her was from the heart. "You are correct that I love you too much. But I honestly didn't think I would have the care of you for this long. I thought a few years at the most. After that, I thought each year would be the last. After ten years, I began to teach you in earnest to protect yourself, because I still thought I wouldn't have you much longer. But I was no longer leaving it to chance. I was alarmed when I learned your father presumed you were dead. I thought about sending your father another missive, to assure him you were still alive. But again, I couldn't be sure it would reach him. So I assumed my old ways of secrecy instead and hired someone who didn't know who I was, didn't see my face, couldn't trace me in any way, and could find out exactly what I wanted to know."

"Did he?"

He nodded. "There had been a mock funeral. There was no pretense of it being otherwise. It was only a formality to put your memory to rest."

"That's — morbid!"

"It was a clear statement that all hope was gone that you would ever be recovered. But the investigation wasn't over, it was renewed with vigor, in fact, as if you had only just been killed. Having lost all hope, your father finally wanted revenge. Understandable, if a bit late. But I was told that an effort was still being made to find out who had set this plot in motion."

"You could have just taken me back. You could have let my father protect me. You should have, when I was still a child, before —"

"He didn't protect you from me, Alana," Poppie cut in sharply to remind her. "You were too easy to get to. I was *not* going to take that chance with a life I came to value more than my own."

Just enough defensive umbrage was in his tone to give her pause. He sounded so sincere, yet *how* could she believe all this? Death plots, assassins, stolen babies. If this tale was true, didn't he realize he'd waited too long to tell her? She was an adult. *This* was her home, not some foreign place that had no meaning for her. And she had no interest in knowing her real father, whom Poppie disparaged as incompetent and incapable of protecting her.

"Why did you wait this long to tell me all this?" she demanded.

"I couldn't tell you sooner. I didn't want you growing up knowing who you were, and thinking you were so important that you didn't need to learn anything from others. I wouldn't have told you now except —"

"Important? *Who* am I?"

"I told you, a Stindal."

"That name means nothing to me," she said in frustration. "Please be more specific."

He tsked at her. "You know. Your studies were thorough. Your father is Frederick Stindal, the reigning monarch of Lubinia."

After all the shocks she'd just absorbed, those words were a soothing balm because they *proved* none of this was real. She even began to laugh.

"This has all been a bad joke, hasn't it? Are you testing my fortitude, my gullibility? Obviously I failed, royally — no pun intended. Good Lord, that's a relief. You really had . . . me . . ."

Her words trailed off. Poppie wasn't laughing with her, and his expression had turned more serious than she'd ever seen it. "This wasn't an easy decision for me. I've been grappling with it for weeks. I always knew I would have to take you back someday to claim your birthright, but not until it was safe to do so. It infuriates me that it *still* isn't safe! Yet I've had news that makes it imperative that we go back now."

She leapt to her feet. "No! I won't leave the life I love here, I won't!"

"Alana, the old regime, the late king Ernest's most fervent supporters, are trying to depose your father. They are using rebels to agitate the people to revolt, spreading lies that the king is ill and might soon die without a proper heir. It will come to war if —"

"Stop it!" she cried angrily, tears running down her cheeks. "I won't listen to any more of this. How could you even ask that of me when you don't care about that country any more than I do? How could you care? You're an — an assassin! Oh, God!"

CHAPTER FIVE

She had run out of Poppie's office and locked herself in her room. He had followed, but she was crying too hard to hear his entreaties to let him in, and eventually the pounding on her door stopped.

She just wanted to wake up, to once again have nothing to worry about other than Lord Adam Chapman and his intentions, and an introduction to society that seemed superfluous now, when she wanted to devote her life to teaching. . . .

The tears wouldn't stop. She wasn't waking up either. This nightmare was real.

Poppie had lied to her all her life. How could he possibly think she'd believe anything he said now, especially something so preposterous. A princess? He should have told her the truth, instead of a ridiculous tale like that. But she believed he was a killer. She tried to deny that, too. She tried so hard! But he wouldn't tell her something that horrible unless it was true. Yet there had to be some other reason he wanted to take her back to Lubinia. It could be as simple as an old betrothal and her future husband was now demanding his bride. And Poppie must have changed his story midway when she'd revealed her contempt for their homeland, and her abhorrence to marrying anyone from it. But a princess? He should have known she wouldn't believe *that!*

"Alana, open the door for me," Annette called out. "I've brought your dinner."

Alana stared hard at the door, then walked over to it and put her wet cheek against it. "Are you alone?"

"Certainly, why wouldn't I be?"

Alana wiped her sleeve across her cheeks quickly and opened the door. She immediately moved away from it toward her bureau. She hadn't put her pistol away yet. She took it out of her pocket now and dropped it into a drawer. So silly that Poppie insisted she carry it with her at all times, just because she knew how to use it.

Her pocket was still heavy. She'd forgotten about the carving Henry had given her — it seemed so long ago instead of just that afternoon. She set the soldier up on the bureau next to the figure of the young lady. Henry was so talented that the wooden female figure did actually look like her in one of her winter dresses minus a bonnet. Henry. Once more, tears filled her eyes. Would she ever see that dear child again? Or would Poppie forbid her to go to the orphanage now?

"You two had an argument?" Annette said from behind her as she slid a tray onto the low table next to the sofa. "I've never seen your uncle so distraught. It must have been very serious."

Annette sounded worried. But Alana held her tongue. She wasn't going to talk about those horrible revelations to anyone. Ever.

"Come, I brought my dinner, too, so I could dine with you. We'll hold our plates. It will be good practice for the parties you will be attending where the hostess feeds you, but won't seat you!"

Now Annette was trying to sound cheerful? There wouldn't be any parties. Alana was probably going to have to leave this house, too. She couldn't stay here knowing what she did about Poppie's past. She'd seek out Lord Chapman. If she wasn't wrong about his intentions, perhaps she could escalate his courtship and make it brief. Surely she could create some plausible excuse not to delay.

"Alana, please. Talk to me. I'll mediate for

you and your uncle so we can put this situation to rights. You'll both laugh about being so silly."

"I don't think I'll ever laugh again."

She said that to herself. She wasn't even facing Annette. The older woman shouldn't have heard her. But Alana heard the gasp.

"This isn't about Adam, is it?"

Alana swung around. "Why would you think that?"

Annette blushed. She looked so pretty. Someone should have snatched her up as soon as her husband died — well, after a decent interval for mourning.

"Because I know what he's up to," Annette admitted. "He's been pursuing an acquaintance with you in an attempt to make me jealous. I'd hoped he'd stop being so foolish so I wouldn't have to tell you what he's doing."

"Did Poppie tell you to say this?" Alana asked suspiciously.

"Certainly not. But your uncle is aware of the situation. I was forced to tell him what I should have told you sooner. Sit down, please. Let me explain."

More revelations today when she was already drowning in them? But Alana sat next to Annette. She even picked up her plate. Eating was the sensible thing to do, but she wasn't sure she could manage it with so much turmoil rolling about inside her. Was Lord Chapman about to be removed as an option, too?

"You know I lost my parents," Annette began. "My cousin was forced to take me in, but she hated having to do so, even for those few years until I came of age. She arranged parties for me. She wanted me to find a husband immediately and be gone from her house. I met Adam at one of those parties. I quickly fell in love with him. And he felt the same way."

"Then why didn't you marry him?"

"I thought we would marry. I was so happy. But then he confessed he felt he was too young to marry. That he hadn't tasted life yet, whatever that meant. I was furious with him. We had a terrible argument. He was breaking my heart because he didn't want to face responsibility yet? And I couldn't wait for him even if I wanted to, not with my cousin insisting I accept the first offer that was made."

"So you married Lord Hensen?"

"Yes, a man I didn't even like. But at least he was kind. My misery was of my own making because I still loved another man. But then my husband died not even a year into our marriage, and his family showed me the door when they came to rip apart his estate. My cousin wouldn't take me back again either. I was forced to find a job, but no one would hire me. I was either too young or too pretty. I sold everything I had of value just to get from meal to meal. Your uncle found me crying in the park. I'd just sold the last of my clothes other than what I was wearing. I was facing a life of poverty — or worse. He spoke to me quietly to find out what was wrong. He offered me this job. He gave me back my dignity and peace of mind. He saved me, and I'll always be more grateful than either of you could know."

Alana didn't want to hear how kind Poppie was. It was all a pretense! Annette had no idea — nor would she. Alana could never tell anyone that she'd been raised by an *assassin.* The founder of an orphanage, the rescuer of genteel ladies, the man who had changed his life to save her from people who wanted her dead — no! Lies, lies, and more lies. What could she believe anymore?

Tears were pouring down her cheeks again. Annette saw them and misunderstood.

"Oh, dearest, he *has* trifled with your affections, hasn't he? This is my fault. I should have —"

"What? No, really. Lord Chapman has

been very proper and polite. He did mention he's ready to marry now, but perhaps he hoped I'd convey that to you? Why exactly do you think he's trying to make you jealous?"

"Because he came here to see me. He begged me to forgive him for his past mistake. He asked me to marry him now. But it's too late and I told him so. He can't break my heart and then show up years later and expect to be welcomed with open arms. So he went straight to your uncle and asked permission to court you. I followed him. He was trying to force my hand. I could see it in his expression. And he did, but not as he hoped. I confided in your uncle instead and told him exactly what I've told you. He showed Adam the door and warned him not to see you again. But he has. Mary has told me how often he stops you on the street."

"Which has made you jealous?" Alana guessed. "And prolonged your anger?"

"No, I —" Annette stopped. She looked embarrassed and confused and regretful.

Alana realized now that Lord Chapman had never been interested in courting her. Compared to everything else she'd learned today, it didn't matter to her all that much. But Alana could see that he meant a great deal to Annette, who hadn't just been one of her tutors and a chaperone all these years, but also a good friend.

"You should forgive him," Alana said. "He's not the man he used to be. He's ready for responsibility now. He's ready to make you happy in the marriage you wanted. Don't throw that away when he loves you and you still love . . . him."

Alana blanched. *You should forgive him. Not the man he used to be. He loves you.* Oh, God, what had she done?

She ran out of her room and downstairs. Poppie was still in his office, but standing in the middle of the room. He looked so broken, so pained, as if he'd lost everyone in the world who mattered to him. And he had. She'd done that by condemning him for what he'd done instead of remembering the man he'd become, the one who had atoned for his past in so many different ways.

"I'm sorry!" she cried as she ran to him, right into his open arms. "I didn't mean to react so — so —"

She couldn't continue because she was sobbing. Annette, who had followed her downstairs in alarm, quietly closed the door behind them, while Poppie held Alana close, gently soothing her, letting her release all of the emotions that were pent up inside her.

"Shh," he finally said. "It was my fault for telling you everything at once. It was too much. And I expected you to hate me now."

"No! I don't! I love you, Poppie. Nothing will ever change that."

"Then you can forgive me?"

It was hard to say yes, but not so hard to say, "I know you're not like that anymore. You're good and kind, and you've helped so many people."

She felt his relief as he hugged her more tightly. She leaned back so he could see she was sincere. His eyes were moist, too, as he tenderly wiped her cheeks with the back of his fingers. She still felt a sense of dread about the other things he'd said. She couldn't let him think she was willing to go to Lubinia when she wasn't.

"Poppie, please, at least tell me that some of what you said was a lie," she beseeched him now. "Please tell me I'm not the daughter of a king."

"I can't do that," he said sadly.

She closed her eyes. "Everything I love is here in London. I don't want to leave. I want to teach. I want to help people as you have."

"Then help your country by preventing a war, princess. Only you can do that, you know. I wouldn't take you back for any other reason except so many lives are at stake now, lives that you can save by standing beside your father to prove he does still have his heir."

CHAPTER SIX

Poppie was taking her home to Lubinia. Her father wasn't dying. He had made numerous public appearances to prove it, according to Poppie's informant. But that hadn't helped, not when his enemies were spreading the rumor that he had a weak heart that wouldn't last much longer. Some people were even blaming his weak heart for his inability to produce another heir in all these years. Many of the commoners who were being agitated were so backward they believed these lies. So only she could put their fears to rest.

Of course she had to go back to Lubinia, there was no question. Her own hopes and dreams were meaningless next to saving lives. But after the rebels had retreated and their lies had been disputed, she was still going to be left with a father she didn't want, and a new life she wanted even less.

There was nothing to keep them from

leaving England immediately. Thanks to Poppie's efforts over the years, the orphanage had a long list of benefactors supporting it now who would continue to run it. And Alana already had a brand-new wardrobe for the London Season that was befitting of a princess. A real princess. No endearment after all. And she never once suspected. How could she have thought the term was more than an endearment when the truth was still so hard to accept?

She knew Poppie didn't plan to return to England himself — because he didn't think she ever would, and he intended to remain close to her. He made it clear they weren't returning when he gave his house to Annette to live in or to sell, whichever she pleased. But when hugging her friend good-bye, Alana whispered, "I'll be back."

She would, too. She'd do whatever she had to do to remove the threat of war from the country of her birth, but then she'd tell her father to get himself another heir. She didn't share these brave thoughts with Poppie, but she held them close in her heart and mind. Otherwise, she'd be terrified of what lay ahead, instead of just nervous.

The only bright spot upon leaving the home she loved was Henry Mathews's crawling into the coach the morning of their departure. With his endearing, cheeky grin, he told her, "I'm goin' with you! Imagine that, eh? Me, crossin' the bleedin' Continent. Who'da ever thought?"

All she could think to do was hug him, she was so delighted. Later at the docks when they had a moment alone, Poppie explained, "I know how fond you are of the boy. I thought he might make this trip a little easier for you. And once you're reunited with your father, he's someone I can trust to get messages to you."

She guessed it might be more that Poppie had grown accustomed to raising a child and Henry would make a fine replacement for her. That saddened and gladdened her equally. But Henry did help keep her mind off what lay ahead for at least some of the trip, especially during the hours she worked with him on his studies, including teaching him the Lubinian language.

She had been taught the two main languages they encountered most frequently on the journey, and a smattering of others. Ever since she'd learned German, she had understood Poppie whenever he had spoken to her in Lubinian, since the two languages were so similar. She hadn't realized he'd been doing it deliberately to prepare her for this unwanted future.

Poppie kept reminding her of her extraordinary future in his efforts to get her to think more kindly of the country he loved. "Lubinia is not perfect, but it can be," he told her. "And in a perfect world, you can have what you want. I see no reason why you can't teach in the palace. Children can be brought to you. I see no reason you can't continue to do so after your marriage."

"Which won't be of my choosing, will it?" she said bitterly.

He sighed, admitting what she'd already guessed. "As a royal, your husband is bound to be handpicked for you, and your marriage will likely be in service of a political alliance that will benefit the country. But you will be reunited with your father. He isn't going to want to let you go off soon into a marriage. And while most royals grow up aware of their responsibilities and knowing what their future holds, you didn't. The king might take that into account."

"And give me a choice?" she scoffed, not believing it for a minute.

"I detect anger. Do you really not want — ?"

"I'm here, aren't I?" she cut in, but then she tried to ease his worry with the truth. "I'm just nervous, afraid I won't like my father or, worse, might even insult him with

74

my disdain."

"This is my fault. Don't make my contempt yours. This plot that involved you is the *only* instance where his leadership has been questionable. But I'm sure there are reasons why it hasn't been resolved, and we will learn of them soon enough. He's a good man, Alana. I was in the streets the day of your birth, when Frederick's heir was shown to the crowds. It didn't matter that you were female, the cheers from the crowd were deafening. Your father has been well loved by his people."

"Then why do they want to dispose of him?"

"Fear. They're being made to think he will die soon, leaving them without a king. Most are willing to wait until that happens. It's the younger men who are being stirred to revolt, those who don't remember why the old regime was overthrown. But this conspiracy will die a quick death with your return. Don't worry, you will love the king. How can you not? He's your father."

What if she did? What if she was so delighted with him that she'd willingly do anything he asked of her, just to please him? That wasn't a kernel of hope, it would be a dilemma!

"I have trained you for this day," Poppie

continued, "for you to assume your rightful place, and for you to be able to protect yourself. But I didn't know *how* to train you to be a ruling monarch. I did my best by giving you the widely diverse education a young nobleman would receive."

"I think you gave me more than that. Diplomacy, the art of negotiating, a firm knowledge of every ruling house in Europe — including my own. I did pay attention to those lessons about Lubinia. The house of Bruslan ruled for centuries, but the last Bruslan to sit on the throne, King Ernest, made such bad decisions for his people that they rose up in a civil war, which ultimately killed him. The Stindals, father and son, ruled after him. Did I remember that correctly?"

"Indeed, but you were not told why the Stindals were chosen instead of one of the Bruslan heirs, and there were *many* Bruslans who might have been chosen. You're actually distantly related to them, though the two branches of the family severed ties long ago and never reconciled. So while the Stindals shared the same royal bloodline, they were viewed as a change from the Bruslans, whom the people no longer trusted. This was why a Stindal was chosen. Tradition was satisfied, and the people were rid of a despised family who'd dominated the throne for too long."

"It sounds as if the Bruslans would have much to gain if there were no Stindals remaining."

"Indeed, and you and your father are the last two. But while it is logical to conclude that the Bruslans instigated the plot to assassinate you, your father would have realized that, too, yet he took no action against them. Until I know why he didn't, I have to conclude he may have other enemies I'm unaware of. Now enough of history. You were taught well, though it still wasn't enough. But your father isn't an old man. You still have many years ahead of you in which to learn anything a royal should know that I've overlooked."

A royal. How could he think she would want this? She *did* want to meet her father though. She couldn't help but be curious about him, more than she cared to admit. But she didn't want the responsibility that might come after that meeting. The thought of having a whole country dependent on her decisions someday was more than she felt capable of dealing with. Nor did she want the restrictions. And she certainly didn't want a complete separation from Poppie, who wouldn't be welcomed with open arms the way she would be.

She was worried about Poppie, too. He was going to devote himself fully now to what her father should have done years ago, finding the person or persons who had hired him to kill her. Until those people were gone, her safety was at risk.

"Did you ever kill again after you brought me to England?" she asked him one night.

They were on the way to the theater in Paris. They had traveled without stopping up to that point, so he was allowing them a day of rest, and a little time to see something of that great old city. The shock of who she was had actually tempered the shock of who Poppie had been. At least she could discuss it now without feeling sick to her stomach.

"No, though there was one instance when I might have had to," Poppie confided. "It was only a few months after I sent that missive to your father. I heard that a couple of men, obviously foreigners, were visiting London's immigrant neighborhoods asking if anyone knew of a Lubinian man with a child or children who had recently arrived. The Londoners weren't very cooperative. I only heard about it, and no one ever showed up at our house."

"So they might not have been searching for me?"

"It could have been unrelated, but I never doubted you would be searched for, despite my assurance to your father. He might have thought that he could protect you better than I could."

She stared at Poppie hard. "So you would have actually killed my father's men?"

"Do not mistake the situation, Alana," he said gravely. "While I was as positive as I could be under the circumstances that my employer was done with the matter, convinced that you had been killed, I wasn't going to completely dismiss the possibility that I could be wrong."

They were traveling halfway across Europe, and it wasn't the best time of year for it, with winter so soon upon them. There would be snow, and lots of it, the higher they got into the mountains. She had been taught about the countries they passed through, all of France, into the Rhineland, where they paused once more in the Grand Duchy of Baden, then on through Württemberg.

Halfway through the Kingdom of Bavaria, they paused one last time, in Munich. There, Poppie suggested she disguise herself as a boy for the last leg of the journey. She didn't think at first that he was serious, but he was.

"You are too pretty," he told her. "You draw attention to us, which we don't want. And it bothers me that I don't know if you look like your mother. It would be the worst luck for you to be recognized before we get to the palace."

"And if I don't look like her? How am I going to prove who I am?"

"With the truth. And with this."

He took a tiny bracelet from his pocket and placed it in her hand. Made of gold and decorated with small gems, it had an engraving on the inside. She could only make out half of it, her name.

"The letters are so small I can't read the first word. What else does it say?"

"It's the Lubinian word for 'princess.' It says 'Princess Alana.' "

She put the trinket in the small, silk-lined box that contained her jewelry and Henry's carvings, which she kept locked and buried deep in one of her trunks. That small piece of her past brought home, more than anything else, that she was Alana, daughter of Frederick, current ruler of Lubinia. She cried herself to sleep that night. Nothing was ever going to be the same again.

CHAPTER SEVEN

They would arrive in Lubinia today. Even though the trip had been long, Alana still thought it was too soon to reach their destination. They were high in the mountains, surrounded by a pristine white landscape. Then a furious snow-storm seemed to come out of nowhere, it was upon them so fast. The trail on the mountain pass they had to traverse grew narrower the higher they climbed. It was so steep that everyone, even the driver, had to get out of the coach and walk in front of it. The sudden snow now made the already slippery trail treacherous.

"It's an ancient trail, rarely used anymore," Poppie shouted above the wind that was blowing the snow in their faces. He was in the lead right in front of her, yet he still had to shout! Behind them, the driver carefully coaxed the coach horses forward. "Not many visitors come from this direction,"

Poppie added.

"Nonetheless, it should still be made less dangerous," she complained as she hugged the mountain rocks on the safe side of the trail. "At least a few fences or —"

"Something you can order when you are queen."

She detected his humor. "Something I can mention to my father," she countered. It made Poppie laugh.

It was so cold she was glad she wasn't wearing a dress, which would have been troublesome in this wind. Her hair was tightly braided and tucked into her coat with its collar raised high. A woolen cap was pulled over her forehead, concealing the rest of her hair. She should have taken a scarf out of her trunks to cover her face though. She could feel her cheeks being pelted by some of the flakes, which were more ice than snow. Fortunately, her britches had been made for weather like this; they were so thick they almost seemed to be padded.

She kept one glove-covered hand on the rocks, while the other tightly clasped Henry's hand. She thought she heard him whistling, or maybe that was the wind. But she knew he was viewing this as an adventure, silly boy. He'd been having the time of his life on this journey, asking questions and expressing fascination about everything they saw. She and Poppie had told him, of course, the reason for the trip, but they'd given him a simplified version that didn't include royalty. They merely said that Alana was going to be reunited with her father, whom she'd never before met.

Henry had gotten new winter clothes in Munich, too. Nothing fancy for either of them. They looked like a couple of peasants, and she'd teased him about that earlier.

Just as they were negotiating a curvy part of the trail, they were almost run over. In the blinding snow and gusty wind, the oncoming horses reared up as they encountered the coach blocking their way. One horse nearly slid off the mountain. Alana screamed as she watched it trying to regain its footing, until she was smashed against the rocks by another horse and lost her breath for a moment. More horses reared as they were yanked back from charging into the others, but their momentum kept them from stopping immediately.

She panicked when she lost Henry's hand, but he'd just scurried up the rocks out of the way, and for a better view of the mayhem. Not that he could see much of it, with the snow still coming down so heavily. But she couldn't see anything at all with one of the horses still pressed against her. She managed to squeeze herself out of that spot and move toward the coach horses where there was still a little room. Poppie followed her and put an arm protectively around her shoulder.

"Say nothing," he warned her. "Your voice is too telling."

Due to the sudden stop, the newcomers' horses crowded the narrow trail. Alana held her breath. Someone or some animal might still be pushed over that dangerous drop.

There were so many horses she couldn't count them all, and that many men mounted on them, all wearing the same long military coats, black, fur-banded caps, and thick scarves wrapped so high only their eyes were visible. They looked like bandits, she thought, though bandits wouldn't all dress alike like this. Were they soldiers? Or perhaps even rebels?

Then she noticed that the men were training their rifles on her, Poppie, and their driver. Instinctively, her hands slipped into her coat pockets to grip her pistols there. She couldn't actually fire them with such thick gloves on. Nor did she dare bring them out. She'd probably be shot instantly.

Some of the men were dismounting and

leading their horses back. One moved to the coach, opened its door, and looked inside it. She didn't see him come around the vehicle, but he suddenly pushed past her from behind. He paused though to grip her chin, but he let go before she could jerk her head away. The man did the same to Henry, who was moving closer to her now.

Then he reported to one of the men up front who had just dismounted, "Two adult males, two children. No one else in the coach."

More horses moved back the way they'd come. Some space had actually been cleared in front of them, but the man she'd just noticed dismounting seemed to fill a good part of it. He was tall, broad, and had an erect military bearing. She couldn't distinguish much of his face. With the snow still swirling around them, it was like looking at him through a white veil. All she could see was a bit of light-colored hair with snow clinging to it and shadowed eyes below the fur of his cap. He removed the glove from his right hand and moved his scarf down below his mouth. A strong nose was revealed, and a firm mouth that was set in a serious expression as his eyes narrowed on Poppie.

"If you rebels are recruiting children, I'll

shoot you right now."

Alana sucked in her breath, but Poppie quickly laughed at the accusation. "We're not rebels."

"Then what the hell are you doing up here in winter if you aren't from the camp rumored to be just over this pass? A rebel camp. It's too dangerous to be up here for any sane reason."

"We're trying to reach our lady's family before she does. She went ahead with her guards the longer way, through the northeastern pass. She was too impatient to wait for us when the baggage coach lost a wheel. But this wasn't a good decision on my part. I was told this way was quicker, but I wasn't warned of the hazardous conditions."

The soldier said nothing for a moment, a horribly tense moment, then replied with a snort, "There's always snow up here this time of year. Who is your lady?"

"She's a Naumann."

That name produced an immediate scowl. "The only female the Naumanns have left is an old grandmother too old to travel. You lie."

Oh, God, Poppie *would* have to choose a name the man recognized. At least five rifles rose up again with that accusation, but Poppie had no choice but to stick to his fabrication and he did so indignantly. "No, my lord, she is not the only one. Our lady is a second cousin who has not lived here for thirty years. This is only the second time I know of that she has returned to Lubinia to visit this branch of her family."

"So just servants, eh? Even the children?" the leader added in disgust. Yet he immediately barked a command, "Search the baggage for weapons."

Did that mean he still thought Poppie was lying? Or was the man just being thorough? The soldiers remained tense and didn't lower their rifles.

Alana would have kept a close eye on the soldier who climbed on top of the coach and opened her trunks and was rifling through them, but Poppie drew her attention again when he said, "My lady doesn't employ my nephews, but she generously allows them to live with me in her household."

The leader of these soldiers, whom Henry had been watching in fascination, was close enough to him to chuck the boy's chin and remark, "You don't look like your uncle."

She didn't think Henry had progressed far enough in his lessons to understand all of that phrase, yet he still mumbled, "Do, too."

Standing next to Henry, Alana heard him

clearly. He'd spoken in English! But, apparently, the leader hadn't heard him due to the wind because he pushed Henry out of his way and was now standing in front of her.

As he reached for her, she stiffened and raised her chin defiantly so he wouldn't have to touch her the way he'd touched Henry. She could see more of his face now. He had dazzling blue eyes and his hard mouth actually turned up at a corner in a half grin.

He glanced back at Poppie. "This one should be wearing skirts, no? Too pretty to be a boy." Guffaws erupted from the soldiers behind him, but he wasn't done yet. He turned her, and before she realized why, he brought his hand down hard on her arse. She was so shocked, she barely felt him squeeze one cheek. "So small, or shriveled from the cold?"

Poppie yanked her away from him before she reacted instinctively and slapped the man. She had no idea what he'd just insinuated, but he and his men were laughing uproariously about it.

"What the deuce did that lout mean about me being shriveled?" she hissed back at Poppie as he pushed her farther away toward the rocks.

"It was nothing, just a way to put his men

at ease."

That had certainly worked, they were all so bloody amused, while she was outraged. He'd smacked her! She couldn't believe it!

"Stay away from him," Poppie warned before he turned back to the leader.

He even grinned to go along with the humor that Alana was bristling over. "The boy knows and eagerly awaits hair to grow on his face."

"Does he?" the commander said, but he'd already lost interest.

The soldier he'd sent to search her baggage jumped down from the coach and reported, "Mostly fancy women's clothes, sir. No weapons."

Of course there were no weapons. Poppie carried his weapons on his person just as she did, and she'd never felt more like using one than she did right then. But the soldiers were obviously only looking for rifles, or they might have searched them, too, for smaller weapons.

She turned away before the brute caught her burning a hole through him with her eyes, but she heard him bark another order. "You. Move that coach out of the way to that wider ledge we just passed, and carefully. Push anyone over the cliff and you'll go with them." Then he addressed Poppie again. "Did you see the rebel camp on your way up here?"

"I saw no one anywhere near the pass, and it wasn't snowing when we started our climb. If there is a camp nearby, it can't be seen from the trail."

"We still have to prove or dispute the rumor. Go about your journey. You'll be out of the snow soon."

That quickly they were dismissed, and they all got behind the coach to follow it down the mountain. Relief should have calmed Alana, but she was still highly indignant over being the brunt of some rude man's joke she didn't even understand. The long line of soldiers passed in single file now as they continued on their way. She couldn't help noting that they were *all* tall, making her wonder if height was a requirement for the Lubinian army, or worse — if her homeland was populated by giants!

CHAPTER EIGHT

Their brush with the military was over, but the snow continued to fall. As soon as the last soldier disappeared in that white, swirling veil, Alana pulled Poppie aside and asked him, "Why did you address that lout as 'my lord'?"

"For no reason other than flavor to support the role I was playing of a menial servant."

"Was he bluffing, or are the Naumanns actually real people that he might know of?"

"They're landowners," Poppie replied. "The same wealthy family mine used to rent from, and the first noble name I could think of to use."

"Ah," she said, but what she really wanted to know was "Is the army here really that coarse and brutish?"

"Lubinia is too small to support a professional army, but the palace guard is extensive, and I don't doubt there has been additional recruitment to deal with the rebels."

"Those were palace guards!" she gasped. "Even worse! It's like they're from the last century, or even before that. Just how backward is our country?"

"There was no newspaper in the capital city when I left," he admitted.

That said a lot. Too much. Was her father going to be a brute, too?

But Poppie added, "You can find coarseness in any military unit, Alana, anywhere. But most of those guards are probably recruited directly from the commoners. They are men of the earth, men who don't easily accept change. Most of the people here treat education as a waste of precious time, but think about it. Even in England education isn't compulsory, and the poor there view education the same way. But there is refinement in some of the noble houses here."

"But not all?"

His answer was a brief shake of his head. But he'd given her something to think about. She'd been comparing those soldiers to Englishmen who had been raised as she'd been raised, in the privileged world of upper-crust London, where refinement and good manners abounded. She had to stop holding to that old disdain of her homeland that Poppie had fostered in her. He'd admitted he'd done it deliberately just so she wouldn't tell anyone where they'd come from.

When the snow stopped as suddenly as it had arrived, a beautiful view was revealed. Green valleys, untouched by the mountain snow, were dotted with farms and villages. And in the distance Alana caught her first sight of the capital city, which shared the same name as this tiny mountain kingdom.

Poppie confirmed that when he put an arm around her shoulders and said with a pleased smile, "There's the capital of your realm, Princess. We're home."

His home, Alana thought. It didn't feel like hers and she was sure it never would.

They arrived in the city just before evening, too late in the day to go directly to the palace. Alana was relieved, even if it was only a brief delay. Now that meeting her father was nigh imminent, her apprehension was back in spades.

They got rooms at an inn on the edge of the city. Without telling him everything, Poppie explained to Henry that he would have to disassociate himself from Poppie when they went into the city. Henry seemed to understand the need for secrecy now, and that he might be followed when he delivered messages to Alana once she moved into the palace. Poppie even took him into the city to find a crowded place where they could meet clandestinely, without appearing to know each other. Henry was thrilled by the intrigue.

All of Alana's trunks were brought inside the inn and would remain there until she had rooms in the palace. Because Poppie wanted her to be at her best in the morning, he made her go to bed early. Sleep? In her current agitation? Somehow she did.

But morning came too soon. Her hands were almost trembling as she dressed in a warm powder-blue velvet gown. Instead of a heavy coat, she picked a dark blue cloak lined with soft white fur and a matching cap. At least she could push the cloak back off her shoulders if she got too warm once she was in the palace. She even managed to pin her long black hair up into a semblance of a coiffure. It was nowhere as neat as Mary's handiwork, but at least the cap made that less obvious.

"Alana?"

When she opened her door for Poppie, he said, "Don't forget the bracelet." He paused as he looked her over. "So beautiful — as always. Your father is going to be so proud today, to claim you as his own."

"I wish I were your daughter instead."

He hugged her so tightly she worried he might think it would be the last time he ever could. "No more than I, princess, but never doubt that you'll always be the daughter of my heart. Now come." He set her back from him. "Fetch the bracelet. You can keep it in your purse for now. And perhaps you should wear that pearl brooch I gave you last year, to complement your dress."

She nodded and moved to her trunks. Her purse was already heavy with the money Poppie had given her and her smallest pistol, but the bracelet was nearly weight-less, it was so tiny. She took out the small jewelry box, but then she gasped, noticing immediately that the latch was bent, completely pried away from the wood.

She swung around. "I — I think I've been robbed."

Poppie came to her side. "Robbed? When?"

"It had to be yesterday. I've been checking my jewelry box every morning before my trunks are loaded onto the coach. The contents are too valuable not to. You look," she said with dread, unwilling to open the box herself.

He did. When she saw his frown, she grabbed the box back from him. It was empty except for Henry's two small carvings. That soldier who'd searched her trunks yesterday! He'd stolen all her jewelry. At least he'd been too stupid to see any value in the carvings, so he hadn't taken them, too.

Poppie was having the same thought. "That man was on top of the coach too long. I should have guessed, should have had you check your belongings before the soldiers got too far away. That commander seemed competent enough in handling his men, if easily fooled. He would have made fast work of getting your jewelry back."

"Unless we were the ones fooled and they were all thieves."

He chuckled. "All angles? Excellent, Alana. That didn't occur to me. Doubtful, but indeed possible. But let's hope not, because your father can easily find out which of his men were sent to that pass chasing rumors and can get your jewelry back. A band of thieves, however, won't be as easily found. And come to think of it, we'd probably be dead now if they had been thieves. It would be all too easy to hide a crime in that pass, with such a deadly drop over the cliffside. But in either case, no one will know what they have in that bracelet."

She was beginning to feel angry over the

loss of not just the bracelet, but every piece of jewelry Poppie had given her over the years. "Simple stupidity?"

"No, a man can be brilliant, but that doesn't help if, like most Lubinians, he can't read, so the inscription will mean nothing to him, even if he noticed it. And he isn't likely to sell the jewelry immediately. He'll want to make sure no fingers are pointed his way when our 'lady' discovers the theft."

"Of course fingers will be pointed. We know exactly who the culprit is."

"Yes," Poppie agreed. "But he'll be confident that his word will outweigh ours because we portrayed ourselves as servants, and servants separated from their mistress are sometimes tempted — you get the idea."

She huffed and put the nearly empty box back in her trunk and slammed the lid down. "That was my proof of my true identity."

"Princess, *you* are the proof. You have the facts and you can still describe the bracelet in detail. Such an expensive trinket was probably given to you by your father before he retreated to mourn your mother's death, so he will remember it. You may also look like your mother. Remember, try to avoid mentioning my real name, but do tell them that Rastibon abducted you as they will be familiar with that name and it will lend authenticity to your account. And keep in mind, the king and his advisers will *want* to believe you because you will put an end to these rebel agitators, when they've obviously been unsuccessful tracking them all down."

CHAPTER NINE

As they rode to the palace, they traversed the main avenue, which was much wider than all the side streets and lined on both sides by shops and one- and two-story homes, no two alike. The shops didn't appear to be as prosperous or as sophisticated as those in many of the other cities they'd passed through, and the homes were by no means as grand. But at least the capital wasn't as primitive as Alana had been expecting.

When she noticed one of the fires burning at the side of the road, flickering from a stone pit, covered by a metal grate, she thought of Poppie's tragic tale. She could almost see it happening, that accident that had changed his life so drastically and had ultimately affected her own.

"Better contained now and not so close to the road," she heard Poppie say tonelessly, having noticed what she was staring at.

"There were no metal grates before."

She cried for the pain he had suffered back then, though she kept her face averted until her eyes dried. It released a little of her tension — until the coach stopped. But then Poppie eased it a little more by letting her see some of his own nervousness.

"Do I appear — normal?" he asked her.

Not like an assassin? was his real question, she realized. "Very dapper," she assured him with a smile. "Like an English nobleman."

"Then I do stand out?"

"No, not at all. Haven't you noticed in our travels that the fashions throughout Europe are very similar to what we're accustomed to?"

Alana wasn't helping him relax, but she didn't think anything would. Her tension didn't stem from anything life-threatening. His did. He was taking a big risk escorting her into the palace, and she hadn't been able to talk him out of it. But any man with her was going to be apprehended immediately as her abductor, once it was known who she was. While he did plan to slip away just prior to her audience with her father, something could easily go wrong. She knew it. He knew it. She wished she had been able to make him see reason, but he refused to leave her on her own until he absolutely had to.

A long line of people and vehicles was before the gates. It was soon apparent the line wasn't moving into the palace yet. Some of the crowd began to disperse as a guard made his way down the line.

When he reached their coach, he brusquely stated, "Only town officials to-day."

"And if our business isn't with the king?"

"Come back next week. Everyone of any import is involved in entertaining the foreign diplomats this week."

He didn't stay to answer any more questions. Alana wondered aloud, "Should we take a town official into our confidence, if they are the only ones who can get in right now?"

"No, only a palace official, and only if you must, as we discussed," Poppie said. "No one is to know who you are until you are safely inside those gates."

This delay had a calming effect on Alana, but just the opposite effect on Poppie. On the way back to the inn he explained the risks of remaining in the city for longer than they'd intended. Old neighbors might recognize him and recall that he'd disappeared the same night the princess did. She might be recognized if she resembled her mother. It would be a good thing if she did, but not before she was secure inside the palace walls.

"You intend to remain in the city afterwards," she reminded him.

"Yes, but I can't assume my old habits of keeping to the shadows and wearing clothes designed to conceal me when there's a beautiful young woman beside me. I will be fine once you are safe with your father. Until then, neither of us is safe."

Which meant *she* wouldn't be leaving the inn. But Poppie made several forays into the city at night, only telling her about them after he returned, so she wouldn't worry.

On one of them, he checked the defenses at the palace, telling her, "The walls are much more heavily guarded than they used to be. It could be because of the dignitaries currently visiting, or because of the rebel threat, or it may have been in effect all these years, ever since you were taken."

"You would have snuck inside if they weren't, wouldn't you?" she scolded.

He didn't deny it. "It would have saved so much time if I could have reached Frederick's chambers to let him know I've brought you home, but it wasn't possible."

Another night he came back to tell her,

"I've visited my father-in-law. I was surprised by his warm welcome, when I had avoided all contact with him during my years of grief. He has agreed to let Henry stay with him. I will take him there the night before the palace opens again. It will be safer to rendezvous with him there, in secret, than out in the city streets."

It was a relaxing week for Alana. Poppie found her books to read. They played games they used to play in London. Henry joined them so they could both continue his lessons. The time didn't drag and was even in her favor, because she finally managed to convince Poppie that escorting her inside the palace was an unnecessary risk on his part.

He did still drive with her to the gates the day after the visiting diplomats left town. They should probably have waited another day or two. He had checked early that morning and the line was even longer than it had been before, with all palace business having been suspended that week, so they didn't leave for the palace until noon. The line was indeed gone by then, and Alana hoped that all the people who had been there earlier hadn't come to see the king.

Poppie put his hand over hers and said gently, "We part here as you suggested."

It was a tribute to her diverse education that he had finally given in to her entreaties, because he knew she could do this on her own. And because she would have others to protect her as soon as she was inside those walls.

"Try to gain an audience with your father without telling anyone else who you are," Poppie continued. "Remember my warning. Trust no one."

He was repeating himself. Did he think she'd been too distraught to retain all his previous warnings?

"And if they won't let me see him without saying who I am, I am to seek out a high official to take into my confidence, one who can arrange a private meeting for me," she finished for him.

"Or bribe one. Your purse is filled with gold, use it at your discretion."

She nodded. Separating from Poppie was much worse than she'd expected. Even though she had insisted this was the safer way, emotion was still choking her. She could barely get out the words "When will I see you again?"

"I will never be far. If — *when* you are safely with your father, send this for repair." He handed her a broken watch. "There is only one watchmaker in the city. This watch will let me know you have succeeded. And if I find out anything you should know, I will send Henry to you."

He suddenly hugged her tightly. "I am very proud of you, princess. You have surpassed all of my expectations. Garner your confidence now. Your blood is royal. Never forget that."

Then he was gone, leaving her alone in the coach. She had a few minutes to cry over their parting before her coach passed through the fortress gate to the palace — and her future.

CHAPTER TEN

Christoph Becker stared at the crackling fireplace that didn't quite heat the main room of his quarters. He would have lit the braziers on the other side of the room if he didn't want his guest to leave. But he did want her gone. And she was still there, angrily pacing behind him, because, out of respect for their past relationship, he didn't want to shove her out the door as she deserved for haranguing him over a pointless issue that was never going to happen.

Christoph had told her no again. It did no good. It certainly wasn't the first time Nadia Braune had tried to reestablish their childhood friendship and seduce him into marriage. With her spoiled temperament, she resorted to insulting him when she failed. This time was no different. He had turned his back on her to dismiss her. Being ignored usually enraged her enough that she stomped off. But she hadn't reached that point yet.

"Why can't you quit this job and get on with your life?" she had railed at him this time. "You've already accomplished what you wanted. You have proven beyond doubt how loyal you Beckers are."

"It's never occurred to you that I like this job?" he had rejoined.

"Don't be ridiculous! Any commoner can do what you do here."

He'd still had enough patience to ignore the insult and remind her, "You have had countless offers. I know most of them. Pick one and, as you have suggested for me, get on with your own life."

"None are as handsome as you."

"Most women marry for wealth, land, or standing. You aren't in a position to do otherwise. And all of the men who have offered for you have had at least two of the three in whatever order, or they wouldn't have had the nerve to approach you in the first place. Would you like me to help you pick one out? I would be happy to if it would mean I won't have to suffer any more of these visits."

She'd actually tried to appear hurt when she'd said, "Now you are being cruel, when you know I love you."

"You don't feel anything of the sort. You

107

just don't want to settle for two out of three of the criteria demanded of your family. But I warn you, ten years from now, you will *not* blame me if you are still unmarried and your offers have dried up. Or must I marry someone else to prove to you that I will never marry you?"

"You wouldn't!"

"Go home, Nadia."

She wouldn't have such confidence that she could change his mind if she hadn't been told that their families had talked the year she was born about how the two would make the perfect match and should be betrothed. But the Lubinian civil war had ended all such talk, leaving him to make his own decision about a wife. It wouldn't be Nadia. Her family hadn't been returned to favor since the war and might never be, considering their ties to the old regime. They had been part of the pack who had encouraged the old king to make such bad decisions that his people finally revolted.

Christoph's family had also been loyal to the crown, though they had argued against the measures King Ernest had favored that had nearly destroyed their country. Which was why the Beckers had been restored to favor. And why he felt he must do even more to keep it that way.

But Nadia knew how close she had come to being betrothed to Christoph, and she refused to accept that it couldn't still happen. When they were growing up, he'd even wished it as well because she was turning out to be so beautiful, blond with brown eyes and unblemished skin only slightly darker than his from her Eastern ancestors.

Yes, he had begun to think they might still marry one day. Until he mentioned it to his father and found out why it was no longer a desirable match for him. That knowledge, and seeing how much it still concerned his father, had influenced him to dedicate himself to earning the king's absolute trust. But then by the time he'd left home, he'd already begun to dislike Nadia's irritating petulance, which had grown worse as she got older. At sixteen, it quite overshadowed her beauty, making him heartily glad of the political obstacles that had kept him from being tempted by her. Now, he didn't even like her anymore, she'd become so obnoxious.

"I'm growing tired of waiting for you to change your mind, you know," she said peevishly now.

"Stop waiting."

"I'm twenty-two years old this month! Who else from the noble houses will have you and forgive you for taking this commoner's job? Who else is as well suited to you as I am? It's not as if there are that many noble houses for you to choose from, Christoph."

He grit his teeth, his annoyance rising. "Who says I have to marry a Lubinian? Or marry at all, for that matter?"

She gasped. "Why must you be so stubborn!"

He swung around so she could see he'd reached the limit of his tolerance. "We enjoyed our childhood together. As neighbors, we were friends, but that's all we ever were. And you tarnish even those memories with this persistent campaign that is utterly useless."

Nadia's young maid tried to make herself invisible in the corner. Once he wouldn't have noticed her any more than Nadia did, but because of his work he'd had to train himself to be more observant.

"It's not useless. If you hadn't moved here before I even came of age, you know our friendship would have progressed to marriage. Come home now, Christoph. You'll see. Your family has regained all their lands and titles. What more do you need to prove by staying in the capital?"

She was never going to understand because she didn't really care. Her family had lost most of their lands, but they still had their wealth. So she had been raised just as she would have been if they hadn't lost their titles as well.

But he wasn't going to jeopardize the favor he had dedicated himself to earning for his family by aligning himself with the Braunes, who were still in disgrace. And he didn't doubt that had more than just a little to do with Nadia's persistence, encouraged, maybe even directed, by her father. Her family had married before to better their standing, and she was the only one left who could do so again.

He had mentioned this thought to her once before, remarking, "I am already redeeming my family's honor, don't expect me to redeem yours as well."

She hadn't denied or admitted it, but she had grasped the opportunity to insult him again instead with her scathing reply: "But you do it so humbly."

A fiasco had ignited the Lubinian civil war, which had changed all their lives, and so unnecessarily. There had been another option, the same one that other small countries and duchies had chosen when Napoléon had demanded money or troops to support his wars on the Continent.

Lubinia should have sent money. They had never maintained an army. It had been ridiculous to create one. But the nobles hadn't wanted to give up their own money to support the Frenchman who wanted all of Europe under his control. And Nadia's father's voice had been one of the loudest in support of sending troops. Nor were the Braunes the only once-noble family still trying to gain forgiveness for that decision. But how do you forgive the kind of stupidity that had nearly toppled a kingdom?

She was still standing there mulishly, refusing to give up. To hell with respect for the past, Christoph decided. They weren't children anymore, and she'd earned his contempt long ago.

"It's a shame you don't listen. I know I've made it clear I don't want you. So must I be even more blunt? So be it. We will never marry, you and I, because I would kill you within a month — or cut out your tongue. One or the other would be inevitable. Now get out."

She actually just glared at him. Even that she didn't believe? His patience snapped. He took a step toward her to throw her out, but he was arrested in midstride by the sudden triumphant gleam in her eyes. She *wanted* him to angrily put his hands on her?

Of course she did. She thought it would lead right to his bed, so she could then run home to her father with the tale, her version of it, and the Braunes would then demand marriage as a consequence. Fools, the lot of them. Did they really think he could be led about that way?

Christoph marched out the door instead and sent two guards to escort Nadia out of the palace. She wouldn't argue with them. They were beneath her notice. Instead she would pretend it was her own idea to leave.

CHAPTER ELEVEN

Alana was shown to a big anteroom in the palace that was furnished with only a few uncomfortable-looking chairs. No one was sitting in those chairs and she didn't sit either. She was still too nervous to relax, almost sick to her stomach with it. She would be meeting her father, the king of Lubinia, *today.* Alana knew that the king would be shocked and overjoyed when he learned that she was still alive and he had a legitimate heir after all. She hoped she would be able to keep her distance from him emotionally, so she could return to London without any regrets as soon as the rebellion here was quelled. But what if she and her father were both overcome with familial feelings and instantly took to each other? That would be wonderful — as long as he didn't expect her to stay in this rather backward mountain kingdom.

She couldn't help comparing this palace

to the one she'd visited in England. This one was so much smaller, and so much more exotic in design. Part of the roof was covered with a magnificent gold dome. Ornate, white columns were in the corridors, and the ceilings were elaborately carved.

The walls themselves were works of art, some of them covered with mosaics that glittered with gold, and others with rose- and cobalt-colored tiles and stones. Like many of the buildings she'd seen in the city, the palace was an odd mixture of Eastern and Western influences.

As she looked around the room, she was dismayed to see more than twenty people waiting to see the king! She was tired of delays. She was tired of keeping her identity a secret. She wanted to be rid of this apprehension that was making her queasy.

Nervously, she walked about the room. That was a mistake. She came too close to a man telling a group of big, brutish-looking men a ribald story that they all laughed at. She got away from them and nearly tripped over a goatherd sitting cross-legged on the floor eating a haunch of something with his hands. And he had a goat with him! Probably a gift for the king, but really, inside the palace?!

As Alana moved farther into the room, looking for a safe place to stand and wait, she noticed the other women there. Most of them appeared submissive to the men they accompanied, and they were dressed so differently from her. She was in the height of English fashion, her long, elegant cloak and cap fur-trimmed for winter. In stark contrast, one of the Lubinian women was wrapped in a toga-like garment, another was wearing a long, shaggy vest that appeared to be made of thick, untreated fur. One middle-aged woman was garbed in a more European fashion, but so gaudily, with half her breasts showing, she was rather obviously of loose morals and happily letting the men know it. Alana did note, however, that not all of the men were giants as she'd feared they would be after she, Poppie, and Henry had encountered that band of big, loutish soldiers on the mountain pass as they entered the country.

With the brightly colored walls, she almost failed to notice the small portrait of a man wearing a crown. She was arrested by it. Could it be? Hesitantly, she asked for confirmation from a man nearby and got the proud answer "Of course that is our Frederick."

My God, her father. Was he really this

handsome, or had the artist rendered him so just to please him? Fascinated, she couldn't take her eyes off the portrait. She had to fight back tears. *Her* father — but he still didn't know that she was alive. She was disappointed that they had no family resemblance at all. He was blond and blue-eyed, while her hair was black as pitch and her eyes were gray. Was this going to make her task even more difficult?

Every so often an official-looking fellow opened the double doors at the far end of the room, which she assumed led to the king's receiving room, and escorted a petitioner or a group of petitioners through them. But more people continued to arrive, keeping the anteroom crowded.

More impatient now than ever to meet her father, she approached one of the two guards standing by those doors to the inner chamber and asked, "When can I expect to meet the king? I've already been here an hour."

He didn't answer her. He didn't even look at her! She asked the other guard the same question, asked it in every language she knew, but he, too, treated her as if she were invisible! Was it because she was an unescorted woman, or was there some custom she wasn't aware of?

Fuming over being treated like that — she was their princess! — she moved to sit in one of the chairs. A brutish man she'd noticed earlier actually approached her after a while. She glanced up expectantly, but he didn't say anything. Instead he boldly fingered the fur on her cloak. Outraged, she came to her feet, but he didn't move away. He just laughed at the glare she gave him. The guards standing nearby did nothing. Fortunately, an old woman showed up to shoo him off.

"Stay away from the men" was all she said to Alana.

Blushing because she hadn't approached that lout, she went back to pacing the room, more certain than ever that Lubinian men had a barbarian streak.

More than an hour later, Alana suddenly forgot about how tired, hungry, and exasperated she felt when a new palace guard entered the anteroom. She was amazed to see the other guards actually speaking to him when they hadn't even spoken to each other, let alone to her. This new guard wore an identical uniform, tight, double-breasted, black jacket with gold buttons, cut short to the waist in front. The back of the jacket was longer, split for ease of movement, she supposed, the two tails reaching nearly to the knees. In contrast, the tall, stand-up collars and the cuffs on the jacket sleeves were stark white, embroidered with gold braid. The tightly fitted trousers were also white.

The gold-fringed epaulets on the uniform made the new guard's shoulders look extraordinarily wide. He was also taller than the other guards, possibly six feet. And something else made him stand out. He was handsome. As if that mattered, but it did cause her to stare at him much longer than she should have. She was still staring when one of the guards pointed her out to him.

She tensed slightly when he glanced her way and then immediately walked toward her. He had better not tell her it was time to leave, not after she'd spent half the afternoon there without having gained an audience with the king.

The thought produced a strong burst of annoyance, so she tried to look away and compose herself. But she couldn't quite manage to take her eyes off him. He was *that* handsome.

He had dark gold hair, worn no longer than his nape, yet it draped off his forehead in soft waves, half covering his ears. She verified that he had deep blue eyes when he stopped before her and gave her a brisk military bow. She had to look up even before he straightened. He was taller than the six feet she'd estimated, and young, probably in his mid-twenties. His face was thoroughly masculine with thick brows, a square jaw, and a strong, lean nose that was perfectly straight. Seen this close, he no longer looked like a common soldier. No, indeed, there was nothing common about him. . . .

"Is there a problem?" she asked when he didn't speak immediately. She'd almost used English, but caught herself in time and addressed him in Lubinian.

"No." A grin slowly formed as his eyes moved boldly over her face — and then lower! "Though my men wonder what such a pretty lady is doing in here."

Was he — flirting with her? Something that wasn't the least bit unpleasant stirred inside her with that thought. She felt so flustered she had to take her eyes off him for a moment to gather her scattered wits.

"Your men?" she asked.

His military bearing became more pronounced. "I am Count Becker, their captain."

Alana felt a surge of relief. *This* was a man she could deal with more easily, a formal official whose mouth was set in a hard, straight line. But why did a man this young wield so much authority? Just because he was a member of the nobility? Or maybe he was older than she'd guessed. The deep timbre of his voice supported that thought. The tone seemed almost familiar to her, though she'd heard so many Lubinian voices today. That had to be why.

"I, too, wonder why you are here," he added in that same formal tone.

"I was led to this room by one of the guards at the palace entrance. Are these other people not waiting for an audience with the king as well?"

He nodded. "Indeed. But there is another room where the nobility wait. It is much more comfortable. Your rich apparel indicates you should have been taken there. So what did you tell the guard that made him show you to the commoners' hall instead?"

CHAPTER TWELVE

Blast it! Alana thought. Had she really wasted so much time because she was being too cautious? Yet what other choice did she have? Poppie had warned her not to tell anyone except a highly placed official why she wanted to see the king. Alana wished this captain had shown up sooner to point out she might have hurried the process along if she had at least claimed nobility.

"I told your guard nothing more than that I wish to speak to the king," she admitted, abashed. "I'm not going to discuss my business here with just anyone."

"Ah, very well, mystery solved."

"What mystery? Is there something else that accounts for my having been kept waiting?"

"If you don't state the nature of your business, you don't get very far," he said simply.

"But I was told that King Frederick had an open policy of receiving his people."

"You aren't one of his people."

"I am more than that."

"Oh?"

As captain of palace security and a nobleman as well, he seemed the ideal person to help her. She wanted to trust him. She just hoped she wasn't being influenced by her strong attraction to him. But he *was* an official, and that decided her.

She leaned slightly closer to him so he would hear her low-voiced entreaty. "Is there somewhere we can go so we may speak in private?"

His demeanor changed abruptly again. His golden brows rose as if she'd surprised him, and his blue eyes gazed at her warmly. When his hard mouth softened into a grin, she felt that fluttering in her stomach again, but more strongly this time. Good God, he was handsome. And as attracted to her as she was to him? Or was he just relaxing, letting down his guard? She wished she hadn't been so sheltered in London and knew more about such matters.

"Come with me," he said.

He grasped her hand immediately, surprising her. She didn't like that at all. It wasn't how an Englishman would behave upon first meeting a lady. But this wasn't England, she reminded herself. Lubinians might think nothing of a man treating a woman this way. It might even be customary here for men to act like barbarians and drag women about. She groaned at that thought. Yet it *did* feel as if he were dragging her, though she allowed that it simply felt that way because his much longer stride was forcing her to quicken her step to keep up with him.

He led her out of the anteroom and deeper into the palace until they came to a side entrance that opened onto a wide courtyard. It wasn't a private courtyard where they could talk, but the ward that lay between the palace and the old fortress walls that surrounded it. Soldiers and even a few opulently dressed courtiers were passing through. A merchant with a small cart was selling meat pies to the guards.

There was still daylight, though the sun had already dipped below the mountain ranges to the west. Alana tried to slow her step but couldn't. Where exactly was the captain taking her?

When he stopped in front of the door to a building that resembled a fancy town house but was adjoined to the ancient fortress walls, Alana took the opportunity to pull her hand away from his, though she actually had to yank a little. He glanced at her and started to chuckle, but it was abruptly cut off when an angry woman swept through the doorway and attacked the captain, pounding on his chest with her fists.

Alana adeptly moved out of the way. The captain didn't even try. The woman, who was young, blond, and finely dressed, pounded on him rather hard, but he gave no indication that he even felt her blows!

"How dare you have me thrown out!" she shouted.

He took her wrists, one in each hand, and thrust her away from him into the ward. Not very gentlemanly, Alana thought, but the woman *had* been attacking him and his annoyance was now obvious.

Yet his voice was absolutely calm when he asked the young woman curiously, "How is it you're still here, Nadia?"

"I hid from your men," she stated rather triumphantly.

"Who will now be disciplined because of it." He waved at two passing guards.

Nadia glanced behind her to see the guards' swift approach, then somewhat in a panic she yelled at Count Becker, "We haven't finished our discussion!"

"Only a fool doesn't know when to quit, so how much of a fool does that make you, eh?" That brought a gasp from the blond woman, but it didn't keep him from adding, "Now, would you finally open your eyes to see that the past will no longer protect you from my contempt?" To the men who had reached him, he said, "Take Miss Braune to the gates. She is no longer to be allowed entry to the palace."

"You can't do that, Christoph!"

"I just did."

Distinctly uneasy now — that had been quite a beautiful woman he'd just dismissed so cavalierly — Alana said, "Is she a former lady friend of yours?"

He took a moment to shake off his annoyance before he glanced at Alana. Once again, his long look took in more than just her face. But then he smiled at her and her breath caught in her throat, it so dazzled her.

"Not as you mean," he answered.

Then he grasped Alana's arm and ushered her inside the building, closing the door behind him. He was gentle with her now, not rough as he'd been with that harridan, not even as firm as he'd been when dragging her here.

She took a moment to glance around and get her bearings. This large room contained two plush, dark-colored sofas with low tables set before each, a chair, several bookcases, a fancy harpsichord, and a small dining table that would seat four. This one room seemed to serve many purposes, but she didn't think it comprised the entire first floor of the building. And then she couldn't think at all.

She didn't realize the captain was still holding her arm until he turned her toward him. His other hand slipped behind her neck and drew her forward, right up against him. Then he bent his head and pressed his lips to hers.

No training she'd ever had prepared her to be overwhelmed by her first kiss.

CHAPTER THIRTEEN

Alana could have drawn away at any point.
The captain didn't rush her into his arms,
he'd been slow about it. He was a man who
savored. A man who sensually coaxed. And
from the second his hand slipped behind
her neck, her senses were arrested in anticipation.

Despite her quick responses, she didn't
think she *could* have moved just then. Or
she simply didn't want to. Lady Annette
might blushingly have explained this aspect
of life to her, but Alana couldn't have
imagined anything remotely close to
this. . . .

With the soft touch of his lips on hers,
Alana's senses were overwhelmed. She felt
her heart racing, and the pleasant fluttering
in her stomach she'd earlier felt was now a
powerful, exciting swirl. Both his hands
were suddenly warm against her cheeks,
caressing her, which meant she was leaning

against him of her own accord! This was madness!

She tried to lean back to take her mouth away from his. For a brief moment she felt something close to frustration when he let her. Opening her eyes, she saw his smile. That was all she saw because she couldn't take her eyes off his mouth, which had just stirred up so many startling, pleasurable feelings in her.

In wonder, she touched her own lips. "Why did you do that?" she asked in a breathless whisper.

She looked up at his blue eyes before he answered. That was a mistake. He was too appealing like this, with the seductive warmth in his gaze and a charming grin on his face. Did he find something humorous in her question?

He raised a brow slightly before he said, "You aren't here looking for a protector? I'm going to be very disappointed if you say no."

He didn't sound disappointed. He sounded confident of himself and amused, as if he were teasing her. Of course, she was here looking for a protector. Her father was going to be her protector. Was she missing something in what he'd just said? Did he mean something else? How could she think with him this close to her?!

She began, "Yes, but —"

He was kissing her again, and this time much more passionately. Now she was thrilled to a new level, every wonderful sensation he'd provoked earlier was back and so magnified, she had to grip his shoulders to keep from falling. He slipped his arm around her back, holding her tightly to him. His mouth slanted across hers, his tongue pushing past her innocence, thrusting deeply, deliciously into her mouth. His other hand was sliding up the side of her leg.

Her gasp was lost in his mouth. Oh, God, what was she doing?!

"Stop!" She pushed away from him, gasping for breath, grasping to keep her balance now that she was no longer holding on to him. She was shocked by what she'd just allowed him to do, what she'd allowed herself to do!

He was watching her with something akin to suspicion in his eyes. "I don't mind a little teasing, as long as we both understand where it ends."

She had no clue what he seemed to be accusing her of, but she'd regained enough of her wits to say stiffly, "I'm not sure what kind of mistake you've made, but it *is* a mistake."

He leaned his back against the door, slamming it hard. "You can't be serious."

He glanced down at her again for an answer. She didn't need to say anything more. Her accusing look seemed to convince him that she was serious. But instead of apologizing, he swore under his breath and moved toward her. She was instantly unnerved. He was much too big and tall to stand that close to her with such an angry visage.

"What sort of ploy is this?" he demanded. "You melt on me like sweet butter, then cry foul?"

She sucked in her breath. That didn't even deserve a response. She pushed around him to get to the door instead. He grabbed her by the waist, stopping her, and even drew her back against his chest.

Her whole body tingled as he embraced her so intimately. "You want to talk terms first?" he asked impatiently. "Fine, I will give you whatever you want. There, we have talked terms. Now melt on me again."

The husky tone he'd ended with made her close her eyes tightly. She was *not* going to be drawn back into his web again. She wiggled out of his hold, hoping to break through to the captain of the guard she'd first met, the polite if mildly flirtatious man she'd been willing to trust. He let go of her as she turned to face him instead of reaching for the door again.

"I asked to speak to you in private because no one else can hear what I was going to confide in you." She sighed. "How could you think I meant anything other than talk?"

A number of emotions crossed his countenance — frustration, self-disgust, finally regret. He turned away, saying, "Your whisper suggested something else."

"What?"

"Many foreign women of quality, mostly widows, come to this court to find a protector," the captain explained, facing her again. "We are not unique in that. We are just one of many courts they visit across Europe, until they find a gentleman of power or wealth to their liking. A few even aspire to be a king's mistress and so they request an audience to make themselves available, yet are too embarrassed to mention it to the guards —"

"I understand!" she quickly cut in. "You thought I was one of those women trying to see the king. You couldn't be more mistaken. I'm his daughter."

"Whose?"

"The king's."

A moment of silence followed. "Are you?"

He said that without inflection, making her realize her wish had come true. She was now dealing with the real captain of the guard, who would actually attend to duty, not that tempting seducer, thank God. Yet why wasn't he more surprised by her revelation? Could he actually be that well schooled in guarding emotions when required? She'd had that training herself, though it had certainly been tested during the last month.

"I can explain," she said, "as it was explained to me. If you aren't surprised, I certainly was. I've only known about this for the last month. I —"

Alana stopped. Was she rambling? She was still in the grip of too many emotions she wasn't familiar with.

She moved to one of the sofas in the room, but not to sit down. She just wanted to put more distance between herself and the captain. And have an excuse to take her eyes off him. After placing her cloak and her purse on the end of the sofa, her heartbeat still hadn't returned to normal. The effect he'd had on her was amazing.

"Would you like some refreshments?" he inquired behind her.

Alana was taken aback by his question, but she quickly seized on his gesture of hospitality. "Yes, thank you. I'm actually quite hungry."

He shouted, "Boris!" — which produced a servant after a few moments. "Tell Franz to serve dinner early, and bring some food immediately for the lady."

He had his own cook, too? "These are your quarters?" Alana questioned as she turned to give him her full attention again. "A bit fancy for a captain, isn't it?"

"I had permission from the king to build this addition. It will be given some other use when I leave."

"Your job is only temporary?"

"It's mine for however long I want it, and in fact I may never leave. It is highly important to me that the king and his family be well protected."

She found those words reassuring, since she was a member of that family. And he didn't seem to mind her questions. His expression hadn't changed at all since his manner had turned professional again. He had to be curious about her revelation, yet he hid it well. Unless he simply didn't believe her . . .

She dismissed that thought. He didn't dare not take her claim seriously. He could just be waiting for her to explain herself. She was hoping she wouldn't have to, at least not until her father was present to hear her tale. The less she said about Poppie to others, the better.

The tall captain moved over to the lit fireplace and stood with his back to it, his hands held behind him. The fire was close to dying. It could definitely use another log, but he didn't take his eyes off her long enough to see to it. He'd even kept his eyes on her as he'd walked over there, his stride and his posture military-erect. She couldn't help but notice he was in prime shape. In fact, she couldn't recall ever before seeing a male physique this superlative. Surely she had, she just hadn't been impressed enough to take note of it. Until now. Because he was so handsome?

The large room felt a little chilly. Of course, she could share that meager fire with Becker, though it might appear a bit too bold for her to close the distance between them. She didn't want *him* thinking about those kisses again.

"Why was I really kept waiting today?" she asked. "I saw at least one man who arrived after me summoned into the inner chamber."

"Bureaucracy," Becker said simply. "If you don't state your business, you are placed at the end of the line."

"So I should have told a mere guard who I am? When my life has been in jeopardy since I was an infant? I was warned not to do that."

He shrugged. "It is of no matter. You would have gone no further in either case. We would merely have had this conversation sooner, since you would have been brought to my attention, not the king's."

She sighed. Such a waste of time. Had she really thought it would be easy to gain an audience with the king? She had hoped foolishly, it now seemed. But at least the captain seemed cordial enough now in his official capacity. And way too cordial when he'd thought she was a widow looking for a lover. But he hadn't had her escorted to the gate as he'd done with his lady friend. And he hadn't dismissed her claim as ludicrous, as he could have done. So apparently he was going to hear her out.

He confirmed her assessment of the situation when he said, "Sit down. Make yourself comfortable. I suspect you will be here for quite a while."

"Not unless my father is scheduled to leave the palace today and I have to wait for his return," she disagreed.

"The king isn't leaving."

"Then can you at least take me to him, so

I don't have to repeat myself? The story I have to tell is not exactly a brief one."

"When you aren't the first princess to show up with this claim? I think not."

CHAPTER FOURTEEN

The food arrived before Alana could say anything, which was fortunate, because she didn't think she could utter a single word, she was so stunned. Someone else had tried to impersonate her?

Poppie hadn't warned her about this, so it must have been kept secret, so secret that not even his paid informant had discovered it. Yet it should have occurred to him, even to her, as a possibility. So much wealth, power, and privilege was involved, of course, some unscrupulous person would try to claim all that. *When you were seven, there was another tidbit, that with so much time passed, it was now presumed you were dead.* She remembered Poppie's words clearly now. There had even been a ceremonial funeral! And that news had opened the door for an imposter to take her place. Who would have dared try something like that before then, when she'd only been "missing" and could have been returned to her family at any time?

"It's appalling and so cruel that someone tried to impersonate me. But I suppose it's not surprising considering what's at stake," Alana said with disgust in her voice. She sat back on the sofa and took a deep breath before she added, "You think I'm going to withdraw my claim now, don't you? I would if lives weren't at stake. I might have been born here, but —"

"What lives?" the captain barked.

His tone disconcerted her again. She sat forward and put her hands on the edge of the sofa in preparation to flee. This man was just too big to yell at her like that.

She told him so. "If you can't keep a civil tone, take me to someone with the patience to hear me out."

He actually laughed, though she didn't hear much humor in it. "You come here to impersonate royalty, but you're not in prison yet, are you? That's how patient I am, wench. Now what lives are at stake?"

His tone was back to normal, but she still closed her eyes briefly against the new fear he'd just stirred. Had that been deliberate on his part? She *hoped* that's all it was. There had been danger outside the palace, but Poppie had assured her she'd be safe inside these walls — no, safe once she was with her father. And this man was standing between her and that safety.

She glanced at him again and summoned her courage. "I was referring to the lives that will be lost in the impending war, if the rebels gain enough support."

"We are dealing with the rebels as we find them."

"By killing them?"

"Of course," he said simply. "What they are doing is treasonous."

She couldn't argue with that, but he was missing the point. "It's the innocent Lubinians the rebels are agitating to their cause that I'm concerned about. In fact, no one else needs to die when the pretext for the rebellion is based on lies. The king does have an heir. Me. My presence will put an end to the sedition."

"You suggest a lie to counter a lie?"

She sighed. "No, I am who I say I am, Frederick's daughter. I wish it were otherwise. I didn't even find out about it until last month. Believe me, I've never aspired to be a princess. I grew up in London thinking I'd marry an English lord someday — well, until I discovered I liked teaching so much, and the nobles at home frown on their wives doing anything so common as

—" She stopped, realizing she was rambling nervously. "That's an old dilemma. My point is, I might have been born here, but I don't consider Lubinia my home, so I don't want to stay here any longer than it takes to avert a war."

"If you were the princess, the choice wouldn't be yours to make."

She jumped to her feet. "I can convince my father —"

"Sit down!"

She didn't. She glanced at the door instead. That made him laugh.

"You're not going anywhere until I decide what to do with you. Perhaps you should have realized that and waited to confess until after I bedded you. A man is much more amiable to a woman he —"

She gasped. "Stop it! Don't say things you'll have to apologize for later, when you realize I'm telling you the truth."

He grinned at the warning. "Apologize for natural urges? Princess or not, I don't think so. But if you are finished amusing me, would you please tell me what makes you think you are a member of the royal family? Shall we begin with your name?"

He didn't believe her, but of course he wouldn't when she hadn't really told him anything yet to support her claim. She took her seat again and explained, "I had a bracelet to prove what I'm saying, but it was stolen when —"

His snort cut her off. "Conveniently stolen, eh?"

She lifted her chin. "I know who took it, one of my father's own men."

He frowned. "When?"

"The same day we arrived in the country. We came —"

He cut in sharply, "Who's we? Who were you traveling with?"

Alana suddenly felt wary. She wasn't calm enough to discuss Poppie yet. "That's none of your concern."

"You are mistaken. Whoever put you up to this and brought you here is plotting against the king, and it is my job to protect him."

Her chin rose. "There is no new plot here, just a very old one — eighteen years old."

He gave her a long, hard look before he said, "Very well, I'll get back to this point. For now, go ahead and continue your story about the bracelet."

She nodded. "To enter the country, we came through a little-used mountain pass and were stopped by a group of very rough soldiers who accused us of being rebels. My trunks were searched for weapons. All of

142

my jewelry as well as the bracelet were gone afterwards. Find out who their loutish leader was and he can tell you exactly who that thief was."

His frown darkened. He directed it at her so long, she couldn't mistake his anger. Why? Because she'd called one of his men a lout?

"Describe the bracelet you think is so important," he snapped out.

She did so quickly and added, "I was wearing it when I was taken from here all those years ago."

She actually thought he was beginning to believe her until he scoffed, "A trinket you could have had made for your purposes? A trinket that resembles the real one and any number of people could have known about? Did you really bother to copy the original, or did you intend to claim it was stolen all along?"

Crestfallen that he could draw those conclusions, she said, "You won't even try to find it? When my father could recognize it?"

"You need to be a lot more convincing for me to accuse a royal guard of theft, when it would be your word against his. No."

He'd just dismissed the tangible evidence that she'd been depending on. She was losing all desire to be cooperative — with him. If he didn't frighten her, she'd tell him so. Good God, she couldn't have picked a worse official in the whole palace to confide in than the head of security.

She grasped at another bit of tangible evidence, asking, "Do I look like my mother?"

"Which mother would that be?"

Frustration entered her tone. "Frederick's first wife, Queen Avelina, of course."

"No."

He gave new meaning to that word. She'd never heard it uttered with such absolute finality.

"No, I don't? Or, no, you're just dismissing the possibility?"

"The monarchs are blond. The other imposters were blond. You aren't. And it is irrelevant. People can be found who resemble each other but are not related. Now —"

"Wait! Did you just say *other imposters?* There were more than one?"

"Indeed, quite a few. Now back to your name."

Good Lord, they were never going to believe her story if she was just one in a long line of claimants. "You expect my name to be anything other than Alana Stindal?"

"Don't answer questions with questions," he warned her.

"I apologize, but I was trained to dissect any given situation and even second-guess an opponent."

"That's probably the first true thing you've said, that you were trained —"

"To be a *queen*," she finished for him. "My guardian knew he would have to bring me back here someday to claim my heritage. So he did what he could to ensure I would be prepared for it, even if he never told me why my education was so unusual."

"Who is this guardian of yours and why would he train you to view the king's protector as an opponent?"

Becker was doing it again, asking specifically about Poppie, probably hoping she'd blurt something out in her nervousness. Realizing that just made her more guarded.

She said simply, "I consider you my opponent because you're acting like one. You're standing between me and the parent I didn't even know I had until just recently. I came here to save people's lives. Tell my father that. Whether you or he believes me or not, he can still use me to prevent a war. Once the rebels slink back into the holes they came from, I'll quietly leave the country and my father can put more effort into producing another heir — and *why* hasn't he done so in all these years?"

She shouldn't have asked that. Her father's lack of heirs was the main focus of the rebels' propaganda. The last thing she wanted was for this man to think that she might be associated with them by bringing up *their* issues. But she blanched, watching his expression alter with that very thought.

She shot to her feet in an absolute panic. She'd almost reached the door when his hand caught her skirt, but he didn't have a good grip and she wasn't stopping. But he didn't let go, his hand just slid down the blue velvet material, right over the pistol in her pocket. She heard him swear, but her hand closed over the door handle and yanked, only to have his foot hit the wooden door in front of her, slamming it closed again. She turned immediately, a fist clenched to hit his throat, one of the moves Poppie had taught her, which she was desperate enough to try despite this man's size. No luck, none at all.

He caught her fist, started to shove it behind her back, which would have brought her hard against his chest and trapped her there. But she foiled that attempt by turning to that same side to give herself leeway to yank her hand back. Unfortunately, catching him by surprise like that didn't work in her favor. She wasn't sure who lost balance, but they both ended up falling to the carpeted floor. At the last second, he rolled to take the brunt of the fall, but then rolled again, pinning her under him. She wasn't getting up from that!

The first thing he did was remove the pistol he'd felt in her pocket and toss it aside. Defensively, before he thought the worst, she exclaimed, "I won't apologize for the weapons. Someone in this country tried to kill me! I need them to defend —"

"More than *one* weapon?" was all he gathered from that explanation. But then he suddenly chuckled. "I think I'm going to have to thoroughly search you, wench. Yes, I can even say it's my duty to do so."

She could see it in his dark blue eyes that he was about to enjoy his job far too much. He was grinning, too, as he glanced down at her breasts. She gasped. He wouldn't dare!

"Stop! You're going to regret —"

"No, regret is the very last thing I will ever feel about this."

He actually did it. He placed his hand firmly over one of her breasts and left it there far too long as he gently squeezed it to make sure she had no weapon tucked in that area. Then he did the same with her other breast! She understood he was obligated to confiscate her weapons, but not like this!

She struggled to push him off her. She'd known that wasn't going to happen. She closed her eyes, too embarrassed to feel anything but fury that his brute strength kept her from stopping him.

"It's good you are cooperating, eh?"

She heard the laughter in his tone and her eyes snapped open to glare at him. "Is that what I'm doing? I could have sworn I said 'stop.' "

He ignored that bit of dryness to say, "I wonder where else you would hide weapons."

She tried to tell him, "In my —"

"Shh." He put a finger to her lips. "You could give up all your hiding places, but, you understand, I would still have to see for myself."

He might as well have just called her a liar. That was what he was implying, that he couldn't trust her to be truthful about it. And he might even be right — when it came to her weapons. But what he was doing was so outrageous, this couldn't be normal procedure in situations like this.

"You could have found a woman to search

me," she pointed out indignantly.

"And shirk my duty?"

His expression suddenly turned distinctly sensual. She was actually arrested, fascinated for the briefest moment. But then he moved to the side, just far enough to yank her skirt and petticoats up so high, one of her legs was completely exposed. She shrieked in outrage.

"Ah, the boot, of course," he said, staring at another one of her weapons.

He bent her leg so he could reach her boot without moving too much. She tried to knee him. All that did was bring her boot closer to his hand so he could take the dagger and toss it aside. Then he ran his hand up her leg, around it, and under it, when he could *see* she had no other weapons strapped there.

"I'm going to scream, and you're going to lose your job," she warned him.

"If you scream, I might have to kiss you to silence you. Not that anyone would dare enter my quarters to investigate, so all it will get you is a kiss. Are you asking me to kiss you?"

"No!"

"You're sure?"

"You're despicable!" she hissed.

"You didn't think so earlier when you

melted on me."

Her blush was instant, and something sweet stirred inside her with the memory of that kiss, but it quickly soured when he flipped her over and ran his hands down her back and her sides, over her derriere, then slowly down her other leg. At least that one wasn't exposed. He chuckled when he came to her other boot.

"Another one?" He tossed the second dagger aside. "Any more?" She clamped her mouth shut, making him add, "That probably means yes."

Her hands were free. She pulled back her sleeve and removed the poniard strapped to her wrist and threw it toward the other weapons. "Are you satisfied now, you contemptible brute?" she said scathingly. "You could have just asked for them! I wouldn't have tried to retain them to protect myself if I had your protection instead. But this isn't my idea of protection."

He stood up abruptly and yanked her up with him. She only caught a glimpse of the furious expression on his face before he tossed her over his shoulder like a sack. His anger frightened her more than his manhandling, and she couldn't imagine what had brought it forth so quickly. Had she merely struck a nerve? Or was it because that last weapon was so well concealed, he probably wouldn't have found it? But she didn't want him to know he was intimidating her.

"You've already behaved like a barbarian. Must you prove it beyond a doubt now? Put me down!"

He didn't. He toted her like that across the parlor and deeper into his quarters. They passed two other rooms in that newer building, then they were inside the old fortress walls and crossing through a long, rectangular storage room that also contained a few cots for sleeping. The meager light came from numerous high windows on the inner wall facing the ward. The outer wall had no openings at all.

The next room they entered was also long, but rows of barred doors were on either side. A place to keep prisoners obviously. It was quiet, so possibly no one was currently being detained. And more fool her to think they would pass through this area as well. . . .

Chapter Fifteen

Alana was set down in the center of a large cell. The wide, barred door was left open, but the captain stood firmly in front of it. His expression was under control, stoic, but she didn't doubt the anger was still there. Why else would he bring her to a prison cell?

"Playtime is over, wench." He was referring to what had just happened out in the other room, amusing for *him,* certainly, but nothing but frustrating for her, since she'd been unable to stop him. He added, "You can remove your clothes or I will remove them for you."

Oh, God, she wasn't expecting to hear *that!* "Why?! I don't have any more weapons on me, I swear!"

"You proved more crafty in your concealment than I gave you credit for. Now we will make sure there are no more surprises." She started to back away from him. "Very well. I don't mind assisting you."

Desperately, she tried to dodge around him to the door, but that only put her within reach of his hands sooner. She fought him when he reached for the fastenings on her dress. They were in the front like on most of the clothes she'd brought on this trip, because she wasn't traveling with a maid. He had to put an arm around her waist to hold her tight to him, so he was working one-handed, but that hand kept brushing against her breasts, deliberately she didn't doubt. The fear she'd felt was gone, outrage taking precedence. She squirmed and pushed to get loose from his arm, slapped or pulled his hand away, but he just patiently brought it back to continue.

Before long she was panting from the exertion of trying to stop him, which wasn't working, making her realize she was only prolonging the inevitable. She hadn't looked at him yet. She was too busy pushing and pulling his hand away. But she didn't want to see the determination that had to be on his face while she was still hoping for a reprieve, and that he'd stop before she was completely naked.

When her dress finally gaped open, she put her effort into holding it closed, which prompted him to say, "You know, we can do this on the bed instead." She made a gasping sound. "No? Too bad."

She looked up at him then. Her breath caught in her throat. No amusement was in his eyes, but something so intense burned there it brought a flush to her skin. He wanted her! That knowledge caused a shiver of excitement to run through her. She had to muster all her anger to fight it down, but all she ended up doing was standing there doing nothing!

Her sleeves slipped down her arms. Several tugs at her waist released her petticoats. Suddenly her dress and petticoats pooled at her feet.

"You're too beautiful," he said in wonder, his eyes moving slowly over what he'd revealed. But then abruptly he schooled his expression again when he added, "What a good job the men who put you up to this deception did in choosing you as an imposter. Deliberate? Did they hope you could seduce me from my duty?"

Her? *He* was the one practicing seduction! But he seemed angry again at the thoughts he'd just expressed. He lifted her off her feet so he could kick the last of her outer garments aside. Then he grabbed the only chair in the cell, set it in the middle of the room, and thrust her down in it.

Sitting there in her chemise, her drawers, her stockings, and her boots, she'd never before been so embarrassed in her life. That brought her own anger back. And the captain's standing in front of her, still looking down at his handiwork, intensified it.

"What is your guardian's name?"

She clamped her mouth shut, glaring at him. Did he really expect her to be cooperative now? She was too furious to be afraid again. The way he'd just treated her was utterly barbaric, confirming her negative opinion of this country.

But her silence made him lean down, putting his face near hers, to tell her in a deceptively soft voice, "Do not mistake what is happening here, wench. You are now a prisoner and you *will* answer my questions. I already regret leaving you these." He plucked casually at the ties of her chemise. "That can be corrected."

She drew in her breath. Oh, God, he would, too. The fear she'd been trying to ignore with her anger wouldn't be ignored any longer.

He stood back to watch her closely, those blue eyes assessing, ready to pounce on the slightest change in her expression. Nothing at all was sensually lambent about them now. Torture was still considered a prime way to extract information from prisoners in many countries, and this country was less enlightened than most. Had that method been used on the imposters when they had shown up? No, surely her father wouldn't allow that — *if* he was told.

She asked abruptly, "You *are* going to inform my father of my presence? Eventually?"

He didn't answer her, bringing home more clearly than ever that only he could ask the questions in this cell. He did move behind her though. That should have given her some relief, to have his eyes off her scanty attire, but it just made her more nervous. Then she felt his fingers unraveling her disheveled coiffure.

"What are you — ?" She raised a hand to brush his away from her head. "Stop it! There is no weapon small enough to hide in my hair!"

He held a long, sharp hairpin between two fingers in front of her face. "No?"

She didn't blush, just insisted, "I don't consider *that* a weapon."

But she didn't try to stop him from removing the rest of the pins. She was actually glad to have her long hair tumble down over her chest, because her chemise was so thin it was nearly transparent. But he didn't remove his hands when he was done. His fingers moved against her scalp in a way that was far too sensual. A shiver moved down her neck that had nothing to do with how cold it was in that cell.

It made her burst out, "My guardian's name is . . . Mathew Farmer. I call him Poppie because he raised me. I thought he was my uncle, that my parents had died in the wars and he was the only family I had left. I thought we were no different than other foreign aristocrats who fled to England to escape Napoléon's rampage, that Poppie had even fought in those wars. I knew we were from Lubinia, but I never once suspected that everything else I believed all my life was a lie. And when I turned eighteen, he still wasn't going to tell me the truth or bring me back yet."

She had hoped that would get his mind back on track and his hands off her, but his fingers kept stroking her as he asked, "Then why did he?"

"Because he heard about what was happening here. That forced his hand to tell me everything, even though he was sure I'd hate him for it."

"To end a war before it begins."

He might as well have just snorted, his tone was so dubious. She tried to turn around to look at him, but his hands on her shoulder and her neck kept her looking straight ahead.

She still demanded, "Why do you doubt such a selfless motive as that? He didn't want to see his homeland ripped apart by lies that he could disprove. He loves this country for some reason I haven't figured out yet." His tightened grip on her shoulders indicated he'd perceived an insult in what she'd just said. She added defensively, "It's not my fault I don't share that love. When I was a child, he reviled Lubinia, made it sound completely barbaric."

"Why?"

"So I'd be too ashamed to tell anyone where we really came from."

"Why?"

"In case someone showed up asking questions — like my father's men or his enemies."

"So he hid you from the king?"

"Of course. Someone wanted me dead. So Poppie wasn't going to allow me to return here until he knew it was safe."

Becker laughed. "And he thinks it's safe now?"

"No, he doesn't. But my presence can save many lives, and that outweighs everything else. And the threat to me personally that he's protected me from all my life, he's going to deal with himself, since my father never did."

Becker was silent for a moment, then said, "So last month your guardian shatters everything you believed about your life, telling you instead that you're royalty? And you simply believed him? Why?"

"Are you joking?" she said painfully. "I didn't believe any of it. It was too horrible, too —"

"Horrible that you're a princess?" he scoffed.

She closed her eyes. She hadn't wanted to tell him this much. His doubt was wearing her down. He still hadn't taken his hands off her, either. And he shouldn't be treating her like this at all!

"No ready answer this time, Alana? — if that's even your name."

The harsh tone he'd been frightening her with turned neutral for that question. His hands left her shoulders, too, though a finger trailed softly down her arm almost in a distracted manner. She shivered. It had to be the cold. It couldn't be his touch.

"Think whatever you like," she said tiredly. "You're going to anyway."

"This is how you are going to save lives?"

Her eyes snapped open again. He was

right. She didn't have the luxury of giving up.

She sighed. "Let me put it this way, Captain. The disbelief you're exhausting me with? Well, my disbelief when Poppie told me I was a royal princess was a hundred times that, and I'm very good with math, so that isn't an exaggeration. Poppie might have called me princess all my life, but I just thought it was an endearment. Of course I didn't believe that I'm the king of Lubinia's daughter. But there's something you should know. Poppie loves me. He changed his life for me. He would never have confessed what brought that about if it weren't true."

"Why?"

"Because he was sure I would despise him for it."

"For stealing you from this very palace eighteen years ago? This *is* what he told you, correct? Or was he actually not involved in that theft? Did this man who raised you merely know the real thief and took you from him or her?"

She was tempted to lie, to remove Poppie from the original crime — and the captain's avid interest. But Poppie had told her to tell the truth, and she had to have faith that it would lead to her being reunited with her father.

"No, it was Poppie who took me directly from the palace nursery, though he wasn't supposed to. He'd been paid to kill me."

"Where is he now?"

"I don't know."

"Where *is* he?"

"I swear I don't know! We stayed at an inn on the edge of town, but he warned me I wouldn't find him there again. I told you. He's going to track down the person who hired him eighteen years ago to kill me."

"When are you going to figure out that I don't like being lied to?"

He was abruptly in front of her again. To see how much he'd been frightening her with those rapid questions? Or so she couldn't mistake how angry he still was?

"I have been telling you the absolute truth and will continue to do so. I really don't have a choice in that."

"There are always choices, and you need to make a better one if you hope to get out of here."

She sucked in her breath. He couldn't keep her locked up. He wouldn't dare. She was his king's daughter! But she began to tremble, half from the cold, half from fear. Yet she *couldn't* let him know how much he was intimidating her. Fear would make her look guilty. He'd never believe her then.

She tried to think like a princess. She tried to embrace the outrage that was the only thing she should be feeling. But all she could manage to say was "I'm cold."

"Your comfort is not —"

"I'm cold!"

Throwing caution to the winds, she raised her chin defiantly. He swore, then marched outside the cell and slammed the barred door shut behind him. The last thing she expected was for him to turn the key in the lock, too.

CHAPTER SIXTEEN

"How dare you keep me in here? I will not forget this, Captain."

Christoph's anger wasn't gone yet. Those words kept it high. Where had she gotten the courage to speak so imperiously? No raised voice. Simple calm laced with ice. But her eyes gave her away, not by expression but by shade. The stormy-gray color lightened to a pale gray-blue when she was frightened.

"You have concocted a tale to bamboozle," he growled at her through the bars of her cell. "But I will have the truth before we are done."

"You wouldn't recognize the truth if it kicked you in the arse."

She uttered that insult in English. He didn't let her know he understood it when hearing thoughts she didn't want him to know of might become a useful tool for him. But he couldn't stay there any longer. Fight-

163

ing desire and anger, he'd end up doing something he would regret.

He told her in parting, "I will get rid of this anger before I decide what to do with you. But I warn you, this" — he waved a hand at her cell — "is nothing compared to what you will face if you do not start telling the truth."

He heard her gasp before she turned her back on him. As soon as he'd left the cell, she'd leapt for her gown and had been holding it up in front of her like a royal shield. But he'd just frightened her enough that she didn't realize she was giving him a fine view of her shapely legs. He left abruptly before he opened that door again.

Her fear mollified him only a little, but enough to make him realize her indignation was partially responsible for his anger. Her situation was too serious. She had to realize she wouldn't be escaping this plot unscathed unless she actually was innocent. If she'd been lied to so convincingly that she really believed what she was saying, then he could be more lenient. The question was, how to determine that?

He was still angry at himself as well for allowing her to distract him from taking the simple precaution of searching her the moment she made her claim. Men were searched at the gate, women weren't. That would change after today.

Desire was a dangerous thing. If he hadn't had a taste of her, it wouldn't be as powerful as it was now. But he'd made an honest mistake when she'd leaned so close to him to request a private rendezvous in such a sexy tone.

Just last month he'd had to deal with a middle-aged widow who had also kept her business at court a secret until she stood before him and confessed she hoped to wile her way into the king's bed. She'd even offered herself to him as payment to arrange a meeting between her and Frederick. Christoph hadn't been tempted. He'd shown her to the gate instead. She wasn't the first who had come there without researching her subject better. It was well-known in Lubinia that Frederick had been lucky to find love twice, with both his queens, and that there hadn't been a royal mistress since he'd married his second wife.

With that foolishness last month so fresh in his mind, it was no wonder he'd given in easily to Alana's temptation — or grasped at that excuse simply because she was young and beautiful and so desirable. Damnation, he'd wanted to be right. He'd wanted her to be exactly what he'd thought she was when he brought her to his quarters.

After giving Boris orders and putting on an overcoat since it had begun to snow again, Christoph went to question the guard Alana had accused of stealing her bracelet. He couldn't leave that stone unturned before he spoke with the king. He was actually a little disappointed to hear the man deny it, which prompted him to instruct another guard to search the man's belongings. He didn't expect the bracelet to prove anything other than that the girl wasn't lying about everything.

Then he went immediately to seek a private word with the king. His stride was quick. He hoped to reach the royal chambers before the monarchs sat down to dinner. Only emergencies could interrupt that, and his business wasn't an emergency — yet.

The royals were entertaining, though, and were in the sitting room with their guests prior to dinner. The king and the queen both greeted him warmly, but Frederick didn't rise immediately to see what had brought him. So Christoph greeted the two guests, with whom he was acquainted.

He wasn't surprised to see Auberta Bruslan there. Norbert Strulland, the doddering, feeble-looking retainer who served as her escort, sat next to her on a gold-threaded, beige sofa. One was rarely seen without the other. White-haired like Auberta, Norbert should have been retired years ago, but Auberta was too kindhearted to dismiss him.

The former queen was often invited to the palace for royal gatherings or private dinners. Both Frederick and Nikola honestly liked the old lady, who was good-natured and had a lively sense of humor. They were also interested in fostering good relations through her with as much of the former king's family as possible. Not all Bruslans were opposed to a Stindal on the throne.

"Christoph, how is your grandfather Hendrik, eh?" Auberta asked him warmly. "I haven't seen my old friend since the sleigh races — it must be ten years ago!"

Christoph smiled. He knew the rumors that Hendrik had been courting Auberta prior to King Ernest's noticing her, and winning her affections, and making her his queen.

"He doesn't come to the city as often as he used to," Christoph replied.

"A shame. I miss his humor. He could always make me laugh. And how is your lovely neighbor Nadia Braune? Have you captured her heart yet? Will we be hearing wedding bells in the near future perhaps?"

Christoph felt like grimacing, but concealed his feelings well. Auberta was no doubt just interested in gossip, but it was too soon after that unpleasant visit from Nadia today for him to answer with anything other than bluntness.

"Nadia and I were merely childhood friends, nothing more."

Auberta seemed surprised, but her escort actually frowned. Christoph had to allow that Norbert was so old that his mind often wandered, and he might not even be following the conversation. The old lady quickly changed the subject to one of her favorites, directing her comments back to Frederick.

"My grandson Karsten has made me very proud again," Auberta said. "He's building up one of the family businesses, creating jobs for the commoners. He's so loyal and devoted to Lubinia, not like his dissolute parents, who do nothing but travel around Europe enjoying a carefree life. But at least they left Karsten in my care."

Auberta rarely had anything good to say about her daughter, Karsten's mother, who had married a Frenchman against Auberta's wishes. But she never tired of talking about her beloved grandson. She rather obviously hoped Frederick, still without an heir, would consider naming Karsten as his successor.

"What brings you, Christoph?" Queen Nikola finally asked a bit nervously. Christoph knew she was always on edge about the rebels so he assured her, "There's no cause for alarm. I merely need to consult His Highness about a private matter that will not wait until morning."

Frederick didn't keep him waiting any longer. He excused himself and took Christoph deeper into the royal suite to his own private office, where they could be assured of privacy. Nearing his fiftieth year, the king was still robust and in good health. Blond and blue-eyed, the same as his first queen had been — one would think the plotters would have found an imposter who at least bore the monarchs' coloring for some semblance of resembling them. The other imposters did. Of course, half of Lubinia did as well.

As soon as the door closed behind them, Christoph got right to the point. "Another imposter has arrived, Highness. Do you wish to see her?"

Frederick didn't even hesitate in replying, "What for? To marvel at their audacity? I trust you to deal with this matter. Find out who put her up to it, then send her on her way."

"She mentioned you might use her to avert a war. This implies she's from the Bruslan camp, sent to encourage you to make a fatal mistake. But that would suggest they have more clever advisers now."

"Possibly, but keep in mind, Christoph, that huge family is the devil's very own to deal with. There are so damn many of them, some of whom are distant blood relations of mine. Many of them are good and decent people, even friends like Auberta is. But I concede some of the young bucks believe the Bruslans should still hold the throne. They resent that Ernest's direct male descendant Karsten wasn't chosen to succeed him."

"Karsten was just a child at the time of his grandfather's death," Christoph said. "The people didn't rise up against King Ernest just to put another Bruslan in his place."

"But enough time has passed since that civil war for the younger generation of Bruslans to forget that. No doubt some of them are funding the rebels. Keep an eye on Karsten in particular. I know Auberta thinks the world of him, but he's a clever fellow and I fear he's duped his grandmother with his sudden shouldering of responsibility."

Christoph nodded. "That would be quite a change in him, when his only interests since he reached manhood have been women and drink."

"Exactly. And actually, she did mention he plans to attend the first races tomorrow. That would be a good opportunity for you to ascertain if he's really making a change for the better — or not. But I also want you to continue to monitor the activities of some of the other noble families, the Naumanns, the Weinsteins, even the Braunes — yes, I know they are your neighbors, but don't let that influence your judgment."

"Of course not, Highness. They lost more than most with the change in regime."

Frederick nodded. "As for this imposter, I suppose she could be a complete innocent they've managed to dupe with tales of heroically saving lives."

"I am keeping that possibility in mind, but there are other unusual circumstances. She entered the palace armed, hoping to gain an immediate audience with you because of her particular story."

"Yet another female assassin?"

Christoph was aware that one of the king's foreign mistresses that he'd kept prior to his remarriage had tried to slit his throat. While it wasn't dismissed that it could have been part of a plot, most believed it to have been simple jealous rage.

Christoph shook his head. "I highly doubt she's capable of murder. She's too young and rather naive. And it wasn't just one weapon but many that she had hidden on her. That's too overdone, so more likely they were just props to support her claim that someone here wants her dead and they were to protect her."

"Be absolutely sure, Christoph. I don't like imprisoning women, much less executing them. Perhaps you can use this to frighten the truth out of her."

"Certainly, Highness, but there is still more. She's English and was secreted into the country in disguise."

"She admitted that?"

"No, but I am aware of it, since I ran across her last week when I was chasing down the rumor of a rebel camp. Two men, two boys, and a fine coach. Unfortunately, it was snowing so hard I wouldn't recognize any of them if I saw them again."

"Yet you now think she was one of those boys? Why?"

"She described the incident to me and has accused one of my men of stealing her jewelry that day. I've already confronted the man. He denies it, but he's new. I don't trust him yet. So I am also sending men to search his family's farm. It is too late for them to leave tonight, so it may be several days before they return."

"Thorough as usual," Frederick commended. "You hope to catch her in the lie?"

"That, yes, but she also described an infant's bracelet that was among her jewelry that was to prove her story."

Frederick was given pause. "There was one bracelet I had crafted for her the day she was born, but there were others. So many trinkets she was presented with in the days following her birth, and so many went missing after Avelina died and the care of my daughter was shifted from the queen's rooms to a new nursery wing. I don't know if the bracelet I gave her was one of the ones that were lost. But it disturbs me that my enemy could know about it and use it against me, when only my most trusted advisers were aware of it. I want answers, Christoph. Use whatever means necessary to get at the truth without actually hurting this young woman — fear, even seduction if you have to. Find out who put her up to this, and we may finally have the name of my enemy."

"Certainly, Highness."

Christoph had had the same thought. His predecessor had dealt with the first three imposters. Mere children they'd been. One had been brought in by a swindler from a German principality. They'd been thrown out of Lubinia and told never to return on penalty of death. Another had been brought in by a money-hungry Lubinian. His tale had fallen apart as well, and he'd been imprisoned and the little girl sent to a convent school. The third pair had been the most convincing, but when the questioning had gotten tough, they had escaped, so the king's guards had never found out who'd been behind that attempt, though Bruslans had been suspected.

Christoph had dealt with the fourth one two years ago. It had been almost comical. She claimed to be sixteen, the age the princess would have been, though she looked more like twenty. He'd no sooner begun his questions than she'd broken into tears. Considering her fearfully distraught, he left her alone, giving her the opportunity to depart with her foolish claim, though he stationed men to discreetly follow her. She took the bait immediately.

Her connection was traced to one of the nursemaids who hadn't gotten the job of tending to the princess all those years ago.

Despite her advanced age, she had claimed to still be nursing her own child, yet a few questions had revealed that child was long dead — and possibly what had addled her mind. After the royal theft had been made known, she had been heard to gloat that she could have protected the princess from being stolen, and that only she could have raised her properly. She set out to prove it by stealing a girl child from town and raising her to think she was royalty.

But the girl had had a harsh childhood, beaten by the old woman each time she questioned why a princess was being raised in such squalor. The girl didn't have the courage to go through with the impersonation. She, at least, had not been part of the plot hanging over the Stindals.

But this girl who had shown up today was something else entirely. The others had been children or stupid. This one wasn't either. But he'd already tried to frighten her, obviously not enough to get a confession yet, so he'd keep that in mind. But seduction? When he had never been anything but straightforward with his women? He was more than willing to get her into his bed, though, and with the king's permission! And it would be interesting to see how she would react to a change in tactics. . . .

CHAPTER SEVENTEEN

If this was how they treated long-lost daughters, Alana could just imagine how they treated enemies. She was actually going to enjoy being a princess just long enough to put Christoph Becker in his place!

She had been contemptuous of this country before, but now she was starting to despise it. If lives weren't at stake, she would withdraw her claim faster than the captain and his palace guards could blink. Closed-minded, primitive lout, how dare he treat her like this when she'd done nothing wrong? Well, she should voluntarily have surrendered her weapons sooner, she supposed, before he discovered them on his own. That did look bad. But he'd rattled her so much she hadn't even thought to do so sooner!

She hadn't grown up knowing any sort of fear. Poppie had taught her how to handle dangerous situations, but not how to deal with this particular emotion. Having her natural indignation over her treatment mixed in with it was a horrible combination that put a painful tightness in her chest.

She was afraid the captain had provoked this fear deliberately so she'd end up telling him exactly what he wanted to hear instead of the truth. God, she couldn't let that happen. Lives depended on *her* steadfast resolve. She needed to regain her confidence. She needed a stronger emotion to outweigh the fear. Indignation wasn't strong enough. She needed to get her anger back, she realized as she stared at the metal-barred cell door. She noticed that the bars were not narrowly set. A man couldn't squeeze through them, but she might be able to.

But the servant Boris arrived before she could test that possibility. "You're not going to shoot me, are you?" he called from the doorway in a jocular tone.

He couldn't be serious. He had to know she no longer had any weapons, so she didn't bother to answer him.

Grinning, he came forward to give her a small lamp first, already lit, thrusting it through the bars and setting it on the floor of her cell. It was welcome because now, in the evening, no light was streaming through the high-set windows in the outer room. The sconces at the door to the detention block, which wasn't far from her cell, provided the only illumination.

Next she heard Boris grunting as he carried a large, heavy brazier, which he placed outside her cell's door. After he lit it, he put a folding contraption around it that funneled the heat into her cell.

"If you hadn't angered the captain so much, he wouldn't have locked you in," the servant told her, "and this could go inside your room."

It was a cell, not a room! she wanted to scream, but she held her tongue. Actually, if not for the barred door, it could be considered a room. It was larger than the other cells she'd passed, and it had been made somewhat comfortable, so she assumed it was for special prisoners of rank or importance. The bed was narrow, void of bedding, but the mattress was softly stuffed. She'd tested it. An oval rug was on the floor, with a pedestal table and that odious chair that she'd left right where the captain had put it before he'd shoved her down in it.

Boris appeared to be waiting for her to reply to his comment. A young man, he was as cleanly shaven as his master, with curly, brown hair worn a little long. His eyes were light blue, sharp with intelligence.

"I expect no less of a barbarian," she retorted.

"I wouldn't say that to him if I were you."

"Why not? He's blind and stupid and doesn't recognize the truth when it smacks him over the head."

Boris laughed and left her alone. Fully dressed now, she had been managing to ward off the chill in that prison block by pacing the floor. She welcomed the heat from the brazier, but not for long.

The room quickly got too warm. She rolled up her sleeves. She opened the bodice of her gown a bit. She took off her boots and stockings, even her heavy petticoats. Still she felt uncomfortably warm. When it occurred to her that this was a deliberate tactic intended to bake a confession out of her, her anger rose with the temperature.

She welcomed her anger. She could control it. Poppie had taught her to control all of her emotions. Look how well she'd done during that outrageous interrogation. Becker wouldn't even see her anger, she could hide it so well. But this heat was too much!

She thought about shouting for Boris, but he wouldn't come back if this intense heat was deliberate, and she was now sure it was. No one in his right mind would funnel this much heat at her by mistake. She thought

179

about trying to knock over the brazier's shield, but it appeared to be out of her reach, and she was afraid she'd get burned if she tried to get close to it. So she stayed as far back in the cell as she could, her back to the heat, and used her petticoat to wipe the perspiration off her face and neck.

Unfortunately, the heat soon exhausted her, draining away her anger. She lay on the bed, and soon the sweat on her cheeks was mixed with tears. Despite what the captain had said, she was afraid he wasn't going to let her out of that cell. But soon she couldn't even summon the energy to feel sorry for herself. She knew she was becoming dangerously listless, but she couldn't muster the gumption to try to counter it.

She was almost asleep when she vaguely heard the door to the detention block open and heavy, military-brisk footsteps approaching. She tried to sit up, but couldn't quite manage it and gave up the effort. She was utterly wilted, soaked with sweat. She opened her eyes only a smidgen to make sure it was the captain. It was, and he looked even bigger and more intimidating because he was wearing a long, shapeless military coat.

She saw him stop next to the brazier and heard him swear, knocking the shield to the floor, where it opened flat, then he shoved the brazier away from the door with his foot. That done, he glanced in the room at her — and drew in his breath sharply.

The long string of oaths that followed were so foul, Alana didn't even recognize them. Not that they would have made her blush when her face was already so flushed from the heat. She knew she should brace herself. He was unlocking the door to come inside. But she was still too drained to care.

He picked her up and carried her out of there. That was at least alarming enough to make her find her voice, albeit barely a whisper, "Put me down."

"I'm taking you to cool off."

"So you didn't mean to melt me?"

"Not like that."

Remembering his earlier remark about her melting *on him* like butter, she actually understood he wasn't talking about that brazier. The cool air from his brisk passage through the storage room didn't pull her out of her stupor either. But the snow did, opening her eyes fully. He'd taken her outside to the ward, just outside his quarters. Darkness had fallen and with it, a steady stream of snow. It melted on her instantly, wouldn't even stick to her warm clothes as it did to his. But that would change soon enough as cold as it was out-side.

"You want me to catch my death?" she gasped.

He snorted. "If it wasn't so early in winter, there would be a pile of snow out here for me to drop you in. It's a healthy way to cool off."

"It's nothing of the sort. Now put me down!"

"In your bare feet?"

Only now was she reminded that she wasn't wearing her boots, though she was more properly attired than when he'd last seen her. But with the snow falling about Christoph's face, she was also reminded of that other time they'd been in the snow together. Good God, he was the brute from the mountain pass! *This* was whom she had to deal with? A man who would touch her so inappropriately just to amuse his men? Of course! She should have known by the way he'd been manhandling her all day! And he knew. Why hadn't he said anything when she'd described that encounter to him and told him her bracelet had been stolen by one of his own men?

He didn't wait for her to answer or didn't expect one, but he did carry her back inside before she did actually catch a chill. He

182

continued down that little hallway off the parlor. She started to stiffen, but he wasn't taking her back to the cell. He stopped between the two doors in the middle of the hall, one of which was open. She only got the briefest glance into the kitchen. The cook saw her and raised a brow. Boris was there, too, leaning against a worktable. She didn't have time to give him a fulminating glare for what he'd done before Christoph opened the door to the other room and set her down inside it.

It was a bedroom, *his* bedroom. Nothing about it was Spartan or military. Richly appointed, it could have been a bedroom in a mansion, if on a smaller scale. It reminded her that he *was* a member of the nobility here and was obviously so rich he could build his own lavish quarters in the palace while he served the king. Too bad his behavior didn't live up to his title.

Despite his having seen her in her underclothes before, she still pointed out, "This is highly inappropriate!"

"What is? That I give you a room where you can repair yourself? Or did you think I was going to stay and watch?"

She abruptly gave him her back again. He snorted, adding, "There's water on the washstand. Return to the parlor for dinner when you are done."

The parlor for dinner? Not back into a locked cell? Well, that was encouraging. But still she was forced to admit, "I will need something to wear. My dress is soaked and will need washing. I actually need a bath. And my boots —"

"Enough. Make do with something in my wardrobe."

She turned again to tell him she wouldn't wear his clothes, only to see the door close behind him. Very well, she didn't exactly have much choice. At least the door had a latch she could turn to be assured of privacy.

With her energy returning, she moved quickly to the washstand, dropped her remaining clothes at her feet, and drenched herself with cool water. The discarded clothes kept a puddle from forming on Christoph's fine carpet. She even poured the last of the water over her head before she ran a towel briskly over her body.

She heard something fall loudly to the floor in the next room, but assumed the cook had dropped something in the kitchen. She was too occupied rummaging through the wardrobe to even start at the noise. Uniforms, shirts, pants that were much too long for her, another winter coat thicker than the one she'd just seen him in, a white robe. She sighed over her choices.

She tried on one of his shirts, which only fell just above her knees. She needed something longer like a nightshirt, but couldn't find one in the wardrobe or the bureau next to it. The white robe and the shirt would have to do. She buttoned the shirt up to her neck and folded the cuffs of the sleeves several times to get them off her hands. Christoph had taken all of her hairpins, so she couldn't repair her coiffure, but she found a comb on the bureau, with which she got the tangles out. She was afraid to find out what she looked like when she was finished, so if there was a mirror in that bedroom, she didn't try to find it.

She took a deep breath before she opened the bedroom door. She had to show that man confidence or he'd never believe her. He needed to *see* her heritage, not that frightened mouse he'd made of her in that cell. Unfortunately, being dressed in his clothes didn't exactly make for a royal bearing. But the outer shell was superficial, she reminded herself. *She* knew who she was.

CHAPTER EIGHTEEN

When Alana stepped into the parlor, it was empty, but only for a moment. "I could cut off the edge of that robe if you like, so it doesn't drag on the floor," Christoph said from behind her.

She swung around to see him coming down the hallway toward her with her boots in one hand. But he paused, his eyes slowly moving over her attire with interest. Her neck and chest were covered with his shirt, but she still felt the need to hold the edges of the robe closed tighter over that part of her body. He suddenly grinned, as if he knew how nervous he could make her with just a look.

She had left his room feeling composed, if a little bit angry, and a little embarrassed over her attire. Yet after his slow perusal of her, she felt something more. His attraction? Hers? Suddenly it was the most powerful emotion in the room, and it shouldn't even be there!

"That won't be necessary," she said stiffly.

"You're sure? I don't think I'd mind kneeling before you — to do that."

So he could see her bare legs under the robe, she didn't doubt, but she promised him, "Someday you *will* kneel before me — as your princess — and regret your treatment of me."

He just chuckled and tossed her boots on the sofa. He had removed his coat and the jacket of his uniform. She wondered if that meant he was off duty now? This certainly wasn't the man who had slammed a cell door shut on her. It would be nice if they could start over, but she didn't think that was possible.

But just in case it was, she offered, "There is a pepperbox pistol in my purse, if you didn't find it yet."

"I have it."

So much for her olive branch. She resisted the urge to check her purse to see if he'd confiscated her money, too, and merely moved to the sofa to put her boots back on. She found her stockings stuffed inside them. She had removed them before they got damp with sweat so she turned her back on the captain to put them back on. Oh, God, this was even worse, wearing boots with a bedroom robe! Could she look any more ridiculous?

Her confidence having fallen a notch, she stood up to find him sitting at the dining table. He extended a hand to indicate she should use the chair beside him. Such a civil gesture seemed wildly out of place in this situation, which was anything but civil.

Before she approached the table, Boris entered the room with two bowls of soup — and a black eye. She wondered if the servant's falling to the floor accounted for the loud noise she'd heard.

Boris gave her an abject look, then abruptly dropped to one knee, incredibly, without spilling the soup. "I swear, lady, I was worried you wouldn't be warm enough even with the heat I brought. That room is cold even in summer."

"She doesn't want to hear what an idiot you are," Christoph snapped at the servant.

No, she didn't, but the man's guilt could be useful. "You can make amends by finding a laundress to clean my clothes," she suggested.

"I will do so myself."

"No, a woman —"

"It will be my honor!"

She gave up and just nodded stiffly. But as soon as he set the soup down and left, she said to the captain, "You didn't have to hit him."

"Yes, I did."

"It wouldn't have happened if you hadn't put me in your prison. Try giving yourself a black eye!"

He raised a brow at her accusing tone. "Anything else you want to get off that pretty chest of yours before we eat?"

He made it sound as if she had no cause to be outraged. "Yes. I know who you are. *You're* that uncouth lout from the mountain pass!"

"So? Why are you bristling over that? Ah, because *you* were the one I tapped on the arse, eh?" He started laughing. "The snow was so thick, I wasn't sure."

She blushed furiously, which made him laugh all the more. Had she thought he would apologize for his behavior that day? More fool her. He obviously had no shame whatsoever over such coarseness. But at least he didn't have to waste time looking for the leader of those men when he was that leader, which meant he already knew who had stolen her jewelry.

"You were gone long enough to confront that thief who stole my bracelet. Did you?"

"He says you lie."

"*He's* lying!"

"*That's* a stalemate — for the moment. But we stopped at his village on the way back to the city that day, so he could have stashed your baubles at his family's cottage there. Men will be leaving in the morning to investigate."

That was something at least. Actually, that was much more than she'd counted on, after his skeptical reaction to her accusation.

She was on the brink of thinking he *could* still be an ally when he added, "Anything else you want to get off that pretty chest? My clothes perhaps?"

Back came the blush. But the way he was watching her, she got the feeling he was testing her somehow. Was he deliberately trying to offend her? Was he trying to provoke her into saying something she shouldn't? How naive she'd been to think she could maintain control over her emotions in a situation like this. But she *could* do better.

Her tone was only a little stiff when she said, "I would like to know why you have closed your mind to the fact that I'm Alana Stindal."

"I haven't formed an opinion yet."

"Yes, you have. I'm going to be absolutely truthful with you. Give me the same courtesy. You would *not* have put me in a prison cell if you hadn't dismissed my claim without reservation. Why? Just because others have come before me? Was one believed to be me? Is that who was buried here when I was seven?"

He ignored her questions and said, "Sit down, Alana. Eat your soup while it is still hot."

"Good Lord, you sound like you're talking to a child," she said incredulously.

"How old are you?"

"You know very well I turned eighteen this year. I am old enough to marry, old enough to bear children, old enough to assume my rightful place — here."

He smiled, reminding her, "I thought you said you didn't want to stay here?"

Tired of his questions and his attempts to twist her words, she sighed and marched to the table and took the seat she preferred, the one opposite him. She reached across for the bowl that had been set at the place next to his and put it in front of herself.

"If I can manage to have a brief visit with my father, which is all I want, I will convince him this is not the life for me. Poppie thinks I must stay here. I don't."

"A good subject to get back to, your Poppie. And in addition to wanting to learn more about him, such as his real name, I'd like to know if the little boy and the coach-man are involved in your scheme."

Her chin rose a notch. "I don't think so, not until you answer me."

He could have insisted. She was amazed he didn't after the earlier browbeating he'd given her. But instead, in an almost conde-scending tone, he said, "Eat, then perhaps I will."

If she weren't so hungry, she wouldn't have picked up the spoon. But before she touched her soup, she reached over and switched her bowl with his. He laughed. She didn't care. At least he wasn't trying to starve information out of her.

Before long, Boris brought in the main course, two large, flaky meat pies. She couldn't identify the meat, which tasted slightly gamy and was seasoned with spices.

"Goat?" she guessed.

"You've had it before?"

"No, but I was told that goatherding is one of the major businesses here. It's not your only source of meat, is it?"

"Centuries ago it was, but, no, not any longer. And what do I call you? That is, what name were you raised with?"

"I suppose Poppie couldn't bring himself to change my first name. It's always been Alana."

She took a few more bites of the delicious pie, hoping it would get the blush off her cheeks. He'd just slipped in that question and she'd answered without even thinking about it! She was going to have to be more careful.

No wine had been served with the meal, for either of them. Was that customary for him, or by his order just for tonight? Was he afraid to cloud his thoughts with even a single glass? If she weren't still upset over what he'd done, she might smirk over that thought.

She finally asked, "Are you testing my patience?"

"Not at all. Just trying not to spoil your appetite."

She didn't like the sound of that and put her fork down. "Like you just did?"

He laughed. "You do make a worthy adversary, but we have not reached that point yet. I will try to keep an open mind and not judge you out of hand. But your tension is obvious and not helping this discussion. Might I make a suggestion?"

Oh, God, the sensuality was back in his eyes, in the sudden soft turn of his lips. She didn't dare ask what the captain had in mind to relieve her tension.

"What?" she heard herself asking anyway.

"If we adjourn to my room and spend some time in my bed, it would —"

She gasped. "That doesn't bear answering!"

He shrugged, but then he actually grinned at her. "You're sure, Alana?"

What was he doing? Using seduction now to get her to admit what *he* thought was the truth? If he was, he certainly wasn't being subtle about it! But could it work? She'd lost her will to him earlier. She'd been dazzled into a thoughtless state. She was out of her depth when it came to the feelings this man could arouse in her. She didn't know and didn't want to find out if powerful feelings like that could be used against her.

She blushed just remembering the kisses she'd shared with him, so it was difficult, but necessary, to remind him, "What happened earlier between us was a mistake. Please don't allude to it again."

"You liked being in my arms."

"I didn't!"

"Liar." He chuckled. "What happened to your being absolutely honest, eh?"

Her blush escalated, but having been called on the carpet as it were, she couldn't keep this particular truth from him. "You are trespassing on a female prerogative now, which is not relevant to this discussion."

All he did was grin, but the passion in his eyes was hot enough to burn.

Desperately she glanced down at the table. "Besides," she managed to add, "I wasn't tense when I came in here, I was angry. There's a difference."

"Your fear goes away and anger takes its place? Do you somehow think you are no longer a prisoner because I am sharing my meal with you?"

That fear he'd just mentioned might have returned if she didn't hear his sigh. She kept her eyes averted, and he said nothing else for several long minutes.

"So which question was I remiss in answering for you?" he finally said.

She relaxed when she heard his calm, professional tone. He was behaving like the captain of the palace guard, not like a seductive rogue.

She was able to match his calm now. "We both know you never would have locked me up unless you'd truly ruled out the possibility that I am Frederick's daughter. After everything I've told you, how can you still be so firm in your disbelief?"

She had to look up to gauge his reaction. He seemed to be hesitating to say anything at all, but then his eyes abruptly narrowed.

"You don't realize the seriousness of what you did. We don't look kindly upon anyone who enters the palace with weapons when we are very much aware that there are people who want to harm our king."

"You can't really be accusing *me* of being an assassin!" she said incredulously.

"I didn't say that. Yet you haven't explained to my satisfaction why you came here so heavily armed."

"I did explain. The pistols were my first defense, the daggers a last resort, but all of them were for my own protection and nothing else. But that doesn't negate your suspicions, does it?"

"I've told you I will keep an open mind."

She nodded, though she didn't believe him one bit. He was too quick to accuse her of other reasons for being there and was flatly discounting the real reason.

Exasperated, she nodded to the rapiers on the wall. "I know how to use those. Would you like a demonstration?"

He burst out laughing. "You want to prove you're an assassin?"

"I believe it would prove I'm not, because *that's* not a weapon an assassin would use, is it? Sword fighting is as much about self-defense as it is about offense."

He was still smiling when he said, "You

appear to have an answer for everything, revealing how quick-witted you are. An excellent memory would go hand in hand with the intelligence you reveal with your every word."

She tsked. "So I am part of some elaborate plot and have memorized my lines well? Is that what you really think?"

He stared at her for a long moment. His humor was gone, and the intensity in his blue eyes was unnerving her again. But she recognized this wasn't passion, this was suspicion. She had to resist the urge to glance away from him.

He finally said, "I apologize."

For his amusement? Or for his pouncing on anything that might support his false conclusions?

She decided to be blunt. "I *was* central to a plot, but my role in it was to die. Poppie foiled that plot by removing me from it."

"What turned a murder into an abduction instead?"

"I smiled at him. Very sentimental I know, but from that moment on, he became my protector. And I owe him my life. Had someone else been sent to kill me, I would be dead." Because the captain was being somewhat cordial again, she also answered his earlier question. "You asked about my other traveling companions. We hired coaches as we crossed Europe, the drivers came with them. The boy, Henry, is an orphan whom Poppie and I are very fond of. There's no scheme, as you put it. We thought it best not to even tell Henry who I really am."

"And your guardian's real name?"

"I gave you his name, it's the name he used all of our years in England, even the name I thought was mine until he told me about my father."

"You call this being truthful? *Farmer* is not a Lubinian name."

"I call it protecting a man who is like a father to me — from you. You don't need him when you have me."

He stared at her for a long moment before he said, "I do have you, don't I?"

He sat back in his chair. His expression didn't reveal if he believed anything she'd said. She really wished he wasn't so strong-willed and carefully guarded. That last remark made her feel distinctly uneasy.

"Boris," he called suddenly.

The servant appeared so quickly, it was obvious he'd been waiting in the hallway — and listening to their every word. And the captain knew that or else he would have shouted the summons.

Alana hadn't wanted anyone else to hear her tale. She was furious that he had allowed someone else to eavesdrop.

"Any dessert tonight?" Christoph asked the servant as Boris picked up the empty plates from the table.

"Sweet or sour?" Boris paused to ask.

"We still have lemons?"

"Sweet, if there's a choice," Alana interjected.

The captain nodded. She waited until Boris left the room to ask, "Do you trust him?"

"Boris? His parents were born on my family's estate, as was he. We grew up together. Despite the difference in our social standing, he is a friend."

"Then why did you hit him today?"

"He's not stupid. The mistake he made was out of good intentions, but an error that would devastate him with guilt. If I hadn't hit him, he would have walked into my fist. Trust him? I do not hesitate to say, with my life."

That was well and good for him, but not for her. "Please warn me the next time someone else is going to be present at your interrogations. What I have to say is for your ears only — and my father's."

"You are here to reveal everything, not to

199

keep your visit secret."

"No, I'm here to reveal everything to my father and prevent a war, *not* make my presence known before then," she said in frustration. "Until I actually have the king's protection, the more people who know I'm here, the greater the risk I face. You do concede this would put me in great danger?"

"I concede that whatever you say will remain behind these doors."

"*Why* can't you just ask my father to come see me? Put me back in that cell, defenseless, unable to touch him, but bring him here to meet me!"

"Do you come to this country thinking we are fools?" he snarled.

CHAPTER NINETEEN

She sucked in her breath. She'd made him angry again. *How?* She felt tears coming on. Oh, God, she'd never forgive herself if she let him defeat her with her own emotions simply because he was so intimidating when he looked like this.

"Answer me!"

"Not if you're going to shout at me!" She had shot to her feet, getting ready to run if he moved toward her.

But he didn't stand up; in fact, she'd definitely given him pause. He leaned back and studied her face for a long moment. He finally sighed before he said, "Against my better judgment, I'm going to tell you a simple fact. While you're here, you are protected — even from me. Nonetheless, it's not wise to provoke my anger."

She almost fell back into her chair, she was so relieved. No, he probably shouldn't have told her that. She could handle all of her emotions except the one he'd just inspired that was so foreign to her. If she didn't have to fear him, she didn't have to be so guarded, so she could speak more freely. She did that now.

"I came to this country thinking it's so barbaric, it might as well be in the Middle Ages. You have reinforced that opinion three times today," she complained.

"Only three? I can do better than that."

Was he joking? No, he probably wasn't. She lifted her chin. "You want the truth, don't be insulted by it. But I didn't call you a fool, you did. And why did you even make that statement?"

"You were resorting to feminine wiles, pleading for me to bring the king to you, appealing to my sympathies because I want you. Do you really think I take my job so lightly that I would ignore my responsibility for a pretty face?"

It registered. He still wanted her, even thinking the worst of her? She took it back; fear wasn't the only emotion with which he could destroy her composure.

She immediately denied, "I did nothing of the sort. Is the king so busy he can't spare a few moments to have a look at me? What if he recognizes me? What if he instinctively knows me? I was merely asking you to be reasonable."

"There is nothing reasonable about putting you in the same room with His Highness — at this point."

"For the record, the tactics you described wouldn't have occurred to me. And considering your suspicions, I even agree with you." She sighed. "I must be too tired, to have even mentioned it again. If there is no dessert forthcoming, perhaps you can show me to a room and we can resume this discussion tomorrow?"

"It's early," he said.

"I have been depleted, drained of my energy today. Perhaps that was not your intention, but it is nonetheless so."

"You don't really think I would give up the advantage of questioning you when you are tired, do you?"

She raised a brow. "So we are going to continue this interrogation all night? Very well, but when I fall asleep in this chair is when we are done. Wake me all you want, but I will say no more."

He didn't acknowledge her warning other than to call out, "Boris, what is keeping you?"

It took another half minute for the servant to rush into the room with two bowls sloppily filled with something creamy. "Apologies, my lord. Franz could not make up his mind." Then, in a whisper: "I think he wanted to impress your pretty guest."

"She's not a guest. Warn him not to be so foolish again." Christoph waved the servant away.

Alana had the thought that the captain had said that for himself, not his cook. But he was going to allow her to eat the dessert in peace. Vanilla, she tasted, but another flavor she didn't recognize.

"Anise, from the southeast," he said, as if reading her mind.

She nodded her thanks. "London gets a wealth of spices; I just never spent enough time in the kitchen to learn the names. But I don't think our cook ever experimented with that one."

Before she set the bowl aside, she couldn't resist running her finger along the inside of it to get the last few drops. Sticking the finger in her mouth, she froze as she caught the captain staring in fascination at what she was doing. She immediately reached for the small, wet towel Boris had left beside her and wiped off the last of the cream instead.

"Please pardon that breach of good manners. I'm partial to sweets," she explained. "Do *not* accuse me of anything else."

"I wasn't going to. I did the same thing when I was a child. Now I just ask for another helping. Would you like more?"

"No, the meal was quite filling. But thank you for offering."

He nodded, even smiled. He was being too cordial again. To make up for that brief bout of anger? If he wanted to make amends, she would much prefer he answer a few questions of her own.

"Exactly how many attempts have been made on my father's life?" she asked. "Is this new plot with the rebels just an extension of the one in which I was supposed to be eliminated? Is it contrived by the same people?"

"You were right. It's late enough for me to be off duty, so no more questions, eh?"

She stared at him incredulously. Just like that? How convenient for him, and utterly frustrating for her. But he probably wouldn't have answered her anyway, she realized. There was and had only ever been one interrogator in the room. He was mindful of that even if she wasn't.

But he wasn't done. "It's still early enough for some amusement though." He pushed his chair back, but only to give himself room to put his legs up on the table and cross them. He then patted his lap. "Come," he

205

said with a slow grin. "I'm sure you can think of something creative to convince me not to put you back in that cell tonight."

CHAPTER TWENTY

With no windows on the high walls and two locked doors, Leonard didn't know the warehouse was abandoned until he picked the lock on the second door and entered at the back of the building. At least the cavernous building wasn't completely empty. Crates, large and small, had been left behind, though only in the back half of the warehouse. All of them were empty, most even broken. Discarded debris littered the floor around them, making his traverse of the room silently a very slow process.

He'd found his target, the man who'd arranged for him to get rid of the royal heir eighteen years ago. The man had a face he'd never forget. Now he also knew the man's name. Aldo. It had taken all day and several more hours into the night to find him. Leonard had actually expected it to take much longer. Luck? He didn't believe in luck. Aldo was simply a man of habit who

207

frequented the one place in the capital where he would hear the kind of news that interested him.

The old tavern where Leonard used to go to "hear" of jobs had burned to the ground, a miller's shop now filling the lot. He'd canvassed the town, checking all the other taverns, spending enough time in each to determine if it was what he was looking for. The last one he'd entered was newer, right on the main street, and much more elegant than the others. A good cover to hide what could really be bought there — death. Even Leonard would have discounted the place if he hadn't recognized an old competitor sitting at one of the tables.

The bartender was as new as the establishment, but likely doing the same job on the side as the old bartender at the old tavern, connecting men who paid for unusual services with those who supplied them. Leonard tried to confirm that by ordering a drink, then telling the man, "I'm looking for work."

"What sort?"

Leonard didn't answer. That used to be all he needed to do to have a few choices mentioned. But this middleman wasn't familiar with Leonard's voice or his manner of concealing his face under a heavy false beard and the hood of his coat. And considering the more prosperous class of customers who frequented this place, Leonard knew the bartender would need to be cautious.

"No jobs here, unless you want to serve drinks?" the bartender said with a chuckle.

"No."

After a moment the bartender said, "Take a seat. Maybe someone will join you."

Innuendos Leonard wasn't familiar with. The man was too cautious. Or a middleman was no longer involved? Or maybe he just wasn't in the right place?

He took his drink to the table closest to the bar, thinking he would have to spend the rest of the night waiting, watching, hoping for something other than the presence of an old competitor to confirm he wasn't wasting his time. And then he had more than that when his target actually walked in and went straight to the bar.

The bartender knew him, even called him by name. "Aldo, what can I do for you today?"

"Just a quick drink. Anything I should know about?"

"Maybe."

"Save it then. No time right now, but I'll be back before you lock up for the night."

That was Leonard's cue to leave the tavern immediately. He barely had time to step into the recessed entryway of the shop next door before Aldo came outside and hurried down the street, then down a narrow side street. Leonard followed. He wanted privacy for his confrontation with Aldo, but it looked as if that would have to wait. The old warehouse Aldo entered would have been suitable and no one else appeared to be there, but Leonard was cautious enough not to approach the man yet. Aldo's rush to get there implied that someone else would soon be showing up to meet him.

Not until Aldo lit a lantern in the open area at the front of the warehouse could Leonard actually see him. Until then, the old building had been too dark for him to locate Aldo other than by the sound of his footsteps. The lantern must already have been on the floor because Leonard hadn't seen Aldo carrying it. This was looking more and more like a secret meeting place Aldo might regularly be using. Leonard might not need to confront him after all, if he learned something pertinent tonight.

He had time to squeeze between two crates fronting the open area where Aldo waited. It was a perfect spot, not close enough for the lantern light to reach him so he was in blackest shadow, but close enough to see and hear whatever transpired.

The first man to arrive was bundled up due to the cold and, unfortunately, didn't shed any of his clothing as he joined Aldo. Hooded, as Leonard usually was, and standing with his back to the crates, the identity of the first man remained hidden. But his voice was distinctive enough, a bit gravelly and subtly confident, that Leonard knew he would recognize it again if he heard it.

"What are you doing here?" Aldo asked the man. "Your job is unrelated to the palace surveillance. I'm surprised you can tear yourself away from it, as luscious as that lady —"

"I have information to report tomorrow," the first man cut in. "It will save you a trip to the stronghold if I bring Rainier's report with me as well. He's late?"

"No, you're early. And you might as well take these with you, too, then." Aldo snickered as he handed the newcomer a small sack. "The herbs the master requested."

"They were requested three weeks ago. They only work in the very first stage. It may already be too late to use them now."

"It's not my fault that Eastern merchant only shows up in the capital every few months," Aldo complained.

"It's never your fault, is it, Aldo?"

"What are you implying, eh?"

Their attention was drawn by another man who came through the front door. A soldier? Leonard was surprised to see the man wearing the uniform of a palace guard.

"Now what are *you* doing here?" Aldo demanded. "It's Rainier's turn to report. Why are you here instead?"

"Rainier suspects he is being watched, so he didn't want to risk coming here now. He was asked today, by the captain of the guard no less, if he had taken some jewelry from a coach he was ordered to search last week. Apparently the captain's prisoner has accused Rainier of the theft."

"Did he steal?" Aldo asked.

"Yes, but it can't be proven. The word of a prisoner against a guard?" The soldier snorted.

The hooded man with the distinctive gravelly voice appeared upset by this news. "More incompetents who can't simply do the job they're paid for? Stealing can draw attention to you! Are you all idiots?"

"Eh, watch your mouth," the soldier growled. "I'm not the one who was tempted to steal. But you'll like hearing what Rainier had to say about it."

"I doubt that. If he's being watched, he's now useless to us."

The soldier was angry enough at the other man's disdain to blurt out, "It was jewelry brought into the country last week by servants, and amongst the baubles was a baby bracelet inscribed 'Princess Alana.' Or perhaps you don't want to hear any more?"

"A forgery," Aldo scoffed. "Rastibon wouldn't have kept it when he killed the princess eighteen years ago, he would have buried it with her. He was the best killer around in his day, which is why I hired him. He didn't make mistakes or keep souvenirs of his jobs. There could be some other plot afoot that we don't know about."

The hooded man ignored Aldo and said to the guard, "I think if you value your life, you should just spit it out."

The soldier backed down immediately, continuing in a conciliatory tone, "Rainier denied the theft, of course, and has the jewels well hidden. He said the captain didn't seem all that concerned over the jewelry, which made him suspect the captain didn't believe his prisoner to begin with. But Rainier didn't actually see her. I did. She's a very beautiful young woman."

"What has that to do with anything?" Aldo demanded impatiently. "The captain could have simply been humoring her to soften her up — if you know what I mean."

"Actually, what you imply begs the question. How do you know she's a prisoner?" the hooded man with the gravelly voice asked.

"She's been detained all day in his quarters, which are connected to the prison block. And Becker isn't a man to dally while he's on duty."

"In other words, you have no clue why he's had her in his quarters all day, do you? You expect me to report assumptions when the master demands facts?"

Aldo had been pacing in agitation, but now swung back to demand, "Tell me more about the woman. How old is she?"

"Young."

"Eighteen years young?"

"She could be that, yes."

"The bastard!" Aldo exclaimed angrily. "He didn't kill the princess! He waited until she was grown and he's brought her back. Go tell the master," he ordered the hooded man. "We shall see what he wants to do about this."

"You make more assumptions than anyone," the hooded man said in disgust. "He's not the master, fool. He's just another lackey like you."

"You dare!" Aldo said in an outraged tone. "You answer to me!"

"Not anymore."

Leonard grit his teeth as he watched his target slump to the floor. In a brief silence, the two remaining men stared at the corpse at their feet.

The soldier finally asked, "Why did you do that?"

"Because I was ordered to. He was old. He was stupid. He's made one too many mistakes. Just by his manner, thinking himself too important, Aldo made his own enemies. He became a liability."

"But what Aldo just said about that old job that . . . might not have been finished, you aren't going to just ignore that, are you?"

"A wild guess on his part, and irrational, if that old assassin was as good as Aldo touted."

"Is that what you really think?"

"I don't discount any possibility just because one looks more obvious than another, something you and Rainier need to start doing if you don't want to end up like Aldo. The young woman in question could have come to the palace merely to report her jewelry stolen, and as Aldo suggested, the captain could merely be humoring her until he's off duty. Rainier could even be wrong about the inscription on that bracelet. Does he even know how to read?"

"I never asked. But as long as you're covering all possibilities, the young woman *could* be the next queen."

The hooded man laughed mirthlessly. "Quick learner. You might not be of Aldo's ilk, after all."

"What about him?" the guard nudged Aldo's leg. "Shouldn't we bury him?"

"Why bother? I never liked this old building as a meeting place anyway, it's too big and has too many hiding places. Return to the palace. You will be notified tomorrow of a new meeting place — and what our employer has to say about all of this."

Leonard didn't move until he heard the front door click closed, then he rushed out the back door and came around the corner of the warehouse just in time to see the two men part ways at the end of the street. He needed to follow the hooded man now. He was going to have to get word to Alana tomorrow to warn her to be on guard, that cronies of the people who wanted her dead might now think she was still alive — because of that bracelet.

Leonard wished she hadn't reported it stolen, but she must have needed to use it as proof for the captain of the guard. If she had taken him into her confidence, why wouldn't he believe her? It was absurd to think he'd imprisoned her, but Leonard couldn't completely discount that possibility, either, though he would find that out for certain tomorrow. But it was much more likely that the captain was just being cautious and thorough in his questioning, and rightly so. He preferred to think the captain had believed Alana and was protecting her by not letting her out of his sight.

CHAPTER TWENTY-ONE

Alana realized that Christoph Becker was a chameleon, able to change his colors before her very eyes.

She didn't exactly like the hard-nosed captain she'd spent most of the day with. He wasn't at all open-minded as he'd claimed he would be. He could frustrate her to the point of screaming. But he'd given her a boon when he'd assured her that she had his protection, so she didn't think he could frighten her again — she hoped. And as long as he kept to a civil tone, she could deal with him.

She didn't like the seducer either. He destroyed her calm in other ways. She couldn't even think when he showed up.

She'd liked the charming man she'd first met in the palace's anteroom, though. Maybe a little too much. But he'd disappeared . . . and would probably never return.

But *this* one, the coarse mountain brute, she liked the least of all. He offended her, shocked her, thought nothing of treating her like a woman of loose morals instead of the lady she was. Sitting there with his feet on the table, suggesting she sit on his lap to entertain him, good God, he infuriated her!

She couldn't keep the contempt out of her tone when she said, "I'll allow that Lubinian aristocrats aren't the gentlemen I'm accustomed to, but *must* you be so vulgar?"

"If you're trying to insult me, wench, you'll have to do better than that."

"You're a barbaric lout and I think you have sense enough to know it. You like behaving in this offensive manner! You don't even *try* to rise above it."

That just made him laugh. He even folded his hands behind his head. So relaxed, so *un*official, so darn handsome. She closed her eyes and counted to ten.

"Thinking about my bed?"

"No!" she exclaimed, opening her eyes.

"I'm disappointed."

He didn't sound it. He sounded as amused as he looked.

Stiffly she said, "I think I've entertained you enough for one day. If you will show me to a room?"

He took his legs off the table and sat

forward. Suddenly he was all business again. "You already know where your room is."

Nothing could have deflated her more. She was going back into a cell? She really was a prisoner. . . .

But then he surprised her by adding, "Boris will have made the room much more comfortable for you by now, including adding coverings to the door for privacy. Hopefully he found some drapes to hang instead of musty blankets."

Comfortable but still alone back there, Alana thought. That stirred some panic inside her. Anyone could yank those coverings down and send a well-aimed dagger through the bars at her, and the captain wouldn't know about it until the morning when they found her dead!

"There's no normal room I can have instead?"

"I *can* be convinced to let you share my room. . . . No? Then I bid you good night."

"What about in the palace? Surely there must —"

"You really are tired, aren't you, to make that suggestion?" He frowned. "Do try to remember the seriousness of the charge made against you."

She drew in her breath. "You've actually made a charge? That I'm an assassin?"

He snorted over her conclusion, clarifying, "That you're an imposter."

He could still say that after everything she'd told him today? "Why don't you just shoot me and have done with it?" she almost snarled.

"I haven't had your confession yet."

She started laughing brittlely. Her frustration was getting to her. *He* was getting to her. Why the devil had he even let her out of that cell if he still thought this?

"Why are you delaying, as tired as you are?" he asked. "I will not be accused of taking advantage of your exhaustion."

"I have returned to the place where I was meant to die. You can't leave me defenseless here. At least give me back one of my daggers for the night. I will return it to you in the morning."

"I think you should say no more. You are no longer thinking clearly, or you'd know that isn't going to happen, not for *any* reason."

"But —"

"What you're doing is making a very good case for me to keep you by my side tonight. You don't have to come up with excuses for it, wench. The invitation is open."

That didn't deserve an answer. "What about this? You lock the outer doors —"

"They will be locked."

"— but give me the key to the cell."

He laughed. "You want to lock yourself in?"

"No, I want to lock you out," she snapped.

While Christoph laughed harder, Alana couldn't suppress a big yawn. Nothing could have pointed out more clearly that she was at the end of her reserves to deal with someone like Christoph Becker. He was indomitable. That might be a benefit to her father, but it wasn't to her.

But she tamped down the panic that had made her argue with him. She didn't really think she was in any danger yet when no one other than Becker knew she was here. And Boris, depending on how much he'd overheard. And possibly her father — that was if the captain had even informed the king about her. He'd had time to do that while he'd left her in that cell. . . .

Christoph snapped his fingers to get her attention on him again. How rude! She would have said so if he didn't warn first, "If I stand up to escort you to your bed, you're going to see just how much I'd rather drag you to mine. Boris!" he shouted, and the servant quickly came out of the kitchen and caught the ring of keys the captain tossed at him. Then Christoph warned

Alana, "For the last time, go now, while I still let you. You will be safe back there, even from me."

She flew past Boris, who had to run to keep up with her. She didn't have to understand everything the captain had just said to recognize his threat was sexual.

She ran all the way to her cell. She didn't enter it immediately. She checked the door at the end of the corridor first to make sure it was locked as he'd said. It was. She came back and had to push the drape aside to enter the cell. She didn't say a word to Boris, who was standing there waiting to lock the door. She cringed as she heard him do so. The bed was fully made up with bedding, and a smaller brazier was lit and tucked into a corner, filling the room with a comfortable heat. How nice. A *cozy* prison, she thought sarcastically.

She dropped onto the bed, too exhausted to think about it anymore. She didn't doubt she'd be asleep in moments, despite . . . She pushed tiredly back to her feet. The captain might not fear for her life, but she had that dread deep inside her, knowing someone had tried to kill her before and would try again. And he'd left her vulnerable.

She glanced about the room for something, anything that she could use as a weapon. She considered the chair. But it was too sturdy, and smashing it apart to obtain a sharp piece of wood would make too much noise. The pedestal table wasn't sturdy. She flipped it over, stood on top of it, and tested each leg. One was loose enough for her to kick with her boot several times, then yank off. The table leg would serve as a club, a clumsy weapon, but she took it to bed with her and tucked it under the blanket.

She prayed she wouldn't sleep so deeply that she'd fail to hear an intruder approaching. She prayed she wasn't a fool for clinging to propriety instead of accepting Christoph's offer to let her spend the night in his bed. But recalling how pleasurable she'd found his kisses before discovering what a barbarian he could be, she knew she wouldn't be entirely safe there either.

Frederick knelt between the two graves, one marked by a large gray stone, the other marked by a small white stone. The snow had stopped falling but had left a layer on the ground that quickly wet his knees. He didn't even notice. The pain in his chest was too strong. They had both been too young to die. Mother and child. Wife and daughter — his!

Avelina had only been twenty when he'd made her his queen, twenty-one when she bore their child. She had been bleeding when he left Lubinia, complications from childbirth. The doctors had known. She wouldn't let them tell him. His meeting with the Austrians was too important because it involved a renewal of their alliance. She thought she would have recovered by the time he returned. She died before he did. And he came so close to losing Alana, too, in his grief over Avelina's death. But he lost her anyway because he'd listened to his advisers instead of following his heart.

"I was afraid you were coming here. You had that look earlier. It breaks my heart to see you grieve like this."

Nikola Stindal had silently approached. She bent and put her arms around his neck, her cheek to his. His second wife, Nikola, had only been sixteen when he'd married her. He'd promised her mother he wouldn't touch her until she was eighteen. That had been difficult. She was as beautiful as his first wife, and while their marriage had been arranged for political reasons, it had soon turned to love. But even her comforting touch couldn't ease this pain tonight.

"I'll give you another child, I swear I will,"

she told him earnestly.

"I know."

He didn't doubt she would. Even now she suspected she was pregnant again, but if she was, he was hesitant to announce it to put an end to the unrest the rebels were perpetrating. It would just terrify her all the more and end the pregnancy prematurely like all the others. She'd wanted her other pregnancies kept secret, as Alana had been kept secret, but he'd refused. After all, that secrecy hadn't helped Alana.

The threat hanging over their lives was a nightmare for Nikola. He'd been told countless times that her fear was what kept her from bringing a pregnancy to fruition, fear that her child would be stolen or killed, too. She hid it so well. Only occasionally did she cry in his arms.

He had been giving serious thought to sending her away this time if she was pregnant again. That was the only thing that might give her peace.

"Come, it's not safe out here in the ward," she said. "You know Christoph doesn't trust all these new men he's had to recruit because of the rebels."

Frederick stood up, but only to turn and embrace Nikola tightly. "You needn't worry about that. The new men are paired with

226

those that are trusted."

She sighed and asked hesitantly, "What has reminded you so strongly of your loss tonight?"

"The arrival of another impersonator who thinks this grave is empty."

"Did you see her?"

"I am afraid to, afraid I will kill her with my own hands for pretending to be my child, when my Alana lies here in this ground!"

"You must stop blaming yourself for that. I know you think they followed you hoping to find you undefended —"

"As they always hope to do! And they saw me with her! They guessed correctly who she was and killed her as soon as I departed!"

"Her fall could have been an accident. It's not your fault!"

"I should not have visited her so often."

"How could you not? She was your daughter."

"I should have brought her home! She would have been better protected here. Instead I listened to those old advisers who were so afraid of my line ending. Hide her, they said. Keep her safe in secrecy. Let my enemies think they succeeded, so there would be no more attempts to take my heir

227

from me. But they found her anyway. My God, I should have killed that whole family, every last Bruslan in Europe!"

"You only say that when you are this deep in your grief. There are many good fathers and mothers in that huge family, innocent children, the old and the feeble, even friends of ours. Yes, some of them might be unscrupulous enough to want to cause us harm. It might even be Karsten, influenced by the other young bucks who are impatient and bellicose. We just don't know! But it is time we did. Give Christoph leave to use harsher measures. Please, Frederick, this nightmare needs to end!"

CHAPTER TWENTY-TWO

When Alana drowsily opened her eyes, she found the light so bright it felt almost painful. She didn't want to wake up yet! Where the deuce was all the light coming from?

She opened her eyes wider, then immediately brought her hand up to shade her eyes. She wasn't dreaming. Bright light was shining directly into her cell from the windows in the detention block because the curtain over the cell door had been pulled open.

"Good morning, Lady — Farmer."

She turned her head to the voice and gasped when she saw Boris standing close to her bed, grinning at her. Yanking the blanket up to her neck, she demanded, "What are you doing in here?"

"I've brought you a very nice breakfast." He set the platter down on the foot of her bed. "I would have brought a table, too, if I had known yours was broken."

She blushed. The table, which was missing one leg, lay upside down on the floor. She wasn't going to explain. She wasn't going to give up her club, either.

"It doesn't feel as though I got enough sleep. What time is it?"

"Very early. The captain asked me to find some clothes for you to wear today." He nudged the sack by his foot, then picked up the table.

"I take it mine aren't cleaned yet?"

"Not yet. And the captain will be here soon, so maybe you should dress quickly, eh? And don't forget to eat!" he called back as he carried the table away.

She noted he had left the door open. Did he forget? Or had Christoph finally figured out that she wasn't going anywhere until she met her father? Boris's tip that the captain would soon be here worried her enough to get her out of bed and emptying the sack of clothes.

She could feel that the clothes were made of coarse materials, but when she slipped the blouse on, she saw they were cut in a risqué style, too. Who in this day and age wore such low-cut garments that didn't cover her breasts decently? The flimsy chemise was even worse as it barely covered her nipples! Nothing in the sack could be used to cover her bosom other than a long, rectangular scarf that was probably meant for her waist, but she draped it around her neck instead.

She had only half-finished eating breakfast when Christoph appeared in the doorway. She got off the bed immediately. He was wearing a long coat, but not the military coat she'd seen him in last night. The material of this coat was not as fine, and because he hadn't buttoned it yet, she could see he wasn't wearing his uniform either. Instead he wore a woolen shirt and loose pants tucked into knee-high boots with wide, furry cuffs. Why was he dressed so informally today?

"Very colorful," he said, running his eyes over her.

She could tell he was trying to hide a grin, but actually she had to agree; she *was* colorful. The skirt was bright yellow, the blouse white, and the wrap was deep red.

"But this won't do," he added.

Thank goodness, she thought, until he stepped forward and pulled the sash off her neck. "What are you doing?!" She put her hands up to cover what he'd just uncovered.

"You need to look authentic, not comical, where we're going." He wrapped the sash around her waist several times before he tied it off. "There, much better, but you'll need a coat. We'll borrow Franz's, he's as short as you. Let's go."

She didn't budge. "Where are we going?"

"I have to attend a festival today in the high country. It's official business. Bad timing, since I need to keep my eye on you as well. So I can tend to both responsibilities by taking you with me."

"I can't go out in these clothes!"

"Of course you can. I was going to introduce you as my maid, but any man who looks at you will know I wouldn't let such a pretty morsel stay out of my bed for long, so . . ."

She sucked in a breath. "Don't you dare introduce me as your mistress!"

"It's only for the day, Alana. We need to blend in at this festival, not show up as obvious nobles who will make the commoners feel uncomfortable. It must appear that we are just there to have fun like everyone else."

The thought of having some fun appealed to her, although she wasn't sure it was possible with *him.* Nonetheless, she stopped complaining and followed his direction when he extended a hand for her to precede him out of the cell. At least she would be given a coat that would cover her appalling outfit.

Now that she understood why he was wearing what looked like rugged work clothes, she couldn't resist commenting, "So, just going to be the barbarian today, are you?"

She was being sarcastic, but he raised a brow at her. "If you insist."

She gasped as his palm whacked her arse. Oh, good grief, that better have only been retaliation for her remark and not a preview of how he was going to behave today!

A lot of snow had fallen during the night. Stepping out into the ward, she was nearly blinded by the sun's reflection on the snow-covered ground. A guard led Christoph's horse to him. He hefted her up into the saddle, then mounted behind her. She was still shielding her eyes against the glare as they rode off, so she didn't notice the little boy standing by the meat-pie cart watching her closely, or see him hurriedly leave the ward as soon as the captain's horse paced through the gate.

CHAPTER TWENTY-THREE

Alana blamed the cook's coat for making the ride to the festival one of the most unusual horseback-riding experiences she'd ever had in her life. The soft fur that lined the inside of the coat was doing the strangest things to her exposed skin underneath it. Every time the horse jostled her even a little, the fur brushed against her breasts. Her nipples kept tightening, and so did Christoph's arm around her waist. It was almost as if he knew the brush of the fur against her skin was arousing her, and he wanted to intensify those sensations. But, of course, he couldn't know. He was merely concerned about keeping her from slipping away from him, so he drew her back tighter against his chest — then the cycle would begin again.

She was quite warm and flustered by the time they arrived. They'd had to ride around a bend in the mountain, then steadily upward to a high meadow. The road was actually clear of snow from so many carts, coaches, and horses heading to the festival, but this area of the country, at a much higher elevation, had obviously been deluged with more snow than the capital had seen so far. Several feet of it lined both sides of the road and circled the meadow near a small village where a fairgrounds had been set up.

The huge tent at the center of the grounds was filled with people — merchants selling food and drink, and people of all ages eating, drinking, and laughing, many seated at long tables. Laughing children were gathered in front of a makeshift stage where a puppet show was in progress. With so many people in the tent, Alana found it so warm she worried that she'd have to remove her coat if they stayed there. But Christoph merely bought each of them a mug of ale before they went back outside to walk around the grounds.

Games and competitions were set up everywhere Alana looked. There were targets for archery, pistols, and rifles, stakes in the ground for throwing horseshoes and other objects large and small, and several wrestling platforms. There were contests of dexterity — an obstacle course a contestant had to cross while carrying a mug of ale on his head! And contests of strength — a footrace in the snow, but each runner had to carry another man on his back. That one, Alana noticed, definitely got a lot of laughs from a crowd of onlookers. Most of the games seemed designed to amuse the audience rather than the competitors, but that was apparently part of the fun.

Christoph kept his arm around Alana's waist as they walked around. Mindful of the role she had tacitly agreed to play, she didn't try to shrug away from him despite the odd tension she felt from his closeness. The effects of that sensually stirring ride still hadn't worn off, and she didn't think they would until she could get rid of the fur that was still tickling her skin. But the alternative was out of the question because the outfit she had been given was much too revealing. Yet because of her agitation, she was far too aware of the man beside her!

She drank some of her ale, hoping it would soothe her frazzled nerves. Christoph bent his head toward hers to say, "You don't have to drink that. It's just another prop to help us blend in."

"Is it common to drink so early in the day?"

"Normally, no." But then he grinned. "At

a festival, absolutely."

"Then I think I'll have a little more of this, if you don't mind." She took a bigger sip.

He laughed. "You can't sound all prim and proper while drinking ale, wench. But you don't need my permission to enjoy yourself."

No, she didn't. He might like to consider her his prisoner, but he was going to get his comeuppance just as soon as she met her father. She took a bigger sip. It *was* helping to soothe her agitation over how possessively he was holding her. She also felt on display. Well, she was, actually, because he was drawing so much attention himself, which meant too many people were looking at her, too. He might have wanted the people to be at ease with his presence, and it appeared to be working — he got a lot of smiles and greetings — but they still knew *who* he was.

"Are you here merely to observe, or to speak with someone, or are you not allowed to tell me?" He didn't answer, which was an answer, so she added, "Well, if you're determined to 'blend in' as you put it, shouldn't you be playing some of these games?"

"Which would you like to try?"

"Me? If I was inclined, I would choose

237

the pistol shooting, and I would win, you know. But I suppose the men might object to being beaten at something like that — by a woman."

"I think you're right. It's fine for women to show off, and they're quite good at it. In the kitchen — and the bedroom."

"Oh, please," she said drily. "You've let the barbarian out again. That's a bad habit you've got."

"Being myself? I should hope so, eh? But in the interest of avoiding embarrassment for the men present today, perhaps I'll take a turn at something for you. What would you suggest?"

She glanced around, twice, but both times her eyes were drawn back to the wrestling platform where the two combatants currently up there were only half-dressed, their chests bare. Yes, she *would* like to see him up there.

She took another sip of the ale, then pointed at the platform. "There you go, that ought to be a piece of cake for you. Show them how it's done."

"Too easy."

"Oh, ho!" She laughed. "So barbarians are braggarts, too?"

He raised a brow. "Are you getting drunk on just a few sips of ale?"

"I wouldn't know, I've never been drunk, but you asked me to choose and I did. Now let's see what you're made of, Captain."

He chuckled. "And said in the form of a challenge I can't refuse, eh? Very well." He started walking them toward the platform.

"The object, I take it, is to throw the other man off the platform and you win?"

"That's about it."

"Well — good luck."

"You think I need luck?"

"You will if you take me up there with you," another male voice said.

They both turned around — well, Alana had no choice with Christoph's arm holding her so tightly. The man who had come up behind them was blond, brown eyed, and handsome. As tall as Christoph and about the same age. Apparently nobles did attend these festivals because the man's rich apparel spoke for itself. He also had his arms around not one but two young women, both clinging to his sides.

"It's good to see you again, Christo," the man said sarcastically. "But I'm afraid you won't have any fun here if you're on a rebel hunt. These are good people loyal to Frederick."

"And to you? There is more than one way to be disloyal to a king, Karsten."

The tension between the two men escalated, with Karsten scowling over that remark. "You aren't actually accusing me of something, are you?"

"Does it look like I'm on duty today?" Christoph countered. "I was curious, though, after hearing such glowing reports about you lately, to see if you really have begun shouldering a few responsibilities for your family. The last time I saw you — when was it, two years ago? You were still carousing your way through your twenties."

Karsten laughed now. "And you didn't?"

Christoph shrugged. "I spent most of those years at the palace. Of course when I'm not on duty . . ."

He bent toward Alana to kiss her neck to make his point. It took every ounce of her willpower not to blush and to put her hand to his cheek as if she welcomed his attention. But that also drew Karsten's attention to her.

Looking at Alana with interest in his eyes, the young noble asked Christoph, "Who is your new mistress?"

"Much too new to introduce to you, so forget it. I'll be keeping her name to myself."

Karsten laughed again. "You've never forgiven me for luring that Austrian wench away from you, have you?"

"What Austrian wench?"

Both men laughed this time. The tension was gone, too. Karsten even nodded toward the wrestling platform again. "Let's give it a turn, eh?"

They moved toward the platform. The last match was over, but the winner was still up there waiting for another challenger. When Christoph and Karsten both stripped down to just their pants and boots, the fellow quickly hopped off the platform to make room for them. Imagine doing this at this time of the year! They ought to be shivering, Alana thought. But neither young man seemed to be bothered by the cold.

Alana tried to look away, she really did. Propriety demanded it! She even half-turned her face from the platform, but her eyes just wouldn't obey and she finally gave up trying. Good Lord, Christoph's body was superb. The noble wasn't skinny by any means, yet there really was no comparison. Christoph had more strength in his arms, across that wide back and muscular chest. His legs were more muscular, too, and from the expression on his face Alana could see he knew he was going to win, there was absolutely no doubt in his mind. But Karsten didn't look worried. Maybe there was more to wrestling than just brawn.

They circled each other, arms out, each making a few false moves. Then the grappling began, the straining, and the crowd started cheering, which brought even more people over to watch. She kept hearing "captain" whispered, but also "Bruslan." Karsten was one of the notorious Bruslans? Good grief, Christoph was wrestling with one of the old king's descendants? Was this his official business here today, to find out what Karsten Bruslan was up to?

She kept getting jostled farther back by the crowd as more and more people rushed over to watch two noblemen playing at one of their sports. It didn't look as if either contestant was abiding by the rules. Christoph had a couple opportunities where he could easily have tossed Karsten off the platform, but it seemed both men would rather win the contest in a more grueling way by actually proving who was the better wrestler.

She was jostled again, more rudely this time. Some of her ale actually sloshed out of her mug. The little she'd drunk had relaxed her nicely, so she didn't want any more of it. She looked for someplace to set the mug down without having to return to that overly warm tent and headed to an overturned crate by one of the games that was presently unattended.

"Your fortune, m'lady?" someone asked behind her.

She turned to decline the offer, then gasped as she realized who it was disguised to look like an old crone. "Poppie?"

"Look at the entertainment, not at me."

"How did you know I was here?"

"Henry told me, but there's no time to catch up. I came to warn you that the man who stole your bracelet is a spy who works for the same people who hired me. They may conclude you are still alive, so be on your guard."

"Can I tell the captain this?"

"Do you trust him?"

"I — yes, I do."

"I had hoped to follow these people to their meetings, but I will leave it to your discretion. I must go, it's not safe for me here."

She heard him slip away and resisted the impulse to watch him go. She felt a pang of loneliness. She wanted to go with him! She sighed to herself. She and Poppie shouldn't have to sneak around like this to meet. She should already be with her father, her protection assured, and Christoph should be working with Poppie instead of working against her. Did she really trust him? Yes, she supposed she did. He was completely devoted to her father's protection, which was why he couldn't simply take her at her word. Knowing about the other imposters, she couldn't even blame him for being so suspicious. And he was even giving her a day of fun to make up for yesterday. Claiming he had to keep an eye on her was an obvious excuse when he could just have left her in that cell all day.

The tug on her coat drew her eyes down to a little girl who pointed in the opposite direction of the wrestling platform and said, "My dog. Help please."

All Alana saw was a group of children playing in the snow beyond the cleared fairgrounds. If their parents had been watching them, they weren't now. Just about everyone at the festival was either at the wrestling match or heading that way. So she followed the little girl.

Alana soon discovered that the girl didn't want help retrieving an actual dog, but a stuffed toy that had been tossed about fifteen feet away from where the children were playing. Some of the boys in that group were old enough to have helped. The child had probably asked them first and they'd ignored her. For whatever reason,

the little girl was afraid to get the toy back
herself.

Alana found out why when she started
heading toward the toy and was soon trudg-
ing through snow that was more than a foot
deep. The children were yelling at her to
come back, that it was dangerous. Wild
animals didn't hide in the snow, did they?
she wondered. She almost turned back, but
the toy was only a couple more feet away,
so lightweight it hadn't sunk into the snow.

She didn't reach the toy. The ice cracked
under her feet and she was suddenly submerged in the coldest water she'd ever felt
in her life.

CHAPTER TWENTY-FOUR

Christoph was getting bored humoring Karsten, but he'd managed to address a few more points while they rolled about the platform, each trying to pin the other. "I heard you're sponsoring the sleigh races today. Will you be racing as well?" he asked.

"No, but I've entered my sleigh — and warned my driver not to win," Karsten replied.

"So you *are* currying favor with the commoners here?"

"Why would that surprise you? I am the logical choice for Frederick to name as his successor. When he does, we will both want the people to be able to rejoice. I'm merely making sure, by my own merits, that they will like me as much as they do him. And no, I am *not* trying to hurry this along. Frederick is a good king. I love him. He's the father I *wish* I'd had."

Christoph grunted as he was slammed to

the floor. Karsten had caught him by surprise with those remarks. Christoph knew that Karsten was actively campaigning to win Frederick's and the people's favor, but he was surprised to hear him admit it.

He bucked Karsten off him and got back to his feet. "And if our king should have a son, all your efforts would be wasted."

"Why wasted? The boy would still need advisers, fresh ones, not those old coots who decry change. I'll help this country in whatever role I'm deemed fit to play, just as you do. We feel the same, you know, when it comes to Lubinia."

Truth or a cunning attempt to ingratiate himself with the king's guard? It was hard to tell with Karsten Bruslan. But Christoph was ready to end this match. He'd looked for Alana and hadn't been able to find her in the crowd.

He was about to shoulder Karsten and simply push him over the side when he saw people at the back of the crowd running toward the lake. Everyone knew the small lake was there and to avoid it. At the next winter festival it would be utilized, but at this first one, the ice wasn't thick enough yet. He could see the hole in the ice where someone had been stupid enough to test it — or someone hadn't known the lake was there. . . .

He leapt off the platform and ran as fast as he could, that last thought producing a gut-wrenching fear. Someone was trying to throw a rope out in the direction of the hole, but no one was there to catch it.

"Break the ice!" he shouted at the small crowd before he ran across it.

He only went five feet before his weight started another crack. He jumped down on the ice and was partially submerged. He used his elbows to widen the hole, then dove down into the icy water to look for Alana. He saw her submerged near the hole she'd fallen through, trying to use the floor of the lake as a springboard to push herself back up, but her heavy clothes were weighing her down. Her movements were too slow, her limbs barely moving. He swam to her and threw her toward the opening above them. There wasn't enough room for both of them, so he grasped the sharp edge of the ice with both hands and pulled another chunk loose. He caught her again when she started sinking, but he was able to get both their heads above water this time. She was breathing, but she didn't even try to hold on to him. He was terrified by how long she'd been in the water.

The men had broken through the ice up

to the hole he'd made, and he saw Karsten there with three others, working to clear more ice away.

"Hold your breath," Christoph told Alana. "We're going to swim underwater a bit because the ice here is too weak to support our weight."

"I — can't."

He hugged her tightly to him. "I'll swim for both of us, it's not far now."

Christoph kept her in front of him as he kicked through the ice-covered water. They had only about six more feet of ice to get past, then another few feet and he was able to pick Alana up in his arms and walk the rest of the way to shore. Women were waiting there with blankets, which they threw around him and Alana. They all ran to the closest cottage, where Christoph laid Alana down on a pile of blankets near a warm hearth. The women tried to shoo him out as they peeled Alana's freezing, wet clothes off her, but he wasn't budging from the room. He could see the numbness was beginning to wear off because she was trembling despite the heated blankets the women kept wrapping around her.

One old woman, shaking her head at him, said, "You know what she needs, Count Becker. She's your woman, see to it."

Thinking she'd made her point, she took all the other women out of the room with her and closed the door. Christoph didn't hesitate. He quickly removed the rest of his clothes and lay down in front of the fire next to Alana, putting her blankets over both of them and wrapping his arms and legs around her. She barely noticed. Her trembling shook them both and continued unabated. It wasn't enough.

He began kissing her gently, first her cheeks, then her neck, sharing his warm breath with her as he hugged her closer and rubbed her briskly with his hands. As he continued to run his hands up and down her body, he noticed a little color returning to her cheeks and her breathing evening out. He also noticed his restraint was becoming painful. He began to sweat. A few minutes later, she did as well.

"I think you should probably move outside the blanket," she finally said in a prim little voice.

He suddenly felt like laughing. "I should, yes, but I warn you, I'm naked."

"I know," she fairly squeaked.

He put a hand to her cheek. "This was necessary, Alana. There's no shame in sharing heat when it's desperately needed. You could have died in that water. When I found you, you were already giving up."

"I wasn't giving up, I just couldn't tell if I was moving or not, and, well, I can't swim, either, so that made it rather awkward. But thank you for finding me. I was out of breath."

"It's my fault, I shouldn't have left your side."

"No, you had to do what you came here to do. I understand. By the way, did you win?"

"No, I jumped off the platform to find you."

"Did you? Then you'll have to challenge Karsten Bruslan again. You would have won."

CHAPTER TWENTY-FIVE

Christoph didn't doubt that his prisoner was fast asleep after her harrowing brush with death today. She'd barely been able to keep her eyes open during dinner. He tried to sleep as well, but he couldn't.

He didn't think he was ever going to get the sight of her naked body out of his mind. Lithe, athletic, breasts proudly jutting. No soft curves, but tight ones. That body had been worked strenuously to become that firm. And yesterday in her cell, her gray eyes blazing at him, long black hair swirling about her hips in her underclothes. But the image that kept coming back to him most frequently was the one of her trying to sit up in that narrow bed in the cell, face flushed, glistening with sweat, hair damp as if she'd just had vigorous sex. That one had kept him awake long hours last night as well. Damn . . .

He was three times the fool for not grabbing the excuse *she* had given him to keep her by his side. She'd even repeated it tonight, that she was in danger, and had pointedly asked, "What if that thief is actually a Bruslan spy? If they get their hands on that bracelet, they'll know I'm alive."

That was a wild accusation, yet the thief in question had actually gone missing today before they'd returned to the palace. Christoph viewed that as a rather firm declaration of guilt, for the theft of the jewelry anyway. Telling her that did seem to relieve her mind a little.

What had stopped him from bringing her to his room where he wanted her? His guilt for not having watched her more closely at the festival? Probably. Her utter exhaustion? That, too. He should ruthlessly have taken advantage of that, but he couldn't do it, even wanting her as much as he did. Why? Because he was beginning to believe she was innocent?

She was too intelligent not to have doubts unless she wholeheartedly believed what she'd told him. That made her the innocent English lady she'd been up to this point, and put the entire plot on her guardian's shoulders. But was her guardian innocent, too, and merely coerced somehow to present this tale to her? That was much more credible than an assassin's turning soft over an infant's smile. But only her guardian could tell him the truth, and Alana would be the lure to catch him. That was assuming the man cared enough about her to find out what had happened to her after she'd entered the palace. So innocent or not, Christoph couldn't release her.

Having finally nodded off, he was awakened by a woman's scream followed by complete silence. He leapt from his bed and headed immediately to Alana's cell to investigate. He found her crossing the storage room. Boris and Franz, who slept there, had also been roused and were trying to help her, but she wouldn't stop until she saw Christoph.

"This is how you protect me?!" she accused him in a high-pitched, nearly hysterical tone.

He barely registered her question because his eyes were riveted on her blood-spattered white robe. He ran the rest of the way to her. "Why are you bleeding?"

"I'm not."

He drew in his breath. "What happened?"

"One of your men tried to kill me!"

"*My* men?"

"I suppose he could have stolen the uniform," she allowed, "but I did see it as he ran out the door."

"Watch her," he told his servants before he ran to her cell.

At a glance, he saw the club on the floor, bloodied, and a trail of blood that led outside the cell straight to the armory.

The door to the armory was wide-open, as was the door to the ward. The trail ended there, but footprints had been left in the newly fallen snow. The man hadn't gotten far; he was bent over, a hand to his head, trying to make his way up the stairs to the parapets, where he could escape over the fortress wall.

Christoph didn't shout for his guards, he wanted the man himself. He caught him at the top of the stairs, yanked him around, and slammed a fist into his face. Completely unprofessional, but the rage inside him for what the man had tried to do to Alana controlled him. Yet he hit him too hard. He heard the crack as the man's back and head went down hard on the stone floor, and he didn't get up. Christoph recognized him. Rainier, the man Alana had accused, had obviously snuck back into the ward tonight, or he'd never really left, had hidden instead. Either that or he'd had help, which was an even more alarming thought.

Christoph swore a blue streak. Two of his

men on patrol in that section of the wall were already running toward him. "A traitor," Christoph told them. "Lock him in the prison. Search him first, you'll likely find the master cell key on him. Assign no less than four guards outside his cell. If he's not there in the morning for me to question, there will be hell to pay."

He went straight back to the storage room. Franz was wringing his hands. Boris was trying to comfort Alana. It didn't look to be working because fear was still etched on her face.

He couldn't blame her for being hysterical and angry. "I caught him," he assured her calmly. "I'll interrogate him as soon as he regains consciousness."

"The thief?"

"Yes."

"I knew this could happen," she said shakily. "But I don't think I ever really thought it would, that I'd actually have to fight for my life."

Inclined to think she really was holding herself together with a thin thread, he moved to take her out of there immediately. Her sudden gasp as her eyes moved over him gave him pause. Had she really only just noticed his lack of clothing?

She was apparently going to pretend that

very thing, primly giving him her back and saying, "How dare you come here like that?"

He was too angry, mostly at himself for not taking her concerns more seriously, to wonder where such absurdity was coming from. She'd just been assaulted while under his protection. She'd also proven she was capable of fending off such an assault.

"You would rather I paused to dress instead of coming immediately to find if you needed my help when I heard your cry?"

He didn't wait for an answer. He took her hand again to lead her out of there. Boris tried to thrust a blanket at him, but Christoph waved it aside. His nakedness was the least of his concerns.

He took Alana to his own room for privacy. He kept his own anger under control, or tried to.

As soon as he closed the door behind them, he said, "Tell me what happened."

"One of your men tried to kill me. I yelled as soon as I knocked him off me."

She seemed to have calmed down, but she hadn't turned around to face him yet. He needed to see her expression, her eyes, to gauge what she was really feeling.

"Kill you how? And look at me."

"Not until you're dressed."

He sighed, but marched over to where

he'd tossed his clothes earlier and thrust his legs into his pants.

"A shirt, too," she said.

His eyes shot up toward her, but she still wasn't looking in his direction. Had she peeked at him, or was she just being thorough?

He slapped his chest. "This is nothing."

She glanced over her shoulder at him, but immediately looked away again to say, "I disagree. Any other man's bare chest might be nothing, but yours is far too distracting."

He stared hard at her back. A compliment in the middle of mayhem? Or was she just trying to soften his mood because she could sense the anger he was trying to keep from her. He put his shirt back on. He even tucked it into his pants.

"Now turn around and tell me exactly what happened, from the beginning."

She turned about slowly. His eyes were immediately drawn again to the blood splatters across the front of the robe, so stark, red on white. If one of his men did this . . .

"Wait," he said.

He moved to his wardrobe to get her another robe. She quickly shrugged off the bloody robe and he helped her into the clean one, lifting her long black hair out from under it. The blood hadn't soaked through to the nightshirt she was wearing. He came around in front of her and tied the robe closed for her.

Before he stepped back, he put a hand to her cheek. "Better? I swear nothing like this will happen again — they'll have to get past me."

"Thank you."

"Can you tell me what happened now?" he asked gently.

She nodded. "I was sleeping. I woke the moment the pillow was yanked from under my head, but I was still too groggy to know I was in danger — until he threw himself on top of me, knocking the breath out of me. And then he thrust the pillow over my face, making sure I couldn't regain my breath. I tried to find his face with my hands, but he was leaning just out of my reach. I was in such a panic by then, I don't know how I remembered the club I'd tucked to my side before I fell asleep, but I did."

"So that was yours?"

"Yes, I broke a leg off the table. I swung it where I thought his head might be. I was hoping to knock him out, but he must have turned, seeing it coming, because it smashed his face instead. But it did knock him enough to the side that I was able to heave him the rest of the way off me."

Christoph was given pause. "He was on top of you? Are you sure he wasn't trying to have his way with you?"

She scowled at that interpretation. "And kill me in the process? He was smothering me! That's murder where I come from."

"Or a means merely to conceal your screams. It wouldn't be the first time a guard has taken advantage of a female prisoner."

"You allow this?" she said incredulously.

"Of course not," he snapped at her. "Any guard caught doing so is publicly whipped nearly to death and kicked out of the palace."

Her eyes were still round on him. "That's all?"

"A disgrace like that ruins a man for life. We take a life for a life. If no life is taken —"

"I get the point! And I bloody well wish I'd killed the bastard — *if* that was his intention. At least I broke his nose. I feel much better now, thank you. But unlike you, I won't dismiss the thought that he came here to kill me."

"I'm not dismissing that thought either."

"Good, because in case it hasn't occurred to you yet, you've been harboring a traitor to the crown. Is that why you're so angry?"

"I'm angry because someone tried to hurt you."

"When are you going to believe I am who I say I am, and that someone, maybe the same people who wanted me dead eighteen years ago, want to harm me now? I — I'm frightened."

He put a finger under her chin. "I will get to the bottom of this. In fact, I think I'll go now to see if that blackguard is awake yet." Christoph grabbed his boots and coat and told her on the way out the door, "Lock this behind me."

He thought he heard her say, "Be delighted to."

It didn't matter. She couldn't lock him out when he had the key in his coat pocket. But he had a feeling she'd be asleep before he returned. Even if his men had managed to rouse that thief, he was going to take his time getting a confession from him. He needed someone to unleash this anger on.

CHAPTER TWENTY-SIX

Alana drifted in and out of sleep. Nightmares had woken her twice. She'd dreamed that she was drowning again, suffocating again. Those two horrible events today had been so similar, she wasn't surprised they'd been blended together in her dreams. But then she reminded herself that Christoph had saved her life today; he'd also caught the man who'd attacked her. She felt so safe when she was with him, and knowing he was there beside her lulled her back to sleep.

The large bed helped. It was so comfortable. She couldn't even feel the robe anymore that had constricted her when she'd crawled into bed. She must have shrugged it off when it got too warm under the covers. But the warmth was perfect now, even with Christoph's body next to her adding to it — and just like today by the hearth in that cottage when his heat had ended that nightmare, a soft orange glow from the fireplace filled the room.

She wasn't surprised that she would want to reexamine the kisses that Christoph had introduced her to, but she wondered how she could remember his taste this strongly. Then she knew. She must have cried out and awakened him. And this was his way of soothing away her fears so she could sleep again. The velvet softness of his lips, the rasp of his tongue, the way her pulse began racing, even the pounding of her heart. Not exactly soothing!

The wintry smell of his hair filled her nostrils when his mouth moved to her neck. Tingles spread down her arms from it. She was feeling everything she'd felt before and maybe a little more.

His hand was on her breast. His *mouth* was on her breast? That was hot, drawing a moan from her as it sent tendrils of pleasure to her core. And between her legs, a friction — oh, God, nothing that had happened before was as exciting as this! She sucked in her breath, again, yet again, and held it tight. Whatever had been building inside her was so wondrous, felt so amazingly good, that even her breath was now held in thrall waiting for it to let her go. Then it did, releasing the most erotic pleasure imaginable. It washed over her in repeated waves, and she expelled her breath in a groan that was loud even to her own ears.

Toes curled, a smile on her lips, she still felt that pulse throbbing between her legs. But she was so drained. So tired, too tired to wonder about it. Tomorrow she would . . .

But the warm cocoon surrounding her suddenly felt heavy. She spread her legs to get them out of the way. Something hard slid across that pulse, making her start, reminding her it was still there.

"Open your eyes, Alana. You melted for me. Now melt with me. I want to give you more pleasure, and I want you to see how much pleasure it will give me to . . . make love to you."

When she opened her eyes, she saw Christoph's handsome face there above her. Lambent blue eyes. A smile on his lips warm enough to melt snow.

"Much better," he said. "I was beginning to think you fell asleep again."

She almost laughed. Sleep through what just happened? But she was still savoring the delicious languor she was floating in. Even his weight felt right now, perfectly distributed on her, a welcome change that put him within her reach.

She gave in to the urge to touch him, putting her hands on his bare shoulders, running them over the thick muscles of his arms, which he was leaning on to keep his chest off hers. He was still naked. Hadn't she objected to that? What could she have been thinking? His golden body was so magnificent, it was stimulating her senses. With such bulging strength he was almost barbarically masculine, yet beautiful. She wondered if she could adequately describe him for Henry so he could make her a carving of him like this. She'd love that.

He was watching her intently. He seemed fascinated by the way her fingers were examining him. She didn't care. She didn't feel the least bit shy.

In fact, she smiled at him and teased, "This is a nice dream."

He chuckled. "I wish my dreams were so erotic." In a deeper timbre, he said, "Actually, they usually are. But let's not wake up from this one, eh?"

He was kissing her so fast, she guessed he didn't really want her opinion on that. She gave it to him anyway, by kissing him back. But sharing a kiss so wholeheartedly with him might not have been a good idea. So quickly, the languor was gone. So quickly, a higher degree of passion was there between them, and it wasn't just coming from him. It was as if she couldn't get enough of him but had to try!

Steam seemed to rise around them. His back was now slick where she tried to grip it, forcing her to wrap her arms around his neck instead. It was slick between her legs, too. That hardness was sliding across the pulse point there so easily, back and forth, briskly stimulating. It was building up again, that amazing tension that kept getting stronger and stronger. But she knew now where it led. She knew . . .

"Are you sure, Alana?"

If he said another word, she'd scream. It was akin to panic, the urgency that was upon her. She dragged his mouth back to hers, then gasped. Had that been pain? It was gone too quickly to be sure. But she was filled with heat, deeply filled with it, and . . . and . . .

"Oh, God!"

The crescendo she'd been heading toward peaked again, but it was different! So much more gratifying this way with that heat still moving in her, prolonging the exquisite pleasure. And such a wealth of tenderness filling her, too, for the man who had given her this gift. A luxury, to briefly allow that emotion. She actually wished it could stay. . . .

But the glow stayed. Even after he shared

in that beautiful gift and collapsed on her completely, she held him close. But he was mindful of his weight. A soft kiss to her neck, her cheek, then he rolled over to the mattress. But he wasn't done with her. He drew her close to his side, even pulled her leg across him before he put his arm firmly across her back to keep her there. A hand, gently smoothing the hair back from the cheek that wasn't pressed to his chest.

She sighed deeply in contentment, so relaxed, sublimely comfortable curled against him. "That was nice," she said drowsily a moment before she succumbed to the sweet languor and drifted away in it.

CHAPTER TWENTY-SEVEN

What an unbelievable day yesterday had been, Alana thought. Had all of that really occurred in just one day, even . . . ? Alana shied away from that thought.

She had no idea what time it was. Christoph's bedroom had no windows to indicate whether it was day or night, just a lamp left burning on the mantel. But she felt calmer, completely refreshed, and was wide-awake the moment she realized it wasn't a pillow her head was on, nor was it a blanket giving such heat to her back and buttocks. He was curled around her! The fireplace had gone cold at some point, but it wasn't needed. *He* was a furnace.

"How are you feeling this morning?"

How did he know she was awake to hear that? She hadn't moved, was barely breathing to keep from rousing him before she could pull her thoughts together.

"I did my best to comfort you last night

after that nightmare woke you," he continued in a reflective tone. "I'm glad you wanted me to. Needing to be close to another human being is a natural urge after a traumatic event."

She tried to get up, but his arm tightened on her and his voice turned firm. "That was no dream, Alana."

"I know it wasn't. I was only teasing last night when I suggested it was. But it shouldn't have happened."

"Yet it cannot be erased. Pleasure like that will linger forever — as beautiful memories do."

She groaned. "Please, can we *not* discuss it?"

Immediately, she was pushed flat on her back. Christoph was now leaning on one arm looking down at her. Just to see how hot her cheeks had become? No, actually, he was smiling at her, a stunning smile that stole her breath and kept her holding it in anticipation as he slowly leaned forward to kiss her.

But all he did was place a peck on the tip of her nose, grin, and say, "Good morning, or perhaps it is afternoon by now."

She released her breath in a whoosh. She should be furious, about everything, but mostly about last night. He'd behaved like a barbarian and enjoyed what had been offered to him. But in the back of her mind, she knew that wasn't so. He'd been sweet and loving to her. She shied away from that thought, uncomfortable with how much she was starting to like him.

"Is it really afternoon?"

He shrugged. "Very likely. I ate some time ago. I was beginning to think you'd never wake, but I suppose you needed the extra sleep."

An understatement. But — wait, he'd been up? But he'd come back to bed to lie with her while she continued to sleep? She hoped that didn't mean he wanted to continue where they'd left off last night. She started to get up. Again his arm tightened around her waist.

But this time he said, "Do you really want me to let you up when you are naked? I suppose you could take the sheet with you, but then you'd leave me here naked. Which would you prefer?"

She groaned. "I would prefer to hide under these covers while *you* leave the room. Can that be arranged?"

He laughed. "No."

She groused, "Why are you still here if it's that late? Shouldn't you be out and about doing your job?"

"No."

"Because I'm your job?" she guessed.

"I am so delighted to say, yes."

Oh, good Lord, she had the charmer in bed with her? That boyish grin of his was devastating her senses. And the arm that was keeping her there wasn't still. His fingers were brushing over her exposed shoulder. So lightly she might not notice? So lightly he might not even be aware he was doing it? She couldn't count on that.

Desperate to distract him, she asked, "Was that actually one of your men who tried to kill me last night?"

He nodded. "It was your thief, Alana."

She drew in her breath. The way he said that, it was obvious he believed he'd solved the matter to his satisfaction.

"Just like that? You think a thief goes from being a thief to a murderer, to hide that he's a thief? Let me guess, you hang thieves here and merely imprison murderers."

Sarcasm and an insult combined, she wasn't surprised he sat up, then got up. And he *was* naked!

She put a hand over her eyes before she felt capable of continuing, "Did he even know I'm the one who accused him? Did you tell him you had me in your prison?"

"Of course not, but he could have easily

drawn that conclusion. You were seen being led to my quarters. He could have assumed you were being detained until the matter was resolved."

Hurt that he could still discount the main threat to her, she said, "Is that really what you believe?"

He suddenly sat down on the other side of the bed next to her and took her hand away from her eyes. She kept them squeezed tight and asked, "Did you put pants on?"

"Yes," he said calmly. "And listen carefully. I'm willing to acknowledge that there might be more here than meets the eye, but so far the man claims he was only trying to frighten you into withdrawing your charge."

"You believe that?"

"No. But consider this, a thief tries to cover his crime by getting rid of his accuser, or, as you are supposing, someone ordered that very same man to kill you when no one knows why you're here except myself and the king? Which do you really think is more likely?"

"So you did tell him?"

"Certainly."

She was crestfallen. Her father couldn't be bothered to come and have a look at her?

Before Christoph could guess how disappointed she was, she asked, "Are you sure the king didn't tell someone else? A member of his family? His closest friends or advisers? Was he alone when you told him?"

The back of his finger brushed her cheek. "Why haven't you opened your eyes?"

Because he hadn't had time to put a shirt on, too! Could she manage to look at his face and no lower? She tried. Oh, good grief, he was smiling! The man had read her thoughts!

"To answer your questions, no, no, and yes, I spoke to him in private."

"And he just shrugged off my claim the same as you have? *Why?!*"

"I've already told you —"

"My arsenal?" she spat out. "That supports *my* claim, not yours."

"You're not an assassin."

"Thank you very much, I was beginning to feel unsure."

He laughed. "You try to make me angry with your sarcasms, but today it won't work. Did I not warn you how amiable I would be after —"

"*Don't* say another word!"

He pretended he was going to flick her nose until she covered it, then with a grin he stood up. "I will agree to that — for now, if you will agree it is pointless to discuss your thief before we finish interrogating him."

He didn't wait for her to answer. He moved to his wardrobe to finish dressing. She should have looked away, but with his back to her, she simply couldn't resist watching him. Those military pants fit him much too snugly. In the dim light, they appeared almost like a second skin, emphasizing how firm and perfectly curved his buttocks were. Her eyes moved slowly up his back, which broadened to his shoulders — then was abruptly covered with his linen shirt. She kept the sigh to herself.

She didn't think he'd heard her, but he did finally glance back at her for her answer to his terms for striking a bargain so he wouldn't allude to their lovemaking again.

"Fair enough," she said.

"Good." He brought his boots to the bed so he could sit to put them on. He then went right back on his word by adding, "As much as I would rather you stay naked in my bed, your trunks are in the other room. They can be brought in here now."

"How did you — ?"

"I sent some men to check the inns in the city yesterday while we were at the festival. I guessed they would find your trunks in one of them."

Her eyes narrowed. "You were looking for my trunks so you could search them, weren't you?"

"Of course! I expected to find two or three more arsenals."

His humor gave her pause, and he *was* just short of laughing again. Teasing? Him?

He even added, "I know, too thoughtful and considerate of me, eh, to think you might like a change of clothes — especially when I liked you wearing mine."

She actually managed not to blush, she wasn't sure how. "You found no weapons," she mumbled.

"No — I didn't find your guardian, Poppie, either."

She raised a brow. "Did you really think you would?"

"I had hoped."

"I told you he doesn't know who hired him to kill me — yet. Why can't you leave him alone to do what he does best, protect me."

"Because he has the answers that you don't have."

What did that mean? But Christoph was already heading around the bed toward the door, and she felt a degree of panic rising that he was going to leave her alone and defenseless once more.

"Wait. I need another weap —"

She didn't even get to finish, he swung around so fast. But it wasn't annoyance in his expression when he said, "I am your weapon. You won't be left again beyond my sight or hearing." Then he grinned as his eyes touched briefly on his bed. "My 'duty' has never been this pleasant before."

CHAPTER TWENTY-EIGHT

It was a good thing she dashed out of the bed to find the robe Christoph had tossed aside last night. She barely got it belted before he returned with Boris, the two of them carrying one of her heavy trunks into the room. They left to get the other two. She didn't move. Bringing her clothes into his bedroom couldn't have made it more clear that she'd be sleeping there from now on — and why Christoph suddenly considered his *duty* so pleasant.

But there wouldn't be a repeat of what had happened last night. He had claimed she had needed comforting, had even called it a natural urge after what had happened to her. She conceded he might be right. But the trauma was over and she had more fortitude than to succumb again to something that improper. Sharing a room would be — difficult — but it didn't mean they'd be sharing a bed, too. He'd just have to bring in a cot or make use of the little sofa in the corner, or she would.

With the last trunk set down against the wall, Christoph waved Boris out of the room and began opening them himself. The locks were broken, reminding her that he'd already searched through her belongings.

"Get dressed," he said. "You have a visitor."

Her eyes flared. "My fa— ?"

"No. A child. He came here early this morning asking for you. My men told him to come back later today. They weren't going to disturb me on a matter they didn't deem important."

"I wish your guards wouldn't make judgments that concern me. I should have been woken."

"You were in my quarters. The judgment was correct and concerned me, not you. Anyone has to go through me to get to you."

She blushed over that reminder. Did everyone know where she was spending her nights?

"But I wouldn't have woken you even if they told me sooner," he added. "You needed the extra sleep."

"But Henry came back?"

He raised a brow. "The boy you traveled with? You said he was an orphan. This boy claims to have a mother who will beat him if he doesn't come home with the gold he was promised for giving you a message. Which is it? Town urchin with an angry mother, or your orphan?"

"I haven't a clue," she admitted, then actually laughed. "Henry would be my guess. He must have thought that tale would get him in to see me sooner. But why don't you leave so I can dress and then we'll both know."

He closed the door behind him. She dressed quickly in a high-necked, lavender day dress that looked deep purple in the dim lamplight that Christoph must have relit that morning. It had to be Henry wanting to see her, even with that improvised tale, but why so soon? She'd just spoken to Poppie yesterday, albeit far too briefly. Had he already discovered something else?

As soon as she stepped into the parlor, Henry flew into her arms. So much for his trying to pretend to be a Lubinian boy from the city who didn't know her. She hugged him close, but she noted Christoph standing to the side watching them with interest.

"It scared the bleedin' 'ell out o' me when they wouldn't take me to you," Henry told her.

"Hush, you just came too early. As you

can see, I'm fine. I have the protection of the head of security here. Nothing can happen to me under his guarding eye."

She was speaking in English to make sure Henry understood perfectly and the captain didn't understand at all.

Henry stepped back to eye Christoph. " 'Im?"

"Yes, him. Now what brings you?"

"Is it safe to say?" Henry whispered at her.

"Yes, he doesn't understand."

He nodded and repeated what he'd been told. "There are two spies 'ere, the thief and another guard. Either one of 'em may try to harm you. 'E wants you to tell 'im." Henry nodded again toward Christoph. " 'E said you won't be safe 'ere until they are both dealt with."

She paled, even though she'd already guessed as much after that attack last night. But her reaction was too obvious for Christoph not to remark on it.

"What disturbs you?" he asked.

She didn't hesitate to answer. This information supported what she'd told him, and she now had Poppie's permission to say how she knew. "What I told you last night, I got that information from Poppie. Yesterday, at the festival."

"He was there?" Christoph said, obviously

surprised.

"For a few moments, yes. He said the thief and one other guard actually work for the same people who hired him eighteen years ago. He was going to follow them to find out more, but he now thinks it's more important that you be told. They know about the bracelet, which means they know I didn't die eighteen years ago as they thought — and they're going to want to correct that."

He sighed. "Or this message was merely prearranged to support your tale."

They'd both had the same thought, but in exact opposite directions. Good Lord, he was exasperating. He'd said he would be open-minded, and yet he didn't even try to be? Why? What did he know that she didn't that had him so convinced that everything she'd said was a lie?

Henry, glancing between them, asked her, " 'E don't believe yer 'ere to stop a war?"

"Not yet," she replied. "But don't tell Poppie that if you see him. I don't want him worrying more than he already does about me."

Henry nodded. "I 'ave to go."

She drew him back for another hug before pushing him toward the door. But he'd no sooner stepped outside than Christoph moved to the door as well. She blanched, afraid he was going to have Henry detained to find out exactly what message he'd brought. She knew just how intimidating he could be when he was after answers. She leapt in front of him.

"Don't. Please."

He glanced down at her. His hand rose to caress her cheek, but didn't quite make it there and dropped to set her aside instead. "It's my job, Alana."

"I hate you and your job!"

That didn't stop him either. He opened the door and immediately motioned the nearest guards to him. "Follow the boy into the city. Keep your distance. I want any men he talks to apprehended."

That was worse than she'd thought! She tried to push past Christoph to warn Henry before he got too far, but an arm snagged her waist, her feet left the ground, and the door was slammed shut.

"He'll notice them following him and will lose them," she said, trying to convince herself more than Christoph.

"I can have the gate closed before he reaches it. Would you rather I have him imprisoned instead?"

She burst into tears. Christoph swung her around to catch her legs with his other arm and carried her back into his parlor. He moved across the room, but not to put her down. He sat on his sofa, still holding her cradled in his arms. She continued to cry, beating on his shoulder until her fist got too sore to continue.

A long time passed. Her tears were spent. Her breath returned to normal. Her fist hurt. Her heart hurt. If he put that sweet boy in one of his cold cells, she'd . . . she'd . . .

Christoph began to talk in soothing tones. "I was just a child all those years ago when the infant disappeared from the nursery. But I know who the suspects were at the time. The Bruslans, King Ernest's family, of course, though it was too soon after the civil war that took them from the throne for them to try to regain the crown. While they had the most to gain in the long run, making sure the Stindal line didn't prosper would merely have been a start for them."

She didn't know why he was suddenly volunteering information she would have liked to have heard sooner. "But they weren't dismissed as innocent?"

"No. They were and still are the king's worst enemies. Don't be fooled by Karsten's charm. He's ruthless in his desire to become king."

"But he was just a child himself back then," she pointed out.

"Yes, but most of his family thought he should have been named the next king after his grandfather died. There were the disgraced nobles, too. A lot of them lost their titles and lands after the civil war. They should have been banished from the country, but Frederick's father, newly made king, was hopeful they could redeem themselves. Some have, but some to this day remain resentful and insistent that they had only done their duty to the old king, Ernest."

"And they'd like to see the Bruslan line back in power, since a Bruslan king would restore their titles and lands," she guessed.

"Yes, so they couldn't be discounted. But then no stone was left unturned. Even the more notorious assassins of the day, those with prices already on their heads, were searched for more vigorously. A few were found and questioned, but none of them appeared to be involved in the abduction. But there was also a man who lived here in the city that disappeared that same night. This got a few of the king's advisers to thinking that the princess's abduction was not the goal of a nefarious political plot but the work of a bold thief taking advantage of the fact that many of the royal guards were away from the palace with the king."

She had a feeling he might be talking about Poppie's real identity. Leonard Kastner did disappear that night, after all. And if they had been looking for a "thief" as the culprit back then, in considering all possibilities it would have been logical to conclude it might have been him.

"Is *this* why no one knows who tried to have me killed? Far too many suspects?"

"Spies were sent into the Bruslan stronghold, but the few who weren't caught and killed returned with no proof. While the Bruslans laughed over Frederick's pain, if the abduction was their handiwork, they were too cautious to claim it. It wasn't even discovered who had taken up the reins in that family, after King Ernest's death. The Bruslans are too numerous. Ernest had two daughters, three brothers, two uncles, all of which have had children, who've had more children. Even his wife, Auberta, still lives."

Alana wanted to know if he knew anything else about Leonard Kastner and steeled herself to hear Poppie's real name before she asked, "And that man who disappeared the same night, I suppose he was never found either?"

"No, he wasn't. With no evidence that the infant was ever killed, and so much time gone by, it actually began to look more and more like Kastner had abducted the princess and was just too afraid to demand his ransom. Does the name sound familiar?"

Good Lord, he was interrogating her yet pretending otherwise! Even though he'd made love to her, he was still doing his job, just with subtlety now, instead of intimidation!

"You think I don't know what you're doing?" she said stiffly, and struggled to get out of his arms. "I've already told you why I was taken and by whom. It certainly wasn't for any ransom, so you're dead wrong in thinking a thief was responsible."

"You haven't actually answered my question, have you? Is your guardian Leonard Kastner?"

"He told me his name. He told me what his occupation used to be. He told me he was hired to kill me by some nameless lackey who worked for someone else. He didn't go into the details of how he got to me, just that it was too easy."

"*Told* you his name? Are we finally getting at the truth?"

"You've had that. I would have told you his name sooner, but you made it clear you wanted to apprehend him. So I decided to wait, to give him a chance to do the job he came here to do, to find out who wants me dead."

"That's *my* job, Alana. Who is he?"

"Rastibon."

"Interesting," Christoph said after a moment's pause. "And actually, convenient for you to say so. That name is quite notorious here. Was it given to you at the same time this tale was related to you — or yesterday when your guardian spoke to you at the festival?"

"What the deuce are you implying now?"

He shrugged. He hadn't let go of her despite her efforts to free herself. He was watching her too closely. He was fishing for something else, but what?

"The investigation into Kastner's disappearance never really ended," Christoph continued in the soothing tone he'd used earlier. "When I was appointed to this post, I thought I could view the mystery from a new perspective and even be the one to finally solve it. I questioned all of Leonard Kastner's old neighbors again, even tracked down those who had moved out of the city. But it was just a formality."

She raised a brow. "So you never really suspected that townsman? Why have you even mentioned him?"

"Of course he was suspected, but he was

287

never thought to be a murderer. A not so common thief, yes, but not a killer. But I did discover that no further deaths were ever attributed to the infamous Rastibon, suggesting that he also retired about that same time. They are one and the same, aren't they, Alana?"

And now she knew what he was fishing for. *He* had come to this conclusion long ago, but he still didn't think either name belonged to Poppie. Convenient? A name given to her yesterday? He was trying to see if she would use what he'd told her to support her claim, *because he still didn't believe her!*

Tiredly she said, "There's nothing more I can tell you about this."

"Or you won't."

This conversation was getting too frustrating. She strained against the arms still holding her tight in his lap. "Let me up."

"I like you in this position."

"I don't."

"I think I can win the argument."

Of who was stronger? Good grief, she noticed it now, the humor back in his eyes. He might as well be sitting there flexing his muscles!

"You know, brute force is for those lacking in wit," she snapped.

He burst out laughing. "You will find it very difficult to get me displeased with you today, Alana mine. I did warn you, eh?"

"Oh, please," she said in disgust. "Stop making sexual innuendos when they are quite out of place right now. Why did you tell me everything you just did?"

"I was curious to see your reaction to the Bruslans."

"You think I've never heard the name before yesterday? My education was as well rounded as that of any young English lord. It included a brief history of all the royal houses in Europe, including this one. I even know what you forgot to mention, that my father is actually distantly related to them, but the two sides of that family became enemies long before he was born."

His humor was gone. "Much more than I expected you to know, which prompts the question now, did the Bruslans steal the infant not to kill her, but to raise her as one of their own and foster in her a love for them? A plot that *would* give them back their power once they get rid of Frederick."

She snorted. "You're really grasping at straws on that one. I promise you, I wasn't raised here, and certainly not by any Bruslan."

"I agree you weren't raised here. I don't

289

agree your Poppie isn't —"

"Oh, good grief." She rolled her eyes toward the ceiling. "So now you think he's a Bruslan, too? Who else are you going to accuse him of being?"

He made a tsking sound, but then he actually grinned. "Do you really expect me to tell you everything about an investigation that is still ongoing? One that *you* are now a part of?"

"Oh, yes, let's not forget *that,*" she groused. "I think our truce just ended."

She clamped her mouth shut so he wouldn't doubt she meant it. He actually let go of her because of it, or so she thought. She leapt to her feet. He stood up just as fast, and before she could put more distance between them, his hands cupped her cheeks.

"We didn't have a truce," he told her gently. "What we have is a relationship, which you'll find more pleasant than a truce. I won't hurt the boy, I give you my word on that. But I will find your Poppie. I don't have a choice in that. But if what I am beginning to suspect is true, *he* won't be hurt either."

She went still. What was he doing, lining up a trap for *her* now? Poppie had a price on his head in this country, and even if he didn't, they weren't going to thank him for stealing and keeping their king's daughter. They were going to execute him. And she wasn't going to help see that happen.

Chapter Twenty-Nine

The captain was making her wait again. As tactics went, it was a good one. She'd no sooner asked him what he meant by that remarkable statement, that he wouldn't hurt Poppie, than he shouted for Boris.

"Feed this woman," he'd told the servant, "and guard her with your life. No one gets in *or* out."

Boris had winced as he moved to lock the door behind his master. So much for making use of his guilt if she deemed it necessary. And too bad Christoph had realized she might try to. But where did he think she'd go if she got out of there? Home? She might as well. She was at her wit's end. She'd told him everything she could, and he still thought her an imposter, so *she* wouldn't be preventing any war.

The food had been waiting for her. It was brought to the table immediately, much more than she could eat. Did they expect

Christoph to return to share it? She didn't. She guessed he'd gone to interrogate the thief again, or to send more men to the city to spy on Henry. But before Henry had come to the orphanage, he'd grown up on the streets of London. He knew how to elude pursuers, thieves, and anyone who was too intently watching him. She hoped he was still adept at it because she didn't really think Christoph would imprison Henry if he didn't get the results he was after.

And then Christoph *did* return while she was still eating. She wondered about his disgruntled look as he sat down opposite her and began to fill a plate from the wide assortment of platters Boris had brought out.

"Did the thief talk?"

"His name is Rainier and, yes, he was much more informative this session, after bargaining for his life in exchange for names. He admitted a man named Aldo paid him to infiltrate my guard just so he could keep Aldo apprised of our movements and anything else that our enemies might find useful. He also gave up the name of the other traitor, who has conveniently already deserted."

"Well, at least you got one name. So why

do you look displeased?"

"Because Aldo was killed the other night, so, in fact, I still have nothing."

"You're rid of two traitors. That's an improvement over the situation yesterday."

"Yes, there is that."

"If Rainier bargained for his life, did he also admit he tried to kill me?"

"No, he maintains he only tried to frighten you. I'm inclined to believe him."

"Believe a confessed traitor instead of me? Thank you very much," she cried angrily.

"You don't even try to see my dilemma, do you? Your tale isn't remarkable. It has been told before with only slight variations."

"I do see your difficulty, it just wasn't anticipated. Poppie was sure that I'd be taken straight to my father, that *he* wouldn't have any doubt of who I am. The bracelet was to prove it. Do you really think something that exquisite could be copied without the original being seen? The detail was too fine, the different gems a rainbow of colors. It was something my father *would* have recognized. But it was stolen, so instead I am faced with you and *your* doubt, which puts me in a similar dilemma."

She ended with a sigh. He chose to ignore it to point out, "You realize of course that according to you, this story isn't even your own but what Poppie told you. What if he lied to you?"

"He wouldn't."

"What if he did?"

She raised a black brow at him. "So he raised me for eighteen years with the intention of feeding me a fabrication? For what reason?"

"A man, any man, who would have the absolute confidence of a monarch would have power. Power is a very potent motivation."

"True," she allowed. "Yet eighteen years is too long, when one of us, me, Poppie, my father, might not have survived. And that would be assuming that in all that time my father doesn't produce a male heir to be the next king." She shook her head. "I know Poppie. He didn't lie to me. I wish he had. Anything else would have been preferable to what he told me."

"Contradicting yourself, Alana? You've already said he wasn't the man you thought he was."

"You're taking what I said out of context and trying to give it a different meaning. His past is what shocked me. My past added to that shock. That doesn't change who he is now, who he has been all the years I've known him."

"You are amazing," he surprised her by saying. "You have a ready answer for everything, don't you?"

She gave him a slight smile. "You might want to ask yourself why. Ask yourself if you ever need to pause to think about the truth. Now if I *was* lying, then, yes, I'd have to agree I'm amazing."

He laughed. "You don't act at all like an eighteen-year-old, you know."

She gave him a curious look for his humor, but merely asked, "What makes you say that?"

"Most aristocratic young women are barely adults at that age, yet there is nothing of the child in you."

She laughed now. "Possibly because I was never treated as a child."

"Never?"

She shrugged. "I suppose, despite how quickly Poppie came to love me, he was still mindful that one day I might be queen and treated me differently than he would other children because of it." But an old memory surfaced, and she decided to share it. "Actually, there was one time he treated me as a child. I had sprained my finger on an outing in one of London's parks. I cried like a baby. I think I was six. It was the first time I ever felt pain that severe. Poppie held me in his arms the whole time the doctor treated my finger, telling me silly things to take my mind off it. I did actually laugh, even with tears on my cheeks."

"You still love him, don't you?"

It was said so gently it almost brought tears to her eyes. Her guard went up immediately. Was this a new tactic on his part, appealing to her emotions? She didn't allow him to know it worked.

She answered him with a question of her own. "How do you stop loving someone you've loved all your life? What he told me he used to do was horrible, but that isn't the man I grew up with. I don't know what else I can say to stress that he's not like that anymore."

"Isn't he? Didn't you say he came here to kill your enemy?"

"That isn't the same thing at all. That's protecting me — *and* my father. That, Captain, is doing your job for you."

He didn't get angry, he actually smiled at her. "That was a very good answer."

She didn't like his smile. It drew her eyes instantly to his mouth and made her think of other things. She wished he wasn't so damned handsome. If he were old or ugly, or didn't have such a finely made body, it would be *so* much easier to deal with him.

But her attraction was too strong. It got in the way too often.

He suddenly said, "We are going to discuss how you might be innocent of all charges."

That was an incredible statement for him and made her instantly suspicious. "So you can let me go?"

"No."

"Then what's the point?"

"The point is keeping you out of prison when this is over — and perhaps your guardian as well."

She sat forward abruptly with a frown. "You mentioned that earlier without an explanation. What exactly are you getting at?"

"I am inclined to think you have been duped, that the Bruslans' advisers are now more intelligent than in the past to think of something like this."

"Duped how?"

"Your guardian has been bought, or coerced, perhaps by threatening your life. He could have been fed this entire tale to use, including the name Leonard Kastner, who is well-known as a suspect in this case, as well as Rastibon, the most notorious assassin of the day. I do believe he's Lubinian, perhaps one of the disgraced nobles who decided to begin anew elsewhere rather than stay here in shame — which would fit what he told you when you were young. He could have kept in touch with old friends here, so the Bruslans could have found out about him and that he has a niece the right age. Think about it, Alana. Everything you have told me *he* told you, and only recently. And if he truly thought they would kill you if he couldn't convince you of this tale, he would have used anything to embellish it, including that he used to be an assassin."

She took a few moments to assimilate that, but it just didn't add up. "If the Bruslans arranged that, then why the rebels, too?" she questioned. "Or are you saying the two plots are unrelated?"

"They are one and the same. Their propaganda has merely set the stage for your crowning performance."

"But war?"

"If they can wrest the crown back, they won't want total destruction. The more people who die, the less people they have to rule. This foment isn't about war, Alana, it's about making the people discontent with the present regime, so they'll be ready to accept a Bruslan on the throne again. You were their final card to play. If you had succeeded, if Frederick actually presented you as his daughter, he would have been denounced for trying to trick the populace with a fake princess. This would have two possible results, an immediate riot that could end in his death, or the demand that he step down from the throne. That was the whole point of this, and you even said it yourself. 'Use me to prevent war.' Weren't those your exact words?"

She was amazed by his theory. It actually sounded plausible, except that Poppie wouldn't have gone along with something like that. He would have told her the truth and gotten her out of harm's way, even if it meant leaving England to go into hiding somewhere else. He certainly wouldn't have subjected her to the complete disbelief she'd been faced with, all based on a lie.

"I can see why you'd prefer this version over mine," she said thoughtfully. "You've compromised your king's daughter. You'll be facing his wrath for that when I am finally reunited with him."

"If that were true, then I would be forced to humbly beg your forgiveness."

He was scowling just at the thought. Why, when he in no way believed that would ever happen?

"Do you even know how to be humble?" she asked curiously, then quickly assured him, "Not that I would forgive you, even if you managed some humbleness."

His scowl got darker. "If you were the princess, then my family would once again be in disgrace because of me, and I would banish myself forever from Lubinia for so failing in my duty. Fortunately for my family, that isn't going to happen."

That absolute conviction that she found so exasperating was again in his voice. "I should agree with you and be done with this," she groused. "But there is one little discrepancy between your theory and actual events which can prove that Poppie did tell the truth. I wasn't going to mention it since he wasn't sure it even reached my father. If it didn't, you would claim that it's a lie, which would have made you dismiss everything else I've said, too. But since that's already the case, and I really can't think of anything else to convince you, you might as well hear this now just in case it *did* reach my father."

"Enough! Just tell me!"

Oh, my, Alana thought, he was definitely angry now. Just because she didn't jump gratefully at his concession that she might be "innocent"? Or because she'd said she wouldn't forgive him? She hadn't realized how important it was to him for her *not* to be the princess at this point because of the way he'd treated her. Could that really lead to his disgrace? She ought to hope so, but the thought didn't actually sit well with her.

"Alana," he said ominously.

"All right! But I warned you this may lead to nothing. Several months after I was taken from the palace, Poppie was moved by compassion to send my father a message. He assured him that he would keep me safe until Frederick found out who wanted me dead. No one else would have known about that missive. If it did actually reach my father, it proves Poppie is who he said he is, and I am who he said I am."

The anger left Christoph's visage. She wasn't sure why, until he said, "You should have mentioned this sooner."

"You know about it?"

"No, but I soon will."

He left the room abruptly. With no doubt where he was going, she started to feel sick to her stomach with apprehension. If that missive did reach the king all those years ago, Frederick would be returning with Christoph. She would finally be meeting her father. . . .

CHAPTER THIRTY

Alana sat at that table in Christoph's parlor too nervous to eat another bite of food, too nervous to even move. She almost hoped Christoph would come back and tell her, "Aha, another lie!"

That must have been his own thought when he left because he hadn't appeared the least bit worried that his job might suddenly be in jeopardy. He'd probably been exaggerating anyway that it could be.

"Would you like a bath, lady?"

Boris had to ask that twice for her to finally notice him standing there. "No, I — yes, actually."

He beamed at her. "The tub is filled for you in the kitchen."

"The kitchen?"

"It is where we all bathe, the warmest room. You will have privacy."

She felt too grimy not to accept. If she was quick, she could be done before Christoph returned. And the room was already empty for her, the large, round tub set near the oven, the pleasant aroma of bread baking floating toward her. She wished she could soak away all her worries, but she didn't dare take any longer than necessary, and she'd never washed so quickly — and still wasn't quick enough.

Even though she wasn't facing the door, the draft on her wet shoulders warned her someone had quietly opened it. She glanced behind her, then sank lower in the tub. Of course it was him. No one else would dare.

"Do you mind?" she said scathingly.

"I don't mind at all."

He leaned against the door frame, arms crossed over his chest, grinning at her. There wasn't enough water to completely cover her, so she pressed against the edge of the tub nearest him to hide what she could and lifted an arm over the rim to point suggestively at the door.

"I'd rather not," he said, but when her eyes shot daggers at him, he sighed and straightened. "I suppose I can take a few moments to blacken Boris's other eye, for putting you in a room filled with knives."

"I heard that!" Boris yelled from the parlor.

She didn't think Christoph was serious,

but Boris must have thought so. The icy draft that soon swept into the room told them both that the servant had run outside, leaving the outer door open. Christoph swore and closed the kitchen door, leaving her alone again. She stood up, wrapped her wet hair in a towel, spared only a few seconds to dry off with another, then quickly dressed before he came back to embarrass her further.

She knew she wouldn't find the king in the other room. Christoph wouldn't have stood there ogling her if he was. And his humor had been obvious, so she had to assume Poppie's missive had never reached her father. Which put them back to square one — no, back to Christoph using her to lure Poppie into his hands.

Disheartened, she walked slowly back to the parlor. Christoph hadn't left to chase Boris down. He had set one of the dining chairs in front of the fireplace, which was crackling strongly with a new log in it, but he wasn't sitting in the chair, just standing beside it.

"Come here," he said.

She raised a brow. "So you can roast me again?"

"I didn't expect to find you . . . wet and naked. You can't imagine how much I wanted to join you in that tub. Even now, it is difficult to keep the thought away."

She sucked in her breath before she wailed, "We had a bargain!"

"I'm not breaking it. This temptation is new and it's not gone yet. So come here and let me occupy my hands drying your hair, then I might be able to keep them off your body."

That did *not* encourage her to approach him. But his words were stirring, making her realize she was in danger of that same temptation.

"That can't happen again," she said to him, but she meant it to be a reminder to herself.

He actually grinned. "Of course it can. Once tasted, there's no longer a reason to deny ourselves such pleasure."

His attitude infuriated her, so self-centered, so unmindful of anything but his own needs and desires. "Easy for you to say," she said sharply. "*You* wouldn't be bearing the consequences."

"A child?" His expression turned intrigued, but ended in a beautiful smile. "I think I would like that. I take care of my own."

"Excuse me while I fetch one of those kitchen knives."

He burst out laughing. "Thank you. That definitely doused the — temptation. Now come here, Alana, and let me dry your hair. You can't go outside until it is fully dry."

She stilled instantly. "Outside? Poppie's missive *did* reach him?"

"Yes."

"Why didn't you tell me the king wants to see me now?!"

"He doesn't."

She felt almost light-headed, to experience such powerful emotions over mere seconds, the final one being utter dejection. She didn't even wonder why that message hadn't resolved this situation for her as it should have.

"Don't look so sad," Christoph said. "I have good news for you."

"Let someone else tell me. I don't like the way you deliver information," she grumbled, but her curiosity got in the way. "What news?"

"Hair first."

"You see!?" she hissed. "You are beyond exasperating. Why do I even talk to you?" She marched to the chair and sat down, but leaned away from him. "And don't you dare touch my hair! I'll dry it."

She reached for the towel on her head, but he whisked it out from under her hand.

"I have the comb — and the towel."

"I have the heat and my fingers will serve as a comb."

"You won't win this argument."

He didn't sound triumphant, just matter-of-fact, yet it still made her want to scream. He already had a fistful of her hair and was pressing the towel to it with his other hand, so she couldn't even get up without his yanking her back down with her own hair.

"I hate you," she said impotently.

"No, you don't, you like me."

"I don't! You have no clue how to treat a lady. And even if you did, an insensitive brute like you wouldn't know when you ought to."

He tsked. "You sound like a brat. I think your Poppie must have spoiled you."

She clamped her mouth shut. Trying to get through to him was a lesson in pointlessness. But he didn't try to provoke her any further. He didn't give her back her hair, though, and the gentle way he was handling it slowly began to relax her.

Quite sometime later, he dropped her hair over each shoulder so she could feel how warm and dry it was. He'd almost put her to sleep, his hair drying had turned out to be so sensually soothing. She couldn't even garner any energy to object when he tilted her head back so he could lean forward and kiss her brow.

But then he straightened and said behind her, "I have the king's permission to tell you the truth and to take you to meet your mother. Dress warmly, Alana mine. She lives high in the mountains."

CHAPTER THIRTY-ONE

"My mother?"

That was all Alana could get out and it felt odd even saying it. Wide-eyed, she tried to comprehend, but couldn't. And Christoph didn't say another word. She swung about to face him, only to have to turn full circle because he was walking out of the room!

"Don't you dare!" she yelled at his back.

He didn't stop. "Your wet hair was an unexpected delay. We need to hurry now or it will be dark before we arrive. You'll find a satchel at the bottom of my wardrobe. Pack us each a change of clothes. I'll be back in a few minutes with my horse. Be ready."

She would have told him to pack his own clothes, but she barely even heard the last of what he said as he was closing the door behind him! She bolted to the bedroom and quickly dug out the thick woolen dress she'd worn for most of the trip across the Continent, gloves, several extra petticoats, some warmer stockings, and her traveling boots. Dressed, she filled the valise he'd mentioned, and not taking the time to put up her hair, she just tied it back and donned her fur cap.

She went back into the parlor with her heaviest coat over her arm, and Christoph's as well since he'd only been wearing his uniform when he left. She could see out the windows on the side of the room that it wasn't snowing. The sun was even out, but she'd felt that icy draft and didn't doubt the coats would be needed.

Alana didn't know what to think because what Christoph had said made no sense at all. Even now, when she had a few minutes to spare before he returned, she merely dropped the valise on the floor by her feet and stood in the middle of the room staring blankly at nothing in particular.

But she snapped to attention the moment the door opened. Christoph didn't close it. She could see the horse standing just outside. The air was icy. She held out his coat to him so she could slip hers on.

He raised a brow at her as he donned his. "Seeing to my comfort? Are you beginning to feel like my woman?"

She snorted. "I was just saving time since

you stressed we must hurry."

He grinned, picked up the bag, and took her arm. "I like my thought better. But come."

He'd only brought one horse. After he'd mounted it, he lifted her up to sit precariously across his lap sideways, prompting her to complain, "You can't really be taking me into the mountains like this. The roads will be covered with snow up there, won't they? Not like that road to the festival."

"Which is why I've already arranged for a sleigh. It's a short ride to where they are kept outside the city."

"A sleigh? Is it enclosed?"

"No, but it will make better time and is safer."

"But we'll be so cold."

"You won't be," he promised.

She didn't try to turn around and look at him to see if he was serious. She didn't blast him with her questions yet either, because she had to concentrate on keeping her perch without having to hold on to him.

They passed through the palace gates and turned away from the city, leaving behind the streets that were kept free of ice and snow in the winter. Snow covered the countryside, including the roads, and no doubt there would be more of it in the mountains, which is where they were going, so she had to allow a sleigh, designed for such travel, might be the better choice — but not if she was going to freeze in it!

About ten minutes later, Christoph helped her into the vehicle waiting for them outside the large sleigh house. He did so by picking her up and setting her in it, it was so high off the ground. Two horses were already hitched to it, tall animals that could make it through snowdrifts without too much difficulty, she supposed. A wide, cushioned seat was in the back, with an elevated seat in front for a driver, which Christoph had also arranged for. The front of the sleigh curved up quite high for a windbreak, but it was still completely open to the elements.

"Just how far are we going that we might not make it by nightfall?" she yelled back at Christoph as he tied his horse behind the sleigh.

He came back around to place his rifle, the valise she'd packed, and a saddlebag on the floor by her feet. She hadn't sat down yet, afraid she'd find the seat wet from a previous snowfall.

"Far enough to need these," he said, taking the armful of blankets one of the sleigh-house workers handed him.

He tossed the pile up at her. She lost her

balance trying to grab them all and dropped down on the seat behind her. She gave him a fulminating glare as he climbed in and sat beside her. He didn't seem to notice, picking up the blankets she dropped and setting them out of the way, then taking the single one in her hands and spreading it across their laps. She would have preferred her own blanket rather than sharing one with him, but she couldn't wait any longer to question him, so she didn't mention it.

The very second the sleigh began to move, she turned to Christoph. "My patience has been extraordinary."

"Yes, it has," he agreed.

With her eye on the driver's back, she leaned closer to whisper, "I was told my mother, Queen Avelina, died soon after my birth. Everyone knew it. This was a lie?"

"You don't have to whisper. I requested this driver specifically because he's deaf." When she leaned away from him again, he shook his head. "I should have waited to mention it."

She ignored that. "My question?"

"Frederick's first wife died, yes, but she wasn't your mother." He put a finger to her mouth when she started to interrupt him. "We know who you are now. You were correct, your guardian Poppie did take you from the palace nursery. Everything he told you recently *is* probably true, even that he is Rastibon — everything except what he didn't know: that it wasn't the princess sleeping in the royal bassinet. It was the daughter of the nursemaid Helga Engel that he carried off that night."

CHAPTER THIRTY-TWO

Alana couldn't stop laughing. She laughed so hard tears came to her eyes. When she caught a glimpse of Christoph's annoyed expression, she laughed even harder.

He waited until she wound down before he said, "You don't believe me?"

"On the contrary, you have just taken an incredible burden off my shoulders. I can go home now. I certainly won't be stopping any war if I'm not the king's heir. Actually, do you still contend this country isn't headed for war now that you know your theory, that the king's enemies were going to use me for a coup, isn't accurate?"

"War, no, we never thought it would come to that. The rebel ploy is to stir up enough fear that Lubinians are soon going to lose their beloved king through illness so the people would either demand a new king or rejoice at having a large family in power again, one with many heirs."

"That sounds as if the Bruslans are setting the scene for my — er, for the king's assassination?"

He smiled at her lapse and Alana realized it was going to take a while for her to stop thinking of the king of Lubinia as her father. But she still had a parent who was alive, one who *wasn't* royal, thank heavens, and one she wasn't the least bit nervous about meeting — well, she was too relieved to be nervous yet.

"Indeed," Christoph answered. "I stopped three assassination attempts last year, so now they try to get rid of me as well."

She started, yet she realized she shouldn't be surprised. "They'd rather someone less competent was in your post?"

He grinned. "Or they're just furious at me for foiling them on every front."

She noted he didn't seem the least bit worried about being one of their targets, so she guessed he'd just exaggerated, maybe to gain her sympathy. *That* wasn't going to happen. Frederick Stindal's difficulties were no longer her concern — and neither were Christoph Becker's.

"What was I doing in the royal bed for Poppie to have made such a mistake?" she asked.

"Your mother switched the two infants

prior to keep the princess safe in her own room."

"So people suspected there was a plot to kill the heir?"

"No, not at all, or the palace would have been better guarded. According to Helga Engel, it was fear that prompted her bold plan. I don't know much else about it. You can ask her when you meet her."

"But it sounds like she sacrificed her own child to protect another. That seems a bit unnatural, doesn't it?"

"Perhaps she thought she was saving her own life. She had sole charge of the royal heir, after all. If anything did happen to the princess —"

"I get it. Execution and all that rot. How could I forget how barbaric this country is."

He frowned at her sarcastic tone. "Not that barbaric, but perhaps, like you, Helga might have thought so."

Alana asked, "What about my father? Is he still alive?"

Christoph sighed. "You should save your questions for your mother, but that one I can answer. Helga came to the palace a recent widow. She had other family, but I don't know if they are still alive. I will say no more other than she was quite the heroine, protecting the princess in the way she did, aware that she could lose her own daughter in doing so. Which is what happened. She thinks you're dead. She'll be overjoyed when she discovers that isn't so."

Alana gasped. "She wasn't told of Poppie's message to the king that I was still alive?"

"No one was."

Alana sighed. She'd come to Lubinia thinking she'd have to convince her father of who she was, but now she wondered if she'd have to do the same for her mother. Or would her mother take one look at her and know instantly who she was — just as she'd hoped would have happened with the king. Ha! Fine joke that would have been on her if she had made it into his presence. At least she didn't have to convince Christoph of anything else. No one could be as stubborn as he was.

She pinned him with a stabbing look. "It's just occurred to me that you've known all along that I couldn't be the princess. *Why* couldn't you have just said so?"

"I did. I called you an imposter, as I recall."

"You know what I mean. *You* knew that the babies had been switched."

He shrugged. "There was always the possibility that you could be Helga's daughter.

I just couldn't discuss what has been a well-guarded secret all these years: that the wrong child was abducted. Your hair, raven black, is mainly why I didn't pursue the possibility. Helga described her daughter as having golden hair, the same as the princess, which made it a simple matter for her to switch the two babies until the king returned."

Alana's brow knitted thoughtfully. "I only ever remember having black hair. Poppie never said if it used to be blond and changed color."

Christoph chuckled. "Are you still clinging to the hope that you're a royal?"

She laughed. "I never once expressed that hope and you know it. I'm just surprised Poppie never mentioned I had lighter-colored hair when I was very young."

"Perhaps he did and you were too young to recall," he said with a shrug. "Or perhaps like my father, he didn't consider it worth mentioning."

"Your hair used to be different?"

"I was nearly a man when I came upon my mother and aunt reminiscing about their children when they were babies. Mother teased me, confessing she used to call me her white-haired angel until I turned three and my hair turned golden."

She gave him a disgruntled look. "And yet you stressed that the color of my hair was why — oh, never mind. That was quite an amazing fact you kept from me, that the king never lost his daughter, so of course that daughter *couldn't* be me. And she's been hidden all these years? He even let his subjects think she's dead? He didn't even bring her out to drop the floor out from under the rebels? When *is* he going to bring her home?"

"He did," Christoph said solemnly. "She's buried on the palace grounds next to her mother."

Alana drew in her breath sharply, remembering the mock funeral Poppie had told her about — and the king's rage at that time. And no wonder, when it hadn't been a symbolic ceremony, as everyone supposed, but a real funeral.

"She died when she was seven, didn't she?"

"Yes. It appeared to be an accident. Frederick thinks otherwise and blames himself for visiting her so often. He can't go anywhere alone, his guards must always accompany him. And naturally this draws attention to him."

"So he could have been followed?"

"Yes, and seen with a child the age of his

daughter. Even if his enemies weren't sure she was his, they would want to be rid of her just in case."

She exclaimed, "That's — !"

"No different than sending an assassin to kill a baby. But due to the absolute secrecy advised back then, to hide the princess, even to pretend she had been stolen so no further attempts would be made on her life, the king told no one about that missive that suggested you were still alive, not even your mother. But after five or so years passed, most people considered you dead. Yet whoever hired Rastibon, as well as all sorts of opportunists, weren't absolutely sure, thus the imposters started showing up."

"No, because of his reputation for never failing, Poppie expected whoever had hired him to conclude that he'd finished the job successfully. The 'disappearance' of the princess supported that."

"But now they think otherwise because of that bracelet," Christoph said.

She stilled. "You're saying I'm still not safe, aren't you?"

"Not as long as enemies of the king suspect you're Alana Stindal."

"Then the king has to admit the truth!"

Christoph gave her a reproving look. "We don't tell the king what to do. But you need only think about it to know that he can't do that, at least, now would not be the time for such a confession. He deceived his people. Some will understand the necessity for it, but his enemies will pounce on it and use it to their advantage. Had the princess survived, that confession would have been cause to rejoice. Now —"

"I understand," Alana mumbled. "And all the more reason for me to go home to London where I can hide safely again. There's nothing else to keep me here."

"Nothing?"

"You mean my mother? I'll take her home with me."

"She lives in grand splendor in the royal chalet," he informed her. "She was given quarters there for life, her reward for the sacrifice she made. She isn't going to want to live in your sooty London."

"How do you know London is sooty?"

"My maternal grandmother lives there."

"Why there instead of here?"

"Because she's English."

CHAPTER THIRTY-THREE

"English?!" Alana exclaimed. "Were you never going to mention that?"

"I just did," Christoph said with some amusement.

"But you're half-English!"

"Only a quarter. My mother is half, though to listen to her flawless Lubinian, you would never think so."

"I bet you speak English, too, don't you?"

"Perfectly." He chucked her chin, then laughed when she swatted his hand away. "I couldn't tell you because you were under interrogation. Now you're not."

"Meaning now you can be honest with me? Too bloody late," she fumed. But she only sat there in stiff chagrin for a minute before her curiosity got the better of her. "How did that happen?"

He chuckled. "My guess would be in the usual way."

"You know what I meant."

"My English grandmother was an artist. Painting was her passion, but she was dissatisfied with her skill. An Austrian painter had inspired her, but he didn't stay in England for very long. English painters were found to teach her but she was already more skilled than they. So before she came of age, she talked her mother into taking her on a trip to Austria to find that old teacher of hers. My great-grandmother didn't object. Her only condition was that they return to England in time for her marriage."

"She was betrothed?"

"Yes. But she fell in love with a young man while in Austria, a Lubinian finishing his schooling there."

"Because there are no schools here?"

"There weren't any then. There are schools now, though we still have no university. The nobles import tutors or send their young out of the country to be educated. But Frederick has had schools built for the commoners. They sit mostly empty."

"So he *is* actually trying to bring this country forward into the nineteenth century?"

"Do you realize how disparaging that question is?"

"You just said the schools sit empty, which I find outrageous, loving to teach as I do.

Never mind. What happened to your grandmother?"

"Are you sure you want to hear this? It
does not have a happy outcome."

It must have been happy at some point,
she thought, if he was a quarter English.
"Yes."

"My grandmother knew her mother
wouldn't allow her to marry the young Lubinian man, so they married in secret before
telling her. And my great-grandmother
wasn't just furious, she refused to recognize
the marriage because my grandmother
wasn't of age yet. Her betrothed was a
powerful earl, a match arranged by her
father before he died. My great-
grandmother took her straight home to
England and forced her to wed the earl."

"Without getting a divorce for her daughter first?"

"Why would she do that when she didn't
consider the first marriage valid?"

Alana rolled her eyes. "Your grandmother
still wasn't of age yet, was she?"

He shrugged. "Some consider a betrothal
as binding as a marriage. My great-
grandmother certainly did."

"And then?"

"My grandmother didn't know she was
already with child. Her second husband

326

knew she was not a virgin when she came to him. Still, he would have kept her — she was beautiful. But the child began to show too soon for it to be his. He kicked her out and *did* divorce her. My grandmother was disgraced. Her mother would have never forgiven her if she hadn't become so attached to her granddaughter, my mother, after she was born."

"Did your grandmother's Lubinian husband ever try to find her?"

"Oh, he tried. He loved her and *his* family recognized the marriage. They considered Grandmother a runaway wife and insisted he bring her home. But, sadly, he never found her because her mother had changed their name and moved them to the country to escape the scandal."

Alana wished she'd stopped him when he'd warned her there was no happy ending. "They were never reunited, were they?"

"No. My grandmother tried to find him after her mother passed on eight years later, but she was too late. He had died the year before. She stayed with his family for a while so they could get to know his daughter, but later that year she returned to London. But every summer thereafter she faithfully brought my mother back to visit her relatives here. On one of those visits, when she was sixteen, my mother met my father. That at least ended happily."

"So your mother actually grew up in England?"

"Yes."

"Then would you mind telling me how *you* ended up with such atrocious manners? A woman who grew up in England would have taught you better."

He grinned at her. "But she did. When I am with the king, I exhibit the manners he expects in his nobles. When I am with my men, I use the manners *they* expect. When I'm with a woman —"

"*That's* far enough."

He raised a brow. "So your opinion of this country still hasn't improved, eh?"

"Nor is it likely to. I was raised in the most civilized country in the world, just as your mother was."

"Then maybe you should ask my mother why she loves this country so much. Do you even know how Lubinia came into existence? Goatherds settled here, prospered, their families grew with each generation, and finally a natural leader emerged, Gregory Tavoris, and with the people's support he became the first Lubinian king. But we are all free men. Never have there been serfs here who grovel to a lord, who are no better than slaves — as your country had."

She blushed furiously, but would have pointed out that comparing today's Lubinia with England's past didn't really support his point that Lubinia was superior to England. But the bullet flying past her ear sent her diving to the floor instead.

CHAPTER THIRTY-FOUR

Alana crouched as low as she could get on the floor of the sleigh. Not an ideal place to hide, but at least the back of the sleigh was high enough to provide cover. Unfortunately, the sides weren't, as they were barely half a foot high. But she realized the shots were coming from behind them when Christoph grabbed his rifle from the floor next to her and shot back in that direction.

Her heart was already pounding, but when she noticed Christoph was too busy returning fire to take cover himself, she was terrified. Kneeling on the backseat of the vehicle, he was exposing half his chest and his head, and his chest made a broad target!

"Get down between shots!" she yelled at him.

He glanced down at her, frowned at what he saw, then said as he crouched a little lower on the seat, "They're cowards, already falling back."

Was her fear that obvious to him? But his remark and the cover he was taking now did relieve her — until she heard the crack of another shot fired, and not from Christoph's rifle. He swore in annoyance and aimed to his right. "They're playing crafty, taking cover in the trees."

"They can play crafty all they like as long as they continue to be lousy shots," she replied.

"Easy for you to say, you weren't shot."

Her eyes flared, her heart skipped a beat. She looked frantically for blood, but couldn't find any on him. But then she noticed the thin rip high on the side of his coat by his shoulder. No blood, though. The coat was thick, as was the corded epaulet on his jacket beneath it in that spot, so the bullet likely didn't even touch his skin.

Relieved without even realizing it, she assured him, "You weren't shot, your clothes were."

Without glancing down at her, he said, "Not the least concern, eh?"

She didn't answer that, afraid she had too much concern. "Do you have an extra weapon I can use in your saddlebag? I'm an excellent shot, and you know I'm not going to use it on you."

"You're not getting up off that floor to

shoot at anything, but you can dig out the ammunition in the bag for me." He added, "One down, one wounded. Two to go."

She quickly did as he asked, but it finally dawned on her that the sleigh hadn't stopped or picked up speed. It was still moving along at a steady pace. She glanced behind her and gasped to see why. The poor deaf driver was still sitting on his perch, oblivious to the sounds of bullets flying about.

"Shouldn't the driver take cover?" she asked Christoph. "He doesn't even know we're being shot at."

"Cover, no, but we need more speed. Tell him."

"How? He can't hear."

"Indicate, and do it without getting up. Also, there is a road coming up on the right. Let him know to turn down it."

She couldn't reach the perch above her without leaning up so she grabbed one of the blankets and flipped it up at the man's back. He glanced behind him. He didn't even see her on the floor, but he saw Christoph shooting and immediately whipped the horses for the needed speed. One down, one to go, she thought. She whipped the blanket at the driver again to catch his eye, then pointed to the right. He nodded as if he understood perfectly, and maybe he did, if he was familiar with the area.

Task accomplished, she glanced at Christoph again. He might be taking careful aim before he fired off a shot, but she hadn't missed that earlier laugh of his. She didn't doubt that *he* was having a great good time fending off these assailants, whether they were after him or her. He might be crouching on the seat, but his head and shoulders were exposed. Someone might get a lucky shot . . .

"*Why* didn't you bring some men with us?" she asked, annoyed.

"I did. I sent them ahead. I was trying not to draw attention to us."

"Well, that worked wonderfully, didn't it?"

He glanced down at her. "Are you always so sarcastic when you're frightened?"

She sighed. "I don't really know. I'm not used to fear. But I'm not actually frightened anymore."

"Why not?"

"Because you aren't."

"I'm terrified —"

"Oh, sure you are," she scoffed.

"— that you'll be shot. Like you, I hide my emotions well."

She snorted. A fine time to be teasing her, she thought. But then he turned around, sat on the seat again, and extended a hand to her.

"They're gone?" she asked.

"Two left behind on the ground, the other two riding off with their wounds. I'll send —"

He stopped to swear foully. She didn't realize why until she was seated next to him again and saw a snowstorm racing toward them. In moments the snow was swirling all around them and moving down the hillside.

"So much for following a blood path," he continued in disgust. "I should go after them myself."

Alana knew that with the snow coming down so heavily the tracks their assailants' horses left behind would soon be covered. She glanced behind the sleigh expecting to see nothing but a sheet of white, yet for a moment she actually caught a glimpse of the sun still shining far below in the lowlands before even that disappeared from her line of sight.

"Go ahead," she suggested bravely as he shook out one of the blankets to spread over them again. "I'll be fine now."

He gave her a sharp look. "I made you a promise. I'm not leaving your side."

Music to her ears — not that she liked his company! She just didn't *really* want to be left alone in the middle of a snowstorm.

She dusted the snow off her shoulders before she pulled the blanket up to her neck. That didn't help her face, which was getting quite wet as the snow melted on it.

"My nose is freezing," she complained, wishing more than ever that they were in a coach.

Christoph immediately drew her closer to him so that her head rested against his chest and raised the blanket over her. She decided not to object. His coat wasn't exactly warm against her cheek, but she didn't doubt it would be in a few minutes.

"I was hoping we could reach the chalet before we ran into one of these mountain storms," he said. "This is not good. The path is treacherous when it isn't clearly visible."

"Let me guess," she mumbled under the blanket. "No fencing to protect a vehicle from sliding over the side?"

"Yes, there's fencing higher up. But it's not sturdy enough to keep a strong horse from breaking through if the driver can't see well enough to steer away from the side. There are no slopes yet, but there will be."

"So we're going back?"

"No."

"But you just said —"

"My home is near here. We've just turned onto the road leading to it. If the snow doesn't blow over within the hour, we may pass the night with my family."

Family?! "Who are you going to tell them I am?"

"My mistress, of course."

She gasped. "The devil you will."

"Very well, I won't mention it."

She tried to get out from under the blanket to see if he was serious. But he held her fast to his chest so she couldn't. Deliberately, she didn't doubt. But before she could decide if it was worth a struggle, the sleigh stopped at his family's estate.

CHAPTER THIRTY-FIVE

When Alana threw off the blanket, she saw that the sleigh had stopped near the front door of the house, close enough that she had to turn her head both ways to see just how far the house extended. Quite far. The large house was several stories high in the center block, with wings spreading beyond that. She'd only seen three other mansions like it on the way to the capital when she'd arrived in the country.

Set off in the higher hills like the Beckers' home, one of those mansions had caught Poppie's eye that day and prompted him to explain to her, "There was a time long ago when the nobles of the land vied to impress each other with bigger and bigger homes, adding wings they had no use for. It might have continued to a ridiculous degree if the king at that time hadn't put a stop to such a frivolous waste of resources. Some say he was merely jealous because a few of those mansions were growing larger than his own palace!"

She knew of ducal properties in England that were just as grand as these mansions, but the majority of the homes in the English countryside were of a more modest size. Here in Lubinia there didn't appear to be anything but cottages for commoners and mansions for noblemen, at least not in the countryside.

"The people don't resent such a show of wealth?" she'd asked Poppie.

"Oddly enough, no. They take pride in the size of their landlord's home. I know my family did. But then competition can be contagious." Poppie had laughed.

Christoph got out of the sleigh and held out his hand to her. She thought he meant to help her down. But, no, he pulled her to him so he could carry her cradled in his arms right to the door. Thanks to his chivalrous behavior, her boots wouldn't get snowy and she wouldn't slip on the steps, which already had several inches of newly fallen snow on them. He stamped his feet just outside the door before he opened it and stepped inside.

But he didn't set her down there, either. When she looked up at him to see why, he captured her mouth with his own. She was startled by the kiss despite the intimacy they'd just shared in the sleigh with her hiding under a blanket against his chest. So much for thinking he'd just made a gentlemanly gesture, carrying her out of the snow.

For some reason her resistance was paltry at best. She shouldn't even have tried to lean away from him. The attempt just tightened Christoph's arms on her and deepened the kiss until she was straining toward him instead of away. She must have been affected by their proximity in the sleigh without even realizing it. How else could this happen again with her showing such complete surrender?

"We would have made a fire in that sleigh if it didn't snow," he said passionately against her lips. "You might want to let your nose get cold when we continue on, or I *will* behave as the barbarian you think I am."

Make love to her in an open vehicle with a driver a mere few feet away? Did she really tempt him that much? If his kiss hadn't taken the chill off her, his words certainly would have because she didn't think he was joking!

"You finally bring a woman home to meet us?" a new deep, masculine voice asked. "When is the wedding?"

Christoph chuckled as he bent to set

Alana carefully on her feet. "Don't embarrass the lady," he told the old man standing there watching them with interest. "I am escorting her. We ran into some trouble on the road. We may spend the night here if the snow doesn't quit soon."

Why would he volunteer so much information? Was he as embarrassed as she was to have been caught kissing her, even by a servant? Unless this wasn't a servant.

Alana gave the old man a closer look. His hair was silver gray, but it wasn't thinning yet. Worn long, some of it was queued, but the rest was loose on his shoulders, giving him a scraggly look. His eyes were light blue, his face craggy with wrinkles. But he was tall, robust of frame, his shoulders barely stooped. And he was oddly dressed. He wasn't wearing a jacket with his dark blue, long-sleeved shirt, but a white fur vest that reached the hem of his knee-high breeches. There were no shoes on his feet, only stockings.

"You kiss all the ladies you escort, eh?" the old man asked.

Christoph laughed. "Only the pretty ones. Lady Alana, this is my grandfather, Hendrik Becker."

Alana wondered if her cheeks could get any hotter. They did a moment later when a middle-aged woman appeared in the open doorway to the parlor.

Seeing her, Hendrik immediately crowed, "Look who's here, Ella. And I caught him kissing this young woman. You should tell him to marry her. He'll listen to you. If they give you a grandchild soon, our Wesley will have a playmate."

"Hush, Henry," Ella said. "You're embarrassing the girl. And Wes has a playmate. You. I have to fight to get him out of your arms." Then she held out her arms to Christoph. "Come here."

He grinned and walked over for a hug. "Introduce yourself, Mother, and make Lady Alana comfortable. I will be back shortly."

"You just got here!" Ella protested.

Alana was speechless. He was going to leave her alone with his family? She was about to protest, too, when he told his mother, "I shot a few men not far from here. I just need to make sure they are dead or cart them here for questioning if they still breathe." Then he turned to Alana and chucked her chin. "I leave you in good hands."

CHAPTER THIRTY-SIX

Christoph walked out the door, every inch the captain, all-business, to deal with his unpleasant task. Alana would still rather have gone with him. She didn't mind meeting strangers, but these people were *his* relatives. Did they have the same barbaric tendencies he displayed? Not his mother, of course, but the rest of his family? He'd been raised in this house, so where else would he have learned such behavior?

But Ella Becker put her at ease immediately with a simple warm smile. She looked no different from most Englishwomen her age Alana could have met in London. Her light brown hair was neatly coiffured, her lavender day dress in the height of English fashion. No taller than Alana was, Christoph's mother had blue eyes as dark as Christoph's, but otherwise Alana noted no resemblance between mother and son.

Ella led Alana into the parlor where a fire

blazed, the room warm enough that she quickly took off her coat, gloves, and cap. The furniture was English in style, dark, polished wood tables and cabinets, tan and brown brocaded sofas and chairs. Alana was reminded that she was in a foreign land when she saw that one entire wall was decorated with a mosaic depicting a mountaintop view of the capital city in summertime. Alana found it breathtakingly beautiful. The windows in the room had tasseled, velvet drapes, which were open. She could see the snow-covered landscape, steep hills and mountains not too far away.

A family portrait hung above the fireplace. Alana wondered if Christoph's grandmother had painted it. She recognized Ella in it easily, and possibly a younger Hendrik. Two other men were in it, another woman much older, and one young boy, blond, blue-eyed, handsome. She didn't doubt the boy was Christoph, and it felt a bit odd, seeing him as a child.

Alana tore her eyes away from the portrait and took a seat, but she'd no sooner got comfortable when Ella asked her frankly, "It's serious between you two? I'd imagine so for Christo to bring you to meet us."

A logical enough question, after what Hendrik had said when he'd caught them kissing, so Alana managed not to blush yet again. But what was she supposed to tell his mother? Christoph hadn't said she could speak freely.

"No, I don't think we would have stopped here if not for the snowstorm. He's escorting me farther up the mountain to a chalet."

"The king's chalet?" Hendrik asked as he walked in to join them.

Alana blinked at his accurate guess, but Ella chuckled at her. "Don't look surprised. The nobles live no higher than the foothills, with estates extending down to the fertile valleys. Only the king has property so high in the mountains that it's not useful for anything other than a retreat." Then Ella frowned. "Forgive my bluntness, but Frederick hasn't finally taken a mistress, has he?"

"No!" Alana gasped. "Well, not that *I* know of. I've never even met the king."

"Good. I would hate to think that the sedition currently being spread in the country would force him to desperate measures for an heir, when the queen isn't barren. She's just been having bloody rotten luck bringing a pregnancy to full term. I sympathize. My luck was just as bad after Christoph was born — until recently," she ended with a smile.

"Recently?"

"Christoph's brother, Wesley, is not even three years of age yet. Quite unexpected he was, arriving so late in our marriage, when Geoffrey and I had long since given up having another baby."

A twenty-year age difference between the two brothers? Amazing, Alana thought. People would think they were father and son, not siblings.

"Your accent is familiar," Ella added. "You're English, aren't you?"

"Like you, I was raised there, yes."

"What brings you so far from home?"

"I came here to meet — a parent I didn't know I had," Alana said carefully.

Hendrik burst out laughing. "That sounds familiar, too, eh, Ella?"

After the story Christoph had related today about his English grandmother, Alana understood that remark. "Christoph told me a little of your family history."

"Did he?" Ella asked with interest.

Alana felt like groaning. The mother was obviously still trying to ferret out the nature of Alana's relationship with her son. Like Hendrik, she'd probably like to see him settled down and raising his own family.

To point out that he hadn't volunteered the information on his own, she said, "I was surprised when I found out he was part

English. I asked for an explanation. Is your mother still living in England?"

Ella tsked. "Yes, she comes to visit us each summer, but I've never been able to talk her into staying. Her art keeps her in London, where she has a comfortable studio in her own home and she can easily obtain the supplies she needs. She has such a long list of commissions for portraits. She's very talented, but thinks that talent would be wasted here, where Lubinians favor a different sort of art. But I'm more hopeful this year she'll change her mind, otherwise she should stop coming. The last few years she's arrived here utterly done in. She's too old to travel such long distances."

"She'll never stop coming here," Christoph said as he stepped into the room. "She's too ornery to think she's too old."

"You're back already?" Alana said in surprise.

Christoph shrugged out of his coat. "It only took a few minutes to see that the two men were dead after all."

"Did you bring those bodies back for your father's wolves?" Hendrik asked. "They can't be buried until the ground thaws, but the wolves can dispose of them nicely."

Christoph laughed at Alana's expression after hearing that. "He's not serious, wench."

"Then your father doesn't really keep wolves?" she asked.

"He does," Christoph answered as he sat down next to her on the sofa. "He breeds them because they are so unique."

She was disconcerted for a moment. He could have sat in plenty of other places, including next to his mother. Ella had noted it, too, her eyes moving back and forth between them.

More as a distraction than a correction, Alana pointed out, "Wolves aren't unique."

"These wolves are. Tell her," Christoph said to his grandfather.

Hendrik grinned. "When his father, Geoffrey, was just a boy, I would take him hunting in the high mountains each summer, where the snow never melts. One year we went higher than ever before. It was a clear day, no clouds on the mountaintops. We found an unnatural creature up there, an albino wolf never seen before in Lubinia, or anywhere else in Europe that I know of. It would have made a fine pelt. I told Geoffrey to shoot it. I wasn't as good with the bow and arrow as he was. But he refused. He wanted to capture it instead and bring it home to tame. I thought it would be a good lesson for him, that the wild should be left wild. I didn't think he would succeed, but in less than half a year the white wolf was obeying his every command. Before she passed on, he found her a mate."

"And he still breeds them?"

"Why not? They're tame, at least, tame for him!" Hendrik laughed. "He uses them to hunt fresh meat in the winter. So many hunts come to a quick end in the high hills because the frequent snow limits visibility. But it doesn't stop the wolves."

She'd love to see these unique animals for herself, but they were probably kept outside and the snow was still coming down heavily, so Alana didn't ask. Instead, she asked, "You actually hunt with bows and arrows here instead of rifles?"

"I've never seen a rifle shot start a snow-slide, but why take the chance, eh, when a bow is as easy to master as a rifle?"

If it were that easy, Poppie would have taught her how to use one, but her eyes still flared wide and turned on Christoph. "*You* could have brought down an avalanche to-day?"

"What choice did I have, eh? But, no, there isn't enough snow down here for an avalanche."

"Who was shooting at you so near here?" Ella asked. "Thieves don't usually waylay people on the roads. Rebels?"

"The king's enemies are my enemies. I've been a target for some time now."

Ella scowled at him. "I could have done without hearing that."

He grinned at her. "You have nothing new to worry about. They only send expendable lackeys after me. But today, we are not sure who they were shooting at, me — or her."

He actually bumped shoulders with Alana when he said *her*. She scooted away from him. What was he doing, behaving so familiarly with her in front of his relatives? Especially after he'd been caught kissing her!

"Why her?" Hendrik asked.

"She's also a target," Christoph said. "But that's a long story and privileged information."

Ella raised a brow at him. "Who is more privileged than your family?"

"Don't ask" was all he said, but firmly enough to make his point.

Ella nodded and changed the subject, asking, "How are Frederick and Nikola faring? Anything interesting happening at court?"

"The queen is still far too anxious over the rebel situation, but at least she's entertaining again, which reminds me." He turned to his grandfather. "Ernest Bruslan's widow was dining with them recently and asked after you. She — um, misses your *humor.*"

Christoph said that so suggestively, he obviously didn't think it was humor the widow was missing, and Hendrik laughed, agreeing with him. "I actually thought about renewing our old acquaintance a while back, but Norbert Strulland was already entrenched as Auberta's 'retainer,' and at my age I didn't feel like competing with that old goat."

"She seems to be paving the way for Frederick to name her grandson Karsten his successor, bragging about all of Karsten's recent accomplishments."

Ella was surprised by that news. "That would certainly solve a lot of the current difficulties, but wasn't Karsten following in his dissolute father's footsteps?"

Christoph laughed. "He was definitely trying for a while and hasn't exactly abandoned the wenches yet, but he's giving a very good impression of having changed enough to shoulder some family responsibilities now — and endearing himself to the commoners in the process."

"So he's paving the way as well?"

"He actually thinks he'd make a good king."

"Would he?" Christoph merely shrugged, so Ella changed the subject again. "As long as you're here, I insist you stay the night. Your father will be back soon from his hunt. He will be annoyed if he misses you."

They all felt the draft as the front door was opened, and Ella added, "That must be him now, though why he would use the front door . . ."

It wasn't Christoph's father who appeared in the doorway to the parlor, but his lady "friend" whom he'd had forcibly removed from the palace grounds. Nadia gave them all a bright smile. Even dusted in snow, she was incredibly beautiful.

Her eyes lit on Christoph and went no further. "How wonderful to see you again so soon, Christo." Then she blushed prettily as if she'd only just remembered her manners and told his mother, "I'm sorry for not knocking, but it was too cold out there to wait. I'm lucky to have made it here at all. I was out riding when the snowstorm rushed down the mountain. I must have gotten turned around in it. I thought I was heading home, but here I am instead."

"That's quite all right, Nadia," Ella said graciously. "You know you're always welcome here."

"No, she's not, not anymore," Christoph

351

countered. "And she knows it."

Ella gasped. "Christo!"

"He's been quite mean to me, Lady Ella," Nadia complained in an aggrieved tone. "He trifled with my — affections — then forbade me to visit him anymore."

Christoph's expression darkened with anger. No one could miss what the blond beauty had just implied. But Alana didn't doubt it was true. How like a barbarian to end an affair as rudely as she'd seen him do.

Elle apparently believed it, too. "Our neighbor, Christo? How could you?"

"I couldn't, so be at ease, Mother. Nadia has merely become vindictive in her old age."

Nadia gasped. Hendrik found something to look at on the ceiling. Ella nodded, believing her son without needing further explanation.

Yet still the gracious Englishwoman, Ella told the young woman, "Nadia, warm yourself at the fire for a few minutes while our coach is readied to take you home. Hendrik, would you mind seeing to it?" But Hendrik wasn't about to leave the room just then and simply bellowed for a servant. Ella sighed. "I could have done that."

Nadia, quite stiff with indignation now

that she knew she wasn't welcome, moved to the fireplace. As she passed the sofa, her eyes narrowed on Alana and then dropped on Christoph.

"Isn't this the wench you took to your quarters at the palace the other day?" Nadia said cattily. "You insult your mother by bringing your mistress here?"

"Why don't you learn some manners, *wench?*" Alana surprised them all by saying. "Or is the captain going to have to throw you out of here as he did at the palace?"

Christoph burst out laughing. All anger gone, he stood up and tossed Alana's coat at her. "Come, *wench,*" he said, laughing again, probably because it was a name he'd called her so many times himself. "I'll show you those wolves you were so interested in."

"I'll join you," Hendrik said, adding with a chortle, "It's probably warmer out there than it is in here right now."

"I'll go, too," Ella said, but she was the last to leave the room, and she paused at the door to tell Nadia, "I don't know why he's annoyed with you. I don't care. But I warn you, don't *ever* try to turn me against my son again as you did here today. Be gone before we return."

CHAPTER THIRTY-SEVEN

Alana needed a few minutes alone to freshen up before she went outside again. The Beckers had a small retiring room downstairs. Hendrik went ahead to clear the path of snow. Ella gave her directions so Alana could follow when she was done, probably because Ella wanted a few minutes alone with her son. Christoph, that barbarian, asked if Alana needed assistance. She closed the door to the water closet in his face.

She didn't expect to find a modern flushing toilet as so few homes had them yet, even in England, but in a contrived semblance of one, a sturdy block of smoothly polished wood cradled a ceramic chamber pot, thankfully empty. She made quick use of it and was washing her hands when the door opened behind her.

She swung around. She wasn't really surprised to see Nadia standing there. The look the blonde had given her in the parlor had been nasty enough to suggest they weren't done with each other. Alana should have kept her mouth shut, but Nadia had attacked her directly in calling her Christoph's mistress. She had responded angrily, thoughtlessly, and now she was going to reap the consequences.

She thought about pushing past the woman and simply ignoring her, but she was too curious to see if Nadia was as malicious as Christoph had implied, or if she was there to apologize for her catty remarks. Alana could understand why Nadia had been upset at the palace. Apparently Christoph had asked her to leave, she'd refused, so he'd had her forcibly removed. But they were neighbors! How close had they been before that argument? He never did say what sort of friends they used to be.

Nadia clarified that rather well when she said stiffly, "Don't think he will marry you. He's soon going to marry me. Our families expect it."

If she hadn't added the remark about their families, Alana could have scoffed that the woman was still just being a jealous shrew. Instead, she felt oddly — deflated.

"He's a barbarian, you're welcome to him," she replied, but then she felt a spark of anger and added, "Though last I saw, he was banning you from the palace, so I doubt *he* thinks he's going to marry you."

What was wrong with her?! She sounded as jealous as Nadia did. Nadia's face turned quite pink at that reminder. Still, Alana didn't expect to be slapped for it, but she'd never been so glad of all those rapier lessons she'd had as she was when her arm rose automatically to block it.

"I warn you, we only had a lovers' quarrel," Nadia hissed. "We've had them before, but we *always* make up and we will this time as well."

"Then what are you worried about?"

"I'm not."

Alana chuckled without humor. "You could have fooled me. Maybe you should be convincing him that you two always make up. I could care less. Now if you'll excuse me, there are some wolves I want to meet, a prospect I find far preferable to listening to anything else *you* have to say."

She brushed past the woman, almost hoping Nadia would try to detain her further so she could *really* give her a piece of her mind. She was furious to find herself in the middle of a lovers' spat. And without warning. But of course Christoph wouldn't tell her he was just using her to make his lover jealous. For Nadia to come to that conclusion so rapidly suggested it wasn't the first time he'd done so, either.

Stepping outside behind the house, she gave Christoph a baleful look. He was close enough to catch it, on his way back to find out what was keeping her.

Grinning as he took her arm to help her along the swept path, he guessed, "You got lost?"

"No, I can follow directions."

"Then — ?"

"You should make an effort to tame that shrew. She's really quite unpleasant."

"Nadia spoke to you again?"

"Yes, she had to make sure I knew that you'll be marrying her — eventually."

"Wishful thinking on her part that will never come to pass, but this is no concern of yours."

"Isn't it? She just made it my concern by trying to slap me a few minutes ago! She's lucky I didn't break her bloody nose."

He choked back a laugh. "Perhaps I should explain."

"Yes, perhaps you should," she huffed.

"As neighbors, we grew up together. At one time she was even my best friend. But that ended long ago, when she became what you met today, a shrew, as you called her. Once I did think of marrying her, but I was still a boy, and she had yet to become the termagant."

Alana blushed, that she'd been so gullible. "So she's not your lover?"

"No, nor will she ever be. The only thing left between us is unpleasantness. She nags me to marry her. She even tries seduction. But her trap is clear. I'm not fool enough to step in it so she can cry foul to her father. Now come and get the foul taste from your mouth with fresh wolves."

She was appalled by the thought. "You killed one of your father's pets?"

He rolled his eyes. "Fresh as in babies."

"Oh, babies!" she exclaimed with a laugh.

Alana had never owned a pet of any sort, nor had any of her friends, at least not in the city, where conditions weren't ideal for them. She thought it was cruel to keep a dog cooped up indoors for most of the day. So her heart opened immediately when she saw the four little wolf pups through the gate, three white, one gray, all the same size, playing with a bone as if it were a toy.

They were in a large pen, with high stone walls, open to the snow. With the snow still falling, it took her a moment to see the white adult sitting in a corner watching her, or the other adult that came out of the cave-like structure attached to the pen to guard her pups. The mother picked up one of the pups by its nape and carried it into the den. Hendrik yelled at her and she dropped it, but that wouldn't stop her for long.

"She's going to hide them all, isn't she?" Alana said with disappointment. "I was hoping to meet them."

"That's probably not a good idea," Christoph cautioned next to her.

But Hendrik grinned. "Sure she can. Give me a few minutes to shoo the adults into the den and close the gate on it. They tolerate me, since I feed them occasionally."

"The adults aren't tame?"

"They are, but only for Geoffrey. I don't have his patience."

"Neither do I," Ella said. "I let him bring one of the pups into the house sometimes. They are adorable at this age. But as soon as they start chewing on the furniture, they go back to the pack."

It didn't take long for Hendrik to get the two adults locked into the den and open the outer gate for Alana to come inside the pen. Despite the cold and the falling snow, she spent a delightful hour playing with the baby wolves. Christoph had warned her to keep her gloves on. Good advice. Their sharp little teeth were catching on her gloves and would have shredded her fingers. But they were just being playful. It was hilarious when she threw snowballs for them. They would chase after each one, then dig around in the snow trying to find the ball that had broken apart as soon as it landed. The mother growled menacingly from the other side of the fence for quite some time, but Hendrik talked to her reassuringly and she finally lay down. She wouldn't take those golden eyes off Alana though.

Behind the gate, Ella noticed Christoph's tender smile as they watched Alana's antics. "So you do like her, eh?"

Without taking his eyes off Alana, he replied, "What isn't to like? She fascinates me."

"Then you aren't *just* her escort?"

"Don't read more into this than there is, Mother. Besides, she doesn't want to stay in Lubinia. Like your mother, she wants to return to England."

"I stayed for a man," she reminded him.

He put his arm around her shoulder. "And *I'm* glad you did, or I wouldn't be here. But there is another reason for you not to get those motherly hopes up. Aside from the fact that she doesn't exactly think kindly of me —"

Ella immediately scoffed, "Women adore you. What did you do to discourage her good opinion of you?"

"Perhaps someday I can explain if you are still curious, just not now."

"There's something else, isn't there?"

He nodded solemnly. "I may have to kill the man who raised her. And she loves him like a daughter would."

Watching the palace gates, Leonard recognized the guard he'd seen at the warehouse the other night. Now the man was walking toward the city. Leonard had followed the hooded man who'd assumed leadership of this clandestine group the other night, but the man had merely gone to an inn to sleep, and Leonard hadn't gotten back to the inn early enough the next morning to see the man's departure. The hooded man hadn't returned to that inn last night, but Leonard planned to check it again tonight. In the meantime, he hoped to learn something interesting by following the guard.

The man wasn't in uniform today and appeared quite nervous. He kept glancing behind him as if he expected someone from the palace to give chase, but he seemed to relax once the palace was no longer within view. Leonard followed on horseback, slowly. When he saw the guard slip into a cobbler shop and flip the sign on the door from OPEN to CLOSED, he tied off his horse several shops down the street and waited. A moment later the cobbler left without locking the door and walked away.

Was this their new meeting place? Leonard checked for a back entrance and found one. It wasn't locked and led directly into the back room where the cobbler worked his trade. It was early in the day. It could take hours for the guard's contact to show up, and the back room offered no place to hide in case the man wandered back there.

He debated whether to get information out of the guard the old-fashioned way, but he resisted the impulse. The guard had worked for Aldo, and from what he'd overheard, even Aldo hadn't known whom he was really working for, so Leonard didn't think he'd get any useful information from the guard. Besides, it was the hooded man he wanted, and all he had was his distinctive gravelly voice to go by.

An hour passed. The guard began to snore in the front room. Leonard glanced around the wall he was hiding behind for a view of the shop's front room and saw the man had settled into a comfortable chair. With a sigh, he resumed his position flat against the wall and continued to wait.

After another twenty minutes the front

door opened and closed, and he heard the distinctive voice he was hoping for. "Wake up, eh."

"Sorry," the guard mumbled. "I didn't know how long you would be."

"Did Rainier follow his orders?"

"He tried to, but he failed."

"Good."

"Good?!" the guard exclaimed. "Did you want him to get caught?"

"No, but that was a hasty decision our employer soon regretted, so don't try to succeed where Rainier failed. They may have other plans for her now. *Was* he caught?"

"Yes, and I'm not going back to the palace. He'll give up my name if he hasn't already. But whether they brand me a deserter or a spy, they'll be looking for me, so I'm leaving the country."

Leonard was furious. They'd tried to kill Alana again, but now had other plans for her? This had to end and soon, so it was time for him to take a more direct approach.

He left the shop silently and retrieved his horse, readying himself to follow his target without losing him this time. If he didn't get a name today . . .

He got a good look at his target when he exited the shop and mounted his horse. The man wasn't wearing a hood today, so Leonard could see he was in his mid-twenties and handsome with black hair and a strapping body.

The target rode south out of the city on one of the more traveled roads. In that direction lay a large Bruslan estate, commonly referred to as the Stronghold because it resembled a small city with many fine homes within the low rock walls that surrounded it. The Stronghold had no gate, and with so much activity in the area, no one asked Leonard what business he had there.

His target disappeared inside the main residence, but so many regal-looking men and women entered and exited the building that Leonard couldn't determine whom the man was reporting to. He wasn't in there that long, though. When he walked out of the building, he was alongside Karsten Bruslan, but the two men went separate ways without a word, Karsten into a fancy coach, the target back on his horse and riding off at a fast clip back to the city.

Leonard wouldn't have known the other man was Karsten, old King Ernest's heir, if he hadn't heard his name mentioned yesterday at the festival and got a good look at him then. Was it a coincidence the two had departed at the same time? He decided to follow Karsten. Actually, the Bruslans' favored heir might have the answers he wanted, but even if he didn't, it was time to stir the pot a little to see what came out.

CHAPTER THIRTY-EIGHT

They had been outside long enough for the Beckers' annoying neighbor to be gone from the house when they returned to it. In the parlor again, Alana was warming herself at the fireplace and didn't see Christoph's father enter the room.

"Kosha seems upset. Did a wild animal get too close to the pack?"

Christoph laughed and nodded toward Alana. "If you want to call her a wild animal."

"I'd rather you didn't," Alana said drily.

Christoph introduced them, though it wasn't necessary. The resemblance between father and son was remarkable. The rest of the day continued to be enjoyable. Unlike Christoph, his family was nice and made her feel quite at home.

Ella wanted to know all about the latest English fashions, which brought a few groans from the men. She merely laughed and invited Alana to come with her to the kitchen so they could continue the discussion without boring the men.

But what she really wanted to know was "You like my Christo?"

Alana didn't blush and managed an evasive reply. "He — takes getting used to."

That made Ella laugh. "I know he's different from the English gentlemen you are accustomed to. Lubinian men, they don't mince words, they get right to the point. But he's a good boy."

Alana chuckled. Only a mother would call a man Christoph's size a boy. She liked Ella a lot. Spending time with her, she couldn't help wondering what her own mother was going to be like. She hoped Helga would be as easy to talk to as Ella was.

She even got to meet Christoph's baby brother — from a distance, when a servant brought him into the parlor. Christoph grabbed him from the woman, tossed him up in the air until the child was giggling in delight, then carried him over to Alana. But the child was too shy around strangers to let her get close, beginning to cry each time she held out her arms to him.

Wesley joined them for dinner. Sitting between his parents at the table, they both fed him tiny bites of the meal. Christoph, smiling at the boy, leaned over to tease Alana. "He doesn't realize what he's missing, to be held in your arms."

At least he had whispered that, sitting next to her, and no one noticed her blush but him. But a distinctly uncomfortable moment came when the hour grew late and Ella said to Alana, "Come, I will show you to a room."

Christoph stopped them and with nothing teasing in his tone said, "No, she will have to sleep in mine. She's in danger. The people who want to kill her are earnest enough to break into a home to get at her."

"We're *not* going to be sharing a bed, Lady Becker," Alana assured his mother.

"No, you certainly will not be," Ella agreed. "She can sleep with me, Christo."

"And where will I sleep?" Geoffrey wanted to know.

Alana thought it was settled until Christoph said, "I'm afraid I must insist, Mother. I'm not going to wake up in the morning to find you both with slit throats. It is my job to protect her, and I'm not going to sit outside your door or mine all night to do it. Propriety is meaningless when a life is at stake."

"You actually think they would break into this house?" Ella asked.

"They broke into my quarters to get to her."

A rather mild version, Alana thought, since she'd been in his prison, which was only connected to his quarters. But he obviously didn't want to clarify that to his family.

Ella finally nodded, but said, "I will have a cot delivered to your room. *You* will use it."

Christoph smiled, having won the argument, and told his mother, "Go ahead and show her the way. I'm not ready to retire yet."

Alana was asleep before he came upstairs. She'd left a lamp burning for Christoph even though the fireplace glowed brightly. After yet another eventful day, she drifted off quickly, staring at the cot on the far side of the room. But when she woke, it wasn't morning yet, and what woke her was Christoph's warm body against hers.

She opened her eyes to see him grinning down at her. "You lied to my mother, telling her we wouldn't share a bed."

If he really wanted to make love to her, he wouldn't tease her with a remark guaranteed to raise her moral defenses, would he? To stop him before she was tempted, she warned, "Touch me and I will scream. Your

369

family will come to investigate. You won't like talking your way out of that one."

"That I made you scream with pleasure?"

"You wouldn't!" she gasped.

"Of course I would. I'm a barbarian, remember? But you've doused the flames. Get some sleep."

But he didn't move! And he was searching her eyes. Was he hoping to see an invitation to stay that she couldn't voice? Was it there? Is that why he was suddenly kissing her? And it was no simple kiss! His tongue thrust past her lips, luring her straight into his passion.

She tried to fight the feelings that rose up so quickly in response, that fluttering, nearly swooning feeling that she didn't quite understand, the flush that raced over her skin and brought the heat with it. But it was too difficult to resist any of that, because she didn't really want to when all her senses were being stirred in such an exciting manner.

He would have to stop this for her, she realized, but she was clinging too tightly to his neck when she said, "We shouldn't." So it was no wonder his mouth was hot on her neck now, shivers spreading rapidly through her body.

He had one leg on top of her, and now he

slipped that leg between hers. Wearing only her chemise and drawers, she felt the friction all too strongly when he began to slowly rub his leg against her. She started, several times, and held more tightly to him.

"You wear only your underclothes." She heard the smile in his voice. "Admit you were waiting for me."

Her eyes flew open. Thank heavens he'd given her the catalyst she desperately needed to kick him out of the bed!

"No," she gasped, then said more strongly, "I merely forgot to bring a nightgown. And you're in the wrong bed."

He leaned back. "Alana, you can't possibly —"

"Really. You're in the wrong bed."

He still hesitated a moment, to gauge again if she was serious. He couldn't doubt it this time. With a tsk and a sigh, he left the bed and went to the cot. He was naked! She clamped her eyes shut and turned over to face away from him.

"Get some sleep," he mumbled. "At least one of us should."

Implying he wouldn't now? She resisted saying she wouldn't either. Somehow she did.

They got an early start in the morning despite his whole family's coming outside

371

to say good-bye. The weather obliged with blue skies for a while. The storm had left a white blanket behind, but the sleigh cut steadily through it.

Christoph didn't say a single word about the previous night. He didn't seem to be annoyed about it either. But her mother took her mind off Christoph during that ride farther up the mountain, especially when the nervousness seized her again.

He noticed and put an arm around her shoulder to draw her closer. "You're anxious again? Why? You should be excited."

"Easy for you to say. You aren't meeting one of your parents eighteen years late."

"I can help you to relax."

She didn't doubt what he meant. "*That's* quite all right."

She fell silent again, chewing at her lower lip. She should probably have let him get her mind off the reunion because her nervousness grew apace, the closer they got to their destination.

It took a little over two hours to finish the journey. It would have been a much quicker ride if the snow on the road weren't so thick. Alana even caught a glimpse of the chalet before the snow arrived again. It had looked like a little castle, sitting on a rocky ledge more than halfway up the mountain.

"You might have mentioned 'grand splendor,' but, really, I wasn't expecting something *that* big up here," she said right before the view was lost. "Chalets are more the size of a farmhouse, aren't they?"

"It used to be small. Over the years, it's been added to again and again. The name merely stuck, despite the size."

"The king comes up here often?"

"He hasn't been here since his first wife died. I've heard she loved it up here, which is understandable, since the views are magnificent — when it isn't snowing. But he avoids anything that reminds him of her. That's why there are no portraits of Queen Avelina in the palace. That's why I don't know what she looked like."

"Why doesn't the king just close down the chalet if he doesn't want to use it?"

"Because it's still useful. Occasionally, he offers it to visiting diplomats. After a few days up here, they return to the capital more relaxed and they are easier to negotiate with."

Alana laughed. "That's quite a ploy."

The sleigh stopped. Her humor departed as Christoph stepped down and reached for her so he could carry her inside, just as he'd done at his home. She was prepared to stop any kissing this time, but he didn't try. He just set her down inside a large room that seemed too big to be a foyer or entry hall, yet it didn't serve any other obvious purpose. A half dozen tall statues, male and female, Grecian in design, circled a mammoth fountain, which currently contained no water, in the center of the marble floor. Large, framed mirrors covered the walls, making the room look even bigger.

"Count Becker, it's good to see you again. Would you like the same room?"

Alana hadn't noticed the servant who approached them until he spoke. She gave Christoph a sharp look over that question. "*You've* been here before?"

He shrugged as he removed his coat and fur cap and handed them to the servant. The room wasn't warm enough for her to do the same. She wondered if he'd admit that occasionally even he needed to spend some time alone, get away from a job that had become more dangerous than it should be.

Once the servant left to put away his coat, he said, "I've brought a few mistresses here." Then, because of her expression: "What? Don't look surprised. You were the virgin when we met, not I."

She blushed immediately. "You're not married. Why bring your women way up here — or were you married?"

He chuckled. "Listen to how indignant you sound, eh? Is that for yourself, or on general principle? Or are you jealous?"

"None of the above," she snapped. "Forget I asked. What you do is your business."

"You want to make it your business?"

"No!"

"You protest too much!" He laughed. "But I will answer your question. When a relationship begins to sour, a lot of arguments can ensue. That usually occurs when a mistress wants a more permanent arrangement, which was never part of the agreement. If I wasn't quite done with her, I would bring her here. It's probably the isolation, knowing they are stuck here with me until I'm ready to take them back to the city, that turns them amiable again. But it only delays the inevitable a little while, so I stopped making that effort."

"If all your relationships end so unpleasantly, maybe you should try a real one instead."

"You mean a wife?" He shook his head. "A wife would require a reasonable amount of my time, which I don't have to give yet." Then he grinned. "But I'll make time for a new mistress — if it's you."

She wasn't going to dignify that with an

answer, but it did occur to her to ask suspiciously, "My mother *is* here, isn't she?"

He laughed again. "You and I don't argue, Alana mine. No, I didn't bring you here to soften your edges. You huff and puff a lot, but I know how to make you purr instead."

She gasped, her cheeks suddenly blazing. No matter how many times he'd said such outrageously inappropriate things to her, she couldn't shrug them off. She knew she should be immune to them by now instead of mortified and angry.

"Good Lord, you make me wish I *was* your king's daughter, just so I could have you clapped in irons. One month for every insult means you'll spend years —"

"Don't expect me to conceal my thoughts from you when I want you as much as I do. Would you rather I pretend you don't affect me? Actually, I doubt I can."

Christoph took her hand and led her out of the room, adding, "Let's find your mother. Maybe she'll be a witch and you'll want my protection from her."

"I wouldn't count on it."

He sighed. "I'm not."

CHAPTER THIRTY-NINE

The servant who showed them the way explained that Helga rarely left her suite of rooms. Alana could understand why because the richly appointed rooms encompassed an area larger than most homes. Helga looked right at home in them. She'd been having a late breakfast. Apparently, the maid who had brought the meal had stayed to talk with her. The two had still been laughing over something even as the maid opened the door for them.

Helga rose from her small dining table at the unexpected intrusion. She probably didn't even think they were there to see her. The chalet was so big it would be easy to get lost in it.

A tender smile broke out on Alana's face. *This was her mother! Her real mother!* Helga was wearing a simple green day dress. Alana noticed she wasn't tall. She was even shorter than Alana by a few inches. No black hair, either. Helga's was blond, her eyes dark brown. Her frame was sturdy, not thick, just big boned perhaps. Alana was small boned. Helga's face had no wrinkles. She must have been a very young mother. She didn't even look forty yet.

"Helga Engel?" Christoph began.

Eyeing them warily, Helga gave a hesitant nod. "You're here to see *me?*"

Christoph smiled to put her at ease and introduced himself formally as captain of the King's Guard. "Indeed, I bring you a wonderful surprise."

Helga laughed suddenly, guessing, "Another gift from the king? He's too kind."

Christoph appeared to be taken aback. "Frederick gives you gifts?"

Helga grinned. "Every year, sometimes twice a year." At his continued surprise, she laughed at him like a schoolgirl. "Oh, nothing like that! Nothing extravagant at all, just little mementos to let me know he has not forgotten what I did for him. It's not necessary. You should tell him that for me. This" — she waved a hand to indicate her quarters — "was already too generous."

Helga's expression turned sad. Christoph cleared his throat uncomfortably, no doubt both he and Helga thinking of the sacrifice she had made. But Alana didn't feel sad.

She was ready for the happy reunion she'd hoped for.

She started to move forward, to give Helga the happy news herself. Christoph suddenly stayed her, his hand on her arm. She glanced at him and frowned as she took in his rigid military demeanor.

Sure enough, he asked Helga in official tones, "You don't feel you deserved this reward?"

"I —"

Helga didn't continue, looking wary once again.

"Stop it!" Alana hissed at Christoph. "You're not here to interrogate her."

"You are."

"No, I'm not."

"You are. You have a thousand questions. I merely asked one."

"You have no reason to unleash that suspicious nature of yours here. It is simple modesty when one denies one is deserving of something. That concept might be foreign to a barbarian like you, but it's something civilized people frequently encounter."

He didn't appear contrite. Of course, the *captain* wouldn't. They'd been arguing in whispers so Helga wouldn't hear them, but that seemed to alarm her even more.

"Would you please tell me why you are

379

here?" Helga asked, glancing nervously between them.

Christoph relaxed. He even smiled again. Alana wondered if her tongue-lashing had really shooed the captain away for now.

"I apologize, Helga," he said. "The surprise I bring you is your daughter, very much alive as you can see."

Helga's eyes touched on Alana for the barest second before they rolled up into her head and she crumbled to the floor in a faint. Alana jumped forward, but she didn't reach her mother in time to break her fall.

Alana glanced back at Christoph. "Good Lord, you have the subtlety of a boar. You could have done that more gently!"

He came forward and picked Helga up off the floor and laid her on the sofa in the west corner of the large room. Alana followed him there and saw some evidence of her mother's artistic endeavors, a few baskets of yarn, a large frame holding a half-finished tapestry set in front of a chair.

"What would you have said, eh, to make it easier for her to hear?" he asked. "It was going to be a shock to her no matter how it was presented."

Alana sighed and leaned over Helga, gently patting her cheeks to wake her. She didn't notice what Christoph was doing until she saw him approach with a glass of water.

She gasped and shielded her mother's face. "Don't you dare!"

He raised a brow. "Why not? It's quick."

"It's rude. Let me try first."

"You are full of complaints today, why is that? Still nervous?"

"I wasn't. Not until you started interrogating my mother. You're not on duty here today. At least, you shouldn't be."

"I am always on duty."

"You're the one who told me Helga Engel is my mother," Alana reminded him stiffly. "If you aren't absolutely sure, you should have said so."

"I am certain."

"Then explain, please."

"She caught me off guard. We had only just spoken of mistresses. Frederick has been faithful to both his wives, but there was a time between those marriages when he went through a number of mistresses. One tried to kill him. It is my job to know them all, even though this was before my time in the palace. I thought I did know. Her remark implied that she and Frederick —"

"I didn't gather that from her remark at all," Alana cut in. "She showed delight that he still remembers what she did for him, even though she claimed his little gifts weren't necessary. That, Christoph, is a female response. Are you really not familiar with it?"

He made a look of self-disgust. "Just wake her so she can give you a motherly hug and you will be too happy to complain anymore."

Alana knelt beside the sofa and continued to pat her mother's cheeks. Without any response at all. She was beginning to worry that Helga might have hurt herself in that fall. But then she heard the slight groan and the catch of breath that followed. Helga's eyes opened, disoriented, but calm, as if waking from a nap — until she noticed Alana. She actually pushed back into the sofa to try to put distance between them, her eyes rounded in horror.

"Get away from me!" Helga shrieked.

But she was too upset to give Alana a chance to move away. She leapt off the sofa, nearly knocking Alana over, and ran around behind it.

"You lie!" she cried, pointing a condemning finger at Christoph.

Christoph frowned. "If you don't believe us, then why do you act like she's a ghost? I assure you her flesh is very warm."

Alana didn't have a chance to reprimand Christoph for his inappropriate remark as Helga loudly denied, "I don't know who or what she is, but she is *not* my daughter. My daughter is dead!"

"Yes, we know that's what you thought, what we all thought," Christoph said gently. "But the proof stands before you that it isn't so."

"Why? Because *she* says so?"

"Actually, she thought she was Frederick's daughter because the man who stole her thought he'd taken the princess and that's what he told her. But thanks to you, he took the wrong child."

"Thanks . . . to me," Helga said brokenly.

She finally looked at Alana — and started to cry. But she didn't appear to be crying tears of happiness.

CHAPTER FORTY

"All these years, I thought he took you to kill you."

Though said hollowly, it was also the first indication that Helga was starting to believe them. Yet the news was apparently still too much of a shock to her for her to express any joy.

Alana managed to get Helga to sit on the sofa again. Christoph offered her a handkerchief for the tears before he stood back, not taking a seat himself. But after initially wiping her face with the handkerchief, Helga discarded it in her lap and didn't seem aware that an occasional tear still rolled down her cheeks.

Alana sat next to her, even tried to hold her hand reassuringly. But she felt Helga tense at her touch, so she took her hand away.

She was feeling a bit rejected by then. Her own brief burst of happiness, when she'd seen the laughing Helga, was gone. Nothing about this reunion was happy — yet. But Alana was still hopeful that once the shock wore off, it would become joyful for both of them.

Some explanation might help in that regard, so Alana said, "He did take me for that reason. He just couldn't do it and raised me instead. He changed because of it. He's no longer an assassin."

"He was an assassin?" Helga gasped.

"Didn't you think so?" Christoph asked.

Helga's eyes dropped immediately to her lap. She obviously didn't like looking at Christoph. He was an official, and he'd been sharp with her.

After a moment Helga said, "Yes, but only you have confirmed it, no one else did."

"He's been like a father to me," Alana assured her mother. "In fact, all these years I thought we were related by blood, that he was my real uncle. He only told me the truth last month."

Helga's eyes flared wide. "He's still alive?"

"Yes, but —"

Helga glanced frantically at the door behind Christoph. "Is he here in the chalet?"

Her fear of Poppie was obvious. Fear instead of hatred for the man who'd stolen her daughter? Alana wondered. She noticed that Christoph was frowning, too.

Alana quickly said, "I'm sure what happened all those years ago terrified you. It's all right, you don't ever have to meet him. Tell me about my father."

Helga's brown eyes came back to Alana, but the fear didn't leave them, not all of it. "He was a good man. We weren't even married a year before he died of fever, so he never got to see our baby." As an afterthought Helga added, "He had black hair."

Alana chuckled. "Finally a relative with black hair! That's been such a bone of contention — with him." She nodded toward Christoph.

"Why?"

"Because I tried to convince Captain Becker I was the princess, which is who my guardian thought I was. And the captain couldn't tell me why he knew that wasn't so. But because of the color of my hair, and your description of me that I was blond, too, like the princess, he didn't once consider that I could be your daughter instead."

"Perhaps the assassin lied to you and you aren't my daughter," Helga said.

That hurt. Helga had even said it bitterly. That could only mean one thing. Helga still had doubts, most likely, because she felt absolutely nothing for Alana. Alana couldn't even blame her for it. Christoph had had the same thought, that Poppie had lied to her.

Christoph said as much, "I thought the same thing at first, but not anymore. If I still had doubts, I wouldn't have brought her here to be reunited with you with the king's permission, of course. Your reaction to her is, however, curious."

"If you say she's mine, then she's mine!" Helga cried defensively. "I just don't *feel* it yet, nor can you blame me for that. It was my baby that was taken from me. You bring me a full-grown woman who doesn't even look like me!"

"Does she look like your husband?"

Helga scoffed. "There is nothing of a man in her."

"No, there isn't," he agreed. "Perhaps you should just be pleased she turned out so beautiful?"

Helga gave him an odd look before she glanced at Alana again and gave her a weak smile. "You are very beautiful. Please don't blame me for my feelings."

"No, I don't," Alana said. "I completely understand. All my life, I thought my parents were dead. When I was told that wasn't so, it was a shock to me, too. It took me a while to believe it. It helped to talk about it, though, and that might make this easier for you as well. Tell me about our family."

Helga sighed. "They're all gone now. Both my parents were still alive when I moved to the palace, but they were old. I came to them late in life. My father died the same year that I lost my baby. My mother moved here to the chalet to be with me, but she died two years ago. I'm sorry, there is only me — and you — left."

"You don't need to be sorry," Alana said, then asked carefully, "Can you tell me why you did it, why you switched the babies?"

Helga immediately tensed. "I was warned never to speak of that."

Christoph interjected, "When we realized who she is, the king gave me permission to tell her the truth and bring her here to you, so she already knows the secret you were to keep. You may speak freely to her."

Helga started to cry again, but now Alana understood why. Helga wouldn't be able to remember that awful time without feeling the anguish over losing her child. Alana thought about changing the subject. She didn't really need to know what had prompted an action that had completely changed her own life. But maybe Helga was reluctant to discuss it because she thought

Alana had suffered, being raised by an assassin.

"I've had a good life with no hardships
whatsoever," Alana assured her. "I was
raised to be a lady in England. I had a fine
education, servants, friends, a loving relative — at least that's what I thought he was.
I've never lacked for anything except a
mother. So nothing horrible happened to
me because of what you did. Truly, I bear
you no resentment for anything."

"I do," Helga said abjectly.

"Then why did you do it?"

Christoph asked it this time, which could
be why Helga answered immediately now.
"I became nervous with the palace nearly
empty, the king away too long in his grief,
and no one even coming to visit the princess. The truth is the princess was neglected.
Only three years had passed since the civil
war when the palace had been attacked and
King Ernest was killed. I wasn't the only
one who thought the Bruslans might try to
regain the throne with more violence. There
was speculation about it in the city even
before King Frederick married."

"Understandable, but the palace wasn't
left undefended," Christoph said.

"You are correct, there were many guards
in the ward, but there weren't many inside

the palace. The two guards assigned to the nursery would check it on their rounds only twice each night! They should have been stationed outside the doors, but they weren't, and they barely even glanced in the royal bassinet when they did come in, always talking and joking with each other. But I didn't switch the babies immediately. It was many weeks before my nervousness turned to fear. The princess was nearly three months old before I did it."

"Were the servants aware of your ruse?" Christoph asked.

"What servants?" Helga scoffed. "There was just one old woman with failing eyesight who came to clean the rooms and bring me meals. The court physician came once a month to check that the princess was healthy and growing normally. But he was an arrogant man who seemed insulted to have been given the task of examining an infant. I caught the scent of liquor on his breath more than once. I begged one of the court officials for more guards and more help. He laughed and told me the palace was secure, but he did deign to hire another nursemaid to help me. But by the time she arrived, a couple of weeks before the abduction, I had already taken matters into my own hands and switched the babies. I was terrified of what would happen to me if anything happened to the princess."

"Why didn't you tell the new nursemaid that you'd switched the babies so she could be on guard as well?" Christoph asked.

Helga didn't answer right away. "First, I wasn't sure I could trust her. And the truth is" — she paused again as her eyes teared up — "I loved being able to spend more time with my own baby."

Alana's heart melted when she heard that.

"Of course, I didn't want the other nursemaid to try the same thing," Helga continued. "The princess's safety was my paramount concern. Even after the new nursemaid arrived, I kept hounding that official to give us more guards. Even just two! He could have prevented *my* loss by doing so. That — that assassin would never have gotten past guards at the door to take my baby. I don't even recall being attacked, but after he knocked me out, he must have tied my hands behind my back." She shook her head sadly. "But the king knew who to blame when he was summoned back, and he was furious."

"I would have felt it was his fault, for being gone so long," Alana said quietly.

Christoph gave Alana a hard look for saying that, but Helga defended Frederick. "It wasn't. He assumed he'd left his heir in good hands. And his grief was so deep, he didn't even know he'd been gone so long. Still, the nursery should have been better protected and had a larger staff. That's why he was so furious. And people were dismissed because of that neglect, but it was too late — for me."

"You came here after that?" Alana asked.

Helga nodded. "I was released from my charge because of my loss. A new nursemaid was hired to travel with the princess to where they hid her. But I stayed with my parents in the city for a while. They helped me through my grief. I came up here after my father died and was able to talk my mother into living here with me."

After a moment of silence, Helga hesitantly touched the top of Alana's hand with her fingers and asked, "Are you really my daughter?"

Alana smiled but didn't get to say anything. Someone was pounding on the door and, so sharply, Helga started and jumped to her feet in alarm.

"That would be for me," Christoph said, and immediately stepped outside the room.

Alana tried to reassure her mother. "He sent his men here ahead of us yesterday. They probably just want to make sure he arrived safely through the storm. And his men, they are rather ba—" She started to say *barbaric,* but realized Helga might not appreciate that, being Lubinian herself, so she amended, "Bossy."

That didn't exactly relax Helga enough to get the color back into her pale cheeks. Alana understood why her mother might fear Poppie, but she hoped Helga wasn't going to feel it every time there was a knock at her door. Alana thought about arranging a meeting between them. It wouldn't be pleasant, but Poppie could assure Helga that he'd meant her no harm.

Then Christoph reentered the room, his expression so grim that Alana rose to her feet. He took Alana's arm and started leading her to the door.

She resisted, pulling back from him. "Don't be so rude. Where are you taking me?"

"We must return to the city. The palace was attacked this morning just before dawn."

CHAPTER FORTY-ONE

Alana was sure Christoph wouldn't have paused at the door to her mother's room if she hadn't chided him for being rude. But he turned to Helga and said, "The king was unharmed, the attack quickly beaten back. I am needed in the city, but I will bring your daughter back to visit another time."

Downstairs, Alana saw that the sleigh had already been summoned, and Christoph's five men were already mounted, ready to follow in their wake. Christoph carried her out to the sleigh, climbed in himself, and after pulling her close to him wrapped the two of them in blankets. As soon as the sleigh shot forward, she said, "So the rebels are bolder than you thought?"

"This had nothing to do with that. King Ernest's grandson Karsten — you remember him, the man at the festival you found so charming — he was severely beaten."

"*He* started the attack?"

"No, some of his men who were furious that he'd been attacked and suspected me or the king of ordering it were able to get into the ward late last night. They were just a handful, but enough to quickly clear the back wall with the immediate help of those ready to climb over it to join them. Because it wasn't quite dawn yet, they actually thought they could slip through the ward, all twenty of them, and enter the palace before they were spotted. Fools. They never got off the wall."

"You're angry because you weren't there, aren't you?"

"No. Every time I leave the palace, it's with the knowledge that an attack could occur. But when I leave, security is doubled, so I was sure if anyone was stupid enough to attack, they would fail. And they did. I am angry that this seems a desperate attempt because of what your guardian has stirred up. He nearly beat the Bruslan heir to death!"

"You don't know he did that," she said uncomfortably.

"Of course he did. No one else would dare."

"If he did, it proves that Karsten isn't responsible. Poppie would have killed him if he thought he was."

"I told you I never thought Karsten knew anything about the abduction. He was a child back when you were taken and he might be a man now, but he's very self-confident and straightforward. It's not his style to deal with assassins and spies. He's the kind who would hire mercenaries for a rebellion." Christoph smiled mirthlessly. "Or launch an outright attack like he just did. No, there are so many elder Bruslans still living who are more likely to have ordered the princess's death."

She tried to point out a bright side. "Well, it was a failed attempt. Maybe they'll stop harassing you with rebels after this."

"Or build a real army, now that they think Frederick has played his hand — to their detriment."

She didn't say she thought that might be a good thing, that it could finally force the king to take action against that branch of his family which he despised anyway. *Her* life had been affected by his reluctance to do so.

Instead, she asked, "Why didn't you let me stay at the chalet to visit with my mother? You don't need me to deal with the aftereffects of that attack."

"I won't — can't leave you alone when your life is still at risk. But you didn't really want to stay there."

She blushed, grateful that he probably wouldn't see it with the blanket half-covering her face. If he was looking. She didn't peek up at him to see.

How had he guessed? She hadn't even fully realized how uncomfortable she'd felt at that meeting with her mother until now. However, she did know that she *would* have wanted to visit longer if she'd felt better about it. Now she felt totally confused.

Not once had the relaxed, happy woman who had laughed over being given gifts by the king reappeared after Christoph had informed her that her daughter was alive. Helga had been fearful the entire time. Because she thought she might lose her place at the chalet now? Alana couldn't re-assure her that wouldn't happen, but why would Helga even worry about it? She'd still saved a princess and lost her own daughter for eighteen years because of it.

Alana tried to explain to Christoph what she was feeling. "It's not that I didn't want to stay, it was — I thought some natural feelings would well up in me when I saw her, like love. And when I first saw her, I actually felt some kind of bond for a few moments. But her reactions . . . I don't know, I just don't feel any closeness to her at all. We are strangers. I should have realized it could be like that. I suppose it's even normal after so many years. She might have given birth to me and has mourned my loss all these years, but she is just a stranger, after all. That is normal, isn't it?"

"My answer would be an opinion, which is irrelevant. I've never seen or heard of a situation such as yours to know how your experience compares. But perhaps the feelings you wanted to have are still missing simply because you always thought your mother was dead. From everything you said, it didn't sound as if you would have had those feelings for Frederick either, though you thought he was your father for a longer time."

"That was different. That was mixed feelings. I wanted to like him, but disparagement kept getting in the way. I think I even told you why, didn't I? It was because Poppie, even loving him and swearing he was a good king, was contemptuous of him for not resolving the matter of who wanted me assassinated years ago. But that doesn't matter anymore. I'm never going to meet him, so I don't need to worry that I might insult him with my disdain. Most of my nervousness had stemmed from that, that I wouldn't be able to conceal those feelings from him."

"You understand now why there was no resolution?" Christoph said. "It was a branch of his own family that was suspected, and it's a large family."

She snorted. "Niceties don't apply when lives are at stake, especially when the two branches of that family have been feuding for generations."

"When we could never say who was pulling the strings? When without proof, banishing that whole family at that time could have brought the country to arms again? The Bruslans were long in power. They have many people still loyal to them, many that would have objected if an entire family was punished for the wrongs of just one of them. Do you really think we are that barbaric?" He added, "Don't answer that."

She sighed. He was correct in the point he was making. She knew he was. But he wasn't the one they'd tried to kill. . . . She blinked. Neither was she. She'd just been an innocent bystander, as it were.

"That's neither here nor there and none of my concern anymore, thankfully."

"It's still your concern as long as the king's enemies mistake who you are and try to kill you."

She frowned. "Which is why I'm leaving

Lubinia as soon as possible. As for my mother, good Lord, I actually felt more comfortable with *your* mother than with mine. But she is my mother. I do want to see her once more before I return to England, and without you standing there making her so nervous. I want to try to talk her into living with me, too, though you seemed to think she won't want to. If she doesn't, I can at least write to her after I'm gone. I'll even come back and visit her next year — *if* you've arrested the perpetrators of this nasty plot, and I expect you to do exactly that now that you have a good reason to point fingers at the Bruslans after that attack this morning."

"Do you?"

She heard the humor in his tone. She'd just complimented him, in a roundabout way. Not deliberately!

"Well, you do have culprits now, the older generations of the Bruslan family. Start your interrogations with them. I'm sure I don't need to tell you how to do your job. You have to anticipate that everything else might well unravel from what happened today, *and* I might add, you'll have Poppie to thank for it if it does."

She glanced over to see how he took *that* remark, only to find his head shaking in disagreement. "His actions provoked an attack on the palace, which is treasonous."

She groaned. "Have it your way. But he *is* a wild card. The Bruslans are going to realize that Frederick had nothing to do with the attack on Karsten, that they actually have someone else to fear now. They might even figure out that it's the very assassin they hired. He's on your side, you know, not theirs, and he'll use any means to get at the truth. Your hands were tied because the Bruslans have managed to keep secret all these years which of them were responsible for the assassination attempt on the princess. Poppie's hands aren't tied."

"If you're done singing your guardian's praises, let's get back to Helga."

"I'd rather not. I'm very disappointed with how that meeting went. I'm going to need a little time to get over it."

"Because you don't think she's your mother."

She gasped. "Of course I do. *That's* why it —" She didn't want to finish.

"What?"

She clamped her mouth shut. But she knew he was waiting, albeit patiently. She finally spat out, "It hurt. It actually felt like she rejected me."

He drew her closer to him. To comfort

her? She did suddenly feel like crying, but that was unacceptable.

So it was more to reassure herself that she said, "It will be better next time."

"If I allow another visit."

"Allow!? Do I need to remind you that I stopped being your prisoner when *you* told me who I really am?"

"That is not exactly true."

She sat up straight and faced him, letting the blanket drop to her lap. "What do you mean?"

"You are still the lure to Rastibon's capture."

"I'm sorry, but that isn't grounds to detain me."

He shrugged. "Here it is."

Was he serious? Alana wondered. She was furious! He pulled her back into the crook of his arm. She struggled against him, but he won. She decided to never say another word to him. How the deuce had the barbarian ended up in the sleigh next to her?

CHAPTER FORTY-TWO

The trip down the mountainside went much faster with no snowfall to contend with. Alana even caught some magnificent views while they were still at the higher elevations, but she was too angry to appreciate them. The sun wasn't shining on the road they traveled because of the clouds clinging to the mountaintops, but it was shining down on the valleys below them.

Christoph let her stew in silence for the rest of the trip. He could have tried to justify keeping her in Lubinia against her will, even apologize for what he apparently felt was necessary. But he didn't. He remained silent as well.

At the sleigh house where the trip had begun, he once again tossed her up on his horse for the short ride back to the palace. Not until his arms were cradling her again did he say without inflection, "You noticed how Helga never addressed *you* by name?

What is her daughter's name?"

No, Alana realized she hadn't caught that. Good God, she didn't even know her real name! She'd been too disappointed by Helga's reaction to the news that she was still alive. Helga didn't even give her one hug! Good Lord, you'd think a mother would at least want to do that.

But still furious at Christoph for wanting to use her to trap Poppie, she merely mumbled under her breath, "She still wasn't convinced."

He snorted. She insisted, "I know you can't help your suspicious nature, but you know very well it's uncalled for here."

"Isn't it? She was frightened the moment I said you were her daughter. That wasn't nervousness, Alana. That was pure fear. She was hiding something. And she was lying. It was obvious."

"What the deuce could she be hiding other than her fear that she might lose her plush residence? That probably accounted for most of it, you know. And you never assured her that wouldn't happen. Instead you demanded answers to what she probably explained long ago to Frederick to his satisfaction. You made her rehash all of that pain! I only wanted to know what had prompted her to switch the babies. Besides, she seemed most fearful when Poppie was mentioned. Of course she'd be terrified of him, after what he did."

Alana thought she'd made perfectly good points that might not have occurred to him, certainly good enough to end whatever maggoty suspicion he was having, because he said no more about it. But when they were back in the ward, he didn't ride his horse to his quarters and leave her there. He stopped in the middle of the ward, handed the mount over to a guard, and, after putting her on the ground and taking her hand, began dragging her straight to the palace!

Immediately she knew why. "Oh, my, God," she yelled behind him. "I know what you're doing. Stop! I don't want to be his daughter, I'd rather be Helga's."

"You don't get to choose."

"Don't you dare tell him! You'll get his hopes up for nothing. There has to be a perfectly good explanation for why Helga was so reticent and afraid that has nothing to do with me. She was just too nervous to say. Probably because *you* were there."

"I'm not going to tell him anything — yet."

"Then why are you taking me into the palace!"

"For you to meet him. He will want to apologize to you himself, for such a long separation from your mother."

Christoph was lying! She knew he was! She fought him really hard, to free herself from his grip. She even slipped on the hard-packed snow so he ended up dragging her on the ground for a second before he stopped to help her back up, then picked her up and carried her the rest of the way.

That's how he took her into the palace, and he didn't set her down once they were inside. Down the corridors he carried her, through the commoners' anteroom, straight into the next chamber. It wasn't the throne room as she'd thought, but a wide passageway with some rooms off it, a carpet down its center, and at the end another set of double doors, which she was pretty certain did lead to the king. As it was early afternoon, Christoph obviously expected Frederick to be in there.

She tried one last time in a pleading voice, "Please, don't."

"I have to" was all he said.

He didn't have to knock to gain entrance; in fact, the guards at all the doors had been opening them immediately for him as he approached. His step was brisk, his expression each time she glanced at him grimly determined. Still Christoph didn't put her down when he passed through the last set of doors. But he barked orders for the room to be cleared. She heard the quick shuffling of feet. Not one complaint. He was head of palace security, after all, so apparently, his business, no matter what it was, took precedence.

Alana didn't look to see who was left in the room with them. She'd hidden her face against his chest the moment those last doors had started to open. But then he did set her down, and she gave him a furious glare that might have lasted indefinitely if he hadn't turned her abruptly about to face away from him.

He didn't need to hold her there. She froze, staring at the man she'd seen in the small portrait in the commoners' anteroom, a bit older, but she'd stared at that painting long enough to recognize him now. He came to his feet on the raised dais where two thrones sat. He was regally garbed, though informally, without a crown on his head. At the moment he was merely looking at Christoph for an explanation. But Christoph didn't say a single word. That's when the king's eyes lit on Alana and moved no further.

"My God," Frederick said, awestruck.

He was looking at her in such wonder, he didn't have to say anything else. She felt it, too, felt it the second she saw in his expression that he knew exactly who she was. It was indescribable, the emotion that welled up in her because of it. She had only hoped to feel a smidgen of this when she came face-to-face with her parent, her real parent. She had no idea she'd be overwhelmed with it.

Papa.

She only formed the word on her lips, was afraid to say it aloud. If her bubble burst and she was somehow mistaken in what she was feeling, based solely on his reaction to her, the disappointment would crumble her. But he was already moving toward her, and she took a few steps to close the distance between them. Then she was engulfed in his arms, and warmth and love were in the word when she repeated it.

"Papa."

She was crying. She couldn't help it. And laughing. She couldn't help that, either. And Frederick wouldn't let go of her, was holding her too tight, but that was all right, too. It didn't even matter to her anymore that he was a king. Nothing could disturb this newfound happiness — not even the vague sound of Christoph swearing behind them.

CHAPTER FORTY-THREE

"When did you know?" Frederick asked.

Christoph didn't answer immediately. He was still swearing! Alana had chosen to stop listening to him after she caught a few of his more vulgar words. So she was standing happily in the circle of her father's arms, her cheek pressed against his chest, oblivious to everything else. Frederick wasn't embracing her as tightly now, but he still wasn't letting go of her, either. She had no idea how long they had stood like that, soaking in the reality of each other.

But she definitely heard her father's question and noticed how long it took Christoph to finally answer. "I wasn't sure," he said. "But our meeting with the nursemaid this morning left a sour taste. I felt you needed to see her for yourself before I tried to make sense of this and explain my suspicions."

"What made you suspect?"

"Helga didn't act as a mother should. She displayed angry disbelief when presented with a daughter returned from the dead, then fearful acceptance, but not once the joy of a mother reunited with her child. She felt it, too, no connection to her," Christoph added, nodding at Alana. "That they weren't related at all."

Alana had to address that and turned to do so. Frederick resisted taking his arms off her so she could, but he put one arm around her shoulder instead, still unwilling to lose touch with her.

"I didn't say that," she told Christoph. "Only that it felt like we were strangers."

He shrugged. "The same thing."

"Send for Helga Engel immediately," Frederick ordered. "I want to know why she did this to me."

"She is already on her way here," Christoph said. "When news of the attack was brought to me, we had to leave before I could voice my doubts to her. But I left a man there to escort her to the palace. Before the end of the day I promise you will have a full account of why she convinced you that her daughter was yours."

Alana interjected, "She did give a reason, you know she did."

"What?" Frederick asked, looking between them.

Christoph answered, "She said she was terrified of what would be done to her if something happened to the princess, that she would be blamed for it. She could have made up that story about switching the babies the very night the princess disappeared, not done so weeks sooner. But there is no point in speculating when we will have the answers today." Then Christoph nodded toward Alana. "I gather she actually looks like your first wife, Queen Avelina?"

"Yes, uncannily so. But I feel it here, too." Frederick put a hand to his heart. "There is no doubt."

Christoph nodded. "I understand. I will leave you alone to get acquainted. I am pleased for you both."

Frederick laughed. "You don't sound pleased."

Christoph waved a hand to excuse his manner. "This was not expected, as you know. I've been wrong before, but not to this extent."

He started to leave, but Frederick's voice stopped him. "Christoph, did you do — what we last discussed?"

Christoph hesitated only a moment before

giving a brief nod. Frederick stiffened. "That is . . . unfortunate."

Christoph merely nodded again in agreement before he walked out of the room. Alana wasn't sure what had just happened, but her father was obviously upset about it.

Staring at the closed door, then at her father, Alana realized that cryptic question had been about Christoph's treatment of her during his interrogations, which had been quite rough.

"He's a barbarian," Alana agreed, as if to say, *What more would you expect?* But then she realized whom she was saying that to and gasped.

But Frederick smiled as he led her to the edge of the raised throne platform, where he sat her down and sat beside her, stretching out his long legs before him and crossing them at his ankles. Such an unkinglike thing to do! Alana thought. It made her relax more than anything else he could have done just then.

"Occasionally, he is exactly that," Frederick agreed with her. "And occasionally, it is useful. But most Lubinians resist change. At least my nobles try to progress, instead of clinging to the comfort of old ways. They set good examples — most of the time. Becker is very good at what he does, in whatever manner he does it."

Alana realized now that she was finally under her father's protection, she wouldn't have to deal with Christoph's high-handed manner ever again. She should complain about him, is what she should do. She owed him a little retribution, didn't she? But it could wait. This was more important. Her father! And for the moment, she had his undivided attention.

They both said at exactly the same time, "Tell me — ," and they both stopped to laugh at each other, for having the same thought.

At his nod for her to go first, she asked for something she really wanted. "Is there a portrait of my mother somewhere? I know there is none here in the palace, but —"

"There is one, a miniature I keep in my bureau. I will show it to you later. My current wife, Nikola, knows I keep it. She doesn't mind if I take it out occasionally and look at it. She's a wonderful woman. I'm not ashamed to say I love them both."

"But my mother, she's —"

"Yes, she's dead. But that doesn't mean I have stopped loving her."

Alana felt tears well in her eyes. That was beautifully said. She hoped a man would feel like that about her someday.

"Now tell me about this man who — raised you. I promise to contain my rage."

She started, though she should have expected her father to feel this way. "Don't hate him, please. Like you just said about your two wives, I love you both."

"Then tell me why you do."

For three hours they talked there in the throne room, alone, without stopping. Alana felt it wasn't nearly enough time. She had a whole life to talk about. So did he. And she found out it was her grandmother, Avelina's mother, who'd had the black hair!

Several officials looked in on them, but only to make sure the king was all right. He shooed them away. A woman came, for the same reason. He shooed her away, too, but with a smile and the promise that he would join her soon with a surprise. His wife, he explained to Alana. She'd guessed as much.

But then Christoph showed up again, and there was no shooing *him* off.

CHAPTER FORTY-FOUR

"We will not get the confession you want today, Highness," Christoph said as he marched briskly across the room to give his report.

Christoph knew he could have waited to deliver this bad news, at least until father and daughter had left this room where they were getting acquainted. He *knew* that he was intruding, but he didn't care. He'd had no idea how difficult it was going to be to lose possession of this woman when he had only just begun entertaining thoughts of a permanent relationship with her.

Yesterday when his mother had looked so hopeful that he'd found someone he could actually bring home to them, who wasn't merely a mistress, he'd begun to think how he might keep Alana. He'd even had a thought that he'd never had before for any other woman: marriage. His family would be delighted by it, and he'd been surprised to feel no resistance to the idea at all. But she hadn't been the princess then. Now she was.

Yet he'd tried to wait to deliver this report. He'd been informed of what had happened two hours ago. He'd waited that long to give them this time together alone.

He couldn't take his eyes off Alana now. Even when she looked down and away from him as soon as she noticed his gaze on her. Even when he continued the report for Frederick, he was looking at her as he spoke.

"A man hiding at the side of the mountain road commandeered the sleigh bringing Helga Engel to the palace. He took my guard by surprise and pushed him out of the sleigh at knifepoint, then raced off in the sleigh with the woman. He might have been on his way to the chalet to see Helga Engel and decided to attack when he saw her in the sleigh coming down the road. My guard described the man as short and thin, his face covered by a hood."

Alana winced at the brief description he'd given of the thief. Christoph had already guessed it had been Rastibon. Who else would want to keep Helga Engel from reaching the palace? Alana's reaction, which seemed to indicate she was having the same thought, confirmed it in his mind.

But Frederick said, "You are searching the city for them?"

"Certainly, but he will expect that. I doubt he will take her there." And to Alana: "Why would your Poppie want to rescue Helga Engel?"

"Why do you assume that was his motive? He wouldn't do something like that unless he was after answers. But I don't see why he would be, unless he somehow found out I went to visit her. You haven't given him any access to me, so he might have thought she could tell him what that visit was about. But there was no way he could have known about it unless he followed us out of the city."

"He didn't follow us, but, yes, he knew."

She frowned. "How?"

"Your young friend came to visit you this morning before we got back. I had hoped he might, so I told the gate guard to tell him where I had taken you before escorting him out of the fortress."

She gasped. "You were hoping Henry would try to reach me again, weren't you? You set that up deliberately!"

Christoph shrugged. "It was worth trying if it would draw out your guardian."

"Who is Henry?" Frederick asked.

"An English orphan Poppie and I are very

fond of."

"They aren't to be killed, Christoph," Frederick said. "She has strong feelings for them, but especially for this man who raised her. I will not have her grieve over him."

"I understand," Christoph said. "But I still need answers from him. He knows things we don't."

"He doesn't!" Alana exclaimed. "I've told you that's what he's doing here, finding those same answers you're looking for. Why can't you just work with him?"

"That isn't an option until he stands before me," Christoph said.

She seemed surprised. "Are you saying you *will* work with him now?"

"Are you saying you will now help to bring us together, for your father's sake?"

"Not if you're going to treat him the way you treated me and throw him in your prison!"

She gasped the second the last word was out, even put her hand over her mouth and looked at her father with wide eyes. Christoph prepared himself for Frederick's wrath. He'd put the princess of Lubinia in prison. He would have had to confess that at some point, but he'd hoped to resolve other issues first before he was dismissed from his job. Alana had warned him she'd make him pay for it. Perhaps she'd forgotten that because she seemed surprised now that she'd inadvertently done exactly that.

Frederick, who had been watching with interest as they argued, left his inscrutable gaze on Christoph.

"It would appear you did your job to the letter?" Frederick questioned.

"Yes, I did."

Frederick turned to his daughter, and notably, emotion slipped into his tone. "Were you hurt?"

"No, not hurt, just frustrated. A lot. And mortified with embarrassment. And, well, frightened a bit whenever he unleashed his barbarian side," she finished indignantly.

Frederick's golden brow rose, but turned on Christoph again. "A bit?"

Tight-lipped, he replied, "She wasn't frightened for long. She had too much courage for that approach to work effectively. Argumentative. Furious. Absolutely insistent on convincing me who — she actually is."

Frederick turned to cup Alana's cheeks in his hands. For a brief moment pride was in his expression at the description Christoph had just given of her, before that expression turned grave.

"You know what we thought, the only thing we could think, given the lie that was perpetrated and believed so long ago," the king told her. "You might have lived out your life, away from here, never knowing who you really are, and I would never have guessed you were still alive. Rastibon brought you back to me. He didn't have to do that. As much as I hate him for what he did, at some point I will summon the generosity of spirit to thank him for keeping you safe all this time. He won't be harmed, I give you my word. I cannot say the same of Helga Engel. Her lie affected many decisions that would have been very different, were the truth known. It was easy to be convinced not to take action against the suspects when we thought they had failed, when that action, at that time, could have provoked another civil war. What you must understand is that Christoph was doing a job he's very good at. I don't want you holding any part of it against him, when he had his orders from me to use any means necessary to get at the truth behind — what we thought was your impersonation."

Frederick turned to Christoph and ordered, "You will guard Alana's safety — and that's all — in the most professional manner until further notice."

CHAPTER FORTY-FIVE

Leonard knew of the abandoned, half-burned-down farm far from the road near the foothills. He'd found it when he was a child and had lost his way home. No one had torn it down back then because no one had wanted to replace it. That was apparently still the case all these years later. He didn't expect so much of it, two of the four walls, to still be standing, though. He was able to hide the sleigh behind them.

After kicking rubble and useless furniture aside for several minutes, he found the root cellar. He lifted the trapdoor and dragged the woman down the old stairs, closing the door behind them. He had unhooked the sleigh lantern and taken it with him, so they had light. It stopped flickering now that they were out of the cold wind. He had to knock ancient cobwebs aside so he could set the lantern on a broken shelf. He laid a blanket on the floor, set the woman down on it, then sat beside her.

He was surprised she hadn't once tried to remove the blanket he'd tossed over her head. He'd just wanted to keep her covered during the swift ride so the wind wouldn't cut into her face. He removed the blanket now and saw why she hadn't done so. She was terrified, and the moment he unwrapped his own face cover, she recognized him and began wailing.

"Don't be afraid," Leonard quickly told her. "I'm not going to hurt you, Helga, I swear."

The fear didn't leave her eyes. He wasn't sure she even heard him. He kissed her gently. Confusion took the place of her fear.

He smiled at her, confessing, "I've thought of you often over the years, more than I should have. I was more fond of you than I anticipated. It wasn't part of the plan for that to happen. In the end, it changed how I performed that job I was hired for. I should have killed you, but I couldn't. I didn't even want you to suffer the horror of waking up to find your charge dead, so I took her with me to finish the job elsewhere away from the palace. Because of you."

"But you didn't kill her!"

His mouth turned wry. "No, I couldn't do that, either. She won my heart with a smile.

It changed me, completely. Because of her, I'm not the man I was."

"You stopped killing?" she asked hesitantly.

"Yes, we lived a fairly normal life."

"You're — not angry with me?"

"Why would I be?"

"You just abducted me! Terrified me! You" — she glanced around her — "bring me to a cellar!"

He touched her cheek gently. "I'm sorry, there was no other way. I'm a wanted man here, and you were with a palace guard. I was on my way to the chalet to speak with you. It appeared you were being escorted to the palace. Once there, I wouldn't have been able to reach you."

"But a cellar!"

"I can't afford to be seen by anyone, Helga. I am being searched for diligently. And now you will be searched for as well until I take you back. I wanted to talk to you in private, out of the cold, without being seen by anyone. I didn't have many options. I remembered this old place, far from the roads, far from any village."

"This cellar is not warm," she pointed out, hugging her arms.

"But it's not freezing, and we won't be here long."

"You intend to take me back to the chalet?"

"If you want to go back, yes."

"Why — did you want to speak privately with me?" she asked cautiously.

"I found out that Alana was taken to the king's chalet to visit you. It was an obvious trap for me. That was too much information to be given of her whereabouts."

"You would have willingly walked into that trap?"

"No, I wouldn't have been able to get to her, not surrounded by guards as she was. But I only found out about her trip this morning, a day after she began it. I saw her returned to the palace before I started up the mountain."

"To see me," she said uncomfortably.

"To see you, yes. I visited your old house, but others live there now. I had no way to find you, until I heard she went to see you and where. Now, I do need to know what that visit was about. And you can tell me how she has fared. You do know, don't you?"

Color drained from her face. She tried to turn around so he wouldn't see it. He put his hands on her shoulders to stop her. He was alarmed now, thinking something bad had happened to Alana.

"Tell me!"

"They — they think she's mine."

"What?" he said incredulously.

"They think she's my daughter!"

"How?" he got out before he realized, "My God, that's why Frederick didn't tear heaven and earth apart looking for her, isn't it? You made him believe you saved his daughter?"

"I had to! I let you in! They would have killed us if they found out!"

His mind was moving frantically ahead. So many other things made sense now. But she was crying again. Keening loudly again.

He asked gently, "What did you tell the other nursemaid when she returned?"

"She knew. She was terrified, too. I convinced her we would both be blamed if she didn't agree I had switched the babies to keep the princess safe. After we agreed, she went to report what had happened. I remembered too late that there was one man who had seen the princess recently, the physician who had been tasked to check on her. Others came first, telling me how sorry they were that my baby was missing. I barely heard them. I knew the truth would come out as soon as the physician arrived. I was paralyzed, they thought with grief, but with fear, because he would recognize that the baby left behind wasn't Alana Stindal."

"He never arrived to do that?"

"He did. He'd been told before he got there that the princess was safe and he looked at my child and said, 'Yes, she is, thank God.' "

Leonard frowned. "Was he part of the plot to have her killed?"

She laughed a little hysterically. "No, just a man who didn't do his job. I thought he'd had a good look at her the day he came to check on her, but I can only guess that he had too many things on his mind, in particular, his anger that a man as important as he was had been sent on what he considered a lowly task. That grievance he made clear with how abrupt he was with me that day."

Leonard was incredulous again that all of that had occurred without his knowing or guessing any of it. "So he confirmed the baby still there was the princess and you went along with it?"

"What else could I do? Admit I snuck the man in who stole her?!"

She screamed that at him. She was too emotional. He put his arms around her. It didn't help, it just produced more crying.

"That must have been a very difficult time for you. I'm sorry, Helga, truly I am. I should have taken you with me, you and your daughter. But you still had her —"

"I didn't! They soon took her away to hide her. They knew that all I did day and night was cry, so they wouldn't let *me* go with her. I begged them to, but they expressly forbid it because I was in such deep grief over losing my baby. They praised me for what I'd done. They rewarded me! But I never saw her again."

"I'll find her for you wherever they still have her hidden so you and she —"

She leaned back to pound on his chest in anguish. "She's dead! She died when she was seven! And for every one of those years I was terrified every single day that as she grew older she might start to look like me and the king might suspect what I had done. She was already lost to me, I would never see her again. And living with that fear for so long, it was almost a relief when she died! It was Frederick himself who came to tell me. Even in his own raging grief, he spared a thought for me, assuring me that what I had done had at least given him seven years to love her."

Leonard sighed with the realization. "So that wasn't a mock funeral after all they had for her."

"No."

"And Frederick let the country think she

was missing so it would never happen again."

"Yes!"

Leonard was stating things tonelessly, not actually asking for confirmation, but then his thoughts continued down the logical path and it finally occurred to him: "My God, they haven't believed Alana's story, who she really is? Instead of convincing them, they've now convinced *her* she's yours? You let her think that?!"

Helga covered her head with her arms, thinking he was going to hit her. He thought he heard her cry, "They'll kill me. I can't tell them, I can't."

"It's all right, you don't have to. I'll let her know even if I have to break into the palace to do so. This can't go on any longer."

"Don't do that. I think he already knows."

"The king?"

"No, his captain of palace security, the man who brought her to me. I could see he was suspicious. And he left a man there to take me to the palace without telling me why. It was to confront me without her being present to hear him! I know it!"

"Hush," he said, trying to soothe her with his hands. "I won't let that happen. I'll take you away from here where you will never

have to be afraid again. I owe you that much
— for trusting in me."

CHAPTER FORTY-SIX

"She's alive!" Nikola said as she returned to the sitting room where she had left Auberta to find out what was keeping Frederick from joining them. "She's with him right now!"

"My goodness, you're so excited," Auberta said. "Who's alive?"

Nikola was so thrilled by this news she simply couldn't contain it. "Frederick's daughter, Alana! He didn't admit it, he only said he had a wonderful surprise for me, that he would join me soon. But he didn't have to say. I've seen the portrait of her mother. She looks just like Avelina!"

Auberta appeared to be in shock, and Nikola realized too late why her friend might not be ecstatic about this news. "I'm sorry," she added gently. "I know you hoped Frederick would name Karsten as his successor, and Alana's return changes everything."

"I am amazed, of course, but — actually, Nikola, I must confess I had a much happier hope so long ago when Princess Alana was born, that she and Karsten, nearly the same age, would make such a perfect couple."

"You mean marriage?"

"Certainly. It would do what we have both hoped for, unite our two families and put an end to all this dreadful hostility and fighting once and for all."

Nikola bit her lip. "I don't know if Frederick would welcome that idea after the attack on the palace. . . ."

"I told you that was a mistake. Karsten didn't even know his men took it upon themselves to avenge the assault on him. He was beaten terribly, the dear boy. He was barely able to get out of bed last night, though he assured me no matter how painful it is, he will come this very night to tell Frederick how appalled he is over this mistake. It was one of his young, hotheaded cousins who rallied his men to blame Frederick for the deed. It was *not* Karsten's doing, Nikola, I promise you. He loves Frederick. He would never do anything to harm Lubinia. And this is the very sort of misunderstanding that will never occur again if our two families are joined in matrimony. You must agree it would be the ideal solution."

"Yes, I do, but —"

"Then use your influence with your husband. He'll listen to you. Remind him of your many miscarriages caused by all this turmoil. By the way, are you pregnant again, my dear? You do look a little peaked. Shall I pour you another cup of tea?"

They weren't going to hide Alana's presence. The palace would soon be buzzing with the news that she'd been returned from the dead, as it were, and she'd been warned to answer no questions about it from anyone, that Frederick would make an announcement later, after conferring with his advisers.

Christoph remained behind with Alana when Frederick left to tell his wife the good news. Alana would be joining the royal couple tonight for dinner after she was settled in her new rooms.

She supposed she ought to thank Christoph. She might have returned to England, blithely unaware that she was Frederick's daughter after all, if not for Christoph's suspicious nature. But he was standing there so stiffly. The word *dutiful* came to mind. Did he find it onerous that he'd been *ordered* to be her protector? He hadn't seemed to mind it before — when she wasn't a

432

princess. He'd even alluded to his duty never having been so pleasant before!

"Is something wrong?" she asked him as he took her arm to escort her to her new quarters.

"What could possibly be wrong? You are where you should be, and I am your humble servant."

Her eyes narrowed at the sarcasm she detected. "So it's to be like that, is it? Are you angry because I was right all along and you obstinately refused to see it?"

He was dragging her along behind him by then in his typical fashion. He didn't answer, probably because it had been an unfair question, asked in annoyance. But she dug in her heels. She didn't like this stiffly silent attitude of his at all.

"What?" he finally said, having stopped when she did.

She glanced up at him. Still so damn handsome he could dazzle her. But the outer shell didn't make a man. What was inside did, and he definitely had a brute inside him that he'd let out much too often. When she was his prisoner, she reminded herself. Well, mostly. But there was that gentle, sweet side of him, too. . . .

She sighed to herself, but said to him, "Nothing," and moved forward again.

The room she'd been given was too lavish, she thought, but then it was fit for a princess, she supposed. She didn't feel like one yet, didn't think she ever would. Big, too much room, two maids already waiting to serve her. All she did was unpack and change her clothes for dinner — and sit on the big, fluffy bed for a while in a daze with her thoughts.

Then the knock came at the door. She was suddenly excited about seeing her father again, and meeting his wife. But it was *him* standing there, just as still and stoic as before, and that just brought her mood back down.

"Why do you have to escort me?" she demanded as she stepped out of the room. "I'm in the palace finally, I don't need you guarding me in here —"

"Be quiet," he cut in, though he didn't appear annoyed. "You complain too much — Princess."

"With good reason! Your attitude has been abominable since you turned me over to my father. If you don't want to protect me anymore, just tell him so. I'm sure you think you have much better things to do, and I even agree."

"I have been given my orders. Do *not* tempt me from them."

She frowned, not quite understanding what he meant. "Tempt you to abandon your duty? Of course you won't. But you obviously don't like having to continue to guard me so closely, even to the point of escorting me about the palace. I'll discuss it with my father tonight if you won't."

That brought a frown to his face as he took her arm to lead her down the hall again. "Leave it go. It's my duty now to protect you, not just my wish to do so, but my duty. *You* need to get over your grievance with me and accept that."

She clamped her mouth shut. Her biggest grievance with him was his treating her like a stranger — no, like a *princess!* Completely annoyed now, she tried to walk ahead of him even though she didn't know where she was going! But when she saw the eight guards standing at attention outside the wide double doors, it was a pretty good guess that she could stop there.

The guards didn't open the door for her, not with their captain by her side. But Christoph didn't either. When she glanced at him, he was lifting off a pouch she hadn't noticed that he'd hung over the hilt of the saber he wore on his hip. He handed it to her.

"This was delivered to me today, found in

the house of the thief's parents."

It was a ratty pouch, not hers, and must have belonged to that guard. When she looked inside it, all she saw was glitter. Her jewelry.

"The bracelet?" she asked.

"No, apparently someone else got there before my men did."

"Guessing I was back wasn't enough, I suppose. They wanted proof."

"You still think Rainier tried to kill you when he's admitted everything else except that?"

"Which is the bigger offense?"

"True."

"Not that it matters now, when my presence is no longer a secret," she said, unable to hide her nervousness over that.

He started to touch her cheek, but drew his hand back. "I won't let anything happen to you, Alana."

He opened the door for her as he said that, but he didn't follow her in. She was so aware of him that as soon as she stepped through the doorway, she noticed he wasn't at her side and glanced back.

"You're not coming in?"

"I wasn't invited."

He smiled and she couldn't even tell what it implied — tenderness, regret? She couldn't tell! But then it occurred to her that he was probably just glad to finally have some time away from her. Annoyed with that thought, she said, "Good," and closed the door on him.

But she had to take a deep breath before she approached her new family, to shake off the bad mood Christoph's reticence had brought on. He was behaving as if they were strangers now, and she was afraid it was because her identity had been confirmed. Did he consider her so high above his station that he could no longer be himself with her? But this cold, stiff alternative was infuriating her so much, it was making her testy about everything.

Nikola, the current queen, didn't wait for her to reach the private dining alcove she and Frederick were seated at. She rose and rushed across the room with arms open, a beautiful smile on her lovely face. She wrapped those arms about Alana with warmth and feeling.

"You cannot know the peace your presence gives me, the weight it takes from my shoulders, that I am no longer solely responsible for carrying on my husband's line." That was said in a whisper, before Nikola released her and added, "You and I, we are going to be best friends, if you will it."

Alana grinned. She hadn't expected to be made that welcome by her father's wife, but she had no doubt the queen had just meant every word. A new friend. Yes, she felt that, too.

Her father, beaming, insisted they join him, and before he seated her, he handed Alana the miniature of her mother. She began to cry as she looked at it. No wonder he'd known she was his daughter the moment he saw her. The portrait could have been her in an old-fashioned gown, except with blond hair.

"Remarkable, isn't it?" he said.

"Indeed." Wiping her eyes, Alana laughed. "If Christoph had just taken me around to find some of the people who had known her, we probably would have met much sooner."

"We were both convinced —"

"I know," she quickly assured him. "It's all right. At least he figured it out in the end."

"He does deserve the credit, I agree."

This wasn't said with glowing praise, and she had the same feeling again that she'd had in the throne room, that her father was angry with Christoph for some reason. She started to ask why, but the door opened again with a new arrival. Apparently this wasn't to be just a family dinner after all.

She hid her disappointment as she was introduced to Auberta Bruslan, and hid her shock, too, when it became apparent that her father and stepmother considered this Bruslan a dear friend! But she soon found out why. Who couldn't like such a sweet old lady? And she wasn't a blood Bruslan, she'd merely married into that family when Ernest Bruslan had made her his queen. Auberta even cried a little, she was so overcome with emotion, genuinely delighted with Alana's reappearance, and so happy for Frederick to have his daughter back.

The dinner progressed pleasantly, but then Alana was surprised again when the talk turned to the recent attack on the palace that had been perpetrated by Auberta's relatives! Apparently, most of her family was appalled by it.

"I'm so glad you were understanding today when Karsten spoke with you, Frederick," Auberta said. "He was so outraged that his men took it upon themselves to avenge him before he even awoke to say who had accosted him."

"I know Karsten had nothing to do with it," Frederick assured her. "Those of his men we captured admitted he hadn't even regained consciousness before they took matters into their own hands. I've asked him to come by to meet Alana tonight, if he's feeling up to it."

Karsten Bruslan arrived when dinner was almost over. Alana was mortified to see how bruised he was, knowing Poppie had done that to him and she had to keep that information to herself. Despite the bruises, he was still handsome and courtly as he bent over her hand to kiss it. But then his eyes widened, recognizing her from the festival.

"Oh, good Lord." He laughed. "That barbarian idiot didn't realize who you were?"

She stiffened over the insult to Christoph, saying immediately, "He was still unraveling the facts. Did you expect him to just take me at my word when others had come before me, claiming to be the princess?"

"Interesting, how quickly you defend him."

She blushed and returned to her seat. But Karsten didn't say anything else disparaging; in fact, he was quickly entertaining them with his wit and charm. The man was actually likable, she soon realized, as much as his grandmother was.

But before the evening ended, her father took her aside, hugged her, and confided happily, "I'm delighted to see you and

Karsten have taken to each other so quickly. It has already been pointed out what a great political union it will be, if you two marry, but also and more importantly, this will unite our country once more, putting an end to the infighting that has nearly brought us to war again."

Alana was speechless with shock. Marry her into the very family that had probably tried to kill her? She groaned inwardly. Did her father have to make it sound as if this was his fondest wish? It couldn't have been worse timing, when right now she felt such a strong desire to please him no matter what. But how could she marry Karsten when she suspected she was already in love with her barbarian — oh, God, was she? Was that why she was so hurt and frustrated that Christoph appeared to want to distance himself from her even though he was forced to still protect her?

CHAPTER FORTY-SEVEN

As tired as she'd been from such an emotional day, Alana stayed with her father much longer than she should have last night. But she kept putting off leaving because she was afraid Christoph was still out there waiting to escort her back to her room, and she didn't want him to sense how disappointed she was that she couldn't think of a way out of marrying a *Bruslan* without having an argument with her father about it, which was out of the question. Did Christoph know yet what her father was planning? No, of course not. He would have said something. She was sure he would at least have warned her, so it wouldn't have been such a shock.

Her ploy to avoid seeing Christoph worked because he wasn't there when she finally left. Two of her father's guards had escorted her to her room instead.

She still didn't get right to sleep last night

with so much on her mind. Poppie had warned her that her father would pick her husband for her, but he hadn't thought it would happen so soon, neither of them did. But oddly enough, that wasn't what was keeping her awake.

She didn't try to fight back the memories of those nights with Christoph this time. She had managed to banish them from her thoughts because, just as she'd told him, she'd never engage in that kind of intimacy with him again. So it would have been pure folly to remember something that wonderful. But now, for some reason, she let herself indulge in a little foolishness.

Her father had mentioned giving her a tour of the palace this morning. When the knock came at the door, she was ready for it and waved back the servant who moved to answer it. Bright and early, the two young women had shown up with platters of food and smiles, ready to wait on her hand and foot. She was going to have to get used to that because they seemed to think they had to stay constantly at her side. She'd tried to shoo them away, but then they'd looked as if she were punishing them!

A guard was standing outside the door, not her father. The two guards who had escorted her last night were standing there at attention, too, plus four new ones! She'd had no idea they would be guarding her door all night. But the new man merely handed her a message. She opened it and stared at a page full of Lubinian text, then asked the guard what it was about.

Christoph came around the corner just then and barked an order at the guard, who quickly marched off. Christoph must just have come in from outside because he was still wearing his long overcoat and fur cap.

"Is there a problem?" he asked her.

"Yes, I was given this without explanation." She handed the note to him.

"It's from the king. He regrets he can't join you this morning and suggests tomorrow morning instead. I was made aware of this and was coming to inform you. But the guard wouldn't have known anything about it. You really shouldn't talk to my men, your father wouldn't like it."

The last was said in such a scolding tone, she demanded, "Why not?"

"Because you're the princess, and soldiers are beneath your notice." But then he sighed. "I think the palace will need to make adjustments, now that a princess is among us."

It sounded more as if he would need to make adjustments, but she couldn't resist reminding him, "You're a soldier. Are you now beneath my notice, too?"

His expression turned slightly annoyed at that, but all he said was "Fetch your coat, you're going outdoors."

One of the maids had heard him and was already rushing forward with the coat. Another came running with Alana's cap. In mere seconds, they had her garbed to venture outside, and Christoph was already walking her down the hallway. She gave him a moment to tell her where he was taking her, but soon realized he wasn't going to! Did he really think he could continue treating her like his prisoner?

"Where — ?" she began, but didn't bother to finish. His stride was too quick, his manner too stiff, and she didn't feel like shouting to be heard.

Outside the main palace entrance, she recognized his horse being held there for him. He mounted and reached for her hand to help her up.

She crossed her arms over her chest instead, a mulish twist to her lips. "You will say where we are going or I'm not going. You can't use this high-handed manner with me anymore. I outrank you!"

He burst out laughing, and swiftly, before she could step back out of the way, he

445

reached down to catch her under her arms, lifted her, and placed her sideways in front of him.

"Rank has nothing to do with it. I'm your official protector, which means, Princess, you must do as I say."

He didn't sound as if he was gloating, but she didn't doubt he was. "And if I object?"

"You can always complain to the king."

"Why don't I complain to you instead? I have a feeling I'll be doing a lot of that."

He bent forward, close enough that she could feel his warm breath on her face. For a moment she thought he was going to kiss her right there in the ward! But he said no more and she realized it was because he'd noticed Henry hurrying across the ward to them. She tried to get back off the horse, but Christoph held her tight.

Stopping beside the horse, Henry looked up at Christoph and beseeched, "A word wi' 'er, m'lord?"

"You're welcome in the palace now," Christoph told the boy. "You can visit her anytime. If what you have to say won't wait, then speak."

Henry looked utterly frustrated for a moment, but then he surprised them both by stepping on Christoph's boot in the stirrup and hoisting himself up farther using

Alana's skirt. He leaned to the side away from Christoph and whispered to her, "Beware the queen," then jumped back down and hurried away.

Alana frowned as she watched Henry go. Christoph didn't move and she realized he was merely waiting for her to explain. "Tell me," he said.

"It made no sense, so I'd rather not repeat it."

"Alana, I will guard your life with my own," he said sternly. "But to do that, you can keep no more secrets from me. Repeat what he told you."

She repeated the message, then added, "Poppie must be on the wrong trail — or is there something about Nikola that I'm not aware of?"

"Queen Nikola is above reproach. She adores Frederick and she wasn't old enough to be involved in that old conspiracy."

She heard the anger in his tone and even agreed, "I would have said the same thing, but —"

"There is more than one queen who resides in this country, Alana."

She almost laughed. He meant that sweet old lady she'd met last night. That was even more absurd, yet she would rather believe that than that her father's loving wife might

447

not be as loving as he thought.

Christoph started moving them slowly toward the gate. Lost in her thoughts over that garbled message — maybe she'd missed some of it — she almost didn't notice the guards in the ward. One by one, as soon as they saw her, they were dropping to one knee and placing a fist to their chests as they bowed toward her. It nearly brought tears to her eyes.

"It didn't take long for them to love you," Christoph said in a soft tone.

Then Alana heard him add, "Just like me." But he said it so softly she couldn't be sure.

CHAPTER FORTY-EIGHT

It took a while for Alana's tears to dry. She waited until they did, unwilling to let Christoph know she'd cried. Then she turned her head to glance up at him. His eyes had already been on her, she realized, when she met his gaze immediately. Such a pensive look, as if he were trying to read her thoughts.

She wasn't sure where he was taking her now, but obviously it was going to require a sleigh again, because he was riding to the sleigh house. A sleigh was again already waiting outside the building for him, the same driver as before already on his perch.

Christoph stopped right next to the sleigh, close enough to lift her carefully down into it before he dismounted to join her. "Don't you think it's about time you told me where you're taking me?" she asked.

"Your father suggested a fun outing for you. I thought you might like to visit the wolf pups again. But if you can think of something you'd rather do . . ."

She'd rather just ride around cuddled in his arms, but of course she couldn't say that. "Seeing the puppies again would be nice, actually."

He nodded and directed the driver where to go before he wrapped her in blankets again.

"Was that really my father's idea, or was it yours?"

"His. He's concerned you didn't take too well something he told you last night."

That was an understatement. Recalling her shock over the marriage he favored for her, she asked, "Did he tell *you* what he suggested?"

"Of course — and he assured me I won't have to guard you much longer."

She sucked in her breath. "He mentioned nothing about *soon!*"

Christoph suddenly put his hand to her belly. "His reason for making haste is valid." His eyes dropped to her midsection as well so she couldn't mistake his meaning.

She blushed furiously, mortified at the realization that her father knew she'd been intimate with Christoph. But there was no evidence that there had been a consequence. Why couldn't they wait to be sure first? And then it really sank in — a baby? Good Lord, she'd never once thought of it before today, and *that* thought wasn't the least bit embarrassing, was actually a wonderful thought. A baby. Theirs . . .

A moment of wonder passed between them, but it was brief. She looked away before Christoph could see how painful she found the thought that her time with him would soon end. Her father might appreciate his work, but he still wouldn't let her marry Christoph, even if she was carrying his child. He was merely a glorified soldier, not good enough for a princess.

"I suppose that's why he's angry with you?" she asked tonelessly.

"He's a father. He's reacting the way any father would."

She had to blame something for this pain, it was starting to choke her. "But how did he even find out unless you told him. Why would you do that?!"

"It doesn't matter how he knows" was all Christoph said.

She sighed and mumbled, "I don't want to marry Karsten, you know."

He turned her face to his so he could look into her eyes. She sensed a sudden change in him. Whatever he saw, it made him smile before he said, "Good, then maybe I won't have to kill him."

She sighed in exasperation. As if that would help anything, but of course he didn't even mean it.

"You didn't tell him how you feel about it, did you?" he added.

"Of course not, he's so bloody happy about the idea, how could I?"

"So his happiness is more important than your own?"

"You don't understand. I've just been reunited with him. I am so incredulous at how that went, how the love was just there, instantly, as if we'd never been separated. I don't want to upset him!"

"If you want to save Karsten's life, you might rethink that."

"Oh, stop it. You aren't going to kill him." She glanced at him, and he actually looked as if he was savoring the thought. She rolled her eyes. "I don't even think this was my father's idea. I mean, he loves the idea, obviously, but I think it was Nikola who suggested the match."

"I'm not surprised. She wants an end to the hostilities more than anyone. There are even whispers that her fears have caused her many miscarriages."

Alana sighed again. "I wish I could talk to Poppie. There must have been more to

Henry's last message and I just didn't hear it all."

"Perhaps you will today."

She looked at him sharply. "Tell me this outing isn't a trap?"

She had hoped for a denial, but didn't get it. "At your father's suggestion. But you aren't to worry. I won't harm him. You've had Frederick's word on that."

"That's all fine and good, but I don't have Poppie's word that he won't harm you!"

Christoph laughed. "You worry for me?"

"Not one jot!" she insisted. "But how is it going to look if he kills you? I don't think my father will be very benevolent if that happens."

He smiled. "It won't happen while you're with me, or did you sing his praises for becoming a new and better man a bit too much? Do you really think he would spill blood in front of you? Now might be a good time to admit that, if it's so?"

"Why? He can't single-handedly stop this sleigh anyway, or were you going to stop it and invite him to join us? Yes, of course you are, all very civil — before you cart him off to prison. You knew Henry was waiting out in the ward for me, didn't you? That's why you rushed me out there!"

"Very persistent, your little friend."

She glared at him. "And once again you didn't tell me?" Then she guessed, "My father didn't really cancel our meeting this morning, did he? You told him Henry had come with another message for me and this would be a golden opportunity!"

She was suddenly so furious she felt like screaming.

Christoph didn't admit or deny it. He didn't say another word, as if *he* saw nothing amiss in what he'd done. It was such a blatant example of his high-handed manner, making decisions for her, proceeding with them regardless of her feelings. But she managed to get her anger under control. His silence helped.

So she was a bit surprised to hear his own thoughts were still with Henry. As soon as the sleigh began heading up into the hills, he said, "I am beginning to like that boy. Very aggressive in his worry over you. Very courageous to argue with my men. He reminds me of myself at that age."

"I doubt that," she said scathingly. "You were probably out smashing something with clubs like all the other little barbarians, while he carves beautiful figures out of wood that amaze and delight people."

He chuckled over her assessment and bent down to take something out of his saddlebag to hand to her. "These are his work?"

It was the two carvings Henry had made for her. She hadn't even noticed they weren't in her trunks that had been brought to her new room in the palace.

"Why do you have them?"

He shrugged. "I told Boris to put them on my mantel after we left the other day. I thought they might make you feel — at home in my quarters. I didn't know at the time that you wouldn't be going back there."

She was incredulous. That was such a thoughtful, nice thing for him to do, not barbaric at all. She wished he would stop showing her glimpses of that side of himself. It made it harder and harder to maintain her original assessment, that he was and would always be a coarse barbarian by nature. And she needed to maintain that, to keep the hurt away from the constant reminder that he would never be hers!

Then he surprised her even further by adding, "The pair, they remind me of us."

She quickly disagreed. "No, the male figure, he's just a soldier, an English one, actually. Henry had never even heard of Lubinia when he carved that for me."

"He thought you should be paired with a soldier instead of the English lord you thought you would have?"

"It was an — odd reason he had for picking a soldier for me, I . . . I don't remember," she lied.

She wasn't about to tell him that Henry had figured it would take a courageous man to marry her because her intelligence could be intimidating. Christoph would just scoff at that, or laugh, since he didn't find her the least bit intimidating, neither before or after she'd donned the royal mantle.

But he obviously didn't believe that she couldn't remember because he said, "Maybe I'll ask him, since you don't want to say."

She drew in her breath. "You didn't detain him?"

"Of course not. He can't deliver the message to Rastibon if he's sitting in a cell. But I know where to find him now."

She stiffened. "I'm going to discuss this with my father. To make sure Henry doesn't end up in one of your cells!"

"You really think I would do that, when I know of your fondness for the boy?"

"You —" She stopped. That question just deflated her anger. "No, I honestly don't think you would hurt a child. But you're so single-minded when you're after answers."

"My job —"

"I know. Your job will always make it so. I even realize your treatment of me was just part of your job. I know it could have been much worse, considering what you thought, what you were so sure of."

He laughed. "You're making concessions for me?"

"No, that doesn't mean I wasn't frightened, and infuriated, and frustrated beyond reason — at the time."

"And you haven't gotten your retribution yet. Are you just waiting for an opportune time?"

Did he actually think that, or was he just teasing her? The latter, no doubt, because he wouldn't worry over something like that, not when he and her father had both admitted he had only been doing his job, what he had leave to do.

All she said was "I happen to recall the other day just before you became absolutely certain that Helga was my mother, your saying that if I *were* the princess, your family would be disgraced and you would even banish yourself forever from Lubinia because of it. Of course when you said it, you in no way believed that could ever happen. And now that it has —"

"Now that it has, instead of incurring the king's wrath for failing to unravel your mystery sooner, I am given his daughter to guard with my life."

She sat forward so she could turn to look back at him. Yes, it was there in his expression, pride in a job well done.

CHAPTER FORTY-NINE

Alana gasped. She couldn't believe what had just happened. Christoph had just taken the two little carvings from her hands and bent down to return them to his saddlebag, saying, "I will hold them until we are back at the palace."

She'd barely heard him. No sooner had he leaned toward the floor to put them away than she saw a man run from behind a tree and leap for the back of the sleigh. It was done so smoothly, the sleigh didn't dip at all so Christoph had no warning — until he leaned back in his seat and the knife was suddenly at his throat.

"Don't kill him!" Alana screamed.

"Hush, princess, I wasn't going to," Leonard said.

"In that case," Christoph began, and with a single hand he yanked Poppie into the sleigh in front of them.

"I should put on more weight," Leonard

said in disgust at how easily he'd just been outmaneuvered by sheer strength.

He said it low enough that Alana guessed they weren't supposed to hear it, but she did. Christoph did, too, which accounted for the slight smile on his lips. Nonetheless, he still bent down to pick up his rifle from the floor and put it on his lap. But he made no attempt to take the knife from Poppie, he just sat there now with a raised brow as Poppie straightened himself into a sitting position on the floor. Alana swiftly dropped to her knees on the floor to put her arms around his neck.

"I've missed you so much! Nothing happened as we thought it would, though it's all right now."

"You now have your father's protection?"

"Yes, we were reunited just yes —"

"This ends right now if you don't move away from that knife, Alana," Christoph cut her off in a furious undertone.

She glanced back at him. "He won't hurt me."

"Not intentionally. I won't accept accidents either. Sit back down. Now!"

Leonard dropped the knife on the floor next to him, apparently agreeing with Christoph. Alana picked it up just to get it out of Christoph's sight before she quickly climbed back on the seat and sat on the edge of it. She knew Poppie would have at least a half dozen more daggers hidden on him, but as long as they weren't visible, Christoph might be able to relax enough so the two men could come to an agreement to work together instead of against each other.

She slipped the dagger in her boot before she held out her hand to Leonard so they could still convey their feelings through touch. The last thing she wanted was for Christoph to deal with Poppie angrily, but he was denying her a proper reunion with the man who'd raised her, just as he'd done with her father.

Christoph still sounded angry when he asked Leonard, "Why did you steal Helga Engel from my protection?"

Leonard snorted. "Admit it, she wasn't under your protection, you were bringing her in to interrogate her. That was obvious."

Christoph didn't try to deny it. "She has a lot to answer for. But how did you find her on this road yesterday?"

"I had been looking for her. I didn't know where to find her until you took Alana to visit her and made sure I learned of it. I was on my way to talk to her at the chalet, to find out why."

"You'll have to turn her over to me. The

king and I need to speak with her. She told us lies. I need to find out what she really did and why."

Leonard shook his head. "No, you don't. She told me, I can tell you. She is under my protection now. I won't allow her to be hurt."

Christoph was silent for a moment. He'd just been told no! Alana held her breath to see if he'd insist on having it his way. But he finally said, "Then tell me."

Leonard did, and Alana's eyes got wider and wider the longer she listened. A romance between him and Helga? And while it wasn't supposed to mean anything to him, because he'd just been using her as a tool for his job, it had turned out to mean more to him than he could have thought possible. It had changed how he had dealt with the nasty job of killing a princess. It had softened his heart before the fateful moment arrived.

It all came out, how Helga had made up the tale of switching the babies that very night when she woke up and found the princess gone. She did it out of fear for her and her daughter's lives. And she got the other nursemaid to go along with her by convincing her she'd be blamed, too. Helga never dreamed the king would end up separating her from her daughter.

Alana squeezed Poppie's hand, letting him know she didn't blame the woman. She might have been separated from her real parent, but she'd had Poppie instead. How different she might be today if she'd grown up a spoiled princess. Impossible to know.

"I bear no grudge," she said when he finished. "You can let her know that."

Poppie smiled at her. Christoph wasn't smiling and pointed out, "The woman deceived the king of Lubinia. She let him love the wrong child. She let him mourn that child when it died. All these years, he's mourned her loss when she wasn't even his."

"He mourned the loss of a loved one, as you say, he loved the girl. Now he loves the right child. I kept his real daughter from him, Helga didn't. And I did that because he and whoever your predecessor was, *and* you, never resolved the threat to her life."

"I wasn't here then."

"You've been at your post long enough to have tried," Leonard reasoned.

"He has tried," Alana found herself saying in Christoph's defense. "The one difficulty in all this time was the suspects are such a huge family, but more to the point, they are the king's own relatives. And despite how many spies were sent into their stronghold,

463

they never found out who was pulling the strings. That secret was too closely guarded. It obviously wasn't the head of the family."

Christoph added, "Nothing could be done back then anyway, it was too soon after the civil war to arrest any Bruslan. It would have led to another war."

"I thought of that," Leonard agreed. "And loving Alana as I do, I didn't mind waiting. But I didn't know it was presumed that Helga's daughter was taken, that it became a royal secret that the presumed princess was safe. I knew none of that until Helga told me. If I had known, I might have brought Alana back sooner — or not. Who is to say in hindsight?" He ended with a shrug.

"About Helga," Christoph said. "It's unacceptable that you've hidden her. I must insist —"

"Don't," Leonard cut in sharply. "I will repeat, Captain, you can't have her. I don't care what she's done, what you think she needs to be charged with. She's been hurt enough, losing her child because of the king's enemies. She's already paid a high price. While I breathe, I won't let you hurt anyone I care about."

The two men stared at each other long enough that Alana became nervous and broke the silence herself, telling Poppie,

"There's something you should know, if you haven't already heard. My father has chosen a husband for me."

Leonard glanced at her with a frown. "So soon?"

"Yes, and the wedding is to take place soon, too."

"Who?"

"Karsten Bruslan," she said with a wince.

"No!" Leonard said furiously. "Give you to the very people who —"

"Frederick was already considering naming Karsten his successor before he knew Alana was alive," Christoph cut in. "He may not have liked the prospect, but it would have been for the good of the country."

"In the meantime," Alana added, "Christoph here is my protector. He's the only man my father trusts enough to keep me safe."

Leonard looked at Christoph for another long moment, then nodded. "Yes, I see it in his eyes. He'll protect you with his life. A much better recommendation for marriage, if you ask me, than a foolish effort to end a feud that many Bruslans don't even remember."

Alana blinked. Poppie would rather she marry Christoph?

"Did you beat Karsten?" Christoph asked.

465

"If I did?"

"I would have killed him."

Poppie actually laughed. "I thought about it, to do this country a service in assuring he'll *never* wear the crown. All their schemes would fall apart without their golden-boy heir standing in line for the throne. But that choice isn't mine to make." And then to Christoph: "So, have I found out more since I've been back than the palace has found out in eighteen years?"

"That depends what you've found out."

In answer, Leonard asked Alana, "Did you get Henry's message today?"

"Yes, but it was garbled, all he said was 'Beware the queen.' "

"Exactly. With those two spies that were in the palace out of the picture, the man carrying out the orders had to hire a new man, and I overheard him filling the new thug in. He made reference to the queen and her connection to some big conspiracy in the past, and passed the bracelet to the new man to deliver it to her. I know Nikola wasn't old enough or tough enough to order an infant's death, but her father wouldn't have hesitated."

"You're guessing now," Christoph said angrily.

"Guesses come first, facts often follow.

And this is a logical conclusion based on past experience."

"No," Christoph disagreed adamantly. "Nikola loves her husband. I have no doubt of this."

"I'm sure she does. But maybe you should ask the king when she was offered in marriage to him? I'll wager Queen Avelina was barely in her grave when Nikola's father approached him on the matter. He would have wanted his own blood relative on the throne, not the daughter of Avelina. It's an old motive I've run into before, when a second marriage occurs yet there are children from the first marriage."

"Who are we talking about?"

"I don't have his name yet, but I'll find out and track him down."

"Speaking of names, you are Leonard Kastner, aren't you?"

Alana quickly shook her head the tiniest bit, to let Poppie know she hadn't mentioned his name. Leonard raised a brow at Christoph. "Does it matter at this point? You and I have the same goal, Captain. To protect our princess. I am also following another lead right now that —"

"And us," Christoph said. "I didn't expect you to — join us so soon."

"Join you? I was surprised to see you coming up this road yet again."

"You didn't follow us?"

"No, I was on my way back down the mountain. I followed someone else up here, the one I told you about who hands out the orders now. He killed the man who hired me so long ago."

"Aldo?"

"So the thief talked to you? The man who killed Aldo implied that the one he reported to, who had always given Aldo his orders, was just a lackey as well. The safeguards they've used to hide the true master — or mistress, as the case may be — are extreme. But I've been following this man for a couple days now. I'm beginning to wonder if he's playing more than one side."

"Where did he go up here? There's not much up here except the nobles' estates on the eastern road. Even my family lives on that road."

"It sounds as if we are speaking of the same one. The estate he visited, the grounds were too open with too many retainers marching about like guards for me to stay there for long. I was able to reach a few windows undetected. One was the right one, his lover's bedroom. It appeared he was going to spend the entire day in bed with her, so I left to pick up the trail on his return to the city."

"What do you expect to gain from him?"

"I'm still hoping to find out who he reports to at the Stronghold. I thought it might be Karsten because they left at the same time, but Karsten knew nothing. The woman my target rendezvoused with up here, though, she obviously knows him well and should also be questioned. But I don't like questioning women. I had hoped I could leave that to you. This was a safe way to tell you that."

Christoph raised a brow. "You call it safe, putting a knife to my throat?"

Leonard chuckled with some genuine humor. "That was only to get your attention."

CHAPTER FIFTY

It went against the grain to work with an assassin, to accept any help from Leonard Kastner at all. Christoph had to keep it uppermost in his mind that Alana considered the man *family.* Yet, Leonard's audacity did amuse him. A lot. He had to admire a man who would confidently put a blade to his throat.

"That's him!" Leonard said suddenly.

Christoph had to stand up to see over the driver's high perch, where Leonard had finally taken a seat for the rest of the ride up the hill. They were nearly to the turnoff and the long road east that accessed so many noble estates, including Christoph's home. He had told Alana he would leave her briefly with his family while he went with Leo to be shown which estate was harboring Bruslan sympathizers. But he saw the man now himself, turning to come down the mountain road. And they were spotted as well.

"Would he recognize you?" Christoph asked Leonard.

"No, but it's possible he doesn't want anyone to see him up here — don't shoot at him!" Leonard amended as Christoph raised his rifle.

The man had left the road to find a different route to avoid getting close enough to them to be recognized, straight down into the wooded hillside. "I won't kill him," Christoph said, still taking aim.

"Just let him go. Let him think his precaution just now succeeded, so he will be confident that he has nothing to worry about."

"Are you placing less importance on him now than you implied?"

"No. I merely know where to find him. I can wait in the Bruslan Stronghold until he shows up. I have an easy access in and out of that place now. If you chase him now and he manages to escape, he'll go into hiding and we will never find who he answers to."

Christoph swore under his breath, but sat back down. Then he noticed Alana's cautionary look in his direction. He took a moment to lean over and kiss her hard on the lips. Not very satisfying for either of them, but then he was only trying to reassure her.

"Don't worry," he said. "I wasn't going to invite bullets to fly your way again."

She started to raise a hand to her lips, but caught herself doing it and put her hand back under the blanket. "I wasn't worried. But it would appear that your reason for leaving me with your parents just took off for the city, so the danger you mentioned is gone. And I already have a feeling I know who that fellow was visiting."

"Oh?"

"Your lady friend who thinks you'll marry her."

Christoph chuckled at the way she put that, but asked Leonard, "How far down the road is that estate you followed the Bruslan man to?"

"Not far."

Christoph told Alana, "Perhaps you're right."

"Then you're not dropping me off first," she said adamantly. "I want to be there when she squirms under your questioning."

He couldn't help grinning. He was sure he knew why, from her disgruntled expression, but he still wanted to hear it. "Why?"

"She was very nasty to me that day at your house. *Very* nasty."

"You think you can get answers out of her that I can't?"

Alana smiled. "No, I just want to sit back and watch. I know firsthand how . . . barbaric you can be when you set your mind to it."

"An interesting remark," he said thoughtfully. "Does that mean you actually think these barbaric tendencies you've been assuring me I have are now deliberate rather than natural as you've been maintaining?"

"No, I —" The blush came this time, a pretty pink. "Perhaps sometimes."

He laughed. "For the record, Princess, giving a prisoner a sense of helplessness is a very useful tool and is quickly accomplished by completely stripping them naked before questioning. Preventing myself from doing that to you was very — difficult. Not very barbaric, eh?"

She sucked in her breath, then glanced worriedly at the driver's perch, where Leonard was sitting with his back to them, to make sure he wasn't listening before she leaned toward Christoph to scold in a whisper, "Hush. This isn't an appropriate conversation to be having at any time, much less here."

"Why be embarrassed about what a man and woman do with each other, or feel for each other."

"I'm soon to be betrothed to another!"

"Do you really want to hold that up as a means to silence me when you admitted you don't want him? I'm happy to say that won't work now."

"Ha!" she replied as indignantly as she could manage. "Besides, that wasn't intimacy between two people you were talking about just now, but a grueling session of questioning."

He ran the back of his fingers along her cheek. "With you, I have to disagree. With you, all I wanted to do was sweep you up in my arms and take you to the nearest bed. So it will not come as a surprise if I tell you how much I enjoyed that interrogation, with you in your underclothes. I enjoyed it so much I was hoping we could do it again someday."

Her blush got brighter, yet she didn't resist looking into his eyes just long enough to confuse him with what she was thinking. Until she laughed, then he was certain that she thought he was teasing, and she even teased back, "Perhaps we can switch places next time."

She wasn't serious — or was she? No, of course not, yet her grin was fascinating. This intriguing suggestion had probably been prompted by her wish to see him on his knees for his treatment of her. He reminded himself she was a princess, after all, and well aware of it now. And soon she would be pledged to another man, he thought in disgust.

This need to keep her at his side had nothing to do with his duty. The king had made it clear Christoph wasn't to touch her again, and he wouldn't have if she'd been pleased with the match being arranged for her. He'd actually thought she would be, as handsome and charming as Karsten was. But she wanted no part of that, and that quickly Christoph's anger was gone.

Now that the danger had just fled down the mountainside, he gave in to his need to have her within his reach and granted her request to be present at the interrogation. If Nadia really was involved, then her father, Everard Braune, wouldn't be there to interfere because Nadia would never have dared to have a lovers' tryst in her bed at home if he was.

CHAPTER FIFTY-ONE

A formally dressed servant showed Alana, Christoph, and Leonard to the parlor in the large Braune manor. Alana hadn't yet had an opportunity to talk to Poppie out of Christoph's hearing, but as they were being shown to the parlor, she had a moment to quickly whisper to Poppie, "You've revealed your face to him. Was that wise?"

"I have a good feeling about him," Poppie said. "He won't betray me."

She'd never really thought Christoph would do that either. He was too straight-forward, too blunt, too honest by far — unless it pertained to royal secrets, of course.

None of them sat while they waited for Nadia to join them. Alana kept herself out of the way because she was only there to observe. She shouldn't even have asked to come. This was now royal business. Her brief moment of wanting to see Nadia get her comeuppance was gone. She realized now it had smacked of jealousy on her part. She hoped Christoph hadn't noticed that.

His childhood friend arrived in a flourish. Nadia wore a delighted expression that abruptly turned to mere curiosity when she saw that Christoph hadn't come alone. She was dressed in dark, bold colors, burgundy mixed with black and a deeper purple, matron colors as they would say in England, where only pastels were appropriate for a young, unmarried woman. But Lubinia didn't follow those customs, Alana reminded herself. She still felt invisible in comparison in her gray coat. The feeling wouldn't have changed if she'd removed it because her dress was pale blue, elegant, yet still nearly colorless.

"What brings you for this visit?" Nadia asked Christoph. "It's been so long since you've stood in this house, I can't even remember how many years it has been."

Christoph had slowly moved toward her the moment Nadia entered the room. He didn't stop until he was positioned halfway between the door and Nadia, so it wasn't obvious that he was blocking her exit. This forced Nadia to turn her back on Poppie, who was on the other side of the room.

"We are going to discuss your recent activities and who you are associating with,"

Christoph replied.

Nadia laughed. "No, we aren't. That's none of your business."

"Actually it is, Nadia, when I have just found out that your lover murdered one of his cohorts. No loss, apparently, just another thug like he is. But I also know he works directly for the Bruslans."

"He's no rebel," she quickly denied.

Christoph said pointedly, "I didn't say he was, but that's quite a revealing statement, that you should connect the rebels with the Bruslans. If I didn't already know, then I have you to thank for confirming that connection."

Nadia's cheeks flushed with angry color. "I have nothing else to say to you!" she snapped, and marched toward the door.

She didn't get more than two steps. Christoph's hand locked on her arm. She started to actually scream for help, until he shook her hard.

"You might want to make this easy on yourself, Nadia, and cooperate. If I have to take you to the palace, you —"

"Get your hands off my daughter!"

Everard Braune stood in the doorway. Blond hair turning gray, well dressed, still wearing the cloak he had just come indoors with. And a pistol in his hand pointed directly at Christoph.

But Christoph wasn't inclined to obey the angry demand. He turned, placing Nadia between himself and her father, making her a shield. It didn't defuse the danger because Everard just pointed the pistol at Alana instead.

Alana gasped and dropped down behind the sofa, crawling her way to the side of it where she could peek out and see where Christoph was standing, and Poppie beyond him. She couldn't see the door and Nadia's father from that position, so she didn't know that Nadia had run to Everard and he'd pushed her out of the room to safety. But it was a good guess that the pistol was back on Christoph, with him just standing there empty-handed now.

She should have demanded her own weapons back as soon as she was moved into the palace, but she hadn't even thought of them since her father's men protected her now. She could have disarmed Braune with a well-placed bullet while Christoph distracted him. Poppie was probably waiting for her to do just that. But all she had was his long-bladed dagger from the sleigh, and unlike him, she was only mediocre at throwing daggers. She'd been taught to use them for defense, but not against a pistol!

She took the long blade out of her boot and showed Poppie that was all she had to work with, then moved to the other end of the sofa where she could peek around at Braune. She might still be able to distract him, long enough for Christoph to take him down. At the very least, she could try to knock the pistol out of his hand.

"Do you even know what your daughter does here while you're away?" Poppie asked the man to draw his attention away from Christoph.

"Who the hell are you?"

"Do you, Everard?" Christoph pulled the man's eyes back to him.

"Yes, I know what she does. She does what I tell her to do. She's an obedient daughter."

"You told her to sleep with a Bruslan lackey?" Christoph asked next.

"No, she merely took a liking to him," Everard said. "I couldn't disapprove when I have kept her from marrying anyone but you."

"Why me?"

"You were supposed to succumb completely to her, that would have neutralized you. But we overestimated her allure."

"We?"

Alana peeked around the other sofa corner for a second before she hid again. Her heart was beginning to pound. Good God, what was Christoph doing, asking so many questions before he had control of the situation? Or did he think he did have control? He *was* armed, though he wasn't revealing anything other than the saber on his hip. But he'd taken two pistols out of his saddlebag and stuck them both in the back of his pants before they'd entered the house. Yet if Braune admitted to an involvement with the Bruslans, he was going to have to kill them all to make sure it went no further than this room, and he still held the pistol!

She positioned the dagger in her hand, then peeked once more. She had a clear shot at that pistol, as well as Braune's wrist and arm, which were extended as he pointed the weapon. She might not be able to knock it out of his hand, but she would definitely distract him long enough . . .

"Nadia and I," Everard said.

Christoph laughed shortly. "So you would have foisted a used bride on me?"

Alana groaned with the realization. Christoph *was* getting a confession, one he might not get if Everard didn't think he had the upper hand. And that's why he'd made no move yet. He wanted that confession! He'd be furious with her if she interrupted it by trying to save him. She moved quickly back to the other side of the sofa to gauge Christoph's intention. She'd actually have a better view of her target from there, all of the man, instead of just his arm. Christoph couldn't get angry if she just helped when the time came.

"That wouldn't have mattered if she had succeeded," Everard said. "In the meantime, it did no harm for her to toy with the young man she likes. She doesn't like you any longer, apparently. And he delivers messages for me, so he is often here. It is difficult, visiting my friends without stirring up suspicions. You have them watched too closely."

"Of course I do, and Karsten Bruslan will soon be arrested for treason."

Everard laughed. "Arrest him, no one cares. He was a fool to let his men attack the palace after someone, I daresay not you and your men, beat him up. Probably some jealous husband."

"The rebels weren't his idea?"

"Of course not. All of you have misjudged the Bruslans. They're rich, and spoiled, and lazy. They like other people to do their work for them. This new generation is not like Ernest and the old guard. They were fighters!"

"You've prodded them?"

"The young bucks, yes. Someone had to so you'd keep your eyes on them. There were only ever two Bruslans who took the initiative, Ernest and his mother. His mother had the right idea, to just get rid of Frederick, and she paid for a number of assassins, but luck remained with Frederick. Then she lost her mind, and her memories, and no one else in that family would take up the gauntlet, they were too complacent. The truth was, no one was left who wanted that throne enough to kill for it."

"I should have known. You were one of the nobles that had been hit the hardest when the Bruslans lost the throne. You had been the most outspoken in advising King Ernest to gain Napoléon's favor with a real army instead of money, which was all that had been asked for. It might even have been your suggestion to begin with."

Everard laughed. "Now you give me too much credit."

"I doubt that. You've kept the flame alive when it might have otherwise faded away."

It was as if the man simply couldn't help bragging. The smirk was in his tone when he said, "Perhaps."

"Why rebels? What did you actually think you would accomplish with that plan?"

"An army, one big enough to storm the

palace, a repeat of history." At Christoph's laugh, Everard added, "Yes, I know. We should have taken that approach before Frederick proved himself such a worthy king. We underestimated how beloved he really is. We instilled fear, that he was sick, dying, but the fools were horrified at the thought of demanding he step down because of it, they would rather have him right up to the day he dies than another in his place. And you!" Everard finished in disgust. "If Nadia had succeeded in seducing you to our side, nothing else would have been necessary. You're the one who forced us to desperate measures because you've made it impossible to get near him."

Leonard spoke up, "Who hired me to kill the princess eighteen years ago?"

Everard gave him a blank look. Alana didn't think it was contrived. He didn't really seem to know.

Drawing the same conclusion, Christoph asked, "Who is the *we* that you mentioned?"

Everard smirked. "Do you really need that spelled out? The other nobles like myself who lost so much when a Stindal took the throne."

"So all these machinations are just to get your land and titles —"

"Our *power* is what we want back. We

want a more pliable, shall we say more wealth-oriented, man on the throne, such as one of the older Bruslans."

"Not Karsten?"

Everard shrugged. "He was our first choice only because he's their first choice, but the boy has become much too industrious lately. Someone else would serve our purposes better. But he's still pliable with the right incentive. Women. He is a philanderer at heart, after all."

Alana wondered if her father knew his choice for her was still such a womanizer. It didn't sound as if Braune knew she had returned either, so maybe Nadia's lover wasn't playing both sides, but merely keeping an eye on what Braune's secret group of nobles was up to for his Bruslan employer, and delivering messages for Braune just to keep the door open.

"Your rebels were a waste of money," Christoph said. "You have an alternative plan?"

Everard actually laughed. "We always have alternatives lined up. And you have conveniently supplied another one. Finally, Frederick won't have you to depend on."

"You really think one bullet can stop me? Make it count, old man, you won't get a chance to fire the other."

Alana was about to stand up, but she heard heavy footsteps pounding into the room, then four bullets were fired! She was still on the side of the sofa where she could see that Christoph was still standing there unharmed. It was Poppie who had to dodge those bullets!

Three Braune men had rushed into the room, obviously summoned by Nadia, but only two of them held double-barreled pistols, the third just a saber. They immediately tried to take out the smaller second man that their lord didn't already have a pistol trained on. Everard began swearing at them for not asking for their orders first. He would have had them shoot Christoph instead to make sure the real threat was ended. But they'd acted on their own initiative, and fortunately, servants carrying weapons they didn't really know how to use usually missed, and they did. Poppie dove and rolled out of the way, and when he came to his feet, he threw a dagger. His excellent aim left only two men charging at him now.

An assassin dealt with shadows and single targets, situations he could control. He didn't do so well in an open fight with more than one opponent. Sabers had been drawn. Poppie only had more daggers to work with.

But Christoph was slowly edging toward the fight to help. Everard must have been watching it as well, or he would have warned Christoph not to move. She wasn't sure why Everard didn't take advantage of the distraction to fire his own pistol, unless Christoph's warning had made him too nervous to try it without his men ready to back him up. Then she saw yet another man outside, looking through the window behind Poppie, raising a rifle and pointing it at his back!

Alana screamed, "The window!"

Poppie was concentrating too deeply on avoiding the two sabers. He might not even have heard her. Christoph did, and the second he saw where the rifle was pointed, he threw his weight in that direction. He tackled Poppie out of the way, knocking over one of the two men, taking a saber slice from the other man to his back that had been meant for Poppie's throat. The shot fired a moment later. Glass broke. The bullet continued across the room. Alana stood up in time to see Everard flinch as it struck the wall next to him, but then with an angry visage he took aim at Christoph, who was still on the floor. She threw her dagger at his chest to stop him. Not even close! But it did embed itself in his upper arm just as his pistol fired, then yet another shot was fired.

It all happened so fast. Everard's aim was thrown off because of the dagger in his arm. Christoph's aim was true. The older man looked down at his chest before he fell to the floor. But it was still mayhem in the other corner of the room. Without wasting time to get up first, Poppie threw another dagger through the broken window. The man out there ran instead of shooting again, the same man he'd followed up here, who must have circled back to investigate what they were doing turning in this direction. Christoph swiped a leg to knock over the last man standing, then pounded a fist into his face to keep him down, before he did the same to the other one.

Christoph had just saved Poppie's life and taken a wound for it. Alana's only thought was to make sure it wasn't a serious wound, yet Christoph wouldn't stop to let her look at it. He moved across the room and leaned down and examined Everard to make sure his chest wound was as serious as it had looked. It was. *Then* he stood up and shook her.

"Next time stay hidden until I say it's safe to get up," he growled at her. "We're not out of this house yet."

"You saved Poppie" was all she said before she threw her arms around his neck.

He squeezed her so tightly, for a moment she couldn't breathe. "Come on, I'm getting you out of here. This was no time to try to make amends to you by giving you your way. Be warned, that will never happen again if danger is even remotely involved. My men can clean up this nest of vipers later."

CHAPTER FIFTY-TWO

Why was she *NOT* surprised? Restricted to the palace until after the wedding!

Her father had been quite upset after Christoph's report because she had been in the Braunes' parlor when bullets had been flying. She hadn't been present for Christoph's account of the surprisingly violent confrontation, but Frederick visited her afterward in her rooms.

After she realized why Frederick was upset, she actually tried to place the blame on herself by pointing out, "Do my orders not override his? I told him I was going with him. We both thought it would be safe."

"I understand what was assumed, but Christoph knows better, and, no, your orders do not override his. Yet this entire unfortunate situation with the Bruslans is now resolved because of it. I may not have to deal harshly with any of them now that we know those younger bucks were instigated to action, that the rebellion wasn't actually their idea. Quite a surprise, that. We knew Braune was up to something, but nothing of this magnitude. If Christoph hadn't gotten that full confession, we may never have known."

"You have Poppie to thank for that," she reminded him, hoping Leonard would get a full pardon now because of it. "He led us there."

Frederick finally smiled. "I am aware of what your Poppie has done." But then his expression got stern again. "But you, daughter, will not be leaving the palace again until after your wedding. Consequently, the betrothal will be formalized tonight at dinner."

She groaned. "Father, please, you can't send me to live with the very people who may have tried to kill me!"

"We don't know who did that yet. If Karsten is your husband, it will assure your safety."

"But I'll know it could have been one of them. I'll never trust any of them. I'll live in constant terror. Is that really what you want for me?"

"I want you protected. This is the way to assure —"

"I've been protected since I arrived!" she

cut in desperately. "Your captain has seen to that."

He got tight-lipped at the mention of Christoph. "I'll see you tonight. Look your prettiest."

She started crying the moment he left. Christoph had been right. Because Frederick knew they had been intimate, he was still furious with his captain. So even if she told her father that she loved Christoph, it wasn't going to make any difference right now. In time it might, but she'd be married to the wrong man before then!

She prepared for the dinner, but she felt as if she were going to a funeral. Christoph arrived to escort her. He didn't look too happy himself, had probably received a tongue-lashing for endangering her, but at least he hadn't been dismissed for it. But her own expression was too revealing.

He lifted her chin. "You told the king you don't want Karsten?"

"He wouldn't listen, and now I've upset him, too. He still thinks this is the only way to assure my safety. I think I need to leave — just go away and not come back. Can you get a message to Poppie? He'll take me out of the country and hide me again."

Christoph took her arm and led her down the hall. "I'll take you away from here, if it's what you really want. But let's see what happens tonight. Sometimes things right themselves."

He said that almost . . . mysteriously. That wasn't like him at all.

"Let's see? Are you actually invited this time?"

"It's a formal matter that requires witnesses. And your father doesn't quite have all the facts yet."

"What doesn't he know?"

"How likely it is that I'll kill Karsten if he agrees to marry you."

There he went again with that silly notion. "No, you won't. I think you even like him. But thank you for making me smile."

They arrived at the royal chamber. Karsten and his grandmother were already there. Auberta was glowing with happiness. Karsten came forward immediately to escort Alana the rest of the way into the room.

"No hard feelings, eh, Christoph, if I walk away with the prize?"

"She's not a trophy, Karsten, another notch for your belt. And if you touch her, you're going to end up on the floor. Everyone will wonder why, and I'll have to mention the three mistresses you're currently supporting. One is never enough for you, is it?"

Karsten actually laughed. "They'll be sent on their way, of course, after the wedding."

"Will they? I doubt it. But there isn't going to be a wedding."

Karsten's visage darkened. "So that's how it is, eh? I think Frederick will disagree."

Alana spoke up before they came to blows. "I'm sorry, Karsten, but he's right, I don't want to marry you. I'm sure you're a fine man, and I've heard very nice things about you, but — someone in your family tried to kill me when I was an infant, and when I returned here, they tried yet again. My guardian has been working diligently to find out who it is, and, in fact, he has uncovered new information that could well exonerate your family, but until we know for sure —"

"No," Christoph cut in.

She gave him a hard look. "No?"

"Leo even admitted it was only a possibility," Christoph reminded her. "He has no facts to support it — it's just a guess, Alana. I even understand why Leonard would draw that conclusion. He's been away from Lubinia too long. It hasn't occurred to him yet that within our borders live two queens, not just one."

Alana's eyes flared wide. Both of those queens were sitting across the room smiling at her at that very moment, the current queen, Nikola, and the widowed queen, who had retired to the Bruslan Stronghold after her husband had been beheaded. Auberta Bruslan.

Alana didn't know what to think now. One queen was too young, the other too nice! But Christoph led them farther into the room to stand before her father.

"I was beginning to wonder if you three were going to join us," Frederick said congenially.

Christoph said, "I withheld information today during my report, Highness, until I could verify it, which I have done. It concerned a message Alana had from her guardian this morning to beware the queen."

Nikola gasped, hearing that. Frederick said coldly, "I think you had better stop there."

"Hear him out, Father," Alana said quickly. "It's not what you think."

"I'd like to hear this myself," Karsten said quietly, standing beside them.

It took a moment for Frederick to nod his approval, but he did, and Christoph continued, "While Leonard was with us today, he told us what he overheard from two Bruslan hirelings. They spoke of a queen who'd been involved in an old conspiracy. And this was to be delivered to her." Christoph handed Alana's baby bracelet to the king. "Do you recognize it?"

"Yes, I still remember the day I gave it to her."

"The person who possessed this bracelet until it was claimed as evidence has twice given the order for Alana to be killed," Christoph said solemnly before he turned toward Auberta. "Would you like to explain what it was doing in your town house, Lady Auberta? I found it there this afternoon."

Nikola jumped up, exclaiming, "There has to be some mistake here. Auberta would never do anything so horrible!"

But Karsten, watching the emotions flickering across Auberta's face, said gently, "Did you really do this, Grandmama?"

She gave him a beseeching look, as if he should understand. "I had to. They took my husband from me, Frederick and his father did. They killed him when he was everything to me! So I took what they loved, a death for a death!"

Karsten looked horrified. "They weren't responsible. They didn't lead that rebellion."

"Of course they did," Auberta insisted, but she looked confused now, then her eyes turned to Alana and she smiled. "I'm sorry, my dear. But Karsten will make you such a good husband. Don't you agree?"

Alana was speechless. Everyone was staring at Auberta as if she were crazy, and perhaps she was, harboring misguided hate like that for so long.

Karsten helped his grandmother to her feet to lead her from the room. Alana found it painful to see how shocked he was. He paused before Frederick and said, "I don't know how she hid this from everyone, but she'll never hurt anyone again. I promise I'll see to that." He also stopped in front of Alana and Christoph long enough to say, "I wish you both a happy life together. I was trying to ignore how obvious it is that you two love each other. But it's all right." He tried to smile, but couldn't quite manage it. "I'm not ready for marriage yet anyway."

Alana blushed, not because of what Karsten had said, but because her father was swearing! "What a fool I was to not see it myself," Frederick said, looking first at her, then at Christoph. "Can you forgive me, Christoph? I know there's no better man for my daughter than you."

Alana was rendered speechless yet again. Did that mean what she thought it meant? She glanced nervously at Christoph, waiting for him to object. He might not have wanted her to marry Karsten, but that had seemed to stem from some old rivalry between them. Not once had he suggested she marry him instead.

Christoph's answer was a formal bow to his king. And just like that, Alana got engaged to the barbarian.

CHAPTER FIFTY-THREE

"Married in two days?!"

Frederick was sharing breakfast with Alana in her suite. He seemed anxious and didn't keep her guessing as to why. He was worried that Christoph didn't feel worthy of being given a princess for a wife. But two days! Of course she knew why her father was rushing the wedding, she didn't have to ask. The possibility of a baby. He didn't have to say it — and then he did!

"I trust him with my life, Alana. There is no one I would trust more with *your* life. Even now, you may carry his child, my grandchild. This is why I was so easily swayed to Karsten at Nikola's urging, though she has admitted now that it was Auberta's idea, not hers. Don't blame her for that, please. She loved that old woman like a mother. She trusted her and never suspected — neither of us did. But this is why your wedding to Karsten would have taken place this soon as well. There can be no question of the legitimacy of the future heirs to this throne."

Alana wondered, could her cheeks get any hotter? Her father was embarrassed, too, but for a different reason.

"If I had not been so angry with Christoph, I wouldn't have distressed you with Karsten." He sighed. "I would have realized immediately that Christoph was the better man for you. I owe him so much. He even saved my life, you know. I was never able to think of a suitable reward for him — until now. And you are in agreement?"

She was getting a say in the matter this time? Despite her embarrassment and worry over the obstacle Frederick had introduced, she couldn't help feeling giddy because she would be getting what *she* wanted.

So she nodded shyly, and he smiled, continuing, "Your mother's gown is being searched for as we speak. The nobles who need to attend are being notified. My only concern now is Christoph. I've given him what assurances I can. I want him to feel welcomed into our family. But I think he needs to hear it from you to believe it."

Christoph might have acquiesced to the marriage last night, but amazing as it seemed, she knew he might decline if he had too much time to think about it. But once again, this marriage was obviously important to her father, and she still wanted to make him happy.

"Perhaps I could invite him to dine with me, if it's permissible for me to be alone with him."

Her father looked pensive for a moment, then said, "As the two of you will be man and wife in two days, I don't see why not. Actually, it's an excellent idea. Tell him what's in your heart, Alana."

She couldn't tell him *that,* not when she didn't actually know what was in his. Karsten had made an assumption when he'd said she and Christoph obviously loved each other. Her father made the same assumption. Whether Christoph loved her was too important to her to rely on assumptions. But she would think of something to tell him, even if she only repeated what her father wanted Christoph to know, that he was being welcomed into the family with open arms.

She sent off the invitation, notified the palace cooks to make something special for dinner, dealt with the ten seamstresses that showed up carrying her mother's wedding dress — it fit perfectly! That left her about three hours before dinner, and she spent all three of them getting ready. She wanted a long bath, wanted her hair washed. She asked one of the maids if her stepmother might have a nice perfume she could borrow, and the girl came back with a basket full of them. She wanted her hair done up just right. She couldn't make up her mind what to wear, though she finally settled on one of her favorites, a pale gold silk evening gown with white and gold trimming.

She didn't even realize how much time she was devoting to her appearance for what should just be a simple dinner until she was reminded that her *fiancé* would soon be there. But she couldn't get out of her mind what she needed to tell Christoph, too, that he didn't have to sacrifice his future happiness simply because he felt compelled to follow the king's orders. She liked him — no, she thought, tears coming to her eyes — she loved him enough to free him from this marriage if that was his wish. No wonder his feelings were more important to her than her own.

She heard a knock at the door exactly on time. The meal had just been delivered. She shooed out the kitchen staff as well as her maids. They all filed out the door past Christoph before he stepped inside. She waited by the table, suddenly feeling more nervous than she'd ever been in her life.

He came forward. His uniform looked different. The colors were the same, but tonight it seemed to shine. She wasn't sure why until she noticed the buttons were reflecting the lamplight like polished glass. The sash of his saber was special, lined with studs. Even the hilt of the saber was fancier than normal. She finally realized this was his special evening wear, and he'd worn it for her!

When he reached her, he bowed formally from the waist. If that didn't amaze her, he also took her hand, brought it to his lips, and kissed it.

She was so surprised, he laughed. "Not barbaric enough for you?"

She blushed immediately, wondering if he would ever let her forget her first impressions of him. It was a good time to admit, "My father has assured me his people are not barbarians. That would include you."

He grinned. "You believed him?"

Her mouth formed an *O* just before he picked her up in his arms, then sat down, placing her in his lap. "What are you doing?"

"I'm going to feed you," he replied. "You can object, but only if you can manage to get off my lap. Do you think you can?"

He was still grinning. She knew very well he could keep her there if he wanted to. "I would guess you're making a point?"

"Several, actually. It's going to give me pleasure to feed you, and I choose not to ask permission because I know you will enjoy it, too. It gives me even more pleasure to keep you on my lap, an unfair advantage over you, but if you would shed the propriety you cling to, you might even admit you enjoy that, too. *You* bring out the barbarian in me, Alana mine. Do you really think that's such a bad thing when I would never hurt you?"

She couldn't get rid of her blush because he was right. If it gave them both pleasure, his taking advantage with his strength shouldn't bother her at all. *Was* she still clinging to propriety, insisting the marriage come first? When they'd already made love, that seemed pretty silly.

"Perhaps some of my beliefs are wrong," she allowed.

He smiled. "No, not wrong, just inappropriate at this point. The moment we had your father's blessing, what occurs between us became no longer a matter of 'Should we?' but instead 'Why don't we?' "

Did that mean what it sounded like? Surely not, but she couldn't bring herself to ask when her blood stirred simply from the thought! And he didn't expect any answer. He leaned closer to her, bringing forth a slight gasp from her, but he was only reaching for one of the platters that had been placed on the table, to slide it within his reach.

With his fingers, he picked up something sweet and put it in her mouth. Dessert first? She almost laughed, but grinned instead.

"That's very good, whatever it is. Try a bite," she suggested.

"You don't want to feed me?"

She drew in her breath again, more sharply. The look in his eyes was fascinating. She did want to feed him, actually. She turned slightly to see if she could figure out which type of sweet he'd just fed her.

He whispered by her neck, "Anything will do. We're going to eat it all — or none of it."

She shivered from his warm breath. None of it? "Did I pick a time too early for you? You aren't hungry?"

"I've been hungry, very hungry."

Even the timbre of his voice was causing a pleasant stirring inside her! "Well then" was the most she could say before she thoughtlessly picked up a dollop of something creamy with one finger. Too late, she remembered the night of their first meal, when she had licked her own finger. She turned, hoping he wouldn't remember that, but she saw it in his eyes, he did. While the intensity in his gaze completely arrested her, he took her wrist and slowly brought that finger to his mouth. She stared, she stopped breathing, while he sucked every bit of that cream off her finger. Something deep inside her began to heat up and flutter, it was such an erotic sensation having her finger in his mouth. When he was done, she still couldn't stop staring at his mouth, and those feelings inside her wouldn't subside, either.

"I'm wondering if I have the strength to feed you, after all."

She didn't mistake *his* meaning. He was talking about strength of will now, because eating wasn't exactly on his mind anymore. But what was on his mind flustered her too much, so she turned again, shoved the dessert platter out of the way, and, stretching, was just able to reach the edge of the platter with a choice of meats on it and pulled it close and picked up one of the plates.

She held it between them and suggested, "Perhaps if we hurry?"

He laughed and picked up a piece of meat with a spicy sauce and held it to her mouth.

"Trying to prove you're stronger than I am?"

She accepted his offering and gave him a piece of the same. "No, I —"

"In this case, I'm sure you are."

"Maybe. Perhaps." She didn't really know what she was saying, but she was staring at his lips too long. "No . . . actually . . ."

She leaned forward and licked a bit of sauce off his lower lip. She could have removed it with her finger, but she wanted to taste him so badly that never occurred to her. His indrawn breath told her he didn't mind, and suddenly she was kissing him! Sweet, spicy, him, an irresistible combination that she tasted fully with her tongue.

When she finally realized what she was doing, she drew back in surprise, suddenly overcome with shyness. He saw it, tilted her chin until her eyes came back to his.

"You have Lubinian blood, Alana mine. Don't be afraid of your passion."

"Is that what it is?" she asked thoughtfully, but then slowly shook her head. "No, I think it's just you."

He groaned, and it sounded like real pain when he said, "I'm trying."

She knew what he meant. He was trying not to overwhelm her with his own passion, to let her decide when they were finished eating. Not very barbaric of him, she thought with a smile.

She said simply, "Stop trying."

He stood up so fast, she laughed. He carried her straight to the bedroom. She braced herself to be tossed on the soft bed. But he laid her down carefully and kissed her once before he stood and started removing his clothes. She leaned up on her elbows to watch him. He was tearing out of his jacket.

"Can I help?" she offered, feeling a strong need to put her hands on him.

"Not if you want to do this half-dressed," he warned. "You've made me wait too long."

"It's only been —"

He cut in with a smoldering look, "Too long, when I want you every minute of the day."

Hearing that, she had to deal with some impatience of her own. She sat up and yanked off her shoes, stockings, and anything else that would just slip off. She unfastened the back of her dress, too, as far as she could reach, then turned her back to him so he could finish it for her.

"I hope you didn't like this dress," he said as he ripped the rest of it open.

She laughed. "No, what would give you that idea?"

He knelt on the bed behind her, his lips

moving from her neck to her shoulder as he pushed the sleeves down her arms, then lifted the dress and chemise off over her head. Whatever pins remained in her hair after that he pulled loose, then ran his fingertips along her scalp.

She leaned her head back against his chest so she could look up at him behind her. He kissed her like that, but it wasn't a satisfactory connection, so he flipped her over and then under him, to do it right. God, it was *so* right, giving her just enough of his weight so she could savor the feel of his body, his mouth slanting across hers at a perfect angle, the kiss deepening, igniting those incredibly delicious sensations again that began to course rapidly through her.

She was being so selfish, to let this happen, to not tell him she'd help him find a way around the king's orders. She couldn't say the words, not after he'd just convinced her that he did want her. Like this. They would at least have this. . . .

He did some savoring of his own with his hands. At least, it sounded as if he was getting a lot of pleasure from caressing her. She'd had no idea she had so many sensitive spots on her body. Maybe she didn't and it was just his touch, his fingers lightly stroking her, that made it seem so. Even his golden hair, brushing against the top of her breasts when his mouth closed over them, made her shiver with pleasure while his mouth drew forth a hot sensation from deep within her.

The muscles of his back and shoulders rippled under her fingertips, too. She even thought she felt him tremble once. She wanted to touch so much more of him, but she wasn't quite bold enough to push him onto his back so she could. She didn't think it would be long before she lost that shyness, but at the moment she was loath to give up the press of his body on hers, his heat surrounding her, and the awe of what was happening inside her. She had no control over it, didn't want to try to control it. She just let it carry her along, aware this time of what this swift buildup of passion was leading to.

Then he gathered her close, so close, his hands in her hair, his mouth back on hers, and he slid so exquisitely into her, filling her with such thick heat. Having him there was such a fulfilling feeling, almost as if her body had always been missing something, but now it was complete. But there was something else, too. She noticed it this time, his touching something so deep in her that it escalated everything she was feeling. Her eyes flew open wide in wonder, her breath froze, her hold on him tightened, waiting, waiting, and then his next thrust found that perfect place again and shot her over the edge.

She cried out, she wasn't sure what. He thrust once more to join her in that sweet ecstasy. She was filled with so much emotion she nearly cried. She smiled instead, couldn't help that upward turning of her lips. He wore the same smile. It was so beautiful! She saw it just before he kissed her tenderly, then carefully took his weight from her.

But he wasn't leaving. He draped her legs over him, made sure she was comfortable, then put his arm around her so she couldn't leave! As if she wanted to move. As if she didn't feel so utterly content right where she was.

CHAPTER FIFTY-FOUR

Alana couldn't believe it was her wedding day! It was amazing how quickly the time flew. She had only seen Christoph once since that wonderful night they'd spent together.

Last night was the traditional dinner for the families of the bride and groom so there would be no doubt both sides were in complete accord over the happy event. It was the last opportunity for any of the family members to express reservations about the match. Alana had actually feared Christoph might say something, but he didn't. Her only disappointment in the evening was that Poppie wasn't there to be included as part of her family.

She did mention to her father when she found a moment alone with him that Leonard and Henry should have been invited. He didn't exactly answer her, but his expression had been poignant. She understood.

He might want to thank Poppie if they ever met for his devoted care of her, but she didn't think Frederick would ever forgive him for keeping her from her real family.

Christoph's mother came to her rooms this morning to help her prepare, the queen by her side. Both women were ecstatically happy for their own reasons, Nikola because the future heir to the kingdom was no longer her sole responsibility.

With the men not there to hear it, Ella felt free to confide, "Geoffrey and I had begun to despair that Christoph would never marry. He felt his job wouldn't allow him time for a wife and family of his own, and he considered his job far more important."

"Then a more perfect solution couldn't have been found for him," Nikola agreed.

"Exactly," Ella said with a laugh.

Job and wife in one, Alana got it. Did Christoph see it as a perfect solution for himself, too?

Alana wished she hadn't been told that. She'd been feeling happy and excited about today. After the other night, she'd stopped having second thoughts. After the other night, she'd caught herself smiling for no reason — a lot. Now, she was feeling misgivings again, and they grew stronger when Christoph's grandfather stopped by with

Wesley on his hip.

Ella took her son from him and asked what was wrong. The boy just smiled at her. Hendrik confessed, "The men were putting him to sleep. They're too solemn. They view this undertaking so seriously. I knew we would find laughter and cheer here with you ladies."

Nikola saw Alana's worried look and said, "Of course they're solemn, they have Frederick with them! He's only just found his daughter and already he's giving her to another man. It will be a while before he can laugh about it."

Was that all? Or was Christoph *finally* having second thoughts?

But Hendrik soon had the ladies laughing again, and the maids blushing. When the summons came at the door that it was time to leave for the royal assembly hall, where the wedding would take place, he asked if he could escort Alana to her father, who would be walking her down the aisle. She already had an escort, her eight guards, the dozen maids it took to carry the long train on her mother's gown, the queen, and her soon-to-be mother-in-law, but the old man's offer pleased her. It almost felt as if he were her grandfather, too. She knew she was going to be blessed in marrying into Christoph's family, already liking them as she did.

Her father was waiting for her at the entrance to the long hall. He didn't look solemn now. He was smiling and shaking his head in amazement at the way she looked. The gown was so grand, the veil so thin it hid nothing of her face. It was fit for a queen, the queen who had last worn it.

"So beautiful you are, and so like your mother," he said as he gathered her close for a hug and a kiss to her brow. "I wish she could see you now."

"Maybe she's watching," Alana said softly.

"Maybe she is," he agreed. He took her arm, but he didn't move into the assembly hall yet. "We are breaking tradition today. Well," he added with a chuckle, "we've been breaking a lot of traditions lately. But this one I think will please you — that we have agreed to both give you away."

She didn't understand until a hand touched her other arm and she turned to see Poppie standing there offering her his bent arm, dressed formally in one of his best English suits. She gave a glad cry as she hugged him, then turned back to her father to hug him, too. Tears of happiness were in her eyes. Frederick couldn't have given her a better gift.

"Thank you so much," she said with great

emotion in her voice.

Frederick smiled. "I thought it only fair since he did raise you. I had to send out criers into the city to find him. There was a chance he wouldn't believe he was invited to the wedding."

"Whether I did or not," Leonard added, "nothing could have kept me away."

"Shall we begin?" Frederick said, formally taking her arm again. "Christoph is nervous enough. Let's not keep him waiting any longer."

Christoph nervous? She didn't believe it. But she was smiling now as both men escorted her down the aisle, her real father, and the father of her heart. Only one thing could complete her happiness with the day: if the man she was walking toward loved her as much as she loved him. But seeing him now waiting to receive her into his care, those misgivings snuck up on her again. He did look solemn, maybe even a little shocked that this wedding was actually happening.

But, oh, God, he looked so handsome standing there in his formal uniform. She suddenly felt like crying. Why couldn't . . . ? She didn't finish the thought. Come what may, they were going to join their lives here today. Unless . . .

"What's wrong?" Christoph asked the moment he took her hand to help her up the last step to the dais.

How did he know? Darn veil, it wasn't thick enough to hide her feelings, or let her lie. She had to say it — for him. "Are you sure you want to do this? I can run away, so my father won't blame you."

He carefully lifted back her veil. He was making sure he missed no nuance of expression when he asked, "What are you saying? You don't want to marry me?"

She cast her eyes down. "Actually, I do — but I fear you don't."

The priest cleared his throat, ready to begin the ceremony. Did it look as if they were ready?! Christoph put up a hand to stay the man, then brought that hand to her cheek. The gathered crowd was beginning to stir. This wasn't exactly the time for them to be having a conversation.

"I knew I should have told you this sooner," he said. "I thought you understood that I wouldn't be here if I didn't want to be. I didn't expect to love you, you know, not so soon. I didn't expect this need to have you in my sight at all times, within my reach, to know where you are every minute of every day."

Had he just said he loved her? Alana wondered. She wasn't sure! But the rest sounded like a complaint. "You take your job too seriously. You don't have to watch me constantly."

He shook his head. "I'm not talking about my job, Alana mine. I'm talking about what comes from here." He put a fist sharply to his chest. "I'm not sure I like it."

Her breath froze. "No?"

"It feels a little obsessive," he admitted with an abashed look. "Something that would beset a frantic old woman."

She let out a sigh of relief before she choked on a laugh. Carefully she asked, "You think that's a bad thing in a marriage?"

"If only one of us feels it, yes, it would be."

"What makes you think I don't feel it, too?"

"When you've made it clear you feel rushed into marriage by your father?"

"I thought you were simply following the king's orders. *You* didn't ask me to marry you, so I thought —"

He abruptly went down on one knee. Some gasps came from the crowd, a few chuckles. What he was doing was rather obvious, so they were probably thinking this part should have been covered before the ceremony.

He took one of her hands in his. "I love you, Alana mine. Will you agree to share your life with me in marriage?"

Tears burst from her eyes, but her smile was so brilliant he couldn't mistake they were tears of joy. "Nothing would make me happier." She bent forward to cup his cheeks in her hands. "I love you so much. I only doubted that you felt it, too."

"You'll never have doubts again. I'm going to spend the rest of my life making sure you know just how loved you are."

She grinned at him. "Then marry me before I think I'm dreaming."

"I like your dreams," he said sensually as he stood up. "I like when you let me share them with you."

With a blush she turned toward the priest. Some sporadic applause came from the guests, then some laughter because of it and quite a few hushes. But the bride and the groom were in complete accord that this unusual wedding — unexpected, rushed, with a proposal at the altar — was perfect — for them.

ABOUT THE AUTHOR

Johanna Lindsey has been hailed as one of the most popular authors of romantic fiction, with more than sixty million copies of her novels sold. World renowned for her novels of "first-rate romance" (*New York Daily News*), Lindsey is the author of forty-seven previous bestselling novels, many of which have reached the #1 spot on the *New York Times* bestseller list. Lindsey lives in Maine with her family.

The employees of Thorndike Press hope you have enjoyed this Large Print book. All our Thorndike, Wheeler, and Kennebec Large Print titles are designed for easy reading, and all our books are made to last. Other Thorndike Press Large Print books are available at your library, through selected bookstores, or directly from us.

For information about titles, please call:
  (800) 223-1244

or visit our Web site at:
  http://gale.cengage.com/thorndike

To share your comments, please write:
  Publisher
  Thorndike Press
  10 Water St., Suite 310
  Waterville, ME 04901